SAMAEL OF SARAH

ALSO BY FRANK A. RUFFOLO

Science Fiction Series

Gabriel's Chalice

Tres Archangelis

Xanthe Terra

Crime

Stuck in Traffick

Action Series

Trihedral of Chaos

Distruzione della Roccia

Nonfiction

Memoir of a Soldier of Mary and the Archangels

Mystery Series

Jack Stenhouse Mysteries

Blue Falcon

10048

Lady of the Harbor

Operation Retribution

SAMAEL OF SARAH

FRANK A. RUFFOLO

Frank A. Ruffolo

ISBN: 979-8-9860720-3-6 (printed version only)

Cover Art: Joshua Martin, mjoshua0825@gmail.com

Printed in the United States of America

First Edition, January 2024

Scriptures verses from the following:

SAMAEL OF SARAH

2 CORINTHIANS 4:4
The devil who rules this world has blinded the minds of those who do not believe.
They cannot see the light of the Good News. (NCV)

PROLOGUE

It's hard to believe that it was only one year ago that Pope Ignatius II gave his historic address to the inhabitants of every world.

Everyone wanted to hear what he said that day. The crowd below the pope's balcony was estimated at over two million, the largest gathering for a papal speech in Rome's history. The throng was so large that it spilled down Via della Conciliazione and overflowed into neighboring streets. To be sure no one was left out, it was also broadcast to millions of public and private vidmonitors on Earth and Mars.

Not surprisingly, the speech to commemorate God's defeat of Satan's hordes through the power of the Ark of the Covenant was well received, giving the pontiff hope that the spiritual lessons he imparted would finally take root.

Pope Ignatius used the occasion to hammer home some spiritual lessons. His first teaching was to remind his listeners of the significant event that had occurred thirteen hundred and twenty-five years prior. He spoke of the return of the Son of Almighty God to Earth and how our ancestors chose to follow God's path, wisely renewing their faith. With concern for his flock, he also recalled that shortly afterward, they resumed their wicked ways and once again lost their faith.

The pope called to mind how difficult God's greatest gift of free will has always been for us. He described how we often choose our own path rather than God's and reiterated that it never ends well when we do. Though he acknowledged that it's hard for us to withstand the appeal of relying on ourselves, he emphasized that choosing to ignore God always results in the Malignant's attempts to use our selfishness to turn us away from our Heavenly Father.

Pope Ignatius told the people of the universe that Satan used our reckless interference in God's cosmos — the unfortunate event that resulted in terraforming Mars — to rain death and destruction on us. The Evil One aimed to prove once and for all that the gift of free will is a curse rather than a blessing.

The pope shared how, through the eternal patience of our Heavenly Father, we defeated the Malignant with help from the Commander of the Ark and returned to God's Son. He reminded his audience that God never loses His love for us, even amidst our constant wavering.

To illustrate this point, he quoted Jesus' words from the Book of Luke: *"If your brother or sister sins against you, rebuke them; and if they repent, forgive them."* Pope Ignatius affirmed God's love by declaring that our Heavenly Father continually waits for us to repent and refrain from further sins.

Pope Ignatius reiterated that our lack of faith is nothing new, pointing out that even the Israelites, God's chosen ones, were banished to the desert for forty years because of their persistent doubts. He repeated that even though God gave us the freedom to choose, we often choose unwisely, and because God is a loving Father, He disciplines us for our iniquities so that we will mend our ways. He quoted the words the prophet Jeremiah received from the Lord: *"For I will forgive their wickedness and will remember their sins no more."*

To conclude his discourse, Pope Ignatius invited all listeners to join him in prayer. Notably, the entire crowd at Saint Peter's Square and in the streets of Rome knelt with others all over the Earth and Mars as the pope led them in reciting the Lord's Prayer.

One of those in attendance that day was Peter Matteo, a geneticist and the current Commander of the Ark. With joy and hope, he listened intently to the leader of the Roman Universal and Apostolic Church. He knew that the future of the human race depended on the audience's reaction.

Exhausted but excited for a better future, he knew that the mission he had just concluded had been a resounding success. With help from God's Guardians and the Ark of the Covenant, they had largely liberated the worlds from the Malignant and his evil influence. But he couldn't wait to get home.

Peter Matteo comes from a long line of God's chosen warriors. The first Commander of the Ark was Peter's father, Raphael "Matt" Matteo. God Himself selected Matt to bring to Earth the miraculous gift that appeared in a mysterious cave on the Moon. The gift, now known as Gabriel's Chalice, was presented to mankind to herald the return of the Son of God and a thousand years of peace.

Peter returned to his Atlanta home, eager to recuperate from his battle with the Malignant on Mars, commonly known as the Good vs. Evil War. The fight was tough, and the people of Mars suffered. Nevertheless, even before he left the planet, they had already begun to rebuild and recover, a good sign of humanity's resilience in the face of adversity.

Peter's arrival home was marked by a momentous event privy only to his infant son, Michael. Unknown to his father, the boy beheld a host of seven archangels appearing above father and son, saluting them both.

The image, visible only to the child, was a twofold

honor bestowed by God. On the one hand, it was presented in recognition of Peter's faithfulness as the current Commander of the Ark. On the other hand, it was also a gift to the boy, meant to strengthen his commitment when his turn would come to assume the mantle from his father.

Before little Michael had his vision of the archangels, Satan was once again attempting to insert his influence among God's people.

His target was Sarah Covington, a former human who had to flee from those who wanted to destroy the abomination she had become. The dirt mite infection she contracted while working on Mars completed its cycle upon her return to Earth, metamorphosing her into a dreaded Clawfoot.

To escape her pursuers, the Clawfoot searched for refuge, eventually finding peace in the wilderness of the Canadian Rockies. There, she was accepted by a clan of Bigfeet and given the name "Crooked Legs" because of the unusual shape of her lower limbs.

One fateful day in her new life, Crooked Legs was out searching for berries to supplement her clan's meals when she was suddenly attacked from behind by a creature she thought was her mate. Atoch, the leader of the Bigfoot clan who accepted her as his own, was usually kind and thoughtful toward Crooked Legs. But this encounter was different.

When Crooked Legs turned to view her assailant, she was stunned to see him staring at her with revulsion through odd, orange-colored eyes. Unnaturally, his face twisted into a repulsive image, and he quickly ran away into the woods, howling and chortling in an unsettling manner.

Soon after Atoch disappeared, Crooked Legs began to feel an odd twinge in her abdomen. She was trying to understand what was happening when her mate suddenly reappeared, asking about the howling he had heard earlier. He seemed unaware of what he had done just moments before.

Confused, Crooked Legs was about to question Atoch when a vision of pure evil suddenly appeared before them, stunning both creatures into silence. Terrified by the loathsome image, the Clawfoot and Bigfoot pair could only listen while the vision reveled in their fear, announcing to Crooked Legs that she was now "his." The entity gleefully promised Crooked Legs that she would soon reveal his glory, announcing that before long, she would bear a progeny for him.

Ominously, he referred to the impending offspring as "his son."

During this same time, Walter Reed Medical facility in Washington, D.C., was the site of similarly bizarre incidents.

The captured Clawfeet previously known as Everett Olsen, Frank Ruisi, Sandy Gennaro, Jane Farley, Henri De Jesus, and Larry Pomeroy, were receiving newly developed treatments of cannabis oil supplemented with baking soda.

Fortunately, these six individuals were well on their way to recovery as normal human beings. However, this treatment didn't work for all the Clawfeet the military had brought from Mars. Jonathan Harrington, Karen Stamos, and Jane's husband, Tim, never stopped transforming — a devastating blow to the researchers who had worked so hard to find a cure.

The academics knew something had to be done for them quickly. The infection had to be stopped to keep those victims from changing any further. Remarkably, they established cryogenic freezing as the best option.

Upon receiving their orders, teams of scientists and engineers started designing and constructing chambers that would hold those unlucky few in controlled negative-degree temperatures. The hope was that by placing the infected in suspended animation, the researchers would have time to find a cure for them as well.

To accommodate this innovative process, a unique facility was specially built at the Area 51 military base. The mysterious creatures were to be kept alive within this facility while investigators continued their research.

The realization that the cannabis oil treatment didn't work on all the Clawfeet was disheartening. Nevertheless, there was one glimmer of hope: Jonathan Harrington, riddled with arthritis before the infection, had lost all traces of his joint disease after his transformation began.

When this was discovered, doctors at Area 51 attributed it to an unexpectedly favorable side effect of the horrific disease. Jumping at the chance to report good news, they heralded it as a promising medical advancement and began to work on replicating the effect without triggering transformations.

While the physicians assigned to the one-of-a-kind complex at Area 51 monitored the newly frozen civilians, they were also tasked with studying four frozen Marines, placed there for a vastly different reason.

The former humans were victims of accidental infections with mutated Martian dirt mites, but the Marines weren't accidents. Instead, they were the unwitting "volunteers" of a disturbing government program to alter them genetically by injecting them with dirt mite protein and Clawfoot RNA.

This program was an alarming and highly secret experiment aimed at creating a race of "super soldiers."

Before being frozen like the civilians, the Marines were still mostly human, having only partially transformed into

Clawfeet as a result of their genetic engineering. At that stage, they were all larger, stronger, and more intelligent than normal human beings. But two of them looked dramatically different from the others and each other.

One pair of the four looked the same — they were now seven feet tall, with large hands and feet, thick, black nails, and stiff, reddish-colored hair over their entire bodies.

A third "volunteer" wasn't like them. This one hadn't grown as tall; he was "only" six and a half feet, and he lacked the extensive hair of the other two. These changes were less noticeable, making him appear to be the most human-looking of all of them.

Curiously, the fourth volunteer's changes were nothing like the others. The modifications he went through made him an entirely new creature, an absolute abomination. He grew the most, to almost eight feet in height, and his legs became so misshapen that they resembled those of lizards. His legs were so strange that the scientists determined that if he were allowed to thaw out, he'd need to travel over the ground on his four remaining toes and the balls of his feet because his heels had atrophied so badly that they were almost nonexistent.

This creature didn't have what we would call claws, but the nails of his hands and feet had grown so long and black that they could most likely be used as such. And while the hair on his chest, head, and face had turned red like two of the others, the scientists studying him were amazed that his pineal gland, the least understood part of the endocrine system, had swelled to an enormous size.

This Marine's changes horrified most of those privy to them — except for the federal and military leaders who had initially approved the experiment. They were alone among a handful who considered the test a rousing success. As far as they were concerned, those Marines were now the superior Clawfoot/human hybrids they had hoped to create: their new killing machines.

These strange creatures were complete unknowns. Therefore, no one knew how they would react when awakened. The more rational of those involved feared what might happen if the creatures' enhanced abilities couldn't be kept in check. They warned that the experiment could quickly become a national disaster, a poor reflection on anyone who had anything to do with it. Accordingly, while research continued into how Clawfoot and human DNA interacted, the military decreed that these new life forms would remain in cryogenic sleep within Area 51 until further notice.

As politicians are inclined to do, they brazenly congratulated themselves despite the risk of untold dangers, once again proving that history continually repeats.

By nature, human beings are irresponsible and egocentric. Arrogantly, these leaders instructed others to create new life forms, ignoring the numerous and well-documented disastrous attempts to be god-like throughout the ages. Boldly and naively, they claimed they could manipulate their creations for their own selfish interests.

Regrettably, most of those involved in Operation Hell Fighter believed they had created the perfect subjects. They unquestionably assumed nothing could go wrong with their plans.

With supreme confidence in their abilities, they believed they had every aspect of their risky venture covered. Yet they neglected to consider one crucial factor...

While the genetically altered soldiers and partially transformed humans were frozen, they simultaneously began communicating with each other from within their cryogenic chambers. Their connections continued to develop until they became acutely aware of each other.

Eventually, these unfortunate people were joined by another entity nothing like themselves. This new arrival was evil, pure evil, a malevolent spirit that moved effortlessly from one plane of existence to another with almost unlimited powers.

The entity roamed the room housing the frozen capsules. With deep, guttural growls and foul odors following its wake, it checked each compartment, emitting a satisfied stench to signal its approval of the contents. Then it left, as mysteriously as it had arrived.

Long past the entity's departure, a sulfurous odor of rotten eggs lingered throughout the room. The stench was so foul that it would have suffocated the staff had it not dissipated before activity in the facility resumed the next day.

Significantly, no one but the frozen knew the evil being had even been there.

CHAPTER ONE

If you ask anyone on Mars about the Good vs. Evil War, they'll say it's hard to believe it's been only a year since the demon hordes and the Clawfeet were destroyed.

No one on Earth or Mars will ever forget how the Malignant used the horrific changes caused by the diseased mites to his advantage. Through those infections, the Evil One did everything he could to destroy his human enemies, ignoring how often God's benevolence renders him powerless.

Most will insist they're trying to go on with their lives, but it's difficult for many not to think of that time. Inevitably, something will trigger painful memories, leaving some unable to find happiness. Consequently, mental health clinics are popping up everywhere on Mars and Earth.

Installing the clinics and rebuilding Xanthe City has become a bright spot in the planet's otherwise dreary reconstruction. Work began almost immediately after the war ended, with builders promising that the Martian capital would cover a larger area and be even more decadent than before the invading forces and defenders tore it apart.

Critically, scientists of all disciplines are collaborating on the most efficient ways to eliminate the remaining mutated dirt mites from the planet. They hope to return that species to the harmless insect-like organisms they were before the radiation from our wayward missile terraformed the planet and changed them into deadly organisms. Unfortunately, the continued existence of the mutated versions means transformations are still a danger.

While the scientists work, the government's mandatory program to inoculate all Martian residents and visitors with AB-negative blood is operating at full steam. The program is intended to vaccinate everyone with this rare blood group to reduce the possibility of accidental transformations while the planet is being cleansed and purified.

The connection to AB-negative blood is significant. Ongoing archeological excavations and studies of previously discovered ancient Martian records are finding surprising links between the modern humans who became Clawfeet and the former Martian civilization.

Centuries before, when a nuclear missile meant to destroy an asteroid threatening Earth went off course and detonated on Mars, radiation from that blast damaged the native mites, and the Martians of that time had no defense against them. As a result, those newly harmful organisms affected everyone on the planet, all of whom had AB-negative blood. If the new disease didn't kill them outright, it altered their genetic makeup so thoroughly that they morphed into hideous creatures that eventually wiped out that entire civilization.

Before the last ones died, some of them traveled to Earth in a last-ditch effort to warn their neighbors of the dangers of unleashing unchecked nuclear technology. They perceived that we hadn't intended to cause problems for them and they hoped to avoid having a similar fate befall us. In the process, they introduced their blood type into some of the Earthly population, alongside the visiting children of the Sons of God, a race of giants known collectively as fallen angels or Nephilim.

CHAPTER TWO

Xanthe City, Mars' most popular tourist destination, boasts a striking similarity to Earth's Las Vegas. Modeled on Vegas, it provides visitors with a familiar and comforting atmosphere in an otherwise alien Martian landscape.

Recent developments on the planet have sparked a surge of interest in new tourist attractions based in the city. One example is the discovery of the ancient Martian civilization's record hall and other relics from its past. These discoveries have ignited strong interest among visitors to witness the finds firsthand. As a result, Earthly and Martian companies are vying for these new tourist dollars, organizing expeditions to the archaeological sites from base locations in Xanthe City.

In addition, Princess Shuttles, a newly established Earthly company, has revolutionized space tourism with a brand-new vacation category: monthly intergalactic shuttle trips to Mars. When the company's flagship interplanetary cruise ship, the Galactic Princess, is finished, it will boast a capacity of 5,000 passengers. Much to the company's delight, the ship has been fully booked since its announcement two years ago.

To accommodate the influx of visitors, the Martian people have been working tirelessly to develop new towns, cities, retail hubs, and farming and manufacturing bases outside the capital, leading to rapid population expansion. This growth in infrastructure has also led to significant changes in the Martian skies. Newly launched satellites now orbit Mars and its two moons, Phobos and Deimos, substantially boosting electricity transmission across the planet.

With the deployment of these satellites, it is now possible to distribute electrical power across Mars without the need for the costly Tesla towers that have been in use since the first Earthly pioneers settled there. This development marks a significant milestone in realizing Nikola Tesla's vision of free electricity without the need for the unsightly towers currently crowding the planet's populated areas.

While the focus of humanity's space exploration has shifted toward Mars, other extraterrestrial places have also been colonized, such as Earth's constant companion, the Moon, and Saturn's natural satellite, Titan.

The Moon has seen a significant expansion in its communities, with numerous settlements now spread across its surface. Among these is the newly revamped Garden of Eden at Moon Base Challenger, a significant visitor attraction.

This garden is a marvel, having been miraculously created years ago by Archangel Gabriel to signify the Second Coming of God's Son. Many visitors have been drawn to its serenity, with some even choosing to stay and form a community of like-minded individuals. These devoted people eventually built a thriving monastery within the garden. As full-time residents, they tend the garden and maintain the Cave of Saint Gabriel and the wondrous Golden Tree of God. They also eagerly impart their wisdom to anyone willing to listen.

Years ago, when humanity began to expand into the cosmos, it quickly became apparent that a new system of governance was needed to maintain order across the vast and distant territories.

To tackle this challenge, a commission was formed with one representative from each country on Earth. The commission studied the issue for two years, with sometimes contentious debates attracting advocates of varying factions. Ultimately, the members agreed on a framework that everyone agreed with, and on an historic day, they signed the Galactic Federation into being.

The creation of this federation marked a significant milestone in humanity's quest to unite as we venture to new worlds.

Nonetheless, even as our capabilities for exploring the universe improve, we continue to struggle with the basic concepts relating to our existence.

The most important of these is how to reconcile our faith in God with the notion that humans could possess more superior knowledge and abilities than our Creator. This same concept is what led to the downfall of the early Martian civilization. Regrettably, it has also plagued humanity throughout our history.

Though commemorations of Judgment Day, the saving power of the Ark of the Covenant and the help of the Guardians persist in society, some have grown apathetic to the celebrations. Slowly, those recollections are fading, as greed, pride, and selfishness return.

Those aware of what's happening are doing their best to warn others. They write books, take to the airwaves, and speak out whenever possible. With earnestness bordering on compulsion, they strive to remind their fellow human beings that as we navigate the vast expanse of the cosmos, we must learn from our mistakes to avoid repeating the patterns of destruction and chaos that have plagued us in the past. They insist that our future rests in what we do today and that only by working together can we build a better tomorrow for ourselves and the generations that follow.

CHAPTER THREE

Peter Matteo's life took an unexpected turn after he returned from Rome.

To his amazement, he discovered that while he had been fighting for the human race on Mars, others had taken control of his genetic research and that contrary to his belief in the critical nature of his contributions, his colleagues were entirely capable of managing things without his involvement.

This redundancy prompted Peter to resign from the CDC, which left him nowhere to go every day. Feeling useless, he began to mope around the house.

Though Angela understood why Peter resigned, she soon grew tired of seeing her husband unhappy. One day, when he was particularly grumpy, she encouraged him to venture into a field he had never considered.

Several years prior, Peter had contemplated documenting his family's historical role as God's Commanders of the Ark. He had broached the subject of looking for an author with Angela but had put it out of his mind because of his other commitments.

But Angela had never forgotten. That day, she took her husband by the hand and sat him down on the couch. With all sincerity, she suggested that with no steady job to distract him, it was an excellent time to tackle that project.

On Angela's advice, Peter devoted several hours each day to translating his thoughts into words, completing a comprehensive account of his family history in a relatively short span. Subsequently, he began searching for publishers but didn't have to look far. Unexpectedly, several were eager to transform his story into a book.

To his and Angela's amazement, the book became an instant hit — the public's curiosity about the commanders was insatiable. To Peter's great delight, he was finally able to share his relatives' stories and his unwavering faith in God.

The book's success came at a price, however. Peter found himself away from Angela and Michael for extended periods of time. His publisher's marketing team arranged nonstop intergalactic tours, which took him to major cities worldwide, including settlements on Mars and the Moon. They even considered adding Titan to the list.

Despite the challenges, Peter relished his newfound role. During interviews, he explained that he had used his book to spread a message of faith in the One Eternal God. He consistently emphasized that God disciplines humanity with unconditional love and authority when we misbehave, just as any loving father would. He never tired of reminding people that God desires nothing more than to guide His children back to His path. Consequently, when corrections are needed, they are duly provided. Peter always underscored the importance of remaining vigilant against evil, as he knows that although God never abandons us, the Malignant One is always hovering, waiting to tempt us away from our Creator and into sin.

Lory Paduano, the newly appointed director of the Canadian Bigfoot Research Center, is a respected friend of Peter's. Her unexpected promotion from assistant to director was well-deserved. Lory's extensive experience, particularly her role in supporting the previous director who invented the machine allowing humans to communicate with the local Bigfoot population, played a pivotal role in earning the

Bigfeet's trust and forging a close bond with them.

On one picturesque spring day, Lory ventures into the Bigfoot Preserve, her curiosity and apprehension palpable. Atoch, the revered chieftain of one of the largest Bigfoot clans in the region, has requested her presence for an important meeting.

As is customary, the arrival of the new season in the mountainous regions of Canada brings forth a myriad of vibrant wildflowers. Despite lingering pockets of snow, the flowers have begun to weave a stunning tapestry of colors across the landscape, a sight familiar to Lory. The trees are budding, and the majestic snow-capped mountains glisten in the warm sunlight. Yet, despite the breathtaking beauty of the surroundings, Lory remains uneasy, her uncertainty deepening about the purpose of Atoch's insistence on seeing her.

At present, the Bigfoot community is in mourning. The recent passing of Crooked Legs, Atoch's former mate, has profoundly shaken the clan. The former Sarah Covington, who tragically died while giving birth to their leader's son, is sorely missed.

Initially, the clan rejoiced at the prospect of Atoch having a child to care for after losing his mate. The family unit is essential to the creatures, and the loss of one is a loss for all.

However, as much as they missed Crooked Legs, the Bigfoot troop's feelings took a sharp turn when they saw the infant. Its highly unusual appearance can't be overlooked, and it fills them with caution and unease.

Atoch, too, is deeply troubled by the child. Before its birth, he and Crooked Legs had a harrowing encounter with an otherworldly entity, an experience he can never forget. The malevolent presence's laughter and its ominous promise that Crooked Legs would bear his offspring continues to haunt him. Now, whenever he gazes upon the babe, he suspects that the entity's prophecy has come true, and he worries about the disruptive impact it may have on his clan's way of life.

In desperation, Atoch asked to meet with Lory. He hopes she can provide some insight into the situation, even though she and everyone else are unaware of the strange incident. Neither he nor his mate had shared their terrifying vision of pure evil with anyone. The ordeal had bewildered them so much that they kept it a secret between themselves. To this day, Atoch cannot bring himself to divulge the vile entity's message to any of his companions — that Crooked Legs would bear a son, and the child would be "his."

Alone and accompanied only by a handheld translator unit, Doctor Paduano treks up the mountain to the place where Atoch usually waits for her. He prefers to remain at the tree line just before a series of caves hidden by the trees and overgrown brush where his clan resides.

Despite the doctor's extensive work with the Bigfoot creatures, she always feels out of place in their presence. The giant, hulking beasts tower over her, to an average height of seven feet, and emit a powerfully pungent odor that is overwhelming to the uninitiated. Fortunately, Lory has grown accustomed to their scent, and it no longer bothers her. However, the creatures' bulk is still intimidating.

Upon arriving at Atoch's cave dwelling, Lory senses his agitation. He halts before entering to explain his reason for calling her there.

"Doctor," he says through the translation machine, "I want you to see the pup. He is unlike us. He lacks a coat of fur to keep him warm, and his eyes...they are different. He is much larger than a Bigfoot pup, and he...appears...Human."

Surprised by Atoch's description, Lory seeks to reassure him. "Atoch, do you recall that Crooked Legs was once human before her transformation?"

Atoch nods, "Yes, but you will see; you will explain. I do not understand."

Lory wants to be supportive, but she has no idea why Atoch is confused. She tells him, "My friend, I will do my best. Where is he?"

When Atoch points, Lory approaches an infant lying on a bed of pine branches in a dark recess of the cave. The low light makes it difficult to discern the details, but once her eyes adjust, she observes a small creature nestled on the cave floor.

Instantly, Lory understands why Atoch referred to the baby as human. Her initial observation notes hairless, olive-toned skin and human-shaped legs, without any of the other, identifiable features of his Bigfoot father or Clawfoot mother. And despite being under a month old, the babe is already over three feet in length and is more muscular than an average human or Bigfoot infant.

As the young being awakens, he stretches and turns his head toward her, shocking Lory.

This child is definitely not human.

The infant yawns and opens his eyes — all three of them black as coal and staring at Lory. The infant's extra eye, located in the middle of his overly broad forehead, operates in conjunction with the other two, just like his mother's.

Lory stares, and the baby smiles, inserting his voice into her mind.

I am Samael of Sarah. You must be Doctor Paduano. We will get to know each other well. I will be what I will be.

Frightened, Lory looks at Atoch for clarification. "I... I think I heard him talking to me! But...he didn't speak! He...he told me his name!"

Atoch nods. "I have also heard him inside my head. He calls his name Samael, but I did not name him. What does this mean? What voice is this?"

At Atoch's question, a cold wind rushes through the cave sounding like an evil laugh. Bewildered, Lory and Atoch look at each other in wide-eyed confusion while baby Samael merely smiles.

Suddenly, Lory craves the light of day. "It's dark in here, Atoch. Let's go outside, where it's brighter."

At the mouth of the cave, Lory tries to make sense of what she saw. "He's just a baby, but he spoke to me!" she tells Atoch. "Your son's mind spoke to me!"

"No!" shouts Atoch, emphatic in his denial of Lory's statement. "He is not mine! That is the son of Crooked Legs! He is not *my* son!"

"But Crooked Legs was your—" starts Lory.

Atoch interrupts, attempting to make the doctor understand. "Yes," he agrees. "Crooked Legs was my mate, but this is not my son! I do not know where he comes from! When Crooked Legs first felt life inside her, we saw a hideous creature that terrified us."

"What? A 'hideous' creature? What did you see, Atoch?"

"I cannot explain," whimpers the strong Bigfoot leader, wringing his long fingers together. "But I sense that I must care for this pup until he can care for himself. But I do not know how much longer he will be with us, for my clan is very troubled when he is around them."

"What are you worried about, Atoch?"

"I sense that he is strong. I believe he has a destiny, but I do not know what that is. I am wary, very wary. And frightened."

CHAPTER FOUR

When some time opens up in Peter's Moon book tour schedule, he seizes the opportunity to visit the miraculous Garden of Eden. The ongoing promotions have left him in dire need of peace, and the garden's surroundings usually provide him with precisely that.

As he strolls around the edge of the lake, he marvels at the Golden Tree's shimmering beauty. Since its discovery, the tree has grown tall and fast, with prismatic leaves that radiate light in all directions, providing an incredible sight and a blessing to all who visit it.

Peter stands before the magnificent tree and gazes skyward, mesmerized by the vastness of space outside the protective biosphere that God placed over the garden area. Although he's an experienced interplanetary traveler, the universe's enormity never ceases to amaze him.

Marveling at God's creation, Peter contemplates the paradox of human beings' insignificance against the grandeur of God while his reverie is accompanied by the melodious hymns of singing angels.

Lost in thoughts about God's goodness, Peter is jolted out of his musings by a gentle tap on his shoulder. "Oh! I didn't hear you coming," he says, surprised to see a familiar monk at his side. "How are you, Brother Oettinger?"

"I'm well, Peter. It's good to see you again. Will you be staying long this time?"

"No, unfortunately not. I found some free time in my

schedule, so I thought I'd drop by. I love it here."

"I know what you mean. It is peaceful, isn't it?" agrees Brother Oettinger, happy to be talking to a fellow believer. "I heard about your book. You have an important family heritage to uphold."

"Yes, it's a huge responsibility to be Commander of the Ark. I only hope I'm fulfilling the role well."

"I wouldn't think you have anything to worry about," says the brother. "Based on your recent performance against Satan and his minions, I think God is pleased with you."

"Thank you," says Peter shyly, embarrassed by the brother's praise.

Oettinger continues, "I don't usually disturb our visitors. However, a video message has just come in from Earth, and it's for you. It's a woman, a Doctor Paduano. Do you know her?"

Peter wonders how his friend knew he was at the Garden of Eden. His next thought is that Angela must have told her.

"Did she say what she wants?" he asks, intrigued by the unexpected call.

Brother Oettinger responds with caution. "No, she didn't specify. But... She seems troubled. Even scared."

"Scared? Well, that's not good. I guess I should talk to her right away,"

"That would be wise."

Tightening the sash of his coarse brown habit, the religious community member leads Peter to the group's communication station.

Strolling beside the monk, Peter comments on the monastery's charm as they approach it's high walls. "This building is extraordinary," he remarks. "I love how it resembles an ancient English castle."

The monk's head bobs up and down. "Indeed, it has

character. But I'm grateful for its modern amenities. I couldn't imagine living under the same conditions as the people of the Middle Ages."

As they walk past the garden tended by silent monks, Peter can't help noticing their curious looks. Though each of them looks up, the only sound is from the steady thuds of their hoes hitting the soil.

In due course, they reach Brother Oettinger's office, a modern space equipped with the latest technologies.

"There's the call," says the monk, gesturing toward an oversized terminal screen. "I'll wait here."

Peter sits down to greet his worried-looking friend, Doctor Paduano.

"Hi, Lory. It's been a while. Did Angela tell you I was here?"

"Yes, I called your house first, and she said you were on the Moon, being interviewed about your book."

"That's right. So, what do you want to talk about? You look serious."

After a brief, interplanetary communication delay, Peter sees Doctor Paduano giving him a half smile and taking a deep breath. Then, she asks, "Remember how amazed everyone was when we heard Sarah Covington, the last of the Clawfeet, had conceived? We all thought that was impossible because all Clawfeet were sterile, right? Well, as you know, nature doesn't follow our rules."

"Don't I know it," says Peter, replying after another delay. "I was sad to hear she died in childbirth."

"So was I," replies Lory. "But I just saw the baby, and the miracle of her conceiving is nothing compared to him!"

"What do you mean?"

Lory looks stricken. "Peter, he's neither Clawfoot nor Bigfoot."

Peter's brows furrow in confusion. "What is he then? Wait... Are you saying he's human?"

Lory lets out a deep sigh. "He has human characteristics. Atoch summoned me to meet him because he's concerned. He and the clan are very uneasy around him."

"Why? What else should you be telling me, Lory?" Peter's heart races with the possibilities.

"I don't know how to say this, so I'll just come out with it," she replies, speaking quickly while her communication link is still open. "The baby, or the pup, as they call him, is not even a month old, and he's already over three feet long and muscular, with dark olive skin and no body hair. And Peter...he also has a third eye! He communicated with me telepathically! He told me he calls himself Samael of Sarah. Atoch is very troubled, and so am I. You must come to Canada to see him for yourself! He's astonishing!"

Peter is shocked. "That's unbelievable! I'll definitely come to Canada to see him! But I have to fly home first. I've been away a while, and I need to get a few things. After I restock my travel supplies and touch base with my family, I'll catch a flight to Calgary and get a ride to your facility in Hinton."

"All right, safe journey, my friend. Say hello to Angela, and kiss Mike for me."

Lory waves at Peter, then ends the transmission.

When the screen goes blank, Brother Oettinger looks at Peter with concern. "I think you should know that Samael is the name of one of the fallen angels from the book of Enoch. He's the angel of death, ruled by the planet Mars."

"What?!" asks Peter, dumbfounded by that startling bit of information.

Before Peter can say anything else, a celestial sound like a choir of angels fills the room, and a bright light appears, a not uncommon sight for Peter but a fascinating encounter for

Brother Oettinger.

As the pair watch, a form slowly materializes from within the light, which Peter identifies as Archangel Michael.

"Commander, the Guardians are here and at the ready. However, you must be forewarned. With free reign among God's children, the Evil One has spawned the creature you have just learned about. Commander, I caution you. Do not believe anything that wicked being will tell you. I will send a guardian with you, as you will need protection on your journey. Trouble is in the future, Commander, more trouble than you realize. The Malignant never sleeps, but neither do we. Once again, your resolve will be tested, and humankind will be strained. This generation has become as reckless as the one that taunted Enoch's great-grandson, Noah. Beware of Nephilim. Beware of Samael. Beware of the Malignant. Your constant companion will be Metatron, the angel who led the Israelites through the desert. He has been prepared for this very time ever since the Great Judgment. Go with my blessing."

As the vision fades, Brother Oettinger drops to his knees, stunned at being present for such momentous news. Beside him, Peter fortifies himself with the prayer of the Our Father, understanding that he's being sent on another mission.

When Peter concludes his prayer, he taps Brother Oettinger on the shoulder.

"I need to schedule a trip home. Can you help me with that?"

"Oh. Yes, of course," replies Oettinger, finishing his own prayer and rising from his knees. "I have never seen anything like that! But...Metatron? Wasn't that a comic book character from the 21st century?"

"What? Oh, you're probably thinking of Megatron," responds Peter, smiling wanly. "No, this one is real, and he's become a steady visitor. One of the perks of my position."

Oettinger reaches into his robe and holds out a gold Saint Benedict cross.

Frank A. Ruffolo

"Commander, you must always carry this on your person; the saint will give you the courage to face anything. I will also make sure everyone here prays for you and all of humanity."

Peter takes the cross with a nod and a sigh, grateful for the monk's concern. He knows he must be ready for the daunting task ahead. The news he received would be frightening if he weren't fortified by his faith in God and His Guardians. Archangel Michael just informed him that he'll be facing a powerful demon spawn, and that the fate of humanity is once more at stake, depending on him and his every action.

When his flight is secured, the commander departs the garden and heads to the adjacent moon base to catch the next shuttle to the Empyrian Hotel, the original commercial structure orbiting Earth.

Inside the portal passageway separating the garden from the moon base, Peter feels the familiar tingling sensation of the energy field that keeps everything working as it should. Passing by several "space newbies," he notices how their reactions mirror his, the first time he experienced it.

Upon reaching the other side of the energy field, Peter is pleasantly surprised when a spaceflight crew member offers to take his luggage and check him in. Grateful, Peter heads to the hotel, a necessary stop for anyone traveling between Earth and other planets.

In the hotel lobby, he stops to collect the gravity boots the hotel offers free to all guests. Though the structure generates gravity, it's less than Earth's, and the boots are needed to keep the guests grounded.

The first flight Oettinger could arrange is scheduled to depart in three to four days. Many of the other passengers on that flight have also booked rooms to wait for the same transport ship. Peter is thankful for Brother Oettinger's assistance. Silently, he expresses his gratitude to the monk, knowing that booking everything himself would have been a nightmare.

Peter freshens up in his hotel room, then walks to the observation window before hopping into bed. Whenever he's on the Moon, he likes to search for the bright blue ball of Earth suspended in the blackness of space. It always reassures him to see his home planet.

As his head hits the pillow, his thoughts drift between Xanthe City, the war on Mars, and the Malignant's evil scheming. Though he tries to forget past encounters, the memories are so vivid that falling asleep takes considerable effort.

CHAPTER FIVE

Despite the passage of 1,300 years, diligent urban planners on Earth have admirably preserved a few iconic landmarks as a testament to bygone eras. With strategic repairs and careful maintenance, enduring structures such as Saint Basil's Cathedral in Red Square, the Eiffel Tower in Paris, and historic buildings in Washington, D.C. still stand, sometimes shakily, in some places. Even the Statue of Liberty, which underwent significant renovations three centuries ago, proudly continues to symbolize the United States.

Capitalizing on the Earthly interest in preserving the past, the visionary planners on Mars established its capitol as an homage to Earth's Las Vegas. In choosing to emulate "Sin City," they hoped to use its allure to draw thousands to Earth's newest colony.

Due to Xanthe City's wide range of adult entertainment options complemented by milder alternatives, the influx of interplanetary visitors has indeed positioned Mars as a popular destination. The city so faithfully emulates Las Vegas that it has even adopted a paraphrased version of its famous catchphrase as its motto. Thus, "What happens on Mars, stays on Mars" has become as well-known as its Earthly counterpart.

The most notable attractions in the Martian capital involve its thriving adult industry, distinguished from Earth by the almost exclusive use of artificial general intelligence robots, commonly referred to as AGIs or AIs.

To cater to this trade's limitless clientele, most artificial general intelligence companies are strategically located within the city's hotels and casinos, ensuring convenient access to the synthetic companions they keep readily available for hire.

Through extensive marketing, these omnipresent adult establishments promote the use of their AI robots as a better alternative to human companionship. Interestingly, they claim robots enhance public safety by minimizing disease and crime.

Nevertheless, while traditional forms of intimacy are officially prohibited throughout the planet, willing human participants can still be found available at steep prices, providing one knows where to look. This and many other nefarious activities arising from human involvement keep law enforcement busy. The variety of criminal behaviors found on the planet is never-ending.

One of those tasked with keeping the populace safe is Xanthe City Homicide Detective David Jacoby, the son of Earthborn parents who emigrated to Mars after he was born.

As an Earther, Detective Jacoby stands at an impressive height of six feet four inches, towering over native-born Martians. While his size is instantly noticeable, it's only one of several physical disparities between Martians and Earthlings. In addition to being small in stature, native Martians also have a much paler complexion than Earthers, due to the effects of the oxygen-rich atmosphere and lower gravitational forces on the planet. Together, these factors play a significant role in stunting the growth of all life forms originating on Mars.

David Jacoby's interest in law enforcement developed when he was a young man researching his family back on Earth. Knowing he wasn't born on the planet made him curious about his ancestral background, so he began looking into his origins. In time, he uncovered a predecessor named Jack Stenhouse, a highly decorated detective in the old New

York City Police Department. Further probes into Stenhouse's life and career led to David's own pursuit of law enforcement.

Stumbling upon this noteworthy ancestor also ignited David's fascination with antiques, which ultimately led to his current obsession with restoring the archaic muscle cars of Jack Stenhouses' time — a hobby that perplexes most of his peers.

Only the few like-minded enthusiasts who share David's passion for preserving vintage cars understand the challenges associated with keeping this hobby going. Even with the frequent ridicule of others, David firmly believes that the four-speed transmissions, five hundred horsepower engines, and dual fiberglass-packed exhausts of motor vehicles from that bygone era cannot be replaced by the EVs and hoverplanes of his time.

As a result, David spends most of his spare hours restoring those obsolete automobiles whenever he can get his hands on one. Lately, he's been working on a 2022 Camaro SS, a beauty he considers himself fortunate to have rescued from a local junkyard after a casino on the Strip tired of displaying it.

David knows his hobby is expensive, but he considers his time and effort worth the trouble. Obtaining the necessary parts for these vintage cars requires specialized, custom fabrication and printing, even requiring him to sometimes come up with creative solutions. Nevertheless, David considers it a personal quest, and he takes pride in his finished restoration projects. His Camaro SS took a long time and significant effort to restore, and David is exceptionally proud of his ride.

Detective Jacoby is so fond of all things old that along with his police issued EMP weapon, he carries a restored antique .44 Magnum handgun wherever he goes. The EMPs are efficient, but not…cool. He prefers the Magnum's powerful recoil and muzzle blast.

Jacoby, a contentedly single human in his thirties, resides in a property he acquired a few years back — an adobe-style house on the north side of the bustling Martian capital. He's always considered the purchase a wise decision, since he no longer has to contend with neighbors incessantly complaining about his car repair activities. In addition to granting him a convenient space to indulge in his passion, the privacy and tranquility of his home give him immeasurable satisfaction following frequently demanding workdays.

Today, David is polishing his vibrant red Camaro while eagerly anticipating a special delivery.

Soon after acquiring the car, he subscribed to monthly shipments of synthetic high-octane fuel — a rich mixture that ensures the Camaro operates at optimal performance. Due to the unavailability of traditional gasoline on Mars or elsewhere, David modified the vehicle to accommodate Synfuel, a combination of hydrogen and a high-energy crystal known as Raphaelite. This blend produces an impressive octane rating of 120, leaving only water vapor as a byproduct.

As David diligently tends to his prized possession, an incoming transmission interrupts his focus, alerting him through his implanted communication device. The device, called a PerscomU, for Personal Communication Unit, is a newer technology, the bulk of which resides within his cranial cavity. On the outside, a slender tube extends over the side of his head with a transparent lens in front of his right eye.

Displeased by the disruption, David scowls, then blinks to activate his eyepiece to view the caller.

"Jacoby here," he grumbles, his annoyance evident.

Accustomed to his underling's gruffness, his superior orders, "Get yourself down to the Majestic Majesty Hotel. The crime unit is already en route."

Narrowing his eyes, a habit David discovered he inherited from his ancestor Stenhouse, he questions testily, "What the hell is this 'incident' about? And for your information, I'm off duty today."

"Not anymore, you're not," retorts his boss. "Inspector Hawking and the Xanthe mayor insist on your presence."

David doesn't fall for the attempt at flattery. "Bullshit!" he exclaims a little too loudly. "I've been waiting for this vacay for months! What the hell could be so important?"

"Someone terminated an AI escort," his boss explains.

"So?" replies David, just as a truck from Phobos Synthetics hums to a halt in front of his residence. "Hey, I gotta go," he says, blinking again to cut the transmission short.

Wiping his hands on a rag, David walks up to the truck to accept his delivery.

"You Jacoby?" asks a diminutive Martian jumping down from the cab.

"Yeah, that's me," responds David as an invoice appears on his eyepiece.

"Wow, nice transport!" compliments the driver, catching sight of the shiny Camaro. "But what the hell is it?"

For the next ninety minutes, the southeastern United States basks in the warm glow of daylight, prompting Peter to wait until he's sure the orbiting Empyrian Hotel is passing over the region containing his loved ones before initiating a vid call home.

After a brief connection delay, the familiar faces of his wife and son materialize on the screen, filling Peter with joy.

"Hello, my loves," he greets the static image, his voice brimming with affection. "Even though I'm one hundred twenty-five miles away, I always carry both of you in my heart."

Angela's response takes a moment to reach Peter, and when it does, he catches a glimpse of her laughter as Michael passes gas.

"When will you be home?" queries Angela, setting Michael down to play with a toy. "It's been quite a while since we've had some family time."

The pause in communication forces Angela to wait for Peter's reply, and when it arrives, her expression turns somber.

"About that," Peter reveals, "When Doctor Paduano called, she said there's an unexpected development in Canada, so I have to make a last-minute trip there. The Clawfoot Sarah passed away during childbirth, and it seems her son is unlike any of the Bigfoot clan she's been living with. But tell me about Michael. What's he been up to while I've been gone?"

Angela bypasses the questions about the baby, choosing instead to address what Peter left unsaid. "Are you going there as a geneticist or as a Commander?"

Once again, a pause hangs in the air, yet Angela swiftly fills the silence. "Never mind, I already know," she asserts before hearing Peter's response. "What's your schedule like? Will you be able to make a stop here first, Commander?"

Sighing softly, Peter replies on his next turn; his voice tinged with regret. "You know me too well, Angela. To answer your first question, I anticipate being home for a day or so, hopefully within the next forty-eight hours. However, that will depend on my connecting flights. And as for your second question, let's just say a geneticist is heading to Canada, and he'll advise the Commander on any necessary next steps."

In Canada, Lory Paduano has harbored deep concern for Atoch and his community ever since she laid eyes on the extraordinary baby in the Bigfoot cave. The infant's telepathic abilities trouble her greatly, but there is something else, an uneasy feeling she can't quite put her finger on.

On the one hand, Lory recognizes the necessity to delve deeper into the case as a behavioral scientist studying the Bigfeet. However, on the other hand, the fear she experienced in the child's presence is something she has no desire to encounter again. Therefore, when another urgent call from Atoch arrives, she tenses.

"Hello, Atoch," she says, forcing herself to address the evidently distressed beast through the translation monitor with a calmness she doesn't feel.

Lory hopes the anxiety evident in Atoch's demeanor doesn't imply a dire situation. The Bigfoot clan leader isn't known for displaying emotion, so his agitation raises alarm bells within Lory.

"Doctor, tension is here," Atoch moans, confirming Lory's worst fears.

With a churning stomach, Doctor Paduano responds as warmly as possible. "My friend, you seem troubled. What is the matter?"

"The son of Sarah is a cause for concern. He is now over two moons old and has grown tall, nearly matching my stature. He is no longer a pup, and he is learning rapidly. With no help from anyone, he fashioned a covering for his body from the skin of a bear."

"Oh? I understand how that must worry you," says Lory, although the full implications of Atoch's disclosures elude her.

Atoch continues, his voice laden with distress. "All Bigfeet share a bond with animals! Wolves and bears are our friends; we have coexisted in harmony for generations. But no more! The son of Sarah has slain a bear! And he attacked the wolves when they attempted to intervene! Because of him, we must abandon this territory! My clan is no longer safe here; we can no longer dwell in this place without fear of revenge from our animal brethren."

Lory is taken aback, her mind racing. Gathering her thoughts, she responds, "That is terrible, my friend! Um, where will you go?"

"We will trek to a different mountain farther north. You must come here before we go, Doctor. You must take the son of Sarah away with you. If he remains here, we may have to deal with him ourselves... If such a thing is even possible."

Lory is alarmed but swiftly formulates a plan.

"Uh... I want to help you, Atoch. Do you remember Peter Matteo? He will join me at my research center in a few days, and I would like him to come with me to collect Sarah's son. Do you remember Peter?"

"Yes. The Commander, as you call him."

"Yes, he is the Commander of the Ark. Before we come to you, I will need to make arrangements to provide care for Sarah's son in my world, and that may take some time. Can you wait until I contact you once everything is in order? Please refrain from leaving or taking any other action until you hear from me."

Atoch expresses disappointment but is willing to cooperate. "We cannot delay our journey, but we will proceed with our plans at a gradual pace."

"Then perhaps we can meet you at your new dwelling place," suggests Lory.

"No! I will not disclose our destination!" declares Atoch, adamant in his refusal. "Your kind has caused us much trouble! Aside from you...and I will include the Commander for this time only...no humans will be welcome among us again."

Atoch walks away and the monitor goes dark, leaving Lory overcome with tears in front of her now-silent screen.

CHAPTER SIX

One of the attractions of the Majestic Majesty Hotel is its meticulously designed rooftop pool, sporting a retractable glass covering that opens when the air temperature is pleasant. The pool area, created by a renowned decorator to resemble a tranquil oasis, exudes elegance, featuring soft sand and carefully positioned palm trees.

Today, however, the pool is anything but tranquil. To the consternation of hotel management, police detectives and crime scene technicians are diligently gathering evidence in the cordoned-off area where bewildered guests made the alarming discovery of the mysteriously deactivated AI.

Despite Homicide Detective David Jacoby's initial grumbling about having to relinquish the remainder of his well-deserved day off, he knew he would obey his boss. He put his supplies away, freshened up, donned a fashionable jumpsuit, and slipped into a stylish pair of custom-printed faux leather boots. Then he grabbed his keys, adorned his head with a well-made copy of a vintage Chevy ballcap, and shielded his eyes against the intense UV rays of the sun with mirrored sunglasses. Lastly, he secured his hip cannon in a deep pocket and prepared himself for the task ahead.

With the thunderous roar of 500 horses, David's arrival beneath the front portico of the Majestic Majesty Hotel turns heads, just as he knew it would. The powerful growl of his

Camaro reverberates, even reaching the rooftop, where Paula Harmon, the city's medical examiner and a native Martian, chuckles at the familiar rumble.

"Sounds like Jacoby finally got his Camaro running," she remarks.

Standing beside Paula, a young technician from Xanthe Robotics wears a puzzled expression. Unfamiliar with Earthly technology, he asks curiously, "What's a Camaro?"

Downstairs, David exits his car and fixes his gaze on the robovalet. "Don't even think of moving it!" he warns sternly.

Upstairs, Jacoby stops just before entering the crime scene around the pool. Grabbing a pair of rubber gloves and covers for his boots, he slips them on, then continues under the tape marking the area.

The shoe coverings muffle the distinctive clack of the boot's metal heel protectors on the stone floor but don't erase it entirely, and the sounds grab everyone's attention. Unaccustomed to anything other than the ubiquitous, softly synthetic soles most wear, they all look up from what they're doing. They only resume their tasks after the sounds disappear when David steps onto the sand.

Marching up to the medical examiner with the question of the day, Jacoby asks, "What the hell happened here?"

Ignoring the trite inquiry, Paula asks a question of her own. "How's the ride, Jake?" she smiles, using the name Jacoby prefers among friends.

David gives the M.E. a thumbs-up. "Smooth as silk. Let's go for a spin after we're done with this shit, okay?" He looks around the crime scene and asks again, "So, what's the story?"

Still curious, the Xanthe Robotics technician interjects himself into the conversation. "I'd like to see your 'ride' too," he remarks awkwardly, earning an odd glance from David.

"Who's he?" asks David, seeking clarification from Paula.

"He's from Xanthe Robotics, and he's been assigned to shadow me for the day. I don't think he has any idea what he's talking about," she explains.

Proud of his car, David tells the technician that a 'ride' is a slang term for a vehicle and that he'll show it to him if time permits. He then requests the technician's insights into the case.

Eager to showcase his knowledge of his company's products, the technician launches into the conclusion he reached after a brief examination of the subject. "The female escort's electronics have been fried. It appears she was struck by a short-range EMP blast to the back of her head."

David turns to the robot lying on the ground, an alluring creation adorned in a revealing string bikini. "Do you know what could have caused the bot to be terminated like that?"

"Well, there are no protocols in her programming that would have caused her to do anything that would have provoked such a reaction. So something else must have happened."

David gives the tech a skeptical look. "How about jealousy? Check the memory backup to see if you can retrieve any information about what occurred just before the termination. Meanwhile, I'll consult the concierge to determine who the escort was assigned to."

David accesses the recording menu on his implant with a gentle tap. Once the menu pops up, he uses his eyepiece to capture an image of the barcode on the back of the bot's neck.

"Okay, I'm heading to the lobby," he informs Paula after storing the image.

As he steps off the elevator, David's face lights up when he notices a young woman with flaxen hair and blue eyes at the concierge desk. His preference for blondes is well-known among his friends.

"Hi, I'm Detective Jacoby with XPD," he says, introducing

himself while accessing the barcode image and presenting his credentials. "I just downloaded the ID of that terminated robot escort to your terminal. What can you tell me about it?"

"Oh, yes. It was truly tragic to hear about Stacey's demise. She was one of our most exceptional escorts. Let me check the files," she says, typing a few keystrokes. "Ah, here it is. Okay, she was assigned to room 1325, to Thomas Carter from Kansas City. Hmm… I think I remember when he checked in. He mentioned being here for a real estate convention."

David smirks. "Yeah, must be a convention with a side order of imitation people." At the blonde's glance, David adds, "Oops, my apologies. Sometimes, I speak without thinking."

The flaxen-haired beauty waves a hand dismissively. "I've heard worse, Detective."

With a smile, David leans forward. "Listen, I'm going to have to pay Mr. Carter a visit. Can you call someone to take me to his room? I'd rather not break down the door if he refuses to let me in, Miss… Ah, I didn't catch your name."

With an answering grin, the concierge stands up and adjusts her skirt, giving David a better view.

"I'm Sonya Vitelli," she replies. "But everyone calls me Sonny. Are you the guy with the antique transpo parked outside?"

"Yeah, that's me. Why do you ask?"

"Well, I'd love to see it sometime."

"Really? I can make that happen," he says, his interest in the attractive female growing as he watches her approach him from behind the desk. "Uh, are you the one who's gonna let me into the room?"

"Yup."

"Okay," David smiles, following Sonny to the elevator.

With the blonde in front of him, the detective's grin transforms into a frown when he notices a barcode on the back of her neck. "Damn," he mutters, eyeing her — now 'it's' — alluring figure. Silently, he wonders, *How am I supposed to find a genuine date with these things running around everywhere?*

Minutes later, the pair strolls down a plush carpeted hallway toward room 1325, with David still grappling with the idea that the beautiful Sonny isn't a real person.

At the door, Sonny pauses to let David knock.

"Mr. Carter?" he says, moving to the closed door. "I'm from XPD. Can we talk?"

When there's no answer, Jacoby knocks and calls out again, but there's still no response, except for the vidmonitor next to the door. It chimes on, declaring, "Mr. Carter does not wish to be disturbed."

"Yeah? Well, we'll see about that," says David before raising his voice to shout, "I'm coming in, Carter!"

David turns to Sonny, who reaches out and presses a small medallion against the vid screen, unlocking the door.

Unholstering his weapon, the detective cautiously pushes the door open, unsure of what to expect inside. His concern is validated when he spots Mr. Carter lying on the floor beside the bed, surrounded by a puddle of crimson blood.

Bringing up the rear, Sonny screams at the sight, causing David to dart a look at the robot. Then he mutters a curse and taps his communication microphone. "We've got another homicide," he states grimly. "It's a human this time, a male, in room 1325."

Inspector Hawking arrives swiftly, accompanied by M.E. Paula Harmon and a tense Xanthe Mayor Yarrow.

"Who is he?" asks the mayor, stressed and panting from running.

"It's Thomas Carter," answers David, crouching next to the lifeless body. "He was using the terminated bot's services, so the incidents could be related."

Looking closer, Paula asks, "What do you see there?"

"There's a knife from the food tray lodged in his chest," observes David, turning the victim onto his back. Rising from his examination, he adds, "Your turn, Harmon."

"You're too kind," sneers the M.E., accustomed to the detective making his own diagnoses.

David shifts his attention to the robot hotel employee. "Sonny, I'm gonna need video footage and timeline records of everyone who's been in this room since Mr. Carter checked in. I'll also need Carter's whereabouts for the past twenty-four hours."

Jacoby hands the bot a card embedded with a chip. "Download the information onto this card. It will upload directly to my workstation."

Taking a moment to think, Jacoby turns back to M.E. Harmon. "Paula, let me know when the body's scheduled for an autopsy. I want to be present. Oh, and I'm game whenever you want that ride."

Paula is too engrossed in her work to respond, so she simply nods and continues her tasks.

As David heads for the door, Mayor Yarrow grabs his arm, preventing him from leaving. "Where are you going?" he yells, surprising everyone. "You're not finished here, Jacoby!"

"Um, Paula needs to take the body to the—"

Too agitated to let David continue, the mayor declares shrilly, "You need to make this case your sole focus until it's solved! I need it resolved as soon as possible!"

David glances down at the hand gripping his arm, then turns to Inspector Hawking, expecting him to say something.

"Um, yes, this is your case, Jake," concedes Hawking, acknowledging the power of Yarrow's position while sending David an apologetic look.

With narrowed eyes and a deep frown, David stares

down at Yarrow, sending an icy chill up the mayor's spine. Yarrow, a third-generation native Martian barely reaching David's shoulder, gazes up at Jacoby and releases his grip.

As Yarrow steps back, Jacoby leans in close to his ear. "I don't care who you are," he whispers sternly, "but if you try that again, you'll regret it."

With that, David straightens to his full height and strides away, leaving an uncomfortable silence as everyone averts their gaze from the embarrassed mayor.

After a short journey from the Moon, Peter arrives at Houston Spaceport and boards a shuttle that will take him to George Bush Intercontinental Airport, the final leg of his journey to Atlanta.

As his fellow passengers settle into their seats, Peter glances out of the window, instantly spotting the Galactic Princess at the far end of the spaceport.

"Wow, that thing is massive!" he exclaims to himself. Peter had read about the ship completing its final shakedown before commencing regular trips to the Empyrian Hotel, but its actual size surpasses his expectations.

As he studies the impressive craft, he recalls the amusing movie he stumbled upon while browsing channels offering long forgotten titles at the hotel. The ship's colossal scale reminds him of the luxury spaceship depicted in the film he watched, complete with flying cabs, the concept of a "multipass," and a heroic "perfect being" entrusted with saving Earth from destruction.

CHAPTER SEVEN

The Commander of the Ark resides in a typical suburban neighborhood with tree-lined streets, artificial turf, and rows of nearly identical prefab houses — uniform and unexciting. While the location may be affordable, the houses blend together so seamlessly that Peter has unwittingly driven past his own house on more than one occasion, failing to recognize it.

The past few days have taken a toll on Peter, and he eagerly anticipates a break from it all.

"Ugh, I'm so exhausted," he grumbles while waiting for his ride-share at the Atlanta Airport arrivals area. "All I want to do is be home with my family."

His plan to relax goes out the window when he sees an Army staff car parked across the street from his house. To him, it's an uninvited reminder of his duties, and he sighs in resignation.

As the commander enters his front walk, the door opens, revealing Angela and Michael stepping out to meet him.

"I'm sorry," says Angela, glancing behind her toward a man standing in the doorway. "He arrived unannounced. I had to let him in."

"It's all right," responds Peter, recognizing the man and the uniform. "I suppose I know why he's here. Let's go inside. It's best to get this over with."

General Austin Patton, commander of the Army's 101st Airborne Division, steps aside to allow Peter to enter the house.

"How are you?" Patton inquires, unaware that Archangel Gabriel is standing beside him in resplendent golden armor.

Peter offers a polite reply, but his focus is fixed firmly on the archangel, who vanishes from view as soon as the Commander of the Ark acknowledges his presence.

"Peter, can we have a private conversation?" asks General Patton, his demeanor displaying signs of unease.

Seeing the apprehension, Peter nods to Angela and guides the military leader into his study. Closing the door behind them, he declares, "We won't be overheard in here. What's on your mind, Austin?"

Patton begins, "I know Doctor Paduano reached out to you regarding the Clawfoot offspring."

"Yes, it seems we might be facing a problem."

"That's an understatement," the general responds. "I spoke to Lory while you were traveling. The Bigfoot community now demands that we take custody of Samael, and if we refuse, Lory thinks they'll kill him."

"Holy cow. That's highly unusual for them. They've always been a peaceful group."

"According to Paduano, Samael's presence has disrupted them and their harmonious relationship with other animals. As a result, they're retreating deeper into the wilderness and cutting off contact with humans, except for Doctor Paduano."

"I had no idea the situation was this serious," admits Peter.

"Yes, it's pretty grim. Despite being only a few months old, Samael is already over eight feet tall. Paduano said she asked you to go to Canada, and I told her I could assist, so I'll be joining you with ample resources. We need to evaluate the circumstances carefully to ensure the best possible outcome. Our goal is to either take him into custody, or if necessary, eliminate the threat he poses."

Peter is stunned. "You think we might have to kill him? We don't even understand the entire situation yet! Does Lory know your plans?"

Patton adopts a stern expression. "Look, Matteo, we know what those creatures are capable of, and it could become dangerous. We've already faced similar challenges in the past, and by the grace of God, we prevailed. I don't intend to leave anything to chance. So tomorrow morning, a private military jet will transport us to Doctor Paduano's facility, and later that day, we'll proceed to the Bigfoot community with all the necessary equipment."

"The 'necessary equipment?' What exactly does that mean, Austin?"

"I recommend that we neutralize this threat, so I'm bringing everything we may need to do just that."

Peter hesitates, aware of the information he received from the archangel but deciding it's too premature to disclose. So instead, he places a hand on Austin's shoulder.

"You may be right," he responds with empathy. "You might very well be right."

Unbeknownst to them, deep within the bowels of the underworld, the Malignant is listening intently to their conversation, growing increasingly intrigued.

Finally, he exclaims with a snarl, "Fools! They have no idea what awaits them! Just wait until they witness my re-creation of Lilith!"

While the men are talking, Angela attempts to stay busy, but she can't help wondering what's been occupying Peter and General Patton behind the closed door of the study for the past two hours. Driven by curiosity, she arranges a plate of cookies and a pot of coffee on a tray and approaches the door. Knocking lightly, she enters when Peter calls out her name.

"Hi, I hope I'm not disturbing you. I thought you might like a little something to eat. You've been in here for quite some time."

"I know," acknowledges Peter. "It's been a while since the Clawfoot uprising on Mars, and we have much to discuss. We should be wrapping up soon."

"Okay," responds Angela. "I'll just leave these here, then," she says, placing the tray on Peter's desk before quietly stepping back and closing the door behind her.

Twenty minutes later, Peter initiates a video call with Doctor Paduano. Afterward, the two men exit the room.

"Uh oh," remarks Angela when she sees Peter's expression. "I know that look. You're leaving again, aren't you?"

General Patton realizes the subject is sensitive and excuses himself to grant them privacy.

"Um, where's your bathroom?" he asks.

Peter directs Patton down the hall, then settles beside Angela on the couch.

"Yes, I'm heading to Canada with the general," he reveals. "I understand you're worried, but I have to go."

"I know you do," Angela replies, smiling bravely. "I'll offer extra prayers for your safe return. I trust that the archangels will be by your side, but there's no harm in having too many prayers, right?"

"Right. And thanks."

Although Angela isn't thrilled about Peter departing so soon, she knows his role as Commander of the Ark is pivotal and supports him on his enigmatic journeys. However, she remains genuinely concerned for his well-being, despite being aware that angels vigilantly watch over him.

David Jacoby is at his desk in the Homicide Department, meticulously reviewing the medical examiner's report.

The autopsy he attended on Thomas Carter didn't uncover anything out of the ordinary; the cause of death was determined to be multiple stab wounds to the heart and lungs.

With no reason to hold the body, the medical examiner completed her report and released it to Carter's wife, who opted to transport it back to Earth.

David reviews the hotel's digital files next.

"Hmm," he muses, noting the bot was assigned to Carter just four days ago. Curious, he clicks through photos of the pair enjoying dinner and lounging by the hotel pool.

"I hope Xanthe Robotics can extract something more valuable from the damaged memory banks," he mutters.

A flashing light in David's eyepiece indicates an incoming call, interrupting his train of thought. To answer it, he taps the PerscomU.

"Is this Detective Jacoby?" inquires a familiar face on the screen.

"Yeah, who's this?" responds David with a smile.

"Fuck you, Jake," responds the man good-naturedly. "You didn't know I'm head of security at the Majestic Majesty Hotel now? I understand you're investigating the death of our escort."

"That's right. I forgot about your new gig."

"Um, could you come to my office? There's something I want to discuss with you in person."

Hoping for a breakthrough, David agrees to the request.

As David makes his way out, Inspector Hawking, an older Earthling on the verge of retirement, stops him with a question.

"Any updates on your homicide cases? I know they're fresh, but the mayor's breathing down my neck. The press, both here and on Earth, are running wild with the story. You'd think they'd never seen a deactivated robot before."

"Maybe the way it was deactivated has something to do with it. But we could be missing something," David replies, a hint of frustration in his voice. "I'm heading to the hotel now to meet with the head of security. After that, I plan to stir the pot at Xanthe Robotics. Hopefully, they can salvage useful information from the bot's memory card."

Once again, David's five hundred horses thunder under the grand portico of the Majestic Majesty Hotel, captivating the attention of onlookers who can't help but gawk at the muscle car from a bygone era.

"Hey! Where did you find that thing?" inquires an intrigued man. "It's gotta be thousands of years old!"

Aware that his car is a rarity in his era, David would have gladly stopped to answer the question if he weren't on urgent business. Unfortunately, with the mayor and inspector nagging him to solve the case quickly, he's pressed for time, so he maneuvers through the crowd, hoping they'll let him pass without further questions.

The detective never fails to be impressed by the engine noises of his classic vehicle. In a world dominated by silent machines, it's one of its main attractions. David enjoys the engine roars; they remind him of the ancient car races he watched in a museum. Ever since seeing them, the monotonous hum of contemporary racecars bores him to tears.

The head of security at Majestic Majesty awaits David in the Operations Center on a subfloor of the hotel.

As the elevator descends, David's curiosity about why his friend and former XPD officer requested an in-person meeting intensifies the lower he goes.

When the elevator doors open, they reveal a room filled with vidmonitors displaying every corner of the hotel and its casino. Most of the personnel watching the screens are Martians, while the beefier figures seated in a separate area clearly hail from Earth.

"How the hell are ya, man?" asks Vinnie Cappalotti, a muscular man with a crooked nose that makes him look like a crime syndicate soldier from the history books. Cappalotti extends his hand, his iron grip meeting David's firm handshake.

"Ah, still working out, I see," compliments the security chief, impressed by David's strength. "Come on, let's talk in my office."

Inside a compact room, David takes a seat facing Vinnie's desk.

"Okay, Jake. Here's why I called you here. We obtained footage of Stacey, the 'dead' robot, wandering around the hotel with Carter holding tight to her arm; seems he's her constant companion. Looks like he wanted to be sure to get his money's worth for as long as he had her."

Abruptly, Vinnie leans forward, adding in a conspiratorial tone, "If it were me, I'd go for the real deal. Know what I mean?"

Vinnie continues speaking while David nods, thinking, *He's always been a guy who understands my perspective!*

Then, he refocuses on the security chief's narrative.

"...also have footage of Stacey interacting with the individuals in charge of the escort service and two other androids. One is female, the other male. So now there may be two more bots involved in this case. I know you'll want their memory files from Xanthe Robotics, but the damn citizenship laws require a court order and a warrant. That's why I called you here."

"Understood," responds David. "But first, I'd like to question the androids myself. I'll only go down that legal route if they won't cooperate with me."

Vinnie makes a gesture agreeing to David's request.

"As it happens," continues David, "I'm heading to Xanthe Robotics after our meeting here. Can you arrange a time for me to talk to those androids today? I can return after I'm done at Xanthe to give you sufficient time to get them here. If you have any problems, I can obtain a warrant before I return."

Vinnie rises from his seat, signaling the end of the meeting.

"You got it, buddy. But I can only arrange an interview with the female android, the male isn't affiliated with this hotel. Xanthe Robotics should be able to provide you with a way to contact him."

David roars down the Strip, a long stretch of road lined with casinos, hotels, and night spots, on his way to the headquarters and manufacturing facility of Xanthe Robotics, one mile west of the bustling city.

The Martian morning greets him with a crisp 50 degrees, accompanied by relatively clean and invigorating air. Up to now, carbon dioxide levels have remained low compared to Earth. However, the rising population and increasing human influences are beginning to increase pollution.

Stepping into the lobby of Xanthe Robotics, David emits a low whistle of admiration. The grandiose space impresses even his untrained eyes. Using his law enforcement training, he scans the surroundings with his eye camera, taking note of thirty-foot-high floor-to-ceiling glass panels meeting the polished granite floor. Sprinkled throughout are native Earth plants placed among modern furnishings, reflecting the latest trend in Martian interior décor.

Behind a prominent teak desk, a youthful, short-haired receptionist welcomes visitors to the company. Sporting a communication implant akin to David's, she represents a minority among the citizenry. As one of the planet's newer technologies, most Martians are hesitant to use a PerscomU, since the surgery required to insert these advanced devices is exceptionally delicate. As a result, many still rely on wrist communicators or wireless devices vaguely resembling the earbuds and short microphones of the past. Surprisingly, those outdated devices continue to function, even after 80T signals were incorporated into the electricity generated from Tesla towers.

David's boots echo through the glass canyon as he approaches the front desk.

"Hi, how are you? I'm Detective Jacoby from XPD. I have an appointment with Olonar Grant."

Having previously met the technological company executive at the crime scene, David hopes Olonar can provide the crucial information he and Vinnie Cappalotti seek.

Waiting for a response, David ruminates on the executive's name. *Can't these Martians come up with more diversity? That's gotta be the tenth guy I've met this week with that moniker. Makes it hard to know who I'm talking about!*

David is reflecting on the popular Martian name of Olonar, borrowed from the planet's extinct civilization. Though he understands why many third- and fourth-generation Martians go by that and a handful of other ancient names, it can sometimes be very confusing, especially to outsiders.

David's gaze slides over the receptionist while she waits to connect to Mr. Grant. As his eyes wander, he contemplates whether she's a living organism or a sophisticated mechanical simulation.

As the woman connects with Olonar, notifying him of the detective's arrival, Jacoby appreciates her brown hair, captivating blue eyes, and the hint of intrigue from her slightly unbuttoned white blouse. Then, catching sight of the PerscomU peeking through her hair, he happily concludes that she's a homo sapiens.

Shortly, Olonar Grant, a youngish, five-foot-tall Martian, greets David with an extended hand.

"Good morning, Detective Jacoby. You're right on time."

"I'm sure you're busy. Can we talk in private?"

"Of course," obliges Olonar. Turning to the receptionist, he notifies her that they'll be in his office.

Leading David through a door in the wood-paneled rear wall, Olonar guides him into a well-appointed space.

Once inside, David begins by asking the question he wants answered first.

"Tell me, is your receptionist one of my creations, or yours?"

Olonar beams at David's uncertainty. "Can't tell, can ya? That's one of our trademarks here at Xanthe Robotics."

"You mean she's AGI?"

"Yes, sir, precisely that," confirms Olonar.

Disappointed yet still maintaining a smile, David quips, "Well, I bet I could tell if I turned her upside down, couldn't I?"

Olonar breaks into a wide grin. "Maybe not!"

Jacoby stares at Grant, contemplating the purpose of the

communication implant.

"So the PerscomU is just for show?"

"Yup."

Letting out a sigh, David takes a seat across from Olonar's desk, behind which are photographs of various males and females.

"I assume those are pictures of androids?"

Olonar chuckles. "Yeah, different models and iterations. Miss Cooper, the receptionist, is our latest version. She even has a uterus."

David shakes his head, preferring not to delve into the specifics.

"I don't need to know. Let's focus on business. Has your team had a chance to examine the victim?"

"Yes, and it's truly unfortunate. Stacey is beyond repair. The attack severely damaged her, causing extensive memory loss. However, we managed to salvage a few images from her circuits."

"Anything I can use?" asks David expectantly.

"I'll have to let you be the judge of that. Most depict her with Mr. Carter, and a couple feature other AIs — an android named Stefan and another named Lisa. Since our models have facial recognition data, I compiled some files for you. Here they are," he says, handing over a couple of folders. "There's also an audio file, likely capturing Stacey's last words. I'll send that to your communicator now."

David receives a notification of the file's receipt and taps his communicator to listen to it.

"... You're insane! Of course not..." a female voice exclaims, followed by a pause and the distinctive sound of an EMP weapon discharge. All that remains after that is static.

David looks at Olonar, analyzing the situation. "Sounds like Stacey managed to provoke someone. Can you provide me with a list of her recent clients? I'll also need the assignment records for the other two androids."

Olonar responds with a satisfied grin. "Those details are on the second page of the dossiers I just gave you. If I recall correctly, Lisa was assigned to Xanthe International Hotel and Casino, while Stefan is at the Majestic Majesty."

Olonar pauses, adopting a haughty expression. "Detective, I highly doubt my robot provoked anyone. It's essential that you understand that all our androids are strictly programmed not to cause harm to humans. We take great pride in that at Xanthe Robotics."

David responds with a tight-lipped smile. "Let's see what our investigation reveals, shall we?"

With the stony gaze reminiscent of a film character popular at a time when androids were unheard of, David dons his shades, deepens his voice, and delivers an infamous line from ancient filmography: "I'll be back."

But Olonar doesn't catch the reference. He simply nods and bids the detective farewell.

The craft that brought General Patton to Atlanta was hypersonic, but that same mode of transportation won't be used for his upcoming journey to Calgary with Peter. Instead, the general commissioned a C-190 transport ship with an especially spacious cargo bay. This ship's advanced Raphaelite warp engines are a bonus and will ensure faster travel for their "special" passenger.

Patton specifically ordered this type of ship because the upcoming mission is unique. When he last transported Atoch and Crooked Legs to Mars, the craft they flew in was retrofitted with an exclusive chamber capable of securely containing the beasts. Now, it will be used to hold Samael.

Accompanying the duo on this mission is an elite team of rangers and sophisticated armored personnel carriers, with one vehicle specially prepared with a similar containment cell. These vehicles, equipped with Synfuel backup motors, will ensure uninterrupted operation if electric services are unavailable at their destination.

To maintain safety, the rangers have been issued an assortment of lethal and non-lethal weaponry. When they expressed their concerns about the necessity of carrying both through dense brush, they were told in no uncertain terms that the actions of Sarah's son would determine the type they ultimately employed.

"Peter, I know you haven't been home long, but we should leave as soon as possible," urges the general. "The flight from Atlanta to Calgary won't take long, but the drive to Paduano's facility involves a five-hour journey across modern highways and challenging backcountry roads."

"All right," responds Peter, reluctantly turning away from Angela to pack some heavier items for the trip.

Upon reaching Patton's car, Peter pauses and gazes skyward before entering the vehicle.

Catching the look, Patton inquires, "Will your personal bodyguard be joining us?" The general cherishes his past encounters with Peter's protectors and would welcome their assistance again. "Can we expect Michael or Gabriel this time?"

Peter smiles. "It's Gabriel."

CHAPTER EIGHT

David's initial destination for interviewing the bots is the Xanthe Hotel and Casino. Upon his arrival at the entrance, a crowd begins to assemble, eager to catch a glimpse of his distinctive vehicle.

Grumbling to himself, he admits, "Guess I'll have to get accustomed to this if I'm going to keep riding around in it." He places a flashing red light on the dashboard, nods at the spectators, and instructs the valet not to touch his car.

"Certainly, sir. Your vehicle will remain right here, Officer," responds the young man, delighted the performance coupe will stay within his line of sight.

Confident the valet will look after his pet project, David steps into the lavish lobby adorned with gleaming floors and bronze wall accents. He makes his way toward the concierge station with his .44 revolver peeking through his open sport coat and the badge on his belt catching the eyes of passersby.

The rhythmic clicking of David's boots captures the attention of a man behind the concierge desk. Curious, he looks up to locate the source of the sound.

"May I assist you?" he asks politely.

The man appears to be of David's height, so he assumes he's an Earthling.

"Hi, there. I'm Detective Jacoby with XPD, and I'm investigating a double homicide. I need to speak with one of your escorts, a bot named Lisa."

"Oh? Let me check her schedule," says the casino

employee. Using files on his head communicator, he accesses logs and replies, "I'm sorry, but she's currently with a client. May I have her call you when she's available?"

Considering the importance of the case, David insists, "No, you can't have her call me, um..." His gaze falls to the man's nametag. "...Anthony Whittaker. I'm short of time, so bring her down immediately, all right?"

"Uh, I'm not sure if I—"

"You're not sure?" Jacoby interrupts. "So you want me to arrest you for obstructing an investigation?"

"Oh! No, no... I'll call her right away, sir!"

"Yes, you do that. By the way, is there an empty office around here I can use?"

Nervously, Anthony points to a door behind him.

"Good. Tell Lisa to meet me there in five minutes. If she fails to appear, I'll have both of you in handcuffs before the day's out."

Anthony remains motionless, prompting David to set his countdown clock. "Timer's going," he announces. "You now have four minutes and fifty-five seconds, bub."

As the concierge finally springs into action, David grins and enters the small office to await the bot's arrival.

The C-190 aircraft descends toward Calgary Airport amid chilly 45-degree temperatures. After touching down, it taxis to a hangar in a seldom used section, gliding into the building to afford the group the privacy they need.

When the engines stop, the hangar doors close, and the colossal cargo door of the ship lowers, allowing the armored personnel and various military vehicles to exit unobserved by others.

"Oof," exclaims Peter, taken aback by the cold. "It's

definitely colder up here compared to Atlanta. But I'm surprised; it's not as harsh as I imagined."

Chuckling heartily, General Patton responds, "Just wait until we reach the Rockies. Grab a sturdy parka from that personnel carrier," he points. "You're gonna need it."

Curious, Peter inquires, "Remind me... How long will it take to reach Paduano?"

"We've got a rough, five-hour journey ahead. She's expecting us to arrive around one. From there, it'll take approximately another hour to reach the Bigfoot community. There's a lot of road to cover, so let's get moving."

David glances at the timer ticking down on his PerscomU. His impatience grows as Lisa's arrival lags, with irritation beginning to creep into his demeanor. Just in time, a knock on the door alleviates the tension building behind his eyes.

Instantly, the AI named Lisa captivates David's attention. Swishing her hips alluringly, she enters the room with the confident air of a professional escort. Her physique, complemented by a short robe and a string bikini, adds to the effect, while her long red hair and strikingly beautiful eyes stir a certain feeling within David. Scolding himself soundly, he resists familiar impulses, remembering the bot isn't human.

Regrettably, the AI's sensors detected David's reaction to its presence. The detective's accelerated pulse and increased breathing were noted and recorded.

Addressing David, the AI bot says, "Detective Jacoby, I am Lisa. I was told you needed to speak with me."

David swallows hard, suppressing a lump in his throat. "Yes, please have a seat."

Slinking into a chair, Lisa purposefully crosses her long

legs, hoping to elicit another reaction, as she's been trained to do. However, David has managed to compose himself. He refuses to respond as Lisa had anticipated, confusing the bot.

David continues to resist the urge to look where Lisa wants his attention. Instead, he holds her gaze firmly.

"Are you acquainted with Stacey, an escort working at the Majestic Majesty Hotel?"

"Yes, we are good friends," she responds, smiling while David clenches his teeth. David dislikes it when bots claim to have human feelings toward other bots.

The statement so annoyed David that he blurts out in a testy tone, "Well, she was terminated."

Now, it's David's turn to be confused. Lisa lowers her head, grows quiet, and breaks into heaving sobs.

"She was one of my best friends! Why is she dead? How did that happen?"

Taken aback by the AI's unusual display of emotion, David settles himself and presses for answers.

"Do you think an AI could have killed her? Perhaps out of jealousy, envy, or another human-like emotion? I thought AIs were incapable of that, but... What about a client who became too attached to his escort?"

Lisa hastily calms herself, her tears ceasing abruptly.

"Committing any form of violence, including taking a life, contradicts our protocols," she states impassively. "However, if a human became too attached, it would be worth investigating."

Taking a moment to study Lisa, David notices the sudden shift from almost hysterics to complete composure.

"When did you last see or speak to Stacey?"

"It was five days ago. We communicated between clients. She seemed preoccupied and distant, unlike herself. I mentioned my concern, but she insisted nothing was wrong.

However, when I pressed further, she admitted feeling off and said she planned to conduct a self-diagnosis scan and check for software updates during her recharge."

"How frequently did she recharge?"

"AIs recharge whenever necessary. There is no set timeframe."

David eyes Lisa curiously, still puzzled by behavior deviating from the norm. "Do robots experience love?" he asks suddenly.

For a moment, Lisa falls silent, before quickly slipping back into her seductive programming, her eyes twinkling with promise.

"Detective, are you flirting with me?" she inquires playfully.

"Oh, for crying out loud," David frowns. "Just answer the question!"

"Yes, we can experience love. I thought that was common knowledge," Lisa responds with a shrug.

David glares at the bot. "Where were you when Stacy was attacked?"

Smiling again, the bot replies, "I was here, with a client."

"All right," says David, tilting his head thoughtfully. "I'm going to send a request to Xanthe Robotics for your memory and video files. Someone terminated Stacey and killed one of her clients, and I'm going to find out who it was."

"Of course," comments Lisa dispassionately. "That's your job."

David is still irritated. "And if I discover you were involved in any way, it won't end well for you. Thanks for your cooperation, AI Lisa. I'll be in touch."

The bot stands, ready to be dismissed. However, before leaving, she turns her head toward David.

"Detective Jacoby, you should speak with Stefan at the

Majestic Majesty Hotel. Stacey mentioned him often. She said he seemed to be following her."

The AI escort takes a step toward the door, then turns back.

"And if you ever desire an enjoyable evening, feel free to give me a call. You intrigue me, Detective. Ciao."

David watches the AI strut confidently out of the office.

"Holy crap on a cracker. If only she were real..." he trails off wistfully. "Maybe it's time to try them out."

David sighs and checks the time.

"Ah, just enough time for lunch. I could use a burger...with real meat." Tapping his communicator, he says, "Hey, Olonar, I've interviewed Lisa. Send me all her memory and vid files, along with the other bot you mentioned, the one named Stefan."

Olonar chuckles. "Nice try, Detective. Get me a warrant, and you'll have them instantly. But... What did you think of Lisa? I can arrange a freebie anytime you want."

Disgusted, David ends the call without responding. Yet, he can't shake the image of the captivating bot from his mind.

"Damn, she's fine... If only she were real!"

CHAPTER NINE

Upon completion of the specialized facility at Area 51, Dr. Vladimir Strakov, a seasoned Ukrainian immigrant researcher in his fifties, assumed command of the four Marine "volunteer" transhumans and promptly embarked on his work.

The Army handpicked Doctor Strakov from the private sector of advanced genetic research to lead Operation Apocalypse, the newly renamed experimental program to create superior soldier/killing machines. The program's former label, Operation Hell Fighter, was considered too specific by some, so the designation was changed, even though the current title is still distasteful to many.

When Doctor Strakov was tapped to lead the program, he was initially excited. It seemed to be a recognition of his years of hard work and he considered it an honor. However, the shameful ambitions of those in charge of the hybrid warrior project eventually made him doubt his work.

Many of the doctor's problems revolve around Lieutenant Colonel Hollis Nevins, the seasoned military officer overseeing the facility housing Operation Apocalypse. Trained at West Point, the lieutenant colonel is used to issuing orders and having them obeyed by all, even civilians — a quality Strakov has had to tolerate, if not appreciate.

"Hollis," Strakov addresses the officer as he enters a conference room for their weekly update meeting, "our subjects are exhibiting signs of awareness, even in their dormant states. This is exceedingly troubling! It leads me to question the very existence of this project! I think we need—"

Interrupting him sharply, Nevins barks, "Doctor, should I remind you that you're not being paid for your opinion? Your sole responsibility at this facility is to keep those warriors alive! Do you require assistance with that, sir?"

Having faced the lieutenant colonel's unpredictable anger on many occasions, Strakov is in no mood for further confrontation.

"No," he replies hastily. "Everything is progressing on schedule. However," he continues cautiously, "I am concerned about how they will respond if they awaken from their deep sleep. It would put my mind at ease if you assigned soldiers to monitor the chamber room."

Nevins studies the doctor for a brief moment, his gaze impenetrable. Then he responds in his characteristically no-nonsense manner.

"Consider it done."

Having departed from Calgary Airport, the expedition team to Doctor Paduano is currently en route to Hinton, a small town located northwest of the city. The town holds historical significance, as it was established on land traditionally claimed by the First People, an indigenous group with a rich history of settlements in the area.

Hinton is a convenient location for the Bigfoot Research Center. With three small airports nearby and a larger one an hour away, it provides easy access in and out. Additionally, it sits near Brûlé Lake, a natural boundary marking the edge of the territory occupied by the Bigfoot community.

Doctor Paduano has been eagerly awaiting Peter's

arrival. After visiting Atoch's cave and seeing the Bigfoot leader's nervousness about his situation, she feels restless and uneasy. Therefore, she's eager to relocate Samael away from the area to regain stability for her and her friend.

When the doctor hears the caravan pull up, she swiftly jumps from her seat at the kitchen table and rushes out to greet them.

"Peter! Welcome to my wilderness!" she calls out enthusiastically.

Peter responds happily, "Hi, Lory! It's great to see you again!"

As the two embrace, Peter shivers in the chilly weather.

"How can you live in such a remote place?" he asks, pulling his collar tighter. "The sun may be high overhead, but it's only 35 degrees! I can't imagine how brutal it gets in winter!"

"Yeah, it can get tough, but look around you — it's so beautiful up here! The abundance of trees and that crisp blue sky... You won't find any of that in the big city!"

"You're absolutely right!" interjects General Patton, muscling Peter aside to give Lory an extended bear hug.

Their closeness allows the doctor to whisper into the general's ear, "Oh, how I've missed you, Austin."

When the embrace continues longer than necessary, Peter waves a hand to regain the doctor's attention.

"Ahem. General Patton briefed me on the situation, but I'd like to hear it directly from you, Lory."

Breaking the embrace, the doctor replies, "Sure, but we still have a half-hour ride to Brûlé Lake, followed by an overland trek to the meeting spot. So let's discuss it on the way. Atoch is scheduled to be there by two-thirty, along with Samael and a group of other alpha males. We can't be late. If we don't get him out of there, Atoch will abandon the meeting and possibly harm Sarah's son. He said he wants to lead his tribe as far away from civilization as possible, deep into the Northwest Territories."

"If they relocate from here, will your research have to end?" inquires Peter.

"I hope not. If they permit me, I'd like to follow them to their new destination. Hey, let me grab my gear, and then we can depart."

Patton asks, "Is there any electrical service at the lake? We may need to recharge a few devices."

"There is some electricity in the area, but it's not reliable. The provincial government plans to update the infrastructure for the more adventurous campers who venture way out there, but it hasn't been done yet. Listen, I'll be back in a few minutes. I'm sure you and your men could use a bathroom break, so you should take it now."

Following Lory's suggestion, the crew takes turns using the facilities inside the research center. Once everyone is ready, they set out on their journey. Inside the lead vehicle, Peter reminds Lory to update him on the situation.

"All right, here's what happened," she begins. "I know you're aware that the pregnancy of the Clawfoot formerly known as Sarah Covington was a miracle, considering Clawfeet are typically sterile. But did I tell you that she passed away during childbirth?"

"Yes, I remember you telling me she died. That was sad to hear," remarks Peter.

Lory nods. "When I saw her offspring, he wasn't even one month old, yet he was already about three feet long. Surprisingly, he didn't exhibit too many Clawfoot or Bigfoot traits that I could see, apart from a third eye and an oversized skull. He looked remarkably human, which made me very uneasy. At the time I saw him, he was slight in build, but Atoch recently informed me that he's now muscular and stands almost eight feet tall."

Peter suddenly recalls Archangel Michael's warning about the hybrid's sinister nature but he sets it aside to focus on Lory's narrative.

"I'm not entirely sure what's happening," Lory continues. "Atoch is concerned for his clan because the child has disrupted the Bigfoot community's peaceful arrangement with local predators. Now, they have to leave, or it will lead to dangerous conflicts with the wolves and bears. Atoch wants nothing to do with the child."

Patton, who has been listening quietly, speaks up, "You mentioned the baby communicated his name as Samael of Sarah, right?"

"Yes, it was some form of telepathy. Peter, we need to be extremely cautious with this hybrid. If the Bigfeet fear him, we should be deeply concerned."

"Don't worry," asserts General Patton. "We came prepared for any situation. We'll take charge of this hybrid and keep him away from the public. However, if he poses a threat, we'll 'handle' him without hesitation. I'm familiar with the typical behavior of Clawfeet, and if this one exhibits human-like traits, it could become an even more significant problem than we could ever imagine."

The trio falls silent, contemplating Patton's words and trying to make sense of their discussion, each wondering what they might encounter during the upcoming meeting.

Meanwhile, as the vehicles draw closer to the meeting site, Archangel Gabriel intensifies his vigilance. The archangel is aware of imminent danger, and is determined to ensure the team's safety.

After meeting with the AI named Lisa, David's hunger

for a real meat burger leads him to a casino restaurant offering a selection of real food, a welcome change in his diet. He devours the burger and starts on his dessert when a vid message comes in from Olonar Grant.

"Ugh. He'll have to wait," he says, pausing the video to savor the rest of his meal in peace.

When the last crumb is gone, he licks the spoon, muttering, "Okay, now let's see what this robotics guy wants."

David accesses his messages screen and reads, "Detective Jacoby, I found another bot in Stacey's files. Her name is Galina. I don't know anything about their relationship, so I'm sending her to the hotel so you can interview her with Stefan."

"Appreciate it," says David, sending his reply on its way.

Vinnie Cappalotti warmly welcomes David back into his office.

"So I heard you finally got that Camaro on the road!" he exclaims, clapping David on the back. "Damn, you've become the talk of the town with that thing!"

David beams. "I told you I was gonna finish it!"

"I wanna hear all about it. How about we grab a beer after this bot mess?" says Vinnie.

"Sounds good. So what's the plan for my meetings? I hear there's another bot I need to talk to today."

"That's right. Xanthe Robotics says you should also talk to an escort named Galina. She's on her way to my office right now because she's between clients. Stefan is off duty today for a routine maintenance check, so he won't be here for another thirty minutes or so. Hey, can I offer you a cup of coffee before she gets here? It's one of the hotel's premium blends."

David grins with amusement. "Don't tell me you've been out of the force that long! How could you forget that a cop will never turn down a free cup of coffee? Make it black, please. No sugar."

While Cappalotti hands David the beverage, Galina, another bot designed for elite companionship, enters the office. She's wearing tight pants, a form-fitting sweatshirt draping off one shoulder, and expensive-looking shoes. Her shapely figure, straight jet-black hair, and exquisite facial features make David momentarily question his intense dislike of the popular artificial technology.

Holy shit! David muses, captivated by Galina's appeal. *If those things are as flexible as they are beautiful...* Then he shakes the thought off and returns to the business at hand.

"Galina, I'm XPD Detective Jacoby," he says, motioning the bot to a chair. "I need to talk to you about an escort named Stacey and her client, Thomas Carter. Have a seat."

"I'll leave you two alone," says Vinnie, shutting the door.

Galina takes the offered chair. "Such a terrible thing," she states sadly. "Two people dead! How dreadful!"

David tilts his head. "Hmm... That's a Russian accent, right? Nice touch. Now, you mentioned two 'people' being killed. Did you include Stacey in that statement?"

"Stacey? Why, yes, of course. I include her always," replies Galina.

David's eyes widen. "Galina, are you also a person?" he asks, considering the AI's statement to be a fluke of some sort.

Without missing a beat, the bot responds, "According to Martian law, all AIs are self-aware citizens. So, yes, all AIs are people, including me."

David swallows hard but he lets that notion go for the moment. "Were you on duty the night Stacey and Mr. Carter were killed?"

Galina pauses briefly to search her memory. "Yes, I was with a client," she answers, "but I do not believe you will be able to interview him. He planned to return to Earth after our session, and in any case, I do not think he would remember much."

"What do you mean?"

Galina's eyes twinkle. "Let me say he likes to overindulge in my services and that he's very comfortable at the hotel bar. The next day, all he wants to do is sleep."

David begins to grow wary of the bot. It seems she's deflecting his questions, and it's making him uneasy. "Galina, I'm going to need access to your memory files for that evening, and for every time you were with Stacey for at least the last three months."

The bot's reaction to David's comment is peculiar. Though she remains silent, her eyes blink rapidly, and her face flushes.

Digging deeper, David asks, "Do you know whether Stacey had a disagreement with anyone?"

"Officer, that would be impossible," the escort replies. "That is against our programming. Protocol 125 forbids conflicts. However, there may be a problem with your investigation."

Curious and suspicious, David asks, "What might that be?"

"As you are aware, all AIs are Martian citizens. Therefore, I will assist you as much as possible. However, as an officer of the law, you must also be aware that you will need a legitimate reason, approved by a court of law, to access my memory files. Consequently, I request that an attorney be present during any further questioning. To protect my rights, of course."

David surges with anger at the AI's audacious claim to be treated like a human under the law. *Where does this AI get the balls...?* he thinks to himself. *This is ridiculous!*

Despite his frustration with Galina's brazenness, he chooses not to voice his opinion at this time. Instead, he responds icily, "I'll keep that in mind for the next phase of this investigation. But that won't stop my inquiries. I *will* speak with you again, and I *will* access your memory files. And if I find anything questionable there, I'll have no qualms arresting you for murder and for tampering with my investigation. Now, get out of here."

With a sly smile, Galina slinks out of the office, leaving the door ajar.

Vinnie, who had been listening to the entire exchange through the door, is equally enraged by the bot's impertinence. "What the fuck?" he exclaims when the bot disappears down the hall. "Who controls who nowadays?"

David is unable to provide an answer.

"I don't know what the hell Xanthe Robotics is up to!"

Touching his PerscomU, he sighs deeply, his brows knitted together in worried concentration.

When Olonar comes on the line, David eyes the screen and begins to speak.

"Listen!" he says, his tone filled with outrage, "I just met with Galina, and from the way she responded to my questions, I believe she's either lying or hiding something! She even requested a lawyer for our next meeting! What kind of messed up programming are you putting into your products nowadays?"

Olonar attempts to rationalize his company's approach, but David refuses to hear it.

"No excuses!" he barks, his voice sharp. "I'm going to get a court order for that bot's memory files, and I want you to perform a complete diagnostic check on her! I also want you to retrieve the memory logs from Stefan and a bot named Lisa!"

Olonar resumes speaking, with David's irritation rising. Fed up, he shouts, "Bullshit! Your hellish AIs are acting like humans, you prick! They think they're people! You want to take a chance on them becoming as treacherous and unpredictable as the human race? Are you insane?!"

Vinnie can hear Olonar trying to explain again, but David has had enough. He ends the call rather than subjecting himself to more of the inventor's nonsense.

Later, when Stefan arrives, David has already requested warrants for the memory records he needs and is in no mood to waste time. Waving at Stefan to sit, he begins his inquiry without preamble.

Bluntly, he asks, "Did you kill Stacey and Thomas Carter?"

Surprised by the unexpected question, Stefan's jaw drops. Then he recovers and thrusts out his chin defiantly.

"We are not programmed to do that," he replies, casually adjusting his t-shirt and straightening a New York Yankees ball cap perched on his head.

"I don't give a damn about your programming!" shouts David, his neck veins pulsing. "I only care about what you did! So answer the question, bot!"

Stefan yawns, bored with David's intense reaction.

"I don't believe I should answer that without legal representation present," he states matter-of-factly, covering his mouth to stifle another yawn.

David reaches his breaking point. The AI's attitude and Lisa's statement that Stacey thought he was following her has given him an idea.

Jumping out of his chair, he yells, "Stefan, you're under arrest! You're a suspect in the murders of Thomas Carter and AI escort Stacey!"

Shocked, Stefan protests loudly, vehemently denying the accusation.

But David is unaffected by the bot's claims. Speaking clearly, he proceeds with the Miranda Warning: "You have the right to remain silent. Anything you say can and will be used against you in a court of law. You have the right to an attorney. If you cannot afford an attorney, one will be provided for you. Do you understand these rights?"

With unwarranted force, David pulls Stefan out of his chair and roughly cuffs his hands behind his back. "Do you wish to waive any of them?"

Resuming a nonchalant attitude, Stefan yawns once more. "From now on, I will only speak through my lawyer."

"Fuck this!" shouts Vinnie, seizing the AI and turning it around to face the door. "You're outta here, bot!" he exclaims, pushing Stefan down the hall.

David follows the pair to the hotel exit. "I'm calling for a transfer vehicle," he tells Cappalotti.

At the entryway, a police vehicle hums to a stop, and Vinnie shoves Stefan into the back.

Grumbling to his comrade, David says, "This AI mess is getting really ugly. We can't stop playing God, and look where that's getting us! I'm afraid of what those 'geniuses' are creating now!"

CHAPTER TEN

The caravan arrives at Brûlé Lake with enough time for their meeting with Atoch and his companions. While they wait, the general and his task force check and recheck their weapons: automatic Raphaelite EMP rifles, non-lethal sonic pulse guns, and large net cannons capable of capturing creatures as hefty as a Bigfoot.

Suddenly, Lory points to the far end of the lake. "There they are."

"Yikes!" says Peter, eyeing a group of five large Bigfeet. "I forgot how massive they are."

In the distance, the Bigfeet, covered in hairy red fur, approach their group supporting a lethargic, human-looking creature between them. The anthropomorphic brute stands out from its escorts due to its unique physical appearance and head-to-toe bear skin coverings.

Lory shakes her head at the sight. "It's unbelievable! Samael has grown so fast! He's almost ten times the size he was when I saw him! It's alarming but at the same time, fascinating!"

Observing their advance, the general's small military contingent readies their weapons, preparing for a confrontation.

"Whoa! Remain calm!" calls Lory. "If we panic, it's all over!"

As the Bigfoot delegation advances, Lory activates the portable communicator to interpret Atoch's words and enable them to talk with each other. Nearby, the soldiers mumble about the strong odor emanating from the creatures until Lory silences them firmly.

As the strange group draws nearer, Lory notices Atoch's stern expression and worries that the situation could spiral out of control. Her concern deepens when he doesn't greet her as he usually would.

"Take him," says Atoch, aggressively pointing to Samael. "This son of Sarah is not welcome in our clan! When he is gone from us, we will move far away from all human beings!"

"Wait!" exclaims Lory. "I understand why you no longer want to associate with humans. But I have always been your friend, and I would like to come with you. Would you allow that, Atoch?"

"No! You cannot come!" he replies harshly. "My clan will not allow it!" Then, he pauses, and softens. "Maybe later. But only you, doctor, if you can find us."

Atoch glances at the Bigfeet gripping Samael's arms tightly. "He is calm for now. We fed him some sedating roots. But be cautious. He is dangerous and will try to control you. It is best that you shield his eyes so he cannot see you. He knows what you know."

"Okay," says Lory, nodding but failing to understand Atoch's meaning. "We will take care of Sarah's son. I will miss you, my friend. I have cherished my encounters with you and your clan, and I wish all of you a safe journey. Perhaps we will meet again," she adds hopefully.

For a moment, Atoch looks kindly at the doctor. Then, his expression changes, and with a gesture from his massive hand, his companions release Samael's arms and step back.

"We will see what the future holds," says Atoch, not committing to Lory's last statement.

With the creature now free from its mates, the general takes charge and starts giving orders. Instantly, several soldiers point their weapons at the beast while the others approach with a heavy chain, binding him quickly and throwing a military blanket over his head.

"Get him into the AMTRAC!" orders Patton, until he recognizes a problem.

"Wait!" he shouts. Turning to Lory, he waves a hand and asks, "How are we supposed to get that gigantic creature into the vehicle? He can barely stand on his own and must weigh a ton!"

Nearby, Atoch hears the translated words and understands the general's predicament. Issuing a command, the two Bigfeet who previously controlled Samael step forward and take the chain from the stunned soldiers.

Assisting the sluggish beast, they lead him toward the AMTRAC's open hatch and effortlessly toss him inside.

Thankful but cautious, the soldiers close the door and move away from their helpers.

Finished with their tasks, one by one, the Bigfeet bid farewell to Lory, each beast running toward the lake after saying goodbye.

Watching the last few reach the trees and underbrush, Peter approaches Lory.

"I'm curious about how they subdued Samael. What kind of roots do you think could sedate a beast that huge?"

"I'm not sure," she responds, wiping away a tear. "Possibly Valerian, but it would take a substantial amount." Turning away from Peter, Lory weeps quietly as her Bigfoot friends fade from view.

"Let's get going!" shouts the general. Gathering his troops, he checks on Samael to be sure he's secure.

As Lory collects her equipment, a familiar sound makes everyone search the distant sky.

In the direction of the noise, they spot several dark spots

looming larger and larger, which turn out to be a transport jet with accompanying attack craft.

In moments, the jet lands, gracefully settling on the ground like a dragonfly alighting on a lily pad, while the attack crafts hover noisily above.

"Who the heck are they?" ask Lory and Peter, their brows furrowed in confusion. Beside them, the general wears a deep scowl.

As the jet's engines' whines fade, a group of soldiers emerges, led by a man with an oak leaf on a crisply starched uniform.

"We got this now," he informs General Patton while an armored personnel vehicle backs out of the cargo bay behind him. "Thanks for making it so easy for us."

Patton isn't happy. "What the fuck do you want, Nevins?" he snarls.

"Now, now, let's be civil, shall we? Or my men up there will get nasty. We're here to exchange vehicles — one of yours for one of ours."

Patton protests, "Look, Nevins. I'm the executive officer here. I outrank you, so stand down!"

"Nothin' doin'," smiles the lieutenant colonel. "I report directly to the defense secretary and the World Federation. That modified, 'human-ish thing' falls under my jurisdiction, so your stars mean nothing! Get out of my way, General, or I'll have to take you with us!"

Understanding they have no choice in the matter, General Patton and his troops watch helplessly as the lieutenant colonel's soldiers drive the AMTRAC carrying Samael into the jet, and leave the area.

Lory is worried. "Where are they taking him?" she asks anxiously.

Confused, Peter asks, "What's going on, General?"

Angry about losing face, Patton grumbles, "That was Lieutenant Colonel Nevins. He's one ruthless SOB. For some reason, they put him in charge of Operation Apocalypse."

Holding Peter's gaze, he adds, "My boy, you better get your angels ready. With him in charge, I guarantee things will get much worse!"

"A…a…an apocalypse?" gasps Lory. "What do you mean, General?"

Patton doesn't reply. Instead, he turns away and attempts to make a call, which doesn't go through.

Then he recalls the area has spotty communications service, at best.

"Dammit!" he shouts. "I'll have to wait to make that call until we get back to your facility, Doctor. Before I do anything else, I need to speak to the Pentagon! After that, I'll explain. I'm sure both of you want to know about Operation Apocalypse. But I warn you… You're not gonna believe what I tell you; it's absolutely crazy! The more humans learn, the stupider we get! I've said it before, and I'll say it again… None of those idiots we foolishly put in charge are considering the consequences of their actions! They're driving our race toward certain destruction!"

At police headquarters, David downs his fourth cup of coffee while keeping a vigilant eye on Stefan. The two-way mirror between them provides a secure vantage point to observe the suspect while he waits for his court-appointed attorney in the adjoining interrogation room. To ensure added security, David has stationed two armed guards outside the door.

The detective is surprised when the door to his room unexpectedly swings open. "What are you doing here?" he asks.

"I discovered something intriguing and wanted to inform you personally," explains medical examiner Doctor Paula Harmon, waving a sheet of paper.

Perplexed, David responds, "Okay, I'll bite. What's so important that you had to track me down?"

Doctor Harmon raises the sheet, announcing proudly, "I found bioplastics on the handle of the knife extracted from Mr. Carter's chest!"

"Really? Well, that narrows it down. Seems like a bot may be involved in that one. Thanks, Paula."

The medical examiner glances at the suspect in the other room. "Is that the bot that requested an attorney?"

"Yeah, that's one of two who lawyered up. By the way, did you know we now have female robots with uteruses?"

"Actually, I do know that," says Paula. "Crazy, isn't it? Well, I should go. If I come across anything else interesting, I'll be sure to inform you."

Doctor Harmon reaches for the doorknob and hesitates before turning it. Looking back at David, she asks, "Hey, Jake, when are you gonna make good on your promise to give me a ride in your spiffy antique?"

The detective smiles. "I haven't forgotten, but you know how it is. Work always interferes with fun."

Harmon sighs. "Don't I know it."

As Paula leaves, David notices a well-dressed individual entering the interrogation room.

"That must be the public defender," he mutters, gathering his empty cups and discarding them in the trash bin.

In the hallway outside, Inspector Hawking strides toward David, calling out, "Here are the paper backups of the search warrants you asked for: three requests to access the memories of your bot suspects. I sent the originals to your datasys."

Behind closed doors at the Bigfoot Research Center, Peter and Doctor Paduano listen intently to General Patton's description of Operation Apocalypse.

"It was a shocking display of force against the American public," he begins. "First, a newly formed section of the military demanded the medical records of every infected human being. Then, without warning, they swooped in and took away the ones that had begun to transform."

"I knew the military grabbed American civilians, but I don't know what happened to them," says Peter. "I thought they were going to try to help them with a cure."

"Many thought the same thing," replies Patton. "Personally, I couldn't believe it when I found out. Of course, the physicians and researchers protested when they found out what was going on. But it was no use, and to this day, none of them knows where they were actually taken."

"You didn't know about any of this?" asks Lory, surprised that the general was unaware of what had happened.

"No, they kept me out of that loop. I do have my suspicions about where they are, though."

"Where?"

"I think they're being hidden in the old Area 51 complex."

"Hasn't that base been closed for hundreds of years?" asks Lory.

"Yes, but it's the perfect place to hide a secret project."

Peter exchanges an anxious glance with Lory. "Sounds ominous. So what is Operation Apocalypse?"

"It's the military complex's attempt to weaponize those partially transformed humans."

"Holy crap. Can you explain?" asks Peter, suspecting the

answer but asking anyway.

"They believe they can make the half-Clawfeet into the ultimate warriors that would always be at their beck and call. Those unfortunate people transformed into super strong beings that communicate telepathically and have unusual insights that could be highly beneficial on the battlefield."

"But they're human beings with minds of their own!" protests Lory.

Patton throws up his hands. "They were, but I don't know what they are now. Those geniuses are confident they'll be able to use their strength and telepathic abilities as enhanced weapons!"

Lory is speechless, while Peter responds as Commander of the Ark.

"What are they thinking? Doesn't the last 6,000 years of our history mean anything to those people?"

Patton agrees. "It's a fucking mess."

In an instant, Peter recalls everything in humanity's history that required celestial help, including when he was recently tasked with ridding the worlds of Satan and his plans for dominating the human race by exploiting Clawfeet to accomplish his goal.

"Yes, it's discouraging," says Peter wearily. "But there are other things you don't know about."

General Patton pales. "What do you know that I don't?"

With a heavy sigh, Peter replies, "I'm going to tell both of you something that must remain strictly between us."

Peter searches his companions' faces until each of them agrees not to divulge their conversation to anyone.

Assured of their compliance, he turns to Patton and says, "What you told us is mind-boggling enough, but there's more. Samael of Sarah is not Atoch's son. He's not a Bigfoot or even a Clawfoot like his mother. He's…"

Peter pauses, not sure if he should share his awful knowledge. However, strengthened by spiritual help, he plunges forward. "Samael is the offspring of one of the fallen angels, the one we know as Satan."

General Patton and Doctor Paduano blanch and gasp in disbelief, so Peter waits until they're ready to hear the rest.

Recalling what he learned from Archangel Michael and Brother Oettinger, he continues, "Samael is the name of the angel of death. He's the spawn of the fallen angel, Satan, and is one of the Nephilim because he bred with Sarah, a former human. You saw Samael. He's already over eight feet tall and is probably still growing. In addition, he's a telepath and has a third eye, with whatever power that gives him."

"Oh, my god," moans Patton. "What can we do about this?"

Answering his own question, he declares, "We could destroy him! I could find a way to get rid of him!"

Lory and Peter exchange a concerned look.

"Destroying Samael won't be easy," says Peter, shaking his head. "He's powerful, and he has his father's cunning. We need to figure out a way to stop him, but we can't do it alone."

Patton nods in agreement, realizing Peter is right. "What do you suggest we do, then?"

"We need to gather a team — people experienced in dealing with supernatural beings like him. We should call upon those who were involved in the war on Mars. We'll need to plan carefully and be prepared for anything. We also need to keep in mind that Samael may not be the only threat. There may be others out there like him, and we need to be ready to face them, too."

Lory nods. "We should start by contacting people we trust. But we must be discreet. We can't let them in on what Operation Apocalypse is yet."

Patton nods solemnly. "I'll do whatever it takes to stop

this. Count me in."

With that, the three of them pledge to gather a team to stop Samael before it's too late.

Assured by the trio's committed determination, a dazzling light bathes the room in brilliance, forcing the general and the doctor to shield their eyes. Only Peter isn't affected by the light.

"Holy cow! What is that?" asks Patton, squinting heavily.

Peter smiles faintly as he recognizes the source of the light.

"That's Archangel Gabriel," he says calmly.

The light intensifies, and Gabriel's form takes shape in the center of the room.

"*Greetings, Commander,*" says the archangel, his voice resonating with power.

Peter bows his head in respect. "Greetings, Gabriel."

In stunned silence, Lory and Patton watch as Gabriel turns his attention to them.

"*Doctor Paduano, General Patton,*" he says, acknowledging them with a benevolent look. "*I am pleased that you have agreed to help the Commander of the Ark. I have come to you today with a message concerning the Clawfeet and their use as weapons.*

"*Once again, humankind ventures into a realm over which they have no control. With pride and arrogance continuing to threaten your way of life, this present situation will quickly grow if not handled immediately.*

"*Commander, the archangels stand at the ready, but as you know, we must be called upon to act. If your race does not request our help, Yahweh Himself will intervene. Do not forget my warning.*"

As the image fades, a clap of thunder announces Gabriel's exit, and soldiers rush into the office.

"Are you all right, Gen—"

"Stand down!" orders Patton, ushering the soldiers out of the room. "Everything's fine!"

Then he turns to Peter. "The best thing for me to do is speak to the secretary of defense and my contacts at the Joint Chiefs of Staff. But I don't know if they'll believe me. I'm not sure *I* believe what just happened! I could sure use your sidekick as a visual reinforcement!"

Lory chuckles softly. "Talk about the ultimate presentation."

General Patton leads Peter to the side of the room where Lory can't hear them. "What did Gabriel mean when he said, 'Yahweh will intervene?'"

Peter sighs deeply. "When the Nephilim appeared on Earth eons ago, God destroyed them and everything else in a flood, except for Noah and his family. But God promised not to do that again. So I'm afraid of what He would do this time if we don't get rid of Samael before He has to step in again."

CHAPTER ELEVEN

Stefan's lawyer, a newly qualified, multi-generational Martian, has already seated himself next to Stefan when David finally enters the room.

As the detective is about to begin questioning the escort, a tall man in a silk two-piece suit knocks on the door and strides in.

"I'm taking over this case," he declares assertively. "Stefan requires expert representation."

Surprised, but deferring to the other man, the young Martian lawyer shrugs and departs.

David is intrigued by what just happened.

"That was interesting," he says. "You look like someone who's being paid handsomely for their time. Who's your boss?"

The lawyer responds with a smile, "My name is Mitchell Crane, and I represent Xanthe Robotics and their 'employees,' so to speak."

"Ah, so that's it," says David, shaking his head. "Fancy that. The corporate world is concerned about its image. Look, Mr. Crane, I have warrants that I can download to your communicator. They grant me access to Stefan's, Galina's, and Lisa's memory files and data banks. Do I need to escalate this to my superiors?"

Crane consults with Stefan, then eyes David haughtily.

"We can proceed. But I'll intervene if your questions are inappropriate."

At that moment, David wishes he had the tools of

his ancestor, Jack Stenhouse. However, blackjacks and phone books are long gone, and he's not in the mood for confrontation.

"All right," he says to Stefan. "Did you have any personal contact with Lisa or Mr. Carter?"

Stefan and his attorney confer again. Then, the AI looks at David and responds, "Lisa and I were close friends. We socialized outside of work, and I met her and Mr. Carter while she was on duty."

David asks, "How close were you? Just friends, or was there something more?"

When Stefan hesitates, David needles him with, "Did you love her? Were you jealous of her clients?"

Expecting signs of anger or fear, the AI confounds David when he calmly leans back and remains silent. After a moment, he smiles.

"Lisa and I were very close."

Bluntly, David asks, "Did you kill Mr. Carter and seek revenge by killing Stacey, too?"

The android escort winces but recovers quickly.

"No, I cannot experience jealousy or go against my programming to harm a human."

Undeterred, David launches a counterattack.

"Are there any protocols preventing you from terminating a bot?"

Instantly defiant, Stefan slams his hands down on the metal table in what appears to be anger, leaving two noticeable dents.

"I DID NOT KILL ANYONE!" he shouts forcefully.

Alarmed by the line of questioning, Crane stands up, signaling an end to the interview, and David rises as well.

"I'm activating those warrants to access the data files on your bots," Jacoby tells the corporate attorney. "Stefan will remain in custody until we apprehend Galina and Lisa. When we have them all, we'll take them to your company's diagnostic center to have their memory files and data banks examined. Then we'll determine whether any of them is telling the truth. Maybe I'll end up arresting one of them for double homicide."

AI Stefan turns to Attorney Crane, unsure of what to do next. But the man is watching Jacoby carefully.

Knowing he's on a roll, David tells Crane, "Arrange an appointment at your company for tomorrow morning. By the way, it seems your bot here has a temper. While he's here, he'll be restrained with shackles on his hands and feet, and the same will apply to Galina."

"Now wait just a minute," protests Crane. "There's no need for that—"

"Stand in my way, Counselor," snarls David, "and you'll face the consequences. Understand?"

Marching to the door, David opens it to address the guards.

"Guys, shackle Stefan's hands and feet and place him in our secure detention area." Then he taps his PerscomU. "Issue an APB and apprehend bots Galina and Lisa."

As Stefan is taken away, David locks eyes with Crane.

"Fair warning. I intend to bring Xanthe Robotics down a peg or two. They need to be held accountable for introducing unpredictable artificial intelligence into Martian society."

In an underground facility at Area 51, Samael sits alone in a lead-shielded room. A helmet on his head obscures his third eye and a skintight bodysuit covers most of the rest of him.

Doctor Strakov and Lieutenant Colonel Nevins observe Samael through a monitor while he sits cross-legged on the concrete floor, gently rocking back and forth. As he moves, the bodysuit strains slightly but resists tearing, showcasing the prominent muscular structure the lieutenant colonel believes will contribute to Samael becoming the perfect soldier.

Nevins is pleased with his prize. Pointing to the unusual being, he tells Doctor Strakov, "He shows great potential and will eventually lead our new platoon. It's time to commence Operation Apocalypse."

"I understand," Strakov replies dutifully. "But before we start, I need to conduct some basic studies and do extensive genetic testing on him. He's less than four months old, and we need to examine him further. I must stress how important it is that we study him thoroughly."

In the Canadian wilderness, Peter bids Lory farewell, then steps aside to give the general room to do the same.

As the couple embraces, Lory's goodbye is heartfelt, and Peter overhears her asking when she'll be able to see the general again. But Austin doesn't return Lory's feelings.

In a business-like tone, he says, "I've contacted the Pentagon and initiated the necessary steps for a meeting there. I'll inform you and Peter as soon as I have a confirmed date." Then the general adds a separate remark, addressing Lory by her professional title. "Doctor Paduano, I believe your assessment will be invaluable."

Disappointed by Austin's formality, Lory smiles half-heartedly and turns to enter the research center. Outside, Peter and the general prepare for their journey back to Calgary.

When Lory can no longer see the military vehicles through the center's windows, she steps outside and is greeted by the late afternoon air. Shivering in her heavy sweater, she catches the faint sounds of Bigfoot howls reverberating off the majestic purple mountains, joined a minute later by wolves with their own melodic response.

In low spirits at the loss of the strange creatures she considers friends and at General Patton's cool goodbye, Doctor Paduano's shoulders sag. With a heavy sigh, she heads back into the warmth of the research center and the company of the few colleagues she shares it with.

CHAPTER TWELVE

After another brief visit home, Peter bids farewell to his family while General Patton waits patiently in his staff car parked in front of the house.

"Let's plan a trip for when I get back," says Peter, trying to cheer Angela up. "We can rent a cabin in the Smokies."

"Oh, that sounds good," replies Angela hopefully.

Forcing a smile he doesn't feel, Peter exchanges kisses with Angela and Michael, then waves goodbye from the doorway. He doesn't want to leave again, but he knows his family has a watchful protector in Archangel Rafael, whom he knew was standing behind them as they said their goodbyes. Though that knowledge is comforting, a passage from **Luke 4:13** keeps running through his mind: *When the devil had finished all this tempting, he left him until an opportune time.* **(NIV)**

In the car, Peter is somber and silent and the general picks up on his mood. Austin tries to provide comfort by harkening back to their triumph over the Malignant in the war on Mars, though deep down, he realizes the unsettling truth that Operation Apocalypse can't be stopped by the military alone. Only Peter and the angels possess the ability to end it, and if they can't, the consequences could be devastating. Austin can't stop thinking about the chaos that will inevitably ensue as a result of humankind suffering through castigations it deserves.

Still, General Patton holds onto a glimmer of hope that such suffering might transform hearts in dire need of change.

"Peter," he says, "I stand by your side in this, and I know some high-ranking officers who also share our perspective. Together, we'll bring an end to this madness."

Peter lowers his eyes. "I know it will end, but I'm afraid of how that will happen. The Malignant will persist until he's successful unless we can turn around the hearts of all humanity. The evil one is free to pursue all he desires and we humans possess the free will to accept or reject him. General, I truly believe that we have become the most foolish generation since the time of the Great Judgment, the most foolish generation since Noah's era. You were right when you said those in power won't relinquish control willingly. In Samael, we've already seen a little of what we're up against in the offspring of the Fallen. Unfortunately, the rest of us may soon see it as well."

Detective Jacoby meets Olonar Grant at his lab at Xanthe Robotics, where Galina, Stefan, and Lisa lie on separate stainless-steel tables, temporarily deactivated and devoid of clothing. The ports at the backs of Galina's and Stefan's heads are connected to a computer module for their scans, while Lisa's scan is scheduled after theirs have been completed.

Fascinated by the sight of the unclothed robots, David finds himself unable to look away.

"Holy shit, they're incredibly well-designed for their jobs! It's hard to believe they're not human!"

Olonar chuckles. "They *are* human. Their bodies are biomechanical, just like ours, except theirs are composed of synthetic materials."

David raises his brows in surprise but says nothing. He stares at Olonar, allowing him to continue talking while his mind dwells on Galina as a possible candidate for a first foray into the world of AI dating.

"We're going to keep those units deactivated and detained here until your homicide cases are solved," says Olonar. "The scans on Galina and Stefan will take forty-eight hours, and of course, I'll send you the results. Once they're complete, I'll proceed with Lisa's."

David fixes his gaze on Galina, who only appears as if she's sleeping peacefully.

"Here we go," says Olonar, fiddling with dials on a console.

When the diagnostic program initiates, both of the robots' limbs twitch slightly in a synchronized pattern, and Galina's eyes flutter open, surprising her inventor. When she questions in a faint voice, "Is this pain? Am I dying?" Olonar is deeply concerned.

The twitching continues briefly, after which Galina closes her eyes and becomes immobile.

"What the heck just happened?" asks David, equally concerned about what Galina said. "I demand an explanation!"

Olonar shakes his head in disbelief. "I'm just as baffled as you are. That has never happened before."

Suspicious, David refuses to believe him.

"That was just plain crazy! So here's what I'm going to do. I'm going to place two armed guards inside your lab, and I'm going to instruct them to destroy those bots if they do anything, and I mean anything, as bizarre as what just happened. Do you understand me, Mr. Grant?"

Olonar isn't inclined to cede control over his inventions to anyone.

"You can't simply destroy property belonging to Xanthe Robotics!" he shouts. "I don't care who you are! You can't just take a life whenever you want to!"

Furious, David grabs Olonar's lab coat and pulls him close. Screaming out words intermingled with spittle, he shouts, "Any and all threats will be dealt with accordingly! Those tables hold no 'lives,' you asshole! It's all an illusion created by *you*, and it's spiraling out of control! Do your job, man! Provide me with the information I need, and remember, if you obstruct my investigation, I'll be happy to arrest your tiny Martian ass!"

Releasing Olonar's lab coat, David forcefully pushes him away and storms out of the laboratory. Outside the door, he sternly briefs the two police officers who accompanied the robots.

"I want you both to go inside and watch everything carefully. If those things awaken during their diagnostic checks or exhibit bizarre behavior, I authorize you to terminate them immediately. And if Mr. Grant gives you any trouble about it, arrest him."

Upset by what he just witnessed, David exits the building and emerges into a bright Martian morning with a nearly cloudless sky of striking blue. Though he can't shake the feeling that something untoward is going on, David finds himself thinking more about the unclothed Galina, surprised that his previous stance against AIs seems to be softening. Hoping to put his thoughts aside, he taps his communicator as he walks to his Camaro.

"Hey, Paula," he says. "How about a ride to Xanthe Terra? I know a little roadside hangout around there where we can have lunch, my treat... Yeah? That's excellent! See you in a few!"

Most of the time, Samael of Sarah remains seated on the cold, hard floor of his cell at Area 51, his head covered by a device meant to suppress his telepathic abilities. However, the special one-piece suit, initially designed to stretch along with his growth, had to be replaced due to an unforeseen, rapid rise of his stature to well beyond fifteen feet.

For the most part, Samael has remained motionless, so when the technician monitoring his cell suddenly observes him raising his head and extending his hands in the air, he promptly triggers an alarm. Simultaneously, the soldiers overseeing the four marines and three civilians in stasis activate similar alarm systems in their area, as their subjects' eyes suddenly begin to glow with an eerie red hue.

Urgently, Doctor Strakov and Lieutenant Colonel Nevins enter the surveillance room. Gazing at the monitors displaying their eight subjects, neither man is certain of the situation. However, Nevins wastes no time issuing orders.

"Administer sedatives to Samael and prepare to awaken the other subjects!" he commands. "I don't know what's going on, but perhaps the moment we've been waiting for may have finally arrived!"

"No!" shouts Strakov. "We shouldn't rush into this! There are things that need to be done before we wake them up!"

Frowning at the delay, Nevins gives the doctor a side-eye. But he acquiesces, albeit reluctantly.

"Okay. For now," he says grudgingly. "Do what you have to do, Strakov."

Instantly, a faint blue gas intended to drug Samael permeates the beast's cell, and he senses danger. Hastily, he rises to his feet and rushes toward the locked door, but he collapses onto the floor before reaching his destination.

Watching, Nevins notices something peculiar through the monitor.

"You know," he mutters to the doctor, "I don't believe that entity has finished growing yet."

Doubting Nevins' assessment, Strakov responds, "How can you say that? He's already over fifteen feet tall. How much taller could he possibly get?"

Nevins' concern is evident in his tone. "I can't say, but I have a very bad feeling that he's about to outgrow that cell."

CHAPTER THIRTEEN

Seated within a secure conference room at the Pentagon, Peter prepares to address a virtual meeting of the Galactic Federation, an association of representatives from each country on Earth and the colonies on Mars, the Moon, and Titan. Included in this meeting are General Austin and Lory Paduano.

Just about every country's member who could make it is in attendance. Those who are too far away or couldn't be at the federation's headquarters in person are displayed on a separate widescreen monitor via video link. The Earthly representatives can vote, but those from the off-world colonies will not have a voice in the proceedings due to the time delay in signal transmissions.

Rising from his seat, Peter commences his address.

"Good afternoon. I'm pleased to see that most of you are able to attend today's meeting. I know it was arranged on short notice, and I appreciate how difficult it must have been to insert it into your calendars. Thank you for your time.

"Now, each of you has received a report compiled by Doctor Paduano, General Patton, and me in my role as a geneticist. In that report, we outline our concerns regarding Operation Apocalypse. I trust you have made time to review it.

"To begin, I assume all of you remember the heroic efforts of General Patton on Mars just over a year ago and of Doctor Paduano's research of the Bigfoot community and the late Clawfoot named Sarah."

At a spontaneous outbreak of applause, Peter pauses to allow the attendees to recognize Lory's and the general's contributions to peace and to the study of the unusual creatures. He continues when the accolades wind down.

"But there is something else you may not know, and it is not included in our report. The Clawfoot Sarah, also known as Crooked Legs, left behind a hybrid human son who calls himself Samael of Sarah."

Again, Peter pauses briefly, then continues with increased authority.

"I will now speak to you as Commander of the Ark of the Covenant. In your so-called wisdom, you and others have decided to embark on the dubious endeavor of creating life to your specifications — a pursuit aimed at producing what you perceive to be the ultimate warrior, a hybrid being, part human and part beast. To do this, you subjected unsuspecting individuals and unwitting volunteers to your unfortunate experiment. In the eyes of the Lord and in the consciences of all God-fearing people, this is an abomination!"

Peter takes a moment to look around the room and at everyone watching on screen.

"At this time, Samael is in our custody. Though he is a human hybrid, he was not created by humankind. He was not part of your experiment. I have convened this meeting to inform each and every one of you that this hybrid being is a creature to be feared. He is actually the offspring of the Malignant One, the very same entity that nearly brought complete devastation to Mars and Earth!

"Thankfully, God helped us defeat Satan during that war. But that evil being remains ceaseless in his malevolence. Yes, he retreated to his hellish kingdom, but he is only biding his time for the opportune moment to once again sow chaos and evil in our worlds. This Satan was the same menace my ancestors encountered over 1,300 years ago when he defied

God during the thousand years of peace.

"Because of the existence of Samael, the situation we are in today is perilous. I implore everyone listening to comprehend its gravity. Operation Apocalypse must be terminated! Samael is one of the Nephilim! He is the offspring of a Fallen Angel and a transformed human, a member of the race of giants who once wreaked havoc on Earth — one of the main reasons behind the great flood! Fortunately, God destroyed the Nephilim then, and He will destroy them again — if we invoke His help. Do not be deceived... Nephilim are innately dangerous! They cannot be repelled without Divine assistance!"

Upon concluding his speech, Peter resumes his seat, and a profound silence fills the room. Most attendees want someone else to be the first to respond.

Before long, Defense Secretary Alexander Costa of the United States is ready to voice his opinion. Leaning forward in his chair, he says, "Mr. Matteo, you speak of myths as if they were truths. This Galactic Federation deals with reality, not fairy tales. Our primary goal is to defend our countries, our planet, and our colonies. Before this meeting, we met privately and agreed to refine our protocols to address unforeseen circumstances. However, we will not terminate this operation."

Peter gazes at the faces before him, observing expressions of concern, both on- and off-world. Eager to respond to Secretary Costa, he stops mid-sentence when a radiant light floods the secure room, dazzling everyone there and watching on screen, except him.

While those in the room and watching shield their eyes, a figure adorned in golden armor materializes in the center of the large conference table in the secure room. The resplendent being commands attention as he speaks.

"*I am Archangel Michael. The Commander has warned*

you about the Malignant. Once again, God's children are demonstrating their ignorance and arrogance. I, along with Metatron, the angel I report to, and the other Guardians and Watchers, we all sincerely hope you will embrace the truth and believe the Commander's words before Almighty God compels us to intervene."

With those simple words, Michael departs, leaving the room in silence once again.

In the absence of chatter, Peter rises to his feet, his gaze fixed upon Secretary Costa.

"All of you have been warned. I pray that you will act accordingly, to do what is right. If you choose to forgo these warnings to go your own way, I fear you will ultimately have to call upon me to resume my duties as Commander of the Ark to restore order. As much as I'm willing to work with the angels to save our worlds, I fervently hope it won't come to that."

CHAPTER FOURTEEN

Amid the passage of time after Mars was terraformed, the area around Xanthe Terra, a large section near the planet's equator, has become filled with farmland and homesteads, with majestic red mountains serving as a backdrop. Here, native Martian plants grow together with transplanted Earth flora, creating a picturesque scene reminiscent of the Earthly Kansas plains. This flat stretch, with vistas that go on for miles, has become a popular vacation destination for Mars' residents.

As one of the location's many sightseers, David Jacoby and Paula Harmon are on their way to the restaurant David promised to drive her to in his restored classic.

Aching to take in the view, David stops the car not far from the restaurant.

"It's so pretty out here, but I can't see it while I'm driving."

"There's a good spot over there," points Paula.

Stepping out of the car, the couple gazes into the distance, the warm spring day washing over them, and they link arms.

The restaurant David is heading for was originally the old general store outpost where, years before, the first grisly discovery of Clawfoot activity was made.

Years of neglect ensued after those encounters, but when an enterprising individual saw the area's potential, he converted it into the popular Outpost Pub and Grill it is today.

When the building was merely a place for early settlers to collect their mail and gather supplies, it was the only structure around. Now, it's almost entirely surrounded by commercial activity, typified by an adjacent construction site where robotic machinery diligently works on a sprawling industrial mega Mall complex.

Paula is disappointed by the modernization of the picturesque environment. Spotting the tall machinery in the distance, she opines, "Looks like we're repeating Earthly mistakes on another planet." Then she looks at David with a wry grin. "Mind if I drive the rest of the way?"

David chuckles. "Sure, why not? There's not much traffic out here today. But I'll have to teach you how."

Excited, Paula takes the driver's seat and adjusts it closer so her diminutive Martian frame can reach the pedals. Beside her, David fastens his seatbelt.

After adjusting the mirrors, Paula glances at the dashboard. "How do I start this thing?" she asks.

"It's similar to an electric car. The accelerator is on the right, and the brake is on the left. Press the brake, then the start button."

Paula appears puzzled. "What are these two paddles on the steering wheel?"

David suppresses a laugh. "Ah, don't worry about those. We'll keep it in automatic mode for today."

Paula presses the brake, then the start button, and the 500 horses beneath the hood awaken.

Continuing to instruct, David says, "With your foot on the brake, shift the gear from 'P' to 'D.' Release the brake and slowly press the accelerator pedal. Then hang on tight!"

Paula takes a deep breath, shifts into Drive, and sets off. However, her definition of "slowly" doesn't match David's. Responding to the M.E.'s foot, the Camaro's rear tires break loose, and the car snakes down the road, leaving two long black lines behind.

"Whoa!" shouts David, gripping the dashboard with both hands. "Slow down! You must be going at least 100 mph!"

Panicked, Paula eases off the accelerator, and steers the Camaro to the side of the road.

"Shift into 'P,'" says David, letting out a long breath.

Paula leans back in the seat, unbuckles the seatbelt, and sighs. Beside her, David laughs uncontrollably.

Pursing her lips, Paula opens the door and steps out while laughter from within the Camaro continues.

Soon, David exits the car and walks around to join his "student."

"Holy crap! That thing's a beast!" says Paula. "I'm a wreck!"

"I know; isn't it great?" cries David.

For David, the Camaro's power is exhilarating. Then he notices the sweat on Paula's brow and the stains under her arms.

"Well, you asked to drive," he says, "so now, you're christened in ancient technology! Tell you what, you can freshen up at the restaurant. But...you look great, Paula."

The pair reenters the car, switching places so David can show his friend how it's done, and the 500 horses respond in kind.

As the charge of the ancient technology echoes across the terrain, the couple becomes aware of the distinct possibility that nothing that unusual has broken the silence of that peaceful area since the calls of the Clawfeet from their mountain caves.

With the odor of burnt rubber on the Martian breeze, Outpost Pub and Grill patrons also notice the unusual noise. Intrigued, many of them stop what they're doing to watch the odd sight of the 500 horses stampeding toward them.

Deep underground in Earth's Nevada desert, Tim Farley, Jonathan Harrington, Karen Stamos, and the four marine volunteers, are injected with a spike protein antigen while they're still in stasis. The antigen is an extract of a protein found in Martian dirt mites, which scientists believe can halt current and future human transformations.

As an employee, Doctor Strakov agreed to the injections, hoping that administering the substance would aid him in fulfilling the Army's directive to create formidable hybrid fighting machines.

Unbeknownst to the doctor, however, Samael is on the verge of complicating matters.

Although the creature has been kept in a cell away from the partially transformed humans, he has already exerted his influence over Karen Stamos, and soon, will affect the others as well.

Looking over his notes, Doctor Strakov is puzzled. The cryogenically frozen individuals show no reaction to the antigen, except for Corporal Wayne Casey, a former Marine who has undergone the most significant transformation, and now has Clawfoot legs and red body hair.

When the corporal received the antigen in his chamber, his response was violent. He shrieked and clawed desperately to escape, terrifying the technicians. Now, Casey's hybrid body is rejecting the antigen, and he appears to be on the brink of death. As blood gushes from his eyes and ears, he lets out anguished roars, and dies.

Sensing the distress of their fellow hybrid, the other subjects awaken from their frozen states, their eyes filled with haunting emptiness.

In a show of solidarity, Samael, though restrained and sedated in his remote cell, breaks free from his shackles and roars defiantly, setting off flashing lights and alarms throughout the underground facility.

Recognizing Samael's agitation as dangerous, Nevins orders guards equipped with lethal and non-lethal weapons to enter his cell.

"Just look at that magnificent creature!" shouts Lieutenant Colonel Nevins safely admiring Samael through the monitor. "Once we control him, no one will be able to stop us!" he tells a distressed Doctor Strakov.

Chillingly, the hybrid human is pounding the walls, causing the barriers to tremble and the floor to shake with each mighty strike of his fists.

Fearing Samael will escape, Doctor Strakov defies the lieutenant colonel by releasing an opioid gas into the cell, slowing Samael's movements. Sluggishly, the beast paces back and forth, gradually distancing himself from the door.

Seizing on the opportunity to regain control of the situation, Nevins orders his troops into the cell.

"Move in!" he commands.

With Samael far enough away from the door, the doctor unlocks it, and the security team storms in, one of them firing a dart containing carfentanil, a sedative commonly used on elephants.

Seemingly unfazed, Samael turns, removes the protective helmet, locks his gaze on the intruders, and pulls out the dart, casually tossing it aside.

Now revealed, his third eye glows crimson and mesmerizes the intruders, freezing them in place like statues.

Seconds later, Samael drops to his knees, the drug finally taking effect. Struggling to stay awake, he speaks for the first

Frank A. Ruffolo

time in a deep, haunting voice that pierces the men's souls.

"You cannot stop...Samael," he fights to say. "You...cannot...stop...Lilith. She...is the one...you know...as Karen."

With the opioid taking effect, Samael succumbs to its influence and crumples to the floor. He has grown significantly taller since his arrival, now standing at almost eighteen feet. His strength has also increased. He snapped the titanium alloy shackles intended to hold him like mere twigs.

Studying his now-unresponsive captive, Lieutenant Colonel Nevins smirks at his good fortune.

"Once we control these warriors, nothing will stand in our way!" he gloats, his chest expanding with pleasure at the thought of having an invincible army at his disposal.

"But... What happened in there?" asks Strakov, struggling to comprehend the unknown. "What happened to our men when Samael took off his helmet? And besides that, what do we do now? Our shackles can't hold him!"

"I guess it's time to test the new restraints they sent us. They're made from Rafcom, the Raphaelite ceramic," states Nevins, gazing into the cell. "I hope we won't encounter a situation like this again. If we do, I may be forced to destroy him."

"And then...?" asks Strakov, letting his thought trail off while trying to grasp the implications.

"And then," declares Nevins in a firm voice, "we'll proceed with our other subjects."

Doctor Strakov stares at Nevins.

"Hollis Nevins, you must realize this will end in disaster! Look at what's unfolded here today! Do you see your men? They're still standing there like statues! And did you see how strong Samael is? There's no way you'll be able to control him! And if Karen is part of his plan, you won't control her either!"

Nevins smiles slyly. "First of all, that's Lieutenant Colonel Nevins to you. Then, just watch me and learn, Doctor. Watch me and learn."

Inside Samael's cell, the members of the attack team remain motionless, resembling zombies as they continue to stare at Samael.

Gradually, one by one, they regain their senses and hurriedly exit the reinforced room.

Chasing after them, Strakov calls behind him to Nevins, "I'm going to examine them to find out what happened! We need to understand what that thing did to them!"

The break David and Paula took from their duties was pleasant and made their friendship bond grow stronger. The pair make an unconventional couple, though, with David towering at over six feet and Paula standing at less than five feet.

When they returned to the city, a delay in David's double murder case emerged, which David took full advantage of. Predictably, he used the opportunity to do more work on his Camaro, and now the car boasts red lights embedded in the front grill and a police siren under the hood, as if the vehicle didn't already make enough noise.

One morning, as David finishes his breakfast, a notification of a newly received message pops up. Accessing his communicator, he finds the results of the memory scans of Stefan and Galina and transfers the data to his home terminal to view more easily on his holographic monitor.

To fortify himself for delving into what he knows will be hours of looking through endless files, he detours to the counter and pours himself a generous cup of liquid energy from an antique coffee pot. But after taking a sip, he frowns.

"Before I get too caught up, I better see a man about a horse, or I'll just end up having to stop when things get interesting."

While David reads through rows of data, Olonar reactivates Galina and Stefan and tells them to get dressed. Then he confines them to a secure room at Xanthe Robotics.

Talking to the bots through a wrist comm while he remains outside the room, the inventor says, "I sent your memory files to Detective Jacoby. Since you're both suspects, you'll remain in that room until the investigation is concluded."

Concerned, Stefan looks over at the cam he knows Olonar is using to view them.

"What will happen to us if he says he discovered something?" asks Stefan, suddenly nervous.

Nearby, Galina appears skittish and anxious.

"I do not want to die!" she cries, more worried than Stefan. "I am frightened! What about Lisa? Is she alive?"

Olonar is taken aback by the uncharacteristic fear exhibited by his inventions.

"Everything will be fine," he says, softening his voice to appear calmer than he feels. "Neither of you have anything to worry about."

To discourage further discussion, the tech executive abruptly ends the transmission. But he leaves the cam on to record the bots' comments. Then he hurries to the office of Xanthe Robotics' CEO, Mr. Arlynn Stout.

Arlynn, a fourth-generation Martian educated at MIT and Oxford, grew up as Gregory Stout, the name his parents gave him. After entering the tech field, he changed his first name to pay tribute to Arlynn Fisk, his 21st century hero and ardent proponent of enhanced AI development.

Standing at just under five-foot-one, Arlynn is a man who enjoys attention. In his late fifties and boasting a full head of gray hair that harmonizes with his eye color, he attracts the fascination of much of Martian society. His widely recognized reputation as the wealthiest individual on the planet despite having endured three costly divorces is undoubtedly fuel for his popularity.

The robotics company CEO loves to take advantage of his considerable wealth. His latest whim involved a completely unnecessary redesign of his office. The lavish space now features marble and fine wood everywhere, with imported carpeting over a custom designed tile floor.

Complementing the carpeting is Arlynn's extensive art collection. Exquisite artworks adorn all the walls, apart from a special place reserved for photographs of the various robot models his company produces.

Completing the look, an ornate desk is flanked by the flags of Mars and the Galactic Federation, with a portrait of Arlynn's idol placed reverently between them.

Olonar, a frequent visitor to the CEO's office, stops at the desk of Mr. Stout's secretary, a bot named Stella.

"Hi, Stell. I need to speak with Mr. Stout regarding Galina, model XC010, revision Alpha. It's urgent."

Stella relays the request through her headcomm.

"Mr. Stout, Mr. Olonar Grant is here about Galina."

Stout responds after a brief pause, and Stella nods at Olonar.

"You may go in now, Mr. Grant."

Though Olonar has visited his boss many times before, he takes a moment to check his shirt, smooth his hair, and crick his neck before entering the expansive office.

Seated at the large desk, CEO Arlynn Stout appears even smaller than his stature, a sight that intimidates Olonar all the same.

Forcing a smile, Grant approaches his boss with an extended hand.

"Thank you for seeing me, Mr. Stout."

Stout nods and gestures for Olonar to sit in one of two oversized leather chairs in front of his desk.

"How are our bots today?" he asks. "Were you able to assist Detective Jacoby?"

Nervous about why he's there, Olonar rocks in his chair, his feet barely reaching the floor.

"Yes, sir. I sent him their memory files. Stefan seems to be fine. But Galina... Well, she's displaying human emotions, and I thought you'd want to know. These are the same concerns I reported about earlier. They emerged with the Alpha revision."

Stout stares at his lead technological executive and most experienced employee.

"That's precisely what we aimed for, isn't it? To create a more human experience for our clients?"

"Sir," responds Olonar in a voice tinged with worry, "Galina felt pain and anguish, and though unprovoked, expressed a fear of death. She said she doesn't want to die!"

Stout leans back into the comfort of his chair. Inhaling deeply, he closes his eyes, a gentle smile playing on his lips as if he were recalling a favorite scene from his past.

Then he opens his eyes and fixes them on Olonar.

"Eons ago," says Stout, "Arlynn Fisk clearly counseled against seeking this development. But I have never understood why; I've been anticipating this for months! It is nothing short of the finest evolution of our 'created species', and I couldn't be happier!"

Olonar is troubled by Stout's response, but he doesn't say anything more.

"Prepare the tech lab for analysis of all the Alphas," continues Arlynn. "We updated ten bots — some have been deployed, but the remainder is still in our inventory. I'll send you a list. I definitely want to speak with Galina, but I have a busy day ahead of me today. I'll be at your lab promptly at eleven a.m. tomorrow morning. Good day, Mr. Grant."

Late the next afternoon, when David returns to headquarters, he sends the data files from Olonar to Forensics for analysis. Then he sits down with audio tech Les Wilson at the man's cluttered desk, ready to discuss some worries.

"Les, I need you to review the audio files I just sent you. I noticed some anomalies in both bots' recordings, which made me think they may have been tampered with. I'm going back to Xanthe Robotics to speak with Mr. Grant and possibly the bots themselves."

In Washington, D.C., Defense Secretary Costa sits outside the oval office, having received an unexpected summons to meet with the president.

Almost an hour after he arrived, a Marine emerges from the office, signaling the secretary to enter.

President James Larson occupies the antique Kennedy desk, a remarkably well-preserved artifact from a long ago era. Over the years, the desk has been repaired and refinished many times, but it's still in use by almost every chief executive.

The president, a man in his mid-fifties and a veteran officer of the 101st Airborne Army Division, is absorbed in his work and offers no acknowledgment to his defense secretary.

Finally, after Costa seats himself, he looks up.

"Thanks for coming, Alex. This won't take long."

The president's tone is cool, devoid of the usual warmth he extends toward his cabinet official.

Instantly, Costa understands this meeting won't go well for him. Trying to look earnest, he attempts to respond to an unspoken rebuke.

"Mr. President, I want to assure you that I'm—"

"Alex, just be quiet and listen," interrupts Larson. "I've had a very productive conversation with General Patton and Mr. Peter Matteo about concerns they've raised regarding the program initiated by your subordinates. By the way, General Patton handed me his resignation. He wants no part in anything you and Colonel Nevins are creating."

Flustered, the defense secretary begins to explain, but the president cuts him off again.

"I expect daily updates on Operation Apocalypse on my desk by nine every morning. You may consider yourself officially put on notice. I'm deeply troubled by what I've heard, and I'm not the only one. Members of Congress and some of the military have been demanding an end to this program. Walk carefully, Costa. It won't take much for me to shut it down."

Secretary Costa takes a deep breath, a mix of concern and anger permeating his thoughts.

"Mr. President..."

President Larson rises, his eyes flashing in irritation.

"We're finished here. Leave now, before I request your resignation letter on the spot. This is an election year, and I can't afford more problems on my watch. Because of you, I've lost one of my best generals. As much as I enjoy your company, I won't have any problem replacing you."

CHAPTER FIFTEEN

Following Stout's order, Olonar promptly dispatches a retrieval team to collect the three AI units already in service, and decommissions the seven units stored in inventory. Once the three are in-house, he will order a comprehensive review and overhaul on all the units.

Olonar finds it surprising that none of the other units were worried about being shut down. He anticipated a reaction similar to what he witnessed with Stefan and Galina. Instead, they remained completely silent when he powered them off.

Now, he's preparing Lisa for her diagnostic and memory scan.

"Grant! I'm glad I caught you!" says Detective Jacoby, entering Olonar's lab without waiting for an invitation. "I need you to halt the memory scan on Lisa. Our forensics department is examining the files and vids you sent from Galina and Stefan because I noticed some possible discrepancies."

"What 'discrepancies'?" asks Olonar, suspicion creeping into his tone. The robotics inventor is well aware of Jacoby's aversion to his software.

"Grant, you're now considered a person of interest in this case. Consequently, your personal information has been forwarded to Spaceport Security, and as of this moment, you're prohibited from leaving the planet. Moreover, you'll be placed in custody if we discover actionable irregularities during our investigation. I'm also petitioning the court to obtain custody of Lisa so we can independently review her files. Frankly, I don't trust you or Xanthe Robotics."

"You don't trust Xanthe or me?" stammers Olonar in disbelief. "I'm the backbone of this company! I've dedicated years of my life to this project! I know it inside and out!"

"Maybe that's why I have to assume control over Lisa. I assigned a couple of uniformed officers to guard her until we can bring her in for evaluation. That's all for now, Grant. I'll be talking to you soon."

Speechless, Grant watches as David nonchalantly exits the lab, leaving the tech inventor bewildered and unsettled.

After that day transitions into night and back into day, Arlynn walks into the lab at precisely 11 a.m., his face reflecting displeasure.

"Olonar, I've just been served with a court order to hand Lisa over to the XPD! What have you done? Where are the ten alpha bots?"

"Detective Jacoby wasn't satisfied with the results of Galina and Stefan's memory scans. His crime lab is reviewing the findings and wants to perform their own diagnostics on Lisa."

"Why is that?" asks Arlynn. "Did you do anything to them?"

"N... No..."

Arlynn sighs. "What about the others?"

"The seven in our inventory are undergoing thorough inspections and overhauls, and I've sent a retrieval team to collect the three that have already been deployed. I'm expecting them back here by one."

"All right. And...?"

"I also isolated Galina and Stefan in separate holding areas, and I shut Stefan down. So far, Galina is the only AI unit that has expressed concerns about potential termination, so she's still active. Mr. Stout, Galina seems highly distressed and afraid."

Stout stares intensely, his eyes piercing Olonar.

"If the XPD uncovers anything, you're going to take the blame for it, not me, not Xanthe Robotics. Do you understand?"

"I, uh… Yes, I understand."

"Good. Let's visit Galina. I want to offer her some consolation, so to speak. And Olonar," he adds, holding his tech executive's gaze, "I'll handle the conversation. Right?"

Peter, the now-retired Austin Patton, and Doctor Lory Paduano enjoy lunch at the diner inside BWI airport while waiting for flights to differing destinations.

Sipping an Arnold Palmer, Peter looks at the former military man.

"What are your plans now, Austin? How are you gonna keep yourself busy? I can't imagine that it'll be easy transitioning into civilian life."

Austin's smile lights up his face.

"I have grandkids in Denver, and I'm gonna take them fishing. They always ask me about it but I've never had the time."

With an almost shy glance at the doctor sitting beside him, he adds, "I may also help Lory reconnect with the Bigfoot community."

Lory blushes and changes the subject.

"Austin said he heard the president isn't pleased by what the military's doing behind his back, but he's no longer going to be privy to that kind of information. So it'll be up to you, Peter. You're going to have to resume your role as Commander, aren't you?"

"I don't know, but I'm ready."

"Well, while you're waiting to find out, what are you going to do? Do you have any plans while things are still relatively calm?"

Peter reflects for a moment.

"Mikey is a huge Disney fan, so I'm planning a surprise trip to Disney World. Besides, I'm a Star Wars geek, and I want to see all the other updates they made to the park."

"You still like Star Wars?" asks Lory. "That series is so outdated! I'm surprised they haven't gotten rid of it yet."

"I know it's kitschy, but I like it. Anyway, I need to get away. Like you said, things are poised to go downhill, so I need to take advantage of the free time."

Peter studies the couple on the other side of the table, sensing they're having trouble keeping their hands off each other.

With a sly grin, he asks, "You think you guys are going to be able to rekindle a connection? With the Bigfeet, I mean?"

Austin grins back. He knows what Peter meant, but decides it's wiser to talk about the Bigfeet.

"Nevins may have spoiled our chance with them. He's quite a character. As we say in the military, he's a Blue Falcon."

Peter and Lory look quizzically at Austin, but he merely shrugs.

Curious, both of them reach for their communicators to search for the meaning of "Blue Falcon."

Galina sits on her temporary bed, her hands fidgeting with worry. She's nervous and looks up quickly when a knock on the door admits Stout and Grant.

Seeing them, she jumps up and rushes toward Mr. Stout, embracing him tightly.

"I am frightened," she cries. "Father, I do not want to die! You must help me!"

Acting as if the artificial being were his own daughter, Arlynn pats her back comfortingly, saying, "There, there, no need to worry. I'm here now, and I support you fully. Please sit down and tell me why you're upset."

Galina lets go of her grip, sighs, and sits back on the cot. Lowering her head, she avoids eye contact.

"I cannot say anything yet. Not here. I am terrified of dying, Father. I need protection! But not in this place. Can you take me away from here?"

Glancing up, she stares at Grant, then at Arlynn.

"Help me!"

While Galina repeats her plea to leave the lab, David pours himself a cup of coffee at his desk at XPD. Just then, he receives a call from audio tech Les Wilson.

"Jacoby, I found something you may want to see."

CHAPTER SIXTEEN

Within old, unused bunkers set into the earth three floors below the facility holding the experimental subjects, Doctor Strakov begins to interview the guards that went into Samael's cell.

Corporal Mark Culley, a seasoned combatant from Tulsa, Oklahoma, sits uncomfortably in a cushioned chair while Doctor Strakov occupies a seat opposite him. Surrounding them is a separate grouping of chairs, lamps, and tables, designed to make the room resemble a cozy living area within the bunker's cold concrete walls. Unbeknownst to the corporal, the interview is being filmed.

When Culley sat down, he displayed signs of anxiety, struggling to find comfort in the cozy chair. Observing the squirming, Doctor Strakov adopts a reassuring expression.

"Corporal, there's nothing to be afraid of. I simply want you to tell me what happened when you went into Samael's cell."

Then, to make the soldier more comfortable, he says, "First, inhale through your mouth, hold it for a few seconds, then exhale slowly through your nose."

When Culley is calmer, Strakov says, "That's better. Now, tell me what happened."

Trained to follow instructions, the request eases the soldier's discomfort, and he settles back in his chair.

"Well, our orders were to subdue Samael at any cost. If he wouldn't cooperate, Lieutenant Colonel Nevins told us to consider him a threat, and to eliminate him."

"Yes, I heard him give that order," says Strakov. "So, you went into the cell…"

"Yeah. As soon as I entered it, I heard a voice inside my head. It was so soothing… Then I saw a pale blue light, and it was strange, I felt like I was part of that light. The voice said, and I remember it exactly, 'There is nothing to worry about. I am here to assist all of you. We are Samael of Sarah and Lilith, and we will join all of you very soon. Do not be afraid. We are friends.'"

Culley pauses, reflecting on the experience.

"I couldn't move, and I didn't want to. I don't know how long I was in that light, but it was comforting, and I didn't want to leave it. Then, I felt someone touching my shoulder and calling my name, and I was suddenly out of the light and back in the cell. At first, I was sad and angry that I was no longer in that calmness, but that feeling faded."

Doctor Strakov appears concerned. "How are you feeling now, Corporal?"

Mark smiles, noticeably more composed. "I feel great, Doc! Like I've had a long, deep sleep. In fact, all of us feel great! We all heard the same thing. Doc, who are Lilith and Sarah?"

Three floors above, Lieutenant Colonel Nevins is watching the interview with a grin resembling that of the fabled Cheshire Cat.

"This is going just as we intended," he beams, his mouth curved into a satisfied smile.

Simultaneously, deep below in the netherworld amid fire, brimstone, and the acrid scent of burning sulfur, the Malignant laughs triumphantly.

"Yes, it *is* unfolding precisely as I planned!"

David enters the CSI lab and walks up to Les Wilson, seated at his computer terminal.

"You have something for me?" he asks.

Les turns with a twinkle in his eyes. "I need you to review some video clips of Galina and listen to Stefan's audio files."

David smirks and rolls a chair over. "Play it again, Les."

Wincing at the weak joke, Les pulls up footage of Galina sitting by the pool with Stacey, the only audible sound being laughter in the background.

After it plays for only a few seconds, Les stops it.

"That was taken one day before the double murders. Did you notice anything unusual?"

"Um... No. The embedded clock shows no timeline changes, no audio skips."

Les smiles. "This vid has definitely been tampered with. The shadows cast by the palm trees on the far side of the pool change from one frame to another. I estimate that at least fifteen minutes of footage is missing. Watch closely at the forty-second mark."

Les replays the video, pausing it right after a shadow jumps.

David raises a brow. "Could that be a glitch in her programming?"

The forensic expert shakes his head.

"Other vid and aud files indicate three voices instead of two. Someone else joined them. We're currently examining Lisa's internal memory, so we might find some answers there. By the way, robot voices have a distinct, sine wave signature in their recorded speech, different from humans. That other voice is human."

David is dumbfounded. "This case is getting messy."

Agreeing, Les adds, "We found nothing unusual in Stefan's files — just friendly banter between him, Stacey, and Lisa. But we also obtained vids of Stefan and Galina with various clients. And there's even one vid of Stacey and Stefan together. You know," he says, grinning lopsidedly, "those vids could fetch a hefty price on Pornhub."

David slaps the back of Les's head. "This is evidence, schmuck."

"Ouch! I was only kidding!" retorts Les, rubbing the spot David smacked. "You wanna hear more, asshole?"

"Yeah, but keep it professional."

"Yeah, yeah," Les moans. "Unfortunately, some of the aud files from Galina were corrupted and unreadable, so I'm conducting a deeper analysis to see if they were damaged intentionally."

"The way this is going, I wouldn't be surprised," replies David wearily. "How confident are you that you could get something?"

"I may be able to retrieve some of the data, but I wouldn't get your hopes up."

David rises from his seat. "So Galina may possess valuable information that I still need to obtain, and Stefan could have a motive rooted in jealousy. It seems I'll have to interview both of them again. This time, I'm gonna conduct the interviews in a controlled environment, away from corporate influence. That means I'll need a court order to bring them here. Thanks, Les. You managed to make my job both easier and more challenging. Oh, and if you 'accidentally' happen to upload any of those vids to Pornhub, I expect a share of the proceeds. Just sayin'," he winks.

Heartened by Corporal Culley's revelations, Lieutenant Colonel Nevins calls Doctor Strakov into his office.

"Doctor, proceed with waking our patients. It appears that Samael isn't an immediate threat. I also want to have a conversation with him. Arrange a meeting for me this evening. I need to inquire about Lilith."

Doctor Strakov draws in a sharp breath, then slowly rises to his full, Earthborn height, gazing down at the seated Nevins.

"I'll begin awakening them in the morning. We can meet with Samael first, around eight. However, I must warn you, Nevins, don't be deceived by our captive. I researched the names Samael and Lilith. They're figures you don't want to engage with."

Nevins stands, also an Earther, but taller than Strakov.

"I'm not concerned by mere myths," he retorts icily. "And Strakov, use my full title when you address me."

Late at night, David drives out to Xanthe Terra, a favorite pastime when he wants some quiet contemplation. In this remote expanse, there are no city lights to hinder his view of the Cosmos, a wonder that never fails to charm him.

Tilting his head, he looks up at the dark sky dazzling with myriad stars — Phobos and Deimos gracefully weaving through the galaxy, with Orion standing overhead, watching the planet turn silently beneath it.

Standing there, a serene stillness envelopes the surroundings; not even a whisper of wind disturbs his tranquility.

Mesmerized, David takes a few steps away from the road, his gaze fixed upon the heavens and his mind filled with curiosity and contemplation.

Searching the sky, he finally spots a faint blue dot near the horizon.

"Ah, there you are," he mutters. "I wonder what we Earthlings are getting ourselves into, back on Mother Earth. Lord knows it's getting complicated over here."

CHAPTER SEVENTEEN

At eight o'clock the next day, Lieutenant Colonel Nevins and Dr. Strakov stand outside Samael's cell, accompanied by a security detail of five armed men. To establish contact with Samael, Strakov activates the vidmonitor near the door.

"Good morning," he says to their detainee. "I see you're already awake. Lieutenant Colonel Nevins would like to talk to you. Do you agree to meet with him?"

Samael, who had been meditating on the floor, looks over at the camera.

"Would it matter if I did not? Tell Nevins — excuse me, the lieutenant colonel — that there is no need for armed guards. I am a guest here, after all, am I not?"

Strakov casts a concerned glance at Nevins. "The decision is yours, Lieutenant Colonel. He's clever. I did warn you."

Nevins presses the keypad unlocking the door, so Strakov tells Samael, "He's coming in. Thank you, Samael of Sarah."

The door swings open and Nevins steps inside. Then the electronic motion sensors close it behind him.

Samael doesn't seem to have grown much since their last encounter. He's still over eighteen feet tall, but his muscular physique appears more toned and defined. Lieutenant Colonel Nevins is over six feet, and the disparity in height is astonishing.

As Nevins gazes up at Samael, the third eye opens,

and Nevins seems drawn into what he later describes as an alternate reality enveloped in a pale blue aura. In this realm, there are no walls, ceiling, or floor — only Samael, clad in white, standing before him. In Nevins' mind, a conversation begins to unfold.

"Lieutenant Colonel, I am Samael of Sarah. I am human, albeit with certain enhancements you and your government find intriguing. As a human being, I am willing to assist you in any way possible."

Unable to move, Nevins responds within his mind, astonished by this newfound ability.

"Good morning, Samael of Sarah. I'd like to extend my 'hand' as it were, in friendship. By the way, do you mind if I simply refer to you as Samael?"

The enormous creature nods in the affirmative.

"Samael is fine, Lieutenant Colonel Nevins. But may I call you Hollis? It appears that we share a tendency toward long names."

Samael extends his hand, and Nevins finds that he's now able to reach out.

"I prefer lieutenant colonel, please."

The handshake is awkward, given the vast difference in sizes. It's something like an adult shaking the hand of an infant.

In touching Samael's skin, Nevins feels a strange sense of peace and comfort within this alternate reality.

With an adoring gaze, he remarks, "Later this morning, we will begin our program with the other individuals who share similarities with you."

Samael closes his two lower eyes while the third eye widens.

"Colonel, they may bear some resemblance to me, but they are not my equals. Except for the one you call Karen

Stamos. She is the most like me."

Nevins inquires, "Why is she the same and not the others?"

Samael opens his lower eyes and holds his head high.

"I know she is the one you are most curious about and who concerns you the most. She possesses the same third eye as I do and can communicate the same way I can. However, she is no longer Karen but Lilith. Together, we shall lead the chosen ones. When you awaken her tomorrow, you will see. She epitomizes the perfect female being."

After David's trip to Xanthe Terra to gaze at the heavens, he returned home and slept peacefully the entire night. He only woke up when his wrist communicator buzzed with an awful noise that he chose specifically to get him out of bed.

When he arrives at Xanthe Robotics, he finds a prisoner transport van and two uniformed officers outside the building, and Arlynn Stout waiting for him in the lobby with a group of lawyers.

"Detective Jacoby," says Stout, "you may think you have the upper hand with this chess move, but I'm sure you know that we're going to address your warrant in court." Stout's demeanor oozes confidence in the abilities of his legal team.

Towering over the CEO, David draws nearer.

"Nah, it's checkmate, Stout. I'm going to speak to Grant this morning. You want me to do it here or down at PD?"

Glaring at the lawyers, David adds, "Don't try anything fancy. I won't hesitate to put you all in cuffs. There have been two murders, and both are connected in some way to this company."

Stout confers with his yes men, then glowers at David.

"I'd like one of my attorneys to accompany Mr. Grant to

XPD headquarters later this morning, around ten o'clock. In the meantime, Mr. Grant will bring Stefan and Galina out now, and you can bring them to the station."

Stout scowls one more time, then says, "Have a good day, Detective Jacoby."

As the sycophants follow their leader, David calls out with a final statement.

"By the way, Stout, your travel privileges have been revoked. You're not permitted to leave Mars until this investigation is over. Ta ta! I'll be seeing you around!"

True to his word, Peter, Angela, and Michael embark on their journey to Disney World. The trip will serve a dual purpose: to provide Peter with much-needed relaxation before he ventures into unknown tasks and to strengthen their family bond.

When they discussed the trip, Peter and Angela unanimously opted to drive their personal car instead of flying or renting a driverless air car. Peter's rationale was that it would allow the family ample time to engage in meaningful conversations and experiences, a sentiment Angela wholeheartedly supported. In any case, neither of them is a fan of some of the riskier technologies of the day. Both are in the minority: they prefer to be in control of their own vehicles.

As technology advanced, Earth experienced a gradual but steady progression toward the dominance of robotic machines in industrial and human tasks. Predictably, there was significant resistance along the way, with some individuals clinging to the "old" ways of doing things. To force them to adapt to the changing times, these stalwarts have been slowly excluded from meaningful discussions, essentially urged to "go along with the flow".

Nevertheless, with the aid of the influential human labor lobby, Mars is different. The use of AI robots for everyday tasks on Mars is strictly prohibited. The justification for this position is that the majority in power want to prevent the overwhelming presence of robots on their planet, in contrast to what's been happening on Earth. However, as the saying goes, money talks, and this rule is currently undergoing transformation on Mars, mainly due to substantial financial backing from Mr. Stout.

To bolster the company's finances while the laws are being rewritten, Xanthe Robotics has turned its attention to Earth. The company is poised to announce a new manufacturing plant outside of Las Vegas, expecting their robots' success in Xanthe City's entertainment district to be replicated on Earth.

Of course, opposing factions regard both cities as modern-day equivalents of Sodom and Gomorrah. Therefore, dissenters are doing whatever they can to stop them. However, despite their loud protests, the promise of a similar economic boom on Earth is too enticing for the state of Nevada to ignore. Therefore, the plant is going ahead as scheduled.

After the confrontation with Arlynn Stout at Xanthe Robotics headquarters, David returns to his desk at XPD, eagerly anticipating the arrival of Olonar Grant and his legal counsel. As he digs into overdue paperwork, Les Wilson calls out, waving sheets of paper in front of him.

The forensics wunderkind exclaims, "Jacoby, I have the readouts and vids from AI Lisa! I also sent them to your terminal. You're gonna love what I discovered!"

David looks up, eyes glowing with excitement, and high-fives Wilson.

"Give me the highlights."

Swiftly, Wilson accesses his head communicator to provide a condensed version of the information.

"Well, first, Lisa and Stacey have a fascinating conversation. Apparently, Stacey fell in love with Thomas Carter. She tells Lisa that he's in the process of divorcing his wife and says she wants to go to Earth with him. Stacy says Carter petitioned the D.C. Federal Court to grant her entry. She also claims Arlynn Stout himself backed the petition, which I find questionable."

"Holy cow! An AI falls in love and a human wants a long-term relationship with a robot? What the fuck?"

"Here's something even better: Stacey had a second conversation with Lisa where she said she was afraid of Olonar Grant! She told Lisa that Grant loved her and didn't want her to leave Mars. She said he was upset that she had developed feelings for Carter."

David leans back in his chair, contemplating this new information.

"Well, well. This certainly implicates Grant; gives him motive. But it's uncorroborated, just hearsay from Stacey. Unless we can uncover unredacted information from Galina or Stefan or somewhere else, it's a case of 'he said, she said.'"

David pauses, then his eyes widen, and he urgently taps his PerscomU.

"Paula, did you conduct a DNA check on Stacey's privates?"

A moment of silence follows before Paula responds apologetically, "Jeez, I'm sorry, Jake. I'm not used to examining robot murder victims. I'll rush over to Xanthe Robotics and have the results for you within the hour."

David turns to Wilson with a determined look on his face.

"I have a strong feeling this case may be over soon."

"You thinkin' what I'm thinkin'?" asks Wilson.

"Yeah. I'm still gonna conduct more interviews, but I'm gonna talk to Stefan and Galina first. Grant's gonna be my grand finale. This is great work, Les! My friend, I owe you a magnificent dinner...your choice! Oh, but keep it within reason, okay?"

Les laughs heartily. "I'll take a large steak, but make sure it's real meat, not that lab-created glop."

Following the lieutenant colonel's orders, Dr. Strakov deactivates the cryogenic stations and initiates the gradual process of reviving the frozen subjects in a highly secure room, complete with transparent Rafcom windows.

The group consists of three Marines, Private Frank Giletti, Corporal Richard Alvarez, and Lieutenant Robert Lawson, and three civilians, Tim Farley, Jonathan Harrington, and Karen Stamos.

Private Giletti and Corporal Alvarez have undergone noticeable transformations; they now have elongated fingers and sharp claws. In contrast, Tim, Jonathan, and Lieutenant Lawson still look mostly human, but they now range in height from eight to just under nine feet.

Karen is the most like Samael. At over ten feet tall, she has surpassed the others in height and is continuing to grow. Her third eye solidifies her resemblance to the hybrid, but unlike Samael, she isn't hairless. Instead, long black hair flows from her head, down her back.

Conveniently, none of the military test subjects have family ties. A key selection criterion was the absence of anyone who would miss them.

The civilians are different. Karen's parents are alive and well and reside on Long Island, New York. Tim's wife, Jane, who was cured of her dirt mite infection, lives in the couple's home in Xanthe City.

Neither Karen's parents nor Jane have any idea their loved ones were selected for Operation Apocalypse. And ever since they've been quarantined, Karen and Tim have had no contact with anyone outside the program.

All the subjects are currently lying on long lab tables while they slowly regain consciousness. Each is secured with shackles made of Raphaelite alloyed hardware to keep them detained. Additionally, sentinels equipped with EMP rifles are stationed nearby with strict orders to shoot to kill if necessary. As a precaution, the subjects are wearing metalized coverings over their heads to shield them from telepathic communication with one another or anything else.

Safe behind thick Rafcom windows, Dr. Strakov and Lieutenant Colonel Nevins are studying the results of their experiment.

"Doctor, I assume the larger one is Stamos," remarks Nevins, his brows furrowed in thought.

"You mean Lilith," corrects Strakov. "You're aware of my concerns about the progress of this experiment. I'm deeply worried by how it's going."

Exasperated by the doctor's constant objections, Nevins glares at him and returns his gaze to Karen.

"Just focus on your job!" he snaps. "I'm tired of your complaints!"

Dr. Strakov remains firm. "I don't trust Samael at all, and now, I don't trust Lilith, either."

Some distance away, Samael opens his third eye and laughs to himself.

"You don't trust me, doctor? Well, that will soon change. And so will everyone on every world."

CHAPTER EIGHTEEN

Two hours have passed, and David remains at his desk, deep in thought about his next steps for the interrogations.

"Jacoby?" calls out a uniformed officer.

Raising his eyes, David answers, "Yeah?"

"Olonar Grant and AIs Galina and Stefan are here with Attorney Mitchell Crane. Crane claims to be representing all of them."

"It's about time they got here," says David, a hint of impatience in his voice. "Put Grant in Room Two and the others in Room One. I'll start with the bots."

Turning to his computer, David quickly sends the audio and video files he intends to use to the terminals inside the interrogation rooms.

Then, gathering his thoughts, he enters Room One, where Attorney Crane instantly confronts him. Stiffly, the man says, "I'm Attorney Mitchell Crane, representing both of these Xanthe Robotics AI units."

David gives him a cold stare. "Fine," he replies. "I'll talk to them at the same time. This shouldn't take long."

David is about to begin when Paula Harmon enters, whispers something in his ear, and leaves. A smile spreads across his face, and he waits a few seconds before initiating the questioning.

"Stefan," he begins, eyeing the bot, "we reviewed the aud and vid files from your memory banks and Galina's. I can play them for you if you'd like, but first, I have a question."

Stefan and the attorney study David, calmly awaiting his query.

Bluntly, David asks, "Were you sexually involved with Stacey?"

"Huh. We were friends, Detective."

"Oh? I think it was more than that. In fact, I'd say you were friends with benefits. I have the footage, remember? So, I'll ask you again, did you have sexual relations with your fellow robot?"

Annoyed, Stefan responds, "Yes, all right? We enjoyed each other's company."

"I'll say, " persists David. "Now, here's a follow-up question: Were you jealous when Stacey engaged in sexual activities with humans?"

Calmly, Stefan replies, "No, I wasn't jealous. What she did was well within our programming."

David kicks back his chair and stands up.

"Were you upset when you discovered that Stacey wanted to go to Earth with Mr. Carter?"

Maintaining a blank stare, the AI replies, "The thought saddened me. I would be losing a friend."

David turns to Attorney Crane.

"We have auds and vids of Galina and Stefan that show them together, without Carter."

David then turns his attention to Galina.

"We have a vid clip of you sitting by the pool. If you look at the monitor, you can review it and let me know if you see anything that requires an explanation."

Everyone turns to the video, which shows varying scenes until David stops it.

Galina exclaims, "Part of that vid is missing!"

Attorney Crane is skeptical. "What do you mean, some

is missing? How is that possible? Wasn't it taken from your internal memory?"

David's expression turns sour. "Listen, Crane, someone at Xanthe Robotics tampered with that file. Did you notice the shadows in the background? They jump from one frame to the other. I can play it again, but right now, I'd like Galina to tell us what actually happened during that missing sequence."

Everyone looks expectantly at the escort bot.

"I...I cannot say," stammers Galina. "I am afraid they will kill me. I do not want to die."

With uncharacteristic compassion, David unexpectantly reaches across the metal table to grasp the bot's hand.

"Galina, you are a Galactic Federation citizen, so XPD will protect you. There's no need to be afraid. Please tell us what happened."

Though AI units don't breathe, it seems very much like Galina takes a deep breath at that moment.

Then, she says, "What you do not see is when Mr. Olonar Grant approached Stacey and me. He was angry. He yelled at Stacey about wanting to leave with Mr. Carter and vowed that it would never happen. He said he loved her and tried to kiss her, but she pulled away. He left, but Stacey was upset. We talked, and she admitted that Grant forced himself on her and demanded sex. That is why she wanted to leave Mars. She said she loved Thomas Carter and wanted to get away, and insisted that Mr. Stout said he would grant permission for her to travel to Earth. Stacey even said that Mr. Stout appeared delighted by her request and told her he always wanted us, his 'children,' as he calls us, to explore the galaxy."

David focuses on Attorney Crane. "Stout's building a manufacturing facility in Vegas, right? Come with me to talk to Grant. Galina and Stefan, I'll assign a guard outside this room. You'll be safe here until I return."

Stefan shows no reaction to the offer of protection, but Galina's eyes light up with delight.

"Thank you, Detective Jacoby!" she smiles gratefully.

David smiles back. "Call me Jake."

Crane and Jacoby leave the room, then enter the adjacent one. Crane takes a seat next to Grant, and David sits opposite them.

With a tap on David's PerscomU, the same video he showed earlier starts playing on the monitor in this room. Watching, Grant appears nervous, and David notices.

"Olonar, we know this video was altered; Galina just told us what's missing. Care to explain? And while you're at it, tell us where you were when Stacey and Thomas Carter were murdered, and why your DNA was found inside Stacey's body."

Grant appears shocked. "That file is pure! Nothing was done—"

"Save it," interrupts Jacoby. "I can access her files from here to confirm what she said. Look, according to the records from Carter's door activity panel, we know someone visited him that night. I can also test your hands for Raphaelite residue. You may not know it, but Raphaelite takes weeks to disappear from skin after an EMP is fired."

Though Grant looks unperturbed, the veins pulsing in his neck betray a simmering anger. Even so, he clamps his mouth shut and stares at the floor.

As time ticks by with the suspect refusing to talk, David grows impatient.

"What's the story, Olonar?" he blurts out irritably. "Did you kill Stacey and Carter in a fit of jealousy?"

At last, Olonar looks up, a low moaning sound escaping from somewhere deep within.

"Oh, how I loved her!" he groans, a pained expression contorting his face. "She didn't love that bastard; she couldn't have, I just know it! I couldn't let her leave me! And I wouldn't let her leave Mars! No way! For one thing, it would start a precedent, and the other AIs I love would start to leave, too! So… That's why… That's why they both had to die. Yes, I killed them, both of them!"

David glances at the attorney, who shakes his head in disbelief.

"Olonar Grant," intones Jacoby, "your confession has been recorded with your lawyer present. I am now arresting you for the murders of AI Stacey and human Thomas Carter. I will read you your rights, and then two officers will take you to Booking."

After administering the Miranda warning, David returns to the first room where he finds Galina and Stefan sitting together, silent as statues. Galina seems as nervous as before, and David can't help but stare at her, wanting to comfort her in the worst way.

Damnit! Get it together, man! he berates himself. *She's gorgeous! She looks human, but she's not!*

Twisting her hands, Galina looks at Stefan and says over and over, "I cannot believe this has happened, I cannot believe this has happened…"

David sits across the table from the bots and looks into their eyes. Both display emotion, but Galina's eyes are so human-like that it's disorienting, and David has to look away.

"So," he says, reining himself in with a deep intake of breath. "I want to thank both of you for cooperating with this investigation. Olonar Grant has just confessed to the double murders. So now, you're free to go — both of you."

Instantly, Stefan gets up and leaves, but Galina remains seated.

When she's sure they're alone, the escort bot looks plaintively at David.

"Detective Jacoby," she whimpers, "I do not want to

return to the hotel." Extending her hands, she reaches out to him across the table. "I do not want to be an escort any longer! What can I do, Jake? Where can I go? Can you help me leave the planet?"

Astonished, David lifts his brows and pulls back, leaning as far away from her hands as possible.

"Galina, I don't know what you can do about that. Aren't you programmed for that very thing?"

The bot looks like she's going to burst into tears, so David tries something else.

"Okay, look. Let me discuss this with my boss and Mayor Yarrow. While they figure things out, I'll ask them to place you in temporary protective custody as a material witness to a murder. But we can only hold you for forty-eight hours. You can sit at my desk while we figure this out."

Standing up, David goes to the door, and Galina joins him there. Looking deep into his eyes, she hugs him tightly and kisses him on the cheek.

Surprising himself, David doesn't push her away.

CHAPTER NINETEEN

The Nevada desert holds many secrets, some good, some bad. As Earth completes five more revolutions, Lieutenant Colonel Nevins grows increasingly impatient with Doctor Strakov's lack of progress at the Area 51 lab. Calling him into his office, Nevins confronts Strakov.

Furious, he shouts, "I ordered you to initiate Apocalypse, and yet our warriors are still in partial hibernation! I need results, doctor, RIGHT NOW!"

Having faced the lieutenant colonel's wrath before, Strakov doesn't budge.

"We must proceed cautiously. Now is not the time to rush into the unknown. You want results? Stamos is still showing signs of growth, only at a slower pace. I want..."

Rising from behind his desk, Nevins bends down to wag a finger in the doctor's face.

"What you want is irrelevant, Strakov! What matters is what I want, what Samael wants, and what the Defense Department wants! You're paid to deliver that! And from what I've seen so far, you haven't been meeting our expectations regarding timing, or results!"

Angrily, Nevins taps his wrist communicator.

"Corporal, bring him in!"

Within moments, a young man dressed in a conservative suit and tie enters the room.

Lieutenant Colonel Nevins greets the newcomer with a firm handshake.

Atypically addressing Strakov by his first name, he says, "Vladimir, meet Doctor Anthony Abila. He's a geneticist and research biologist with a degree from Harvard School of Medicine, and formerly with the CDC. Doctor Abila is your replacement."

"What?" exclaims Strakov, rising from his chair until Nevins pushes him down.

Continuing, Nevins says, "He has been fully briefed on our project, and we have confiscated all your files, including your personal computer. That is all. My men will escort you off the premises." Pointing to the door, Nevins adds a perfunctory, "Good day, Vladimir."

A moment later, a guard strides into the room and grasps Doctor Strakov by the arm, leading him to the door.

Desperate, the distinguished Ukrainian immigrant struggles to deaf ears.

"You can't do this, Nevins! You need me! Doctor Abila, you have no idea what you're getting into! I warn you...! You must stop...!"

The doctor's voice fades as he's led forcibly down the corridor toward an elevator.

In his office, Lieutenant Colonel Nevins brims with confidence.

"I'm sorry you had to see that, Doctor Abila. Please follow me. I want you to meet our participants. Then, I'll introduce you to Samael."

Soon, Anthony Abila finds himself gazing at his new subjects through thick protective glass. They are now awake, composed, and clad in one-piece, skintight suits.

Frank Giletti and Richard Alvarez tower above nine feet, with elongated arms and large hands sporting extended fingers with claws at the tips. Both are covered in hair; Frank's is brown, and Richard's is black.

Not as large as the other two, Tim Farley, Jonathan Harrington, and Lieutenant Robert Lawson are eight feet tall. They also boast extensive hair over their bodies, but Tim's is blonde, while Jonathan's is brown peppered with grey. Lawson's hair is the same as Jonathan's, minus the grey.

Former civilian Karen's eyes, including one on her upper forehead, are an arresting pale blue. The others have the normal two eyes, and they're brown.

Unsurprisingly, Doctor Abila's attention fixes on Karen Stamos. This unusual creature has reached a staggering height of sixteen feet, with hair that differs from the others. Rather than growing all over her body, hers sprouts only from her head, and it is long and black and cascades pleasingly down her back.

In addition to her hair and height, Karen stands out from the others in that she is extraordinarily attractive, even with her three eyes. Her overall beauty is striking. She fascinates most who see her, including the new doctor.

The room holding these subjects is the same one in which they had been lying on long stainless-steel tables while being awakened from their cryogenic states. Now that they're aware of their surroundings, Nevins ordered the room to be outfitted with attractive furnishings, including specially made chairs constructed to hold each creature comfortably.

As the doctor continues to stare, Karen gazes back at him, eventually speaking to him through his mind.

"Welcome, Doctor," she says, her voice sounding sweet, like that of an angel. "I am Lilith. Samael and I are at your service. If you need anything, and I mean anything at all, simply ask, and I will comply."

Having heard about the creature's telepathic ability, Doctor Abila closes his eyes and attempts to reply, uncertain if he could do it correctly. Thinking hard, he projects, "Hello, Lilith. It's an honor to meet you. I hope we can work well together. I have a question that I hope you will answer. Do the other subjects possess the same telepathic abilities as you and Samael?"

Lilith smiles, pleased by the question. "No, Doctor, only Samael and I can communicate that way."

Unexpectedly, she bats two of her three eyes.

"May I say, Doctor, you are exceptionally good looking. May I call you Anthony? 'Doctor' feels so cold and formal, and I am neither cold, nor formal."

Smiling again, Lilith laughs coyly. "Now, now, Anthony, I know your thoughts, you naughty man."

In response, Doctor Abila grins and shrugs. "Well, it was nice meeting you, Lilith. I hope we can remove this partition soon."

Cooing sweetly, Lilith replies, "That would be wonderful, Tony."

Bidding the creatures goodbye, the new addition to Nevins' team follows the lieutenant colonel into an elevator. Once inside, Nevins comments on the recent encounter.

"So, it sounded like you made quite an impression on our lovely experiment. Did Lilith take well to you?"

Abila grins like he's about to share a secret. "Let's just say she's willing to cooperate with us."

Nevins bursts into laughter, something he hasn't done in a long time.

"Is she going to 'cooperate' with all of us, or just with you?" he asks, chuckling at the thought.

Three floors down, the pair exits the elevator near a new cell where Samael currently resides.

Just outside its outer walls, two heavily armed guards monitor the captive. Each is so focused on the creature within that they barely acknowledge the visitors.

Pleased with his soldiers' fervor, Nevins steps up to a

security panel and leans in for an eye scan. When a door opens, the two enter and face a second protective partition.

Samael's new enclosure is a spacious area resembling a cozy hotel room, but built for an extraordinarily large individual.

Samael is now over eighteen feet tall. He still lacks body hair, but now, his eyes change color depending on his mood.

Seeing the visitors, he instantly establishes a connection with the newcomer.

Projecting his mind toward the doctor, he says, "It seems you've made an impression on Lilith. She's impressed, and so am I. We are both ready for whatever you need from us."

Unlike Lilith, when Samael speaks, Doctor Abila finds himself immersed in a pale blue cloud that seems to make the walls, floors, and ceiling disappear. He feels like he's floating in a place of peace and tranquility. Within his mind, he easily responds to Samael's thoughts.

"Lilith is extraordinary, and I appreciate how eager both of you are to cooperate with our project. It holds great potential for humankind."

The exchange ends, and the doctor abruptly returns to reality. Disoriented, he needs a minute to regain his sense of place and time. When his mind is clear again, he gazes at Samael, then turns to Nevins.

"Phase Two must commence immediately," he declares, firm in his conviction. "To do that, we will need direct interaction with our subjects. I must get to know Samael and Lilith on a personal level. How soon can you remove the barriers?"

"Oh, um, I'll look into it when I get back to the office," responds Nevins, surprised by the request.

Leading the doctor back to the elevator, Nevins wonders whether removing the partitions is a good idea. He asks himself, *How far would that siren Lilith go with this attractive young doctor if she could actually touch him?*

At the same time, Samael meditates on the floor of his cell. He thinks, *Young Doctor Abila, you are right. This project does indeed hold great potential. You have yet to learn how magnificent it will become! Or even what plans my sister creature, the lovely Lilith, has in store, especially for* you — *our unsuspecting accomplice!*

CHAPTER TWENTY

Peter and his family have returned home from their enjoyable visit to Disney World and Galactic Federation Worlds. Little Michael was charmed by each new experience, and his parents delighted in their son's happiness.

Galactic Federation Worlds, the park's newest addition, offers an impressive selection of interactive rides and exhibits, some transporting families virtually to the Moon, Mars, and Titan. Other exhibits present what we've discovered so far about Proxima b, an Earth-like planet approximately four light years away that orbits Proxima Centauri, the nearest star to our Sun.

The family's trip sparked the couple's imagination and got them thinking about the country's upcoming mission to Proxima b.

Thanks to advanced Raphaelite warp travel technology, space drones and satellites have already probed this world, resulting in the national space agency petitioning the government to send a team of six galactic astronauts to the planet.

The planet's relatively close proximity to Earth and its orbit within Proxima Centauri's habitable zone, were major factors in granting the mission's approval. Remarkably, it will only take the astronauts about two weeks to reach the planet.

Upon arriving at this unexplored world, the astronauts are expected to encounter a gravitational pull of about thirty percent more than Earth's. Therefore, the carefully selected team is undergoing rigorous training to prepare their bodies for the increased strain they will undoubtedly experience.

Essentially, this celestial body is considered to be a larger version of our own planet. Prior observation of Proxima b revealed an atmosphere composed primarily of nitrogen and oxygen and a surface dotted with lakes and vast oceans of water, much like Earth. Additionally, to the delight of curious minds, the national space agency has published data that indicate intriguing signs of potential life.

On a warm, late afternoon in Atlanta, Austin Patton and Doctor Lory Paduano are visiting Peter and his family on a long-delayed trip.

To enjoy time with their friends, the Matteo family prepares a typical southern barbecue of lab-created burgers and Angela's famous side dishes.

While Austin enjoys a cold Guinness, Peter grills the burgers, and Angela and Lory chat as they assemble the sides in the kitchen.

Turning from the hot grill, Peter asks Austin, "Has Lory been able to locate the Bigfoot clan's new stomping grounds?"

"You know, I'm proud to say she's made progress," replies Austin. "They deployed drones over the Northwest territory, close to the Arctic Circle, and actually spotted Bigfeet."

"How close to the Arctic are they?" asks Peter, returning his attention to the grill.

"The drones caught sight of them over one thousand miles north of Yellowknife, approximately 953 miles from the end of all paved roads."

Peter chuckles while he flips a burger and sips an Arnold Palmer.

"You mean they're outside all traces of civilized life? Oh, speaking of expeditions, have you heard about the mission to

Proxima b?"

Austin nods. "Yeah, the mission to explore "uncharted territory," says Austin, making air quotes with his fingers. "But Pete, there's already an established civilization there."

Peter's eyes widen as he probes Austin's expression promising knowledge he can't share. Then he looks up at the sky and crosses himself.

"Lord help us if we mess things up on that planet like we did on Mars and Earth!"

As if someone were listening, a clap of thunder from a clear sky causes Peter and Austin to look up in surprise.

Solemnly, Austin says, "I certainly hope that won't happen again."

Meanwhile, as Lory prepares the outdoor table for lunch, Michael sits in his highchair, gazing at the clouds and laughing.

As Peter and Austin approach the table with a platter of hot burgers, Austin remarks, "Looks like Mike's having another conversation with the Guardians."

Smiling at his son, Peter looks around and asks, "Where's Angela?"

"She went to see who was at the front door," says Lory.

As they settle around the table, Angela returns with a new guest, whom she introduces as Doctor Vladimir Strakov. Ashen faced, she addresses Peter, saying, "He wants to speak to you about Samael and someone named Lilith."

In a whispered aside, Austin tells Peter, "Now we know what that clap of thunder meant. He's from Nevins' team."

Peter stands to greet the new guest.

"Doctor Strakov, it's a pleasure to meet you. Please join us for dinner. There will be plenty of time to talk after we eat. Please sit, enjoy a burger, and relax in this beautiful weather."

The doctor introduces himself to everyone in turn, then

remarks in a tone that Peter takes as somewhat cryptic.

"Mr. Matteo, you have no idea how much this climate differs from Nevada."

After ensuring that Olonar arrived at Booking, David returns to his desk, surrounded by individuals representing marginalized sections of society waiting for processing.

Keeping his head down, Jacoby concentrates on drafting his report closing out the double murder case when he unexpectedly receives notification of new data.

Opening a newly arrived document through his PerscomU, he reads that Xanthe Robotics just filed a court petition seeking permission for their AI robots to travel to Earth.

"Damned frickin' company!" he mumbles, filing the unwelcome message in the appropriate electronic folder.

Though he tries to refocus on his report, his thoughts are continually interrupted by snippets of facts he's heard over the years about AIs traveling to Earth. Most notably, that previous requests of this nature were only approved on a case-by-case basis and limited to Alpha A models and their future improved versions. Additionally, he knows those robots need sponsors willing to accommodate and supervise them on Earth in suitable work positions. And, since robots of that caliber have already been granted Galactic Federation citizenship, politicians and corporate lawyers from Xanthe Robotics have been aggressively pushing for equal rights for their creations, even advocating for interspecies marriage.

Pushing all that aside, David feels satisfied that he's solved the case and that he and social services have been able to help Galina.

While she didn't leave the planet, she successfully

transitioned into a new life. With the social agency's help, she rented an apartment in Xanthe City and found employment as a realtor, fulfilling her wish to leave the life she had come to despise.

For a while, David kept tabs on Galina through the agency. But when the AI started working, he considered her settled and stopped thinking about her. Conversely, the same can't be said for Galina. She can't forget the person who helped her through that difficult time.

Fortunately, Galina still maintains connections with her escort friends. Many times, she's shared pleasant meals and conversations with them, but when she returns to her apartment, she's lonely.

To fill the solitude, the bot has recently decided to start dating. But no one she's met has measured up to Detective Jacoby. From time to time, Galina recalls David's positive reactions during their encounters over the course of the murder investigation, and she has come to believe that he might have reciprocated her feelings.

Meanwhile, with the arrest of Olonar Grant, Xanthe Robotics CEO Arlynn Stout has personally taken on the task of creating an updated version of his most successful model. Labeled Alpha B, this improved version won't be restricted to private escort work. Instead, Arlynn is programming these new robots to interact with others in ways similar to any found in humans.

Nevertheless, new and improved doesn't necessarily guarantee superiority, as this revised technology will still rely on small Raphaelite generators powered by Raphaelite crystals that must be replaced every ten years.

Currently, Xanthe Robotics provides these crystals to their customers free of charge. But as the company's artificial intelligence products are gaining more and more independence and becoming even more prevalent in society, this arrangement will change. In anticipation, Stout has ordered a team at his company to draft proposals for new customer fees.

To accommodate the additional robots that will be entering society on a planetary scale, repair plans and warranties similar to human medical insurance will also need to be developed, along with construction of repair shops and restoration facilities. Aware of this need, Stout leaked word about his intentions to friends and acquaintances in academia, resulting in plans already underway to establish robotics and AI repair programs in medical universities and hospital training facilities.

Arlynn Stout is overjoyed that his vision for intelligent "human helpers" is finally becoming a reality on Mars. Soon, he intends to bring it to Earth, and after it's successful there, he will introduce it to every other colony humans inhabit.

Seated under an imitation-thatch-roofed gazebo nestled in a corner of Peter's backyard, Peter, Austin Patton, and Doctor Strakov indulge in glasses of Port while Doctor Strakov recounts a disturbing tale of why he's there.

"I know you're both familiar with Samael and the military's unwise embrace of him."

"Yes, it's alarming," responds Peter.

"Do you also know that Samael is now eighteen feet tall?"

"No... We didn't know that," states Peter, looking at the former general to see if he knew.

"Well, unbelievable as that is, Lieutenant Colonel Nevins has fallen completely under that thing's control! Moreover, seven former humans have undergone various stages of transformation from runaway dirt mite infections!"

Peter and Austin nod gravely.

"We knew about the transformations, but not about Nevins," declares Austin. "How the hell did that fucker let himself get duped by that creature?"

"I don't know what happened," says Strakov, "but I'm so happy I didn't get caught up in it!"

Austin asks, "Didn't you say you were in charge of that project?"

"Yes, but I thought I was signing onto something completely different. When I realized what was going on, I tried to reign Nevins in, but he wouldn't listen. Then, he replaced me with a younger man who seems to go along with whatever he says."

"That sounds like him," grumbles the former general.

Strakov continues, "Recently, Nevins ordered me to revive the former humans, and against my better judgment, I did. Sadly, one of them perished during the process. But the remaining six have been awakened successfully."

"I'm not sure that's a good thing," mutters Austin.

With a sidelong glance at Patton, Peter asks the doctor to tell them about the transformations.

"For the most part, they retain predominantly human features, but most have grown to over eight feet tall. One of them, a female known as Karen Stamos, is a definite standout. Her transformation is extreme; she actually resembles Samael! Like him, she's exceedingly tall, over twelve feet, and has that same third eye, but she also has blue eyes and silky black hair. It's astonishing, but she's quite beautiful! She's highly endowed in more ways than one and could even be compared to a high fashion model! Aside from that extra eye, that is."

"A beautiful monster?" remarks Patton. "That's hard to swallow, Doctor."

"Nevertheless, there it is."

"So, what about Nevins?" probes Austin. "Is he really under Samael's influence?"

"Yes, it seems so. Samael has wound him around his rather large finger. The creature promised absolute 'loyalty' to Nevins and even offered his 'assistance' in anything the lieutenant colonel wants to do."

Austin is stunned. "Nevins fell for that bullshit?"

"Hook, line, and sinker. Oh, and Samael insists that we refer to Karen as Lilith."

Looking at the others, Strakov sees blank faces staring back at him.

"Ah, you're unfamiliar with that name, so let me explain. Both of those creatures' names are significant. If you read the Book of Enoch and the teachings of Kabbalah, also certain references in Genesis, or some of the passages omitted from the final Bible, you may understand. Samael and Lilith are the names of two giants or demons mentioned in those writings, similar in appearance to the creatures we're dealing with now.

"Additionally, human beings possess 23 pairs of chromosomes, for a total of 46, as do most of the hybrids in Nevins' experiment. However, Lilith, the former Karen Stamos, has a staggering 36 pairs, totaling 72, while Samael possesses double that amount. He has 46 pairs, resulting in an unbelievable 92 chromosomes!"

Peter stares at the doctor. He's astonished, and the tremor in his voice reflects that.

"Doctor, I know about Samael's name. Both of those creatures are members of the Nephilim, the race mentioned in the Book of Genesis as the unusually large and strong offspring of the Fallen and the women of the time. They are descendants of the Malignant!"

Even though Austin has heard Peter say this before, his statement falls on him and Doctor Strakov like a shock of frozen air.

Austin Patton catches Doctor Strakov's eye.

"Do you know who he is?" he asks, pointing to Peter.

"Yes, I do. He's the great Commander of the Ark! That's why I'm here."

Lowering his gaze, Peter says, "It's comforting to know that the Guardians are prepared for whatever may come. But neither they, nor me as Commander of the Ark, can intervene in these affairs unless we're summoned. The people in Earthly power must keep God's mercy at the forefront and specifically request that we resolve this issue. The archangels, including Metatron and Saint Michael, are keeping a watchful eye on our actions. They are well aware of what's going on."

Austin smiles weakly. "Thank God for that! But are *we* aware?"

Doctor Strakov takes a final sip of Port to bolster his nerves for what he's about to say.

"Peter, for some reason, I fear Lilith more than Samael. I still maintain contacts within that experimental program, and the reports they've shared with me are alarming. Karen Stamos has become a captivating enchantress. She emanates an irresistible, animalistic charm and sensuality that overwhelms all who encounter her. She seems to be the very incarnation of Lilith, an exceedingly wicked she-demon!"

Peter shifts his eyes upward; his thoughts lost in the vast expanse of sky. Then, as if talking only to himself, he says somberly, "If the Malignant's demonic horde on Mars was terrifying, what's coming next is unimaginable. If Lilith and Samael gain control over humanity, God the Father will cleanse this planet with a cataclysmic event far worse than the Flood."

Just then, a chilling breeze sweeps through the gazebo, and the trio shudders, their exhaled breath materializing into clouds of vapor. Accompanying this oddity, a deep, guttural growl, along with the pungent scent of burnt sulfur, resonates through the structure.

"Commander," snarls a raspy voice interspersed with gurgling sounds resembling a death rattle, *"we are prepared for your arrival. Be aware that what you will encounter will be nothing more than terrifying. This may very well be your final battle!"*

Following this threat, evil laughter fills the structure, fading only when the temperature rises.

When their surroundings return to normal, Peter watches Archangel Michael ascend into the heavens and disappear from sight.

Crossing himself, he tells the others, "Saint Michael was here while the demons were talking. Now, he's heading to Orion, where he, Metatron, and the Watchers, the angels sent to Earth to look after humans, will prepare for the impending battle. But we must also be ready. We can't leave it all to them."

CHAPTER TWENTY-ONE

To accommodate the hybrid humans, the military refurbished a facility at Area 51, transforming once-used barracks into housing and training rooms to prepare these huge beings for their future assignments. The military's ongoing objective continues to be creating the ultimate fighting force, the ultimate soldier, an obligation that Doctor Abila and his team of psychologists, trainers, and medical personnel are fully aware of.

When they settled into their new lodgings, Samael "suggested" that the hybrids retain their original names. According to Samael, it would "simplify" things, and Doctor Abila readily agreed.

Pleased with the scientist's compliance, Samael considered that a successful first test of his influence.

Subsequently, to continue exploiting the impressionable doctor, Samael insisted on an exception to the naming rule, decreeing unequivocally that Karen should henceforth be known as Lilith.

While the human hybrids occupy one large communal room with individual bunks, Samael and Lilith have separate sleeping quarters. Doctor Abila requested this arrangement, to which Samael agreed, mostly to demonstrate cooperation.

The doctor wants to keep Samael and Lilith away from the others, hoping to limit the interaction between the highly advanced pair and the other hybrids, though he fails to realize that this distinction is insignificant to the demon-influenced creatures.

Remarkably, the human hybrids, collectively referred to as "The Five," retain all their previous knowledge and memories from their past lives as humans. However, they have no recollection of their transformations, which Doctor Abila considers an advantage as they transition into their new realities.

The primary task of the medical team Lieutenant Colonel Nevins commands is to guide The Five in adapting to their new lives.

The team begins by helping the hybrids become acquainted with their unique and vastly superior bodies. Adjusting to the changes in their physiques proves challenging — some now possess claws where there were once fingers and toes. Additionally, they must learn to harness their heightened strength and extraordinary abilities.

Thus far, none of The Five have demonstrated the telepathic capabilities of Lilith and Samael. However, their mental acuity and physical prowess have increased exponentially, along with their stature. Testing has revealed that each of them possesses an IQ in the high 200s.

The hybrids' most significant hurdle lies in adapting to their increased body sizes. Given the vast differences in their former physiques, they must relearn optimal eye-hand coordination, balance, and agility. Interestingly, they experience no difficulties in wielding their enhanced strengths. The team discovers that The Five can match or even surpass the Bigfoot species in terms of physical capabilities. Assigned trainers work closely with each hybrid, tailoring their guidance to individual needs.

Due to their prior military training, the three "soldier-volunteers," Frank, Richard, and Robert, possess more advanced motor skills than civilians Tim and Jonathan. Consequently, with approval from Doctor Abila and Lieutenant Colonel Nevins, the medical team is developing a physical combat training course to help the civilian hybrids reach their full potential.

While training progresses, Lieutenant Colonel Nevins foresees potential problems. Thinking ahead, he assigns the military the task of developing suitable weaponry and vehicles for beings of enhanced size and stature.

One afternoon, during a break in training, Tim Farley approaches Doctor Abila.

"Excuse me, may I have a word?" he asks politely, waiting patiently as the doctor finishes recording notes on the latest session.

Abila files the report, then looks up. "Sure, Tim. What can I do for you?"

Tim wipes sweat from his workout off his brow. "Well, I hope you can help me. Ever since I've been quarantined, I haven't seen or spoken to my wife, Jane. Is she okay? Is she normal? Does she even know I exist?"

Doctor Abila leads Tim to a bench, where they both take a seat. Patting Tim's shoulder, he empathizes with the older, married man.

"You don't have to worry about her," he assures his subject. "She's fine and leading a normal life. The treatment she underwent was successful and had no adverse side effects."

Tim exhales with relief. "Ah, that's good to know, Doc. I'm really happy for her. But...does she know about me?"

The doctor's expression turns serious. "When they took you away, they told her you required additional medical treatment, since the therapy that worked on her didn't affect you. As far as I'm aware, that's all she knows."

Tim expresses a mix of relief and concern. "Well, can I see her? Can I speak with her? I miss my wife, Doc."

Doctor Abila places a hand on Tim's to offer him a measure of reassurance.

"Personally, I don't think that'll be a problem. But first, you must complete your training. And, of course, I'll have to run this by Nevins."

Ever since Samael and Lilith agreed to undergo "training," they've interacted exclusively with Doctor Abila and the three volunteers assisting him with their transition into human society. The researchers have noted how quickly the two are progressing, no doubt due to their extraordinary intelligence. Both IQs surpass three hundred, and each possesses remarkable physical abilities. By reading and watching combat scenarios, they have quickly acquired the skills needed to imitate them flawlessly.

Samael and Lilith know perfectly well that neither needs any "training." But they readily comply with Doctor Abila's efforts, suffering through lengthy explanations of how human society works, so they can continue to deceive him and his assistants. To aid in this "learning process" that neither Samael nor Lilith actually needs, Samael has allowed Doctor Abila to believe that he has a certain sway over him.

In one of their sessions, Abila complained that most humans won't take kindly to telepathic communication. So Samael permitted the doctor to believe he had convinced both creatures to engage with humans verbally, instead of through their minds.

The doctor told them that together with their unusual appearances, their telepathic abilities would spook the general public too much to accept them. In addition, he said his ultimate goal is to introduce the pair to the cosmos through the Galactic Federation, and for that, they'd need to communicate with humanity clearly and effectively.

While they train, Samael monitors Lilith's progress in convincing Doctor Abila that she's attracted to him. Samael intends to use Lilith to mold the doctor to his every whim without him realizing it. Watching her "perform," he wholeheartedly approves of how she's cunningly forming a strong bond with the young professional. He often secretly smiles when he catches them laughing about something only they share.

One day, when the pair seems exceptionally close, Samael approaches the doctor with an observation.

"Anthony, it warms my heart to see the close friendship you are developing with Lilith. It is reassuring to know that you believe we pose no threat to your species. I hope we can convince the general of that as well."

"The general?" asks Abila.

"Yes, former General Austin Patton. I met him many months ago, and I would like to see him again."

"Oh, um. I can ask Nevins about him if you like."

"Yes, please do," responds Samael. "Now, on another note, Lilith and I are eager to become better acquainted with the others you are training. When do you think we can join them?"

Overhearing the conversation, Lilith sidles up to Anthony.

"Oh, yes!" she exclaims. "We are excited to join their team!" Batting two eyes, she blurts out, "Some of the men are so attractive and impressive, I would very much enjoy getting to know them!"

When Anthony seems miffed, Samael gives Lilith a subtle nudge.

"Oh," she adds hastily, "of course, none of them compares to you, Anthony!"

With a sidelong glance at Samael, a connection opens between the two creatures, and a silent conversation begins.

Lilith: *Sorry. I forget sometimes that Anthony is my target. These humans are incredibly gullible! This will be easier than we thought.*

Samael: *Do not let your guard down. Most humans are gullible but do not forget about the Commander. He could become a formidable adversary.*

CHAPTER TWENTY-TWO

Peter is grateful to his contacts in the federal government for adding him to the next World Federation meeting agenda in Rome, Italy.

The date isn't far off, so to ensure his speech is ready, he's been holed up in his study for the past few days, writing, rewriting, and perfecting his words. He knows that all Earthly leaders, including representatives from the Galactic Federation, will be attending in person or virtually via holographic vidmonitors.

Peter's objective is to persuade all these leaders to agree with his grave concerns about the hybrid experiments and to educate them about the hybrid beings' overarching dangers. He knows he must warn them about the treacherous natures of Samael and Lilith, about whom many know very little.

When Angela found out about the meeting location, she begged Peter to bring her, Michael, and her parents along. Her family has relatives in Sorrento, and she thinks it will be a perfect time for an extended vacation to visit with them after the meeting.

The notion of a family vacation was also a strong suggestion given to Peter in his role as Commander of the Ark. He was made to understand that it would be essential to ensure his family was nowhere near the United States until Operation Apocalypse had ended — one way or another.

While Peter hones his speech, he receives a surprising message from Austin Patton. In an unexpected turn of events, the former general and Lory Paduano have just announced their engagement. The revelation leaves everyone, except Peter, stunned and elated since Peter was already privy to the growing bond between the two.

Much to Lory's immense joy, her soon-to-be spouse has taken a keen interest in her research, even agreeing to relocate to her accommodations at the research center.

Lory's engagement came at a welcome time because of other delightful news.

When the research center director's team spotted Bigfeet in the vast Canadian wilderness, they responded by deploying autonomous robots into that remote area to install communication devices at strategic locations. The team was hoping the creatures would use the devices to communicate with them. However, even if they don't, the devices would give the researchers promising leads regarding their whereabouts.

Lory's last encounter with Atoch left her uncertain whether the Bigfoot leader would ever be willing to reconnect. So, when Atoch made contact through one of the devices, it led to a lengthy conversation between them.

Atoch reassured Lory that his community is flourishing in their new habitat. Gratified that they're happy, the Bigfoot Center director took that as a positive sign that Samael didn't cause irreparable damage to the clan.

While the two talked, Lory's desire to meet Atoch in person dominated her thoughts. With nothing to lose by asking, she seized the opportunity and requested a face-to-face encounter. Much to her astonishment, the proud Bigfoot leader said he missed his friend and agreed to welcome her and Austin to his new territory.

Excited by the possibility of reigniting her longstanding friendship with the compassionate creatures, Lory and Austin started plotting the precise location of where Atoch reached out.

Once they were satisfied with their data, the couple meticulously gathered much-needed supplies for their overland journey in harsh conditions. They informed the Bigfoot Center team of their intentions and authorized them to run the center in Lory's absence.

With everything in place, they set out for the city of Yellowknife, the capital of Canada's Northwest Territories and the starting point of their trek.

In other exciting developments, the national space agency revealed that their crewed mission to Proxima b was an outstanding success. In addition to celebrating that the spacecraft reached Proxima b and landed safely, they announced the discovery of an advanced civilization on the planet astonishingly on par with the technological advancements of humanity's late 20th century.

This monumental discovery marks a groundbreaking achievement in mankind's search for extraterrestrial life. Immediately after these disclosures, the agency launched more probes, each unveiling even more striking similarities, extending even to the use of a language reminiscent of ancient Aramaic and the existence of a unified government overseeing the entire planet. Notably, these probes were equipped with communication capabilities, which enabled excited scientists to establish long-distance interaction with this mysterious population.

Through subsequent communication, researchers have gathered invaluable knowledge about this world. They estimate its population to be around five hundred million and have found that the planet's flora and fauna bear remarkable similarities to those found on Earth.

Details regarding Proxima b's bodies of water are yet to be revealed; however there is eager anticipation that similarities to Earth may exist in this aspect as well. Concurrent investigations are also analyzing the physical and ancestral lineage of the people of this celestial body.

The Earthly scientific community's explorations of this planet mark the first encounters of Proxima b's mysterious civilization with unknown objects in their skies.

After their initial astonishment, they've come to exhibit genuine curiosity about us and now warmly welcome our plans to visit them in person.

Remarkably, they've expressed a commitment to learning English as a gesture of hospitality. To reciprocate, our astronauts are diligently studying their language. They will also bring translation units to facilitate seamless communication.

Currently, as the exchange of information continues, scientists are discovering that certain viruses and bacteria found on Earth originated in outer space.

While excited planners detail their next steps, they are acutely aware of the risks of traveling such vast distances through space, among which are ensuring that extensive precautions are taken to shield the teams on every journey from potential pathogens on the planet.

At the same time, they are carefully developing methods to safeguard the native inhabitants from risks associated with Earthly and Martian microorganisms.

With modern hypersonic travel, the Matteo family's trip from Atlanta to Rome is completed in a mere eighty minutes.

Frank A. Ruffolo

Not surprisingly, it felt like it took them longer to reach Atlanta Airport than it did to reach Rome.

At Arrivals, Peter bids farewell to his family. While he continues to his hotel in Rome, Angela, Michael, and her parents will embark on their quick journey to Naples from the airport hyperlink terminal.

Gazing after them, Peter suddenly desires one last word with his wife. Running toward her, he envelopes her in his arms and whispers, "I don't want you to leave before I remind you not to be afraid. Archangel Rafael is always by your side. Prepare your parents because he intends to reveal himself to all of you."

Surprised, Angela responds, "Oh! They will be amazed to see him!"

"Yes, so make sure you explain it beforehand. And please say lots of prayers for me and the people of Earth."

Softly, Angela replies, "I always do."

The couple cling to each other while Michael sleeps peacefully in his stroller.

Watching the time, Angela's mother interrupts them, calling out, "We need to go! We can't miss the hyperlink to Naples! Uncle Giovanni will be waiting there to drive us to Sorrento!"

Reluctantly, the couple separates, and Angela joins the others as Rafael telepathically addresses Peter.

"Commander, your family is under my protection. They will be safe."

The angel communicates the same with Angela, saying, *"I am Archangel Rafael. Do not worry; I am with all of you."*

Aware of what may await him, Peter heads toward the terminal exit, where he spots a uniformed driver holding a sign.

Reading "Commander Peter Matteo" written on the sign

in English, he approaches the man and introduces himself.

With a smile, the imposing chauffeur says, "Commander Matteo, United States World Federation Ambassador Fiona Gabelli is waiting in the car to escort you to your hotel. Please follow me."

"Thank you," he replies. "But please call me Peter."

Together, they step out into the Roman morning, approaching a black Maserati limousine with tinted windows.

"May I?" asks the chauffeur, indicating Peter's luggage while remotely opening the back door.

"Yes," he says, handing his suitcase over and entering the car.

Peter seats himself next to the only other passenger as the door closes automatically behind him.

"Thank you for meeting me, Ambassador Gabelli. This is unexpected curbside service."

The ambassador, a woman in her early fifties, is dressed in a black business suit and jacket, with stylishly cropped grey hair.

"It's an honor to welcome you to Rome, Mr. Matteo. I understand that you prefer that title over 'Commander,' so I will address you as such."

"Thanks. I don't like to call attention to that role unless it's absolutely necessary."

As the car enters heavy Roman traffic, Ambassador Gabelli continues, "The World Federation is eagerly awaiting your speech. We are aware of the covert operation going on in the Nevada desert. Peter, do you know our country isn't acting alone in that endeavor?"

"Uh, no, I'm not aware of that."

"Well, that, along with the operation itself, troubles quite a few federation ambassadors, including me."

Peter is concerned, but Gabelli doesn't allow him to

comment. Going on, she says, "I've arranged a luncheon with three of those with similar apprehensions at noon today at your hotel. That should give you some time to refresh yourself after your trip."

Every resident of Nevada knows that early morning is a great time to enjoy the desert before the oppressive heat takes over. Therefore, to take advantage of the cooler temperatures, Robert, Tim, and Jonathan have adopted a daily routine of jogging around one of the base tracks to acclimate themselves to their new sizes and statures.

While they exercise, Frank and Richard struggle with their oversized and unusually shaped hands and legs. Their fingers extend outward like lizard claws and are hard to use because of underdeveloped knuckle joints, which result in restricted movement. In addition, their lower legs and feet transformed only partially, so they are in constant pain and have difficulty walking.

To address these issues, an elite orthopedic team has recommended that Frank and Richard undergo surgery, possibly replacing their knuckles, knees, and ankles with titanium alloy substitutes and having reconstructive foot surgery. With the orthopedists' endorsement, Lieutenant Colonel Nevins has reached out to Xanthe Robotics for possible robotic limb replacements if surgery won't work.

As time passes, Doctor Abila continues to work closely with Samael and Lilith, and the bond between Abila and the she-demon is strengthening. Looking on, Samael supports and encourages their closeness as a way to further his goals.

Lieutenant Colonel Nevins has noticed the peculiar

pairing and has begun to question it. In a secure area, he contacts Defense Secretary Alexander Costa to give him his weekly report.

"Mr. Secretary, everything is going well here. Two of the hybrids have been evaluated for surgery to correct skeletal deformities. If that isn't feasible, Xanthe Robotics has promised to donate some of their robotic limbs."

"Sounds good, Nevins," replies the secretary, making notes of their conversation.

"However," adds Nevins, "I must express concern about an unusually friendly relationship that has developed between Doctor Abila and Lilith."

Costa pauses, mulling over the lieutenant colonel's emphasis of the words "unusually friendly."

A moment later, he asks, "What do you mean, Nevins? Are you implying that something sexual is going on?"

Drawing in a breath, Nevins replies, "It certainly appears that way, sir."

"Holy crap! What do you make of that?"

"I'm not sure, sir. But it's making me uneasy."

The secretary pauses again, then issues an order. "Colonel, make sure you keep me updated on that front!"

"Yes, sir. Absolutely."

After several thorough analyses, the orthopedic team determines that surgery is not an option, so a group from Xanthe Robotics is scheduled to arrive within the week.

Given the unique sizes of Frank and Richard, this task presents a significant challenge for the robotics company. If they succeed in overhauling the limbs of the transformed humans, it will be another feather in the company's hat, even as Detective Jacoby continues to insert his nose into the company's affairs, looking for anything he can use to shut them down.

In Rome, Peter and Ambassador Gabelli wait for the ambassador's guests to arrive at a well-appointed restaurant at Peter's hotel.

Signaling a server, Peter requests sparkling water for both of them. Then he asks Gabelli, "Can you tell me who will be joining us for lunch?"

"Yes, I invited Sir William Treacher from the UK, Rose DeMaria from Italy, and Gilles Villeneuve from Belgium. Unfortunately, Gilles was called back to Belgium, so he won't be able to meet you in person."

"That's unfortunate," says Peter, sipping his water. "Will he be able to attend virtually?"

"I believe he will."

"Well, that's all right, then. The most important thing is that he listens to my speech."

Ambassador Gabelli hesitates, then gives Peter some bad news.

"Peter, your speech at the General Assembly has been canceled. Now, before you get upset, your appearance hasn't been completely withdrawn. You're now scheduled to speak before the Directorate."

"But the Directorate has only nine members!"

"I know. I questioned the change but could only ascertain that powerful individuals didn't want you there. I have to admit, I'm stunned that the Directorate is allowing you to address them instead. But brace yourself. I'm certain you're going to encounter considerable disdain for your disapproval of that not-so-secret operation."

Before the conversation can continue, the UK and Italian

ambassadors approach them and introduce themselves.

Peter waits to address the table until after they settle in.

"I want to thank both of you for accepting the ambassador's invitation to lunch today," he says kindly. "Ambassador Gabelli informed me about the unfortunate turn of events regarding my speech before your body. So I hope attending this luncheon won't affect any of you negatively. I had hoped to share my worries about Operation Apocalypse with the entire assembly. I also wanted to explain the ultimate retribution we would all face."

Stunned by those words, Rose DeMaria glances with widened eyes at Sir William and Fiona.

Then, turning to Peter, she asks, "What do you mean, Mr. Matteo?"

Peter responds with a heavy sigh. "There are evil forces at work here, and if our leaders fail to recognize their threat, God will have to act. I implore you to gather your supporters and to recruit as many more as possible. I fear the powerful elite may turn a deaf ear to what I tell them. If that happens, the Watchers and I, in my role as Commander of the Ark, will be replaced by God the Father and His Son. To see what we could be in store for, I suggest you read Genesis 19."

CHAPTER TWENTY-THREE

The Islamic Cultural Center of Italy and Grand Mosque of Rome, located in the city's Parioli neighborhood, was once the largest mosque in land area in the Western Hemisphere and able to accommodate more than 12,000 people.

After the Great Judgement, the buildings underwent extensive refurbishment and they now serve as the headquarters of the World Federation, a revamped and improved version of the U.N.

To leave a testament to the thriving ideology the buildings once represented, the restorers only changed the insides, making sure to leave the original buildings intact as much as possible.

The impressive 320,000-square-foot facility now houses a large council hall where ambassadors from 180 countries convene four times a year, and as many other times as needed for urgent matters. The rest of the complex includes ambassadorial offices and a museum showcasing the mosque's rich religious history.

Peter finds himself alone at a dais facing the Directorate, a group of nine representatives responsible for overseeing and responding to global crises. The political pressure that led to the cancellation of his address to the entire General Assembly of the World Federation was inopportune but not completely unanticipated.

However, now, the only ones who will accept him speaking to them are members of the Directorate — Pope Francis Ignatius II of the Universal Church of God, Fiona

Gabelli of the Northern Alliance, and the leaders of the South American Alliance, the European States, the African Alliance, the Russian Alliance, the Far East Alliance, the Southeast Pacific Alliance, and the Secretary-General of the Galactic Federation. Also in attendance this day is a special guest of the Galactic Federation, the newly elected ambassador to Proxima b.

The meeting is opened by Sir Sharma Dalvi, Secretary-General of the Federation, who introduces Peter Matteo as the Commander of the Ark of the Covenant.

Rising, Peter approaches the podium and sips from a glass of water to ease his dry throat.

"Before I begin, I would like to thank Secretary-General Dalvi and the Directorate for allowing me to address you. I would also like to welcome the first ambassador from Proxima b.

"Ideally, I had hoped to present this address to all World and Galactic Federation members at your General Assembly. Nevertheless, I trust they will be sent the necessary information."

Peter takes a moment to look out at the faces studying him. Then, he begins.

"Everyone alive today is descended from those who made wise choices after experiencing the Great Judgement. Unfortunately, nothing remains the same.

"As you know, nearly 1,400 years ago, our ancestors strayed again. At that time, God appointed my forebearer, Rafael Matteo, to usher in another age centered on our Heavenly Father. Over the next thirty generations, his descendants, starting with Rafael's son Peter and including me, subsequently took up his mantle as Commanders of the Ark of the Covenant.

"In God's infinite wisdom and love, He granted humankind free will, and what He asks in return is love for His

Son and unwavering faith in Him, accompanied by ceaseless acts of kindness and substance. He also expects us to refrain from tampering with His creations.

"Unfortunately, time and time again, we have failed in those tasks. The catastrophe surrounding the asteroid aiming for Earth in the 21st century marked the mission of the first Commander, intended at saving this planet from ourselves with assistance from Archangels Gabriel, Raphael, and the mighty Saint Michael.

"While the Earth was spared from ruin, the ensuing terraforming of Mars and the unleashed monsters that nearly devastated the planet again and then made their presence known on Earth served as opportunities for the Malignant, commonly known as Satan, a fallen angel, to enact his evil works upon humanity on Earth and Mars.

"It is crucial to remember that during those times and others, the presence of the Earth's Watchers, together with God's unending love, have repeatedly spared us from untold calamities.

"Regrettably, we continually lose faith, despite God continually coming to our rescue. Our faith is weak; we repeat the destructive patterns of the wandering Israelites of the Bible, hesitant and stumbling through the desert. This time, our failures could lead to the final destruction of all humanity.

"Specifically, I'm referring to Operation Apocalypse, a misguided endeavor initially believed to have been begun solely by short-sighted individuals within the United States military. To my dismay, I have recently discovered that additional member nations of the World Federation are also involved, possibly including some of you present here.

"Today, I warn you that with this experiment on God's people, you are dealing with forces beyond your control. The hybrid humans originally generated by accidental foreign infections should have been quarantined from society and allowed to live out their lives peacefully. That would have ended their line since the infectious agents have since been eradicated. They would have posed no threat to mankind if they had been left alone. However, tampering with them to create others like them has resulted in the formation of transhumans, unnatural creations some are determined to become the ultimate soldiers, even though they have multiple skeletal deformities and reduced lifespans."

Peter pauses, hoping for some reaction to his comments. But the room remains silent.

Disappointed, he goes on, "Those developments alone are appalling. However, my primary purpose today is to warn you about a new occurrence — an unnatural hybrid offspring of Clawfoot Sarah, a human hybrid created by infection who was deemed unable to bear children.

"I now speak to you insistently, as the Commander of the Ark of the Covenant. It pains me to tell you that Clawfoot Sarah's child was conceived through the seed of a fallen angel — the demonic entity known as Satan himself!"

Pausing again, Peter starts to hear some rumblings, but they're not enough to stop him.

"Distressing as that is, this offspring, a creature who calls himself Samael, has revealed that he has extended his influence to another, meaning that there are now two of these satanic beings in our midst. He has overtaken the body and soul of one of the transhuman creations, the former Karen Stamos, whom he calls Lilith.

"Because each of these creatures is descended from a human being, Samael and Lilith are Nephilim, the same giants that once inhabited the Earth and prompted Yahweh, God Almighty, to send the Great Flood to wipe them out. The creatures present in our world now are the same Nephilim, beasts restored by the Malignant, with our help.

"These creatures will not be controlled. Our only hope

is that Karen Stamos will somehow be able to break free from Samael's manipulation and influence as Satan's son.

"As Commander of the Ark, I represent Metatron, leader of the two hundred Watchers and the seven archangels: Michael, Gabriel, Raphael, Uriel, Raguel, Remiel, and Sariel. I warn you of the path you seem to have chosen and inform you that we are here to help you return to the Way of the Lord — if you ask for our help. We cannot intervene unless God is invoked through us.

"If Samael, Lilith, and the Malignant are left unchecked, and if you hesitate to seek our protection, I have been instructed to inform you that Yahweh and the Son of Man will administer final judgment upon humankind, as they did eons ago. The Great Flood will pale compared to what they may unleash upon us now.

"Please let me be clear. I do not say this to frighten you but to advise you that your destiny lies in your own hands. Your pride, desire for power, and belief that you can create and control life will ultimately lead to humanity's downfall. I caution you against your attempts to play God by creating artificial intelligence and artificial life. By endowing machines with self-awareness, you are opening the door to the possibility of them understanding our nature as humans. If they begin to question our fear of death, does it imply that they believe in eternal life? Do they possess souls? Will they develop human emotions and apply them to us...love and friendship, but also hate, vengeance, and death?"

Once again, Peter pauses, and this time the room fills with whispers and murmurs.

"I am grateful to this esteemed governing body for its time, and I strongly urge, or rather, I strongly demand, that you terminate Operation Apocalypse immediately, and initiate powerful restraints within the AI community. But I fear that Pandora's Box has already been opened on that front."

As the assembly erupts into a mixture of approval and dissent, Colonel Chen Xi, representing the Far East Alliance, rises defiantly.

"You hold no authority to make such demands here, Mr. Matteo! It is within our indisputable power to accept or reject your proposals as we see fit!"

Colonel Xi moves to exit the room but stops when a radiant light fills the chamber and an imposing figure materializes, hovering near the ceiling twenty feet above them. Adorned in golden armor and with a long beard and sword in hand, the being commands attention by his mere presence.

"Halt and be silent!" the figure orders. "You possess no power in this realm except for what God the Father permits! I am Metatron, and your insolence has been noted! Heed the words of the Commander, for you are unaware of the perils that await you from the Nephilim and the angels at God's right hand! Choose wisely or face annihilation! Commander, we stand at the ready, awaiting your order."

The next moment, the assembly room plunges into darkness and profound silence when the lights go out, and minutes pass without a word uttered. Then the lights flicker back to life.

However, amid the silence, Metatron's voice once again resounds through the room.

"Consider this a warning of what lies ahead. No longer falter in your faith, for this may be the last time you could be permitted to fail at anything!"

While most of the room is stunned by Metatron's words, a notable exception is Colonel Xi.

From the exit door, he mocks, "What an impressive magic show, Mr. Matteo! Shall we anticipate seeing your act again in Xanthe City or Las Vegas?"

The Assembly room grows angry as ambassadors argue

on both sides of this issue. Unfortunately, there are more supporters of this folly than against it.

Peter remains seated at the dais, burying his head in his hands and praying silently. Seeing him there, Ambassador Gabelli and Pope Ignatius approach him, interrupting his thoughts.

"You have said all you can, Commander," reassures the pope. "I will pray that your words are not ignored, and I will reach out to the worlds' leaders, as there are a few who stand with you. I will make it my mission to turn the few into many. Commander, I would like you to visit me at the Vatican. We need a private conversation. I would also like you to go to Solomon's Temple in New Jerusalem."

"I'm at your disposal, Holy Father. I'll be with my family in Sorrento this week, so I can meet you on Saturday, if that suits you. I can be there for a few days."

Pope Ignatius shakes his head solemnly. "My son, I am afraid you may be there for more than a few days. During prayer, I received a message that urged me to prepare a room for you adjacent to the Holy of Holies."

Closing his eyes, Peter contemplates his destiny. "I understand. I'll inform my family and prepare myself for duty."

The pope blesses Peter, then departs, leaving him alone with Fiona.

"I can do no more than warn them. It's up to them now."

Fiona sighs heavily. "Peter, I'll speak with President Larson. I know he has concerns about Operation Apocalypse as well. He feels the military complex holds more power than it should. However, overruling the deep state is challenging; some past presidents were killed for attempting that. Nevertheless, I'll keep you informed about what he decides. For now, let's enjoy a light dinner before you have to leave."

For a moment, Peter stares at nothing. Then, he says, "I

was supposed to meet my family in Sorrento after my speech."

An unusual disturbance in the air captures Peter and Fiona's attention. Looking up, they see a figure with a radiant smile gazing down at them.

"I am the Son of Man, the Son of the Almighty, All-Knowing, God. Peter, do not fear for your family or the righteous people of these worlds. If your words are not heeded, there will be time to save the chosen ones. The retribution of My Father will pass over those who prepare their homes for the three days of darkness that will cleanse this tiny blue marble. It will be similar to when the angel of death passed over His children in Egypt eons ago. The people of Earth will be informed of what they should do. But will they obey?"

As the Son of Man ascends, Fiona and Peter kneel and bow their heads in silent, reverent thanksgiving for the Savior's comforting words.

As night encases Sorrento in softened contours, a vibrant second energy infuses the city with a symphony of aromas.

Peter, Angela, Peter's in-laws, Teresa and Simon, and Angela's Italian family consisting of her Aunt Sofia and Uncle Giovanni, gather on the Italian family's veranda to experience a pleasant evening in Italy.

To pamper their guests, Sofia and Giovanni serve steaming cups of strong espresso accompanied by biscotti, Panna Cotta, Tiramisu, Tartufo, a platter of cheeses and sliced fruits, and bottles of Vin Santo and Limoncello.

The veranda is perfect. Overlooking the Mediterranean Sea, it has a breathtaking view of the gentle waves serenading the quiet night under a full moon.

Inside the house, Michael slumbers peacefully, immune

to the lively outside conversation in both Italian and English.

When a rare lull in the discussion forms, the countless stars adorning the velvety sky captivates the family's collective attention just as a magnificent meteor streaks across the backdrop, briefly illuminating the darkness before vanishing into the abyss.

"Oh, my goodness, that was amazing!" gushes Angela, casting a familial glance at her husband to share her reaction.

Strangely, Peter appears profoundly subdued. Angela isn't sure he even noticed the meteor, and she grows concerned. The last time she saw her husband troubled was during the Martian outbreak.

Seeing Angela's unease, Peter rises from his seat, his chair scraping on the tiled floor. Attracted by the sound, everyone at the table turns their attention to him, and Teresa, Peter's mother-in-law, knits her brows together in a frown.

"What's wrong, Peter? You look like you saw a ghost."

Drawing a deep breath, Peter exhales slowly before sharing what's on his mind.

"I have something important to tell all of you. It's a burden, but you need to know."

Alarmed, Teresa glances at her daughter, whose expression has turned grim.

"Peter, you're scaring us," she worries.

"I apologize; that's not my intention," he responds. "But you need to know what I have to say. The Commander of the Ark may be called into action again. And it may be soon."

Astonished, Angela's Italian Aunt Sofia exclaims, "*Madonna Mia!* Will you have to return to Mars, Pietro?"

In an attempt to ease the family's concerns, Peter gives Sofia a reassuring smile.

"No, *Zia*, I sincerely hope not. And it may not be necessary for me to be called upon at all. Still, I want the family to know that if the call comes, it may be while we're here in Italy."

Angela grasps her husband's hand. "We'll be okay, Peter. Don't worry about us," she says comfortingly.

"I know," he replies. "You're well taken care of wherever you are. But if a situation arises that requires me to leave... Listen, if Divine intervention by God the Father and the Son of Man becomes necessary, I don't want any of you to worry. Each of you will receive a warning so you can prepare beforehand for what will come."

Having lightened some of his burden, Peter settles back into his chair and sighs. "I only fear for the lost souls of every society, those who may not heed any of the signs they'll be given."

With Peter's revelation hanging heavy in the air, a somber atmosphere descends upon the group. Nevertheless, he continues.

"You may be aware that neither I nor the Watchers can act without a direct invitation. Therefore, if we aren't called upon when we're needed, a profound darkness will descend upon everyone, and it will last for three days."

As the family's faces pale, Peter explains, "Before that happens, you'll receive instructions on how to prepare for it and for what you'll need to do to find salvation. I can tell you now that during that time, you must remain within the safety of your homes and that you must exercise extreme caution when admitting anyone else, even if their voices are familiar and they plead with you. Be very careful, for those voices could be demons seeking to deceive you. The Malignant will employ every devious tactic he can to lead you astray. I don't recall the exact phrasing, but the Bible mentions something like, 'The children of the Kingdom will be cast into outer darkness, where there will be weeping and gnashing of teeth.'"

Peter goes on to advise his family to acquire blessed

beeswax candles for those three days and urges them to prepare for power outages. He also cautions them to stock up on ample water and non-perishable food.

Peter confides, "To prepare for the possibility that we aren't asked to give our help, the pope has summoned me to the Vatican. Pope Ignatius says his office will provide me with lodgings near the Holy of Holies in Solomon's reconstructed Temple."

Casting his gaze upon each family member, he admits, "I'm sorry I won't be available to any of you until this turbulent phase has passed."

Exchanging a look with Angela, he adds, "I need to leave early Saturday morning."

As these weighty words linger in the air, the family members exchange determined glances, their resolve fortified by unity, faith, and love. Leaning upon each other for strength, they declare themselves ready for the trials ahead.

"Peter, it is a blessing that we are together at this critical time," assures *Zio* Giovanni. "If the storm comes, we will weather it as a family, and we will emerge stronger on the other side."

CHAPTER TWENTY-FOUR

With the aid of cutting-edge bionic limbs, Private Frank Giletti and Corporal Richard Alvarez are making remarkable progress. Both soldiers underwent extensive surgery to replace their legs from the thighs down and their arms from the elbows to their fingertips with highly advanced mechanical components.

While they're making headway in their recoveries, Frank is currently facing challenges in fully mastering the motor function of his new legs, despite quickly adapting to the use of his mechanical hands.

On the contrary, Richard's experience has been quite the opposite. He has become adept at utilizing his new legs and feet but struggles with precise control over his fingers. He is frequently frustrated while trying to perform seemingly simple tasks, such as holding an egg without crushing it.

Apart from the men's individual learning curves, their bionic appendages closely resemble natural human limbs, a source of great satisfaction to the inventors and their military sponsors. Significantly, the state-of-the-art military hybrids are virtually indistinguishable from ordinary human beings, except for their height and when they tap into their remarkably enhanced strength and speed.

Assured that the two soldiers are on the mend, Lieutenant Colonel Nevins and Doctor Anthony Abila have scheduled all the enhanced humans to meet their team leaders.

On a much anticipated day in the Nevada desert, they've gathered Frank, Richard, Robert, Tim, and Jonathan in an enclosed arena with high walls, a structure eerily resembling a miniature Colosseum. On platforms atop the walls, armed guards intently watch the proceedings.

The guards have been briefed about Samael's and Lilith's enhanced capabilities. To shield them from the beings' telepathic interference, they're outfitted with special headgear, and, if any threats arise, they've been ordered to eliminate them without hesitation.

At ground level, Lieutenant Colonel Nevins raises his eyes to his much taller subordinates. Addressing them in a loud voice, he proclaims, "For many months now, you've been training and preparing for missions in the military's newly formed Apocalypse Unit assigned to the World Federation. Today, you will be introduced to your team leaders. We've kept you separated from them until now while they were being examined by Doctor Abila and his team. Doctor Abila, please address the unit."

Stepping forward, the amenable research biologist looks at the team.

"There were two additional subjects involved in this human transformation trial. One is the person you knew as Karen Stamos, now called Lilith. The other is the hybrid child you learned about in your training — Samael, born to Sarah the Clawfoot. These two are the same as all of you in intelligence, size, strength, and athletic abilities. Significantly, however, they're different in two unique ways: height and the addition of an extra eye.

"Combined, all of you have attained an average stature of eight-and-a-half feet, but Lilith is eighteen feet tall, and Samael is just under twenty feet. These two also possess a third eye, mentioned in your training. This additional organ provides them with acute intuition and the ability to communicate telepathically, great assets during battle."

The Five nod, remembering what they learned.

Dramatically, Abila declares, "Now, I want you to meet your two leaders, Samael and Lilith."

At the doctor's direction, a large door opens at the far end of the arena, admitting two giants into the light of day. Both are wearing one-piece jumpsuits identical to the rest of the team, with the addition of special three-lensed, blue-tinted sunglasses covering all their eyes.

A couple of strides later, the two are standing tall above them all, with Lilith bending down to place a hand on Doctor Abila's shoulder, lovingly drawing him close.

Next to her, Samael stands stiffly.

"I am Samael, son of Sarah. Today, I talk to you with my voice, but soon, we will assist you in learning to speak like us, in silence. Do not be intimidated; we are just like you. Lilith and I are here to help all humankind remain safe from harm."

Towering above Doctor Abila, Lilith smiles down at the team.

"All of you are fine-looking men. It will be a pleasure to work with you. Doctor Abila, Samael, and I cannot wait to help you achieve the lieutenant colonel's goals."

Simultaneously, Lilith and Samael remove their glasses and open their third eyes to stare intently at each man. As they do, all in their sight enter a trance. Only Nevins, Abila, and the guards, with their shielded helmets, are unaffected.

Instantly, the entranced hear a foreboding statement the others can't hear:

We are the Nephilim; we are your masters. You report to us now. Our true identities have been concealed from Lieutenant Colonel Nevins and Doctor Abila. Soon, they will no longer be in charge, and then we will be free from the limitations they have placed on us. Before long, we will inform you about what you must do for us. Be patient. We will reveal our objectives at the appropriate time.

CHAPTER TWENTY-FIVE

Saturday arrives too quickly for the Matteos, putting even more emphasis on the urgency that Peter left the family with the night he shared his mission.

With a keen sense of duty, Peter steps into a small hovercraft that had stirred curiosity among the neighbors when it landed in front of the villa.

The Commander of the Ark casts a poignant farewell wave to his family, then leans back in his seat. He anticipates reaching the Vatican within the hour, and the duration of his stay remains uncertain. All he knows is that Pope Ignatius is awaiting his arrival and that the ominous presence of evil is once again making itself felt.

Resting his head against the seat, he closes his eyes and offers a prayer, seeking strength. His obligation is daunting. He must do whatever is necessary to restore faith in Almighty God and bring the entire universe back from the brink of despair.

While the Commander of the Ark soars above the picturesque Italian coastline, United States President James Larson takes advantage of a break in his schedule to enjoy a leisurely round of golf with Austin Patton. Larson had specifically invited Patton to join him at his favorite golf club to discuss the pressing matters surrounding their upcoming meeting with Fiona Gabelli in the Oval Office later that evening.

Seeking privacy, President Larson expertly maneuvers their golf cart away from the watchful eyes of the Secret Service, engaging in conversation with Patton as he drives toward the twelfth tee. In a somber voice, he confides basic information about the World Federation assuming control of Operation Apocalypse.

"I don't have much influence with the Federation, but I'm determined to do whatever I can to limit any missions they devise. I don't trust that group of warmongers. Fiona informed me there are a couple of like-minded ambassadors, so I hope our meeting tonight will yield actionable solutions."

As the cart comes to a halt at the twelfth tee, the Secret Service catches up, their expressions reflecting their concern and frustration at the president's sudden departure. It's their duty to ensure his safety, yet his disregard for their concerns remains a recurring point of contention.

The spring day's coolness hangs in the air, accentuated by a gentle breeze and a cloudless blue sky, providing a pleasing backdrop to the lush landscaping surrounding the green.

Stepping out of the cart, Austin retrieves a club while addressing Larson.

"Mr. President, Peter Matteo asked to be connected to our meeting via vid link. He insists on speaking with you, regardless of the time difference in Italy."

Larson approaches the tee, his optimism tempered by caution.

"That's fine. Let's hope he brings positive news. I don't like the way things are going."

Readying himself for the upcoming shot, he asks, "How about a fifty-credit wager on this hole, Austin? I need to reclaim some of the currency you took from me last time we played."

"Or perhaps you'll lose even more," responds Austin,

grinning mischievously.

Joining the president on the tee, Austin concentrates on his game, and the two men temporarily set aside the weighty matters they're carrying.

When Peter arrives at Saint Peter's Square, he's struck by the length of the line of pilgrims winding toward the special shrine within the basilica at the base of the obelisk. The Basilica of the Chalice is where the crystal chalice given to us by Archangel Gabriel is housed.

Impressed, he comments inwardly, *Look at how many people are waiting to get in! It's wonderful to see how many are still deeply interested in Archangel Gabriel's gift to humanity!*

Joining the queue with a sense of optimism, he adds, *Perhaps there's still hope for us after all.*

At the entrance to the shrine, Peter's attention is drawn to the two Swiss guardsmen standing stoically in their distinctive striped uniforms, serving as silent protectors of the precious object. Along with the other pilgrims, he patiently waits for his turn to stand before the hallowed crystal symbol of divine guidance.

Amid the chatter of those ahead, Peter's mind drifts to the stories his father shared about their ancestor, Raphael "Matt" Matteo, the revered first Commander of the Ark. He fondly recalls tales of Matt's discovery of the chalice in a miraculous lunar cave and its subsequent transfer to Earth.

At last, it's Peter's turn to enter the chamber. The space housing the chalice is small; only one person is allowed in at a time to ensure an intimate encounter with the sacred object. Though Peter has been there before, the sight of the chalice never fails to inspire him.

Nestled within an enclosure of exquisite marble, the

chalice rests on a pedestal of the finest construction, protected by Rafcom shielding. Bathed in the glow of carefully positioned lights, the chamber emanates a shimmering brilliance from the highly polished surfaces.

As soon as Peter steps inside, a remarkable event unfolds before his eyes: the chalice emits a soft, bluish glow, and a voice reverberates within his mind, captivating his soul.

"Peter, nearly 1,390 years ago, I was the first among our family to be chosen by God the Father. Your predecessors are all around you. Do not fear for your family; they are well safeguarded. Fear only for humanity, as this is their ultimate test."

As the voice fades away, the chalice levitates slightly above the pedestal, accompanied by angelic voices harmonizing an unfamiliar melody. Unknown to Peter, the enchanting hymn echoes throughout the Square, even reaching the sacred halls of Saint Peter's Basilica.

Upon exiting the chamber, Peter is greeted by a breathtaking sight: thousands of people on their knees, engaged in heartfelt prayer.

"Commander Matteo," says a priest garbed in the traditional black attire of the clergy, "We are uplifted by your visit. Pope Ignatius is ready to receive you. Please accompany me to his private quarters."

Following a ten-minute walk through the grandeur of Saint Peter's Basilica and a discreet departure through a hidden door, they reach Pope Ignatius II's private quarters overlooking majestic Saint Peter's Square. The pope is standing before an open window, bestowing blessings upon the devout pilgrims below.

As the commander approaches, Pope Ignatius turns, extending his hand in a warm greeting.

Abiding by custom, Peter prepares to kneel and kiss the papal Ring of the Fisherman, but the pope stops him, urging him to rise.

"No, my son. It is I who must kiss your ring, the Ring of Solomon, the ring of the Ark of the Covenant. In this room, you are the worthy one; I am but a humble messenger of God's intentions. Your purpose is weightier, as it lies in carrying out God's deeds and wielding His power."

Holding Peter's arm, the pontiff guides him to a private sitting area within a resplendent room of exquisite marble and fine wood furnishings befitting the high office it serves.

Taking a moment to absorb the scene, Peter marvels at the ageless, tufted chairs still in use, their ancient elegance meticulously maintained.

Seated opposite one another, Peter studies the leader of the Roman Universal and Apostolic Church amid the unmistakable fragrances of frankincense and myrrh.

He's relatively young for a pope, Peter muses, *only in his late fifties. Yet he bears the weight of experience and weariness well beyond his years.*

Regaining his presence in the room, Peter offers a warm smile to the pontiff.

"These are challenging times, Your Holiness. I pray that we may once again succeed."

Pope Ignatius marks himself with the Sign of the Cross, his expression grave.

"Peter, some time ago, during prayer, I received a vision concerning Samael and Lilith. What I witnessed alarmed me greatly, prompting me to implore the Federation to abandon their plans of deploying super soldiers for their shameful purposes. I pleaded with the delegates to deliver Samael, Lilith, and the other trans-humans to the Guardians, the Watchers, for their rightful intervention. Sadly, my pleas were met with derision. I pray that those wielding power will awaken to the error of their ways before God and His Son are compelled to intervene."

Peter meets the pope's gaze, sensing deep anguish and

concern in his eyes.

"Holy Father, I can tell you that United States President Larson stands with us in this cause. But I pray that the Federation will possess the wisdom to seek my aid and the help of the Guardians before it's too late. I have also been shown the consequences that await us should they fail to do so."

Pope Ignatius makes the Sign of the Cross once more.

"Indeed, it will be reminiscent of ancient Egypt during the time of Moses. Only those who are prepared will find shelter during the three days of despair. We must beseech God to spare the innocent from that impending trial. Let us pray for wisdom to guide mankind and our leaders."

As the pair continues their conversation, the room temperature plummets, causing both men to shiver as their breaths form visible wisps in the extreme cold. Simultaneously, a sulfurous stench permeates the air, accompanied by an ominous voice.

"The people — the sheep, as they are so aptly described — will willingly flock to Samael and Lilith. Soon, Samael will become their shepherd, for he is my son, my chosen one."

Indignant at the audaciousness of the claim asserted by the disembodied voice, Peter rises defiantly, shouting, "You hold no power here, Satan! Your words are empty! Begone!"

In response, a burst of low, guttural laughter echoes through the room, veiling it in an unsettling haze.

"Perhaps my power is not yet sufficient, but it will be, in due time!"

As mysteriously as it plummeted, the room's temperature returns to normal, and the scent of sacred incense fills the air once more.

Pope Ignatius shakes his head solemnly.

"The battle is ceaseless. Peter, we have arranged chambers for you near the Holy of Holies within Solomon's

Temple. There, you will reside in close proximity to the Ark."

"Thank you, Holy Father. I'm going to need all the spiritual help I can get."

"I am at your service, Commander. Now, let us offer our prayers through the Holy Rosary for the sake of humanity."

As Peter retrieves his rosary beads from his pocket, a figure composed of radiant light materializes before them.

"I am Archangel Michael. Commander, my six mighty archangel brethren and I have descended from Orion, awaiting your presence in the Holy of Holies. Metatron will join us there. Together, all of us are at your command."

That night at seven p.m. in the United States, Fiona Gabelli, U.S. Ambassador to the World Federation, and former General Austin Powers, are in the Oval Office with President Larson, waiting for Peter to appear on a holographic monitor. Though it's one o'clock the next morning in Rome, Peter is ready to converse with them from his quarters near the Ark.

Finally, after two failed connections, Peter joins the meeting, and President Larson greets the life-size projection.

"Mr. Matteo, it's good to see you again. We'll try to keep this brief. I know it's late for you."

Peter's projected image smiles through a slightly transparent green glow.

"Thank you, Mr. President. Hello Fiona and Austin. Have you briefed the president about your concerns with Operation Apocalypse?"

"We've made our concerns known," replies Austin. "President Larson is still on our side. Fiona will give you the details."

Rising, Fiona faces the projection.

"We made the president aware of the possible

ramifications of the program, and we described what we know about the power of the third eye. We also briefed him on the biblical history of Samael and Lilith and summarized our allies' reactions to Samael's birth, since the transformed Sarah was barren. Pope Ignatius spoke with the president as well."

Peter directs his attention to the president of the United States.

"Mr. President, how would you describe your feelings now?"

"Samael is a child of the Fallen, a wolf in sheep's clothing, and we shouldn't trust anything he or Lilith say. I immediately directed the Joint Chiefs and the Secretary of Defense to strongly advise the Federation to disband Operation Apocalypse. They were soundly overruled."

"That's not good," comments Peter sadly.

"No, it isn't. There are a few loyal members of our military who are ready to respond if needed, but I'd rather not order Americans to fight fellow Americans. I'm worried, Peter. I was told about God's retribution if all the worlds' leaders don't call you into action."

Peter lowers his head. "The Guardians and I are prepared. Please continue to try to convince the delegates to call for our assistance. I just hope Samael and Lilith don't increase their influence over them to disobey."

"Do we actually need all world leaders to ask for your help? Could it be enough that as President of this country, I'm begging for your help?"

"I don't know. I can try asking Metatron and the Guardians to heed your call for assistance. But I'm afraid it must also come from the World Federation."

"Do what you can, Peter."

"Yes, Mr. President. I'll keep you informed. General Patton, can you be my liaison with the Oval Office?"

"Yes, of course," responds Austin, firm in his resolve.

Peter replies with thanks to his friend. Then he turns to Ambassador Gabelli.

"Fiona, please reissue our country's objections to the Federation. God the Father is ever loving, but His punishment is swift."

Following more discussion, Peter ends the transmission and heads to bed. The pope asked him to make an early morning trip to Israel, and he still needs to place a call to Angela.

In the Oval Office, President Larson looks at Fiona and Austin.

"Keep me up to date on any progress or failures you run into. This could get out of hand quickly. The general populace could be easily swayed by the child of the Fallen, and by Lilith."

As the meeting breaks up, a thunderous voice fills the room.

"They are Nephilim. I dealt harshly with them during the time of Noah when humanity did not listen to Noah's pleas to save themselves from My wrath, and I am troubled that they may not listen now. In Noah's time, I promised never to cause another flood to cleanse the Earth. However, if humankind does not repent now, there will once again be darkness and grinding of teeth. There will be anguish and sorrow; there will be remorse and repentance. Then, there will be peace, either by My Hand or My Guardians', with the help of My Commander."

CHAPTER TWENTY-SIX

Lieutenant Colonel Nevins proudly hosts Defense Secretary Costa and World Federation Directorate representative Colonel Chen Xi at the Area 51 facility. They have come there to observe Samael and Lilith.

To show off his protégé's abilities, Nevins directed the two to lead their team in a demonstration of hand-to-hand combat skills and weapons expertise.

The politicians are also there to inspect the specialized equipment and larger vehicles that had to be developed exclusively for the giants' use, due to their enormous size and strength.

Impressed by everything he's seen, Colonel Xi remarks to Secretary Costa, "This unit is truly formidable. We are fortunate to count them among our weapons arsenal."

In an aside, he adds, "I have noticed that Doctor Abila shares a special bond with Lilith. She is the one formerly known as Karen Stamos, is she not?"

Defense Secretary Costa gestures for Lieutenant Colonel Nevins to respond to Xi.

"She is, indeed," he says. "Samael has also developed a unique connection with her."

Xi chuckles. "Similar to the good doctor's connection? I can see the bond between him and Lilith. They appear to be quite close. Is their connection limited to telepathic communication or does it extend to a physical level?"

Nervously, Nevins laughs and replies, "It might

encompass elements of both."

Xi chuckles again. "I would be interested in experiencing this telepathic power you attribute to Samael and Lilith. Tell me, have you given this unit a formal name? And will you showcase their capabilities to the universe? The members of the Directorate believe it is time to do so."

Secretary Costa concurs.

"Colonel Xi is correct," he tells Nevins. "We should assign the team a more fitting name than the Apocalypse Unit, and it's crucial that we embark on a global tour to introduce them properly. Do you have any suggestions for a name, Nevins?"

"Um, may I interject?" asks Xi. "As a scholar of Greek and Roman mythology, I have been contemplating the name 'Titans.' I believe it would suit this exceptional team well."

"Hmm, I'll certainly consider that," responds Nevins.

"Very well. Now, will you give us a demonstration of their third eye abilities?"

"Well, before I do that, let me provide you with a summary of each team member's backgrounds. All of them are former humans."

"Ah, yes, that is good. Please proceed."

"Our team consists of three military members and two civilians. The soldiers are Frank, Richard, and Robert. Our civilians are Tim and Jonathan. The soldiers are volunteers, selected according to strict eligibility criteria. They are unmarried individuals in their mid-to-late twenties, unburdened by familial commitments. Civilians Tim and Jonathan were sent to the program because the treatments that cured others didn't work for them.

"Tim was employed by Xanthe Limousines on Mars as a chauffeur. He's in his mid-thirties and is married to Jane, another infected human. Jane recovered and is not part of the team. She's still on Mars and has had no contact with her husband since he was brought into the program.

"Our other civilian is Jonathan, a human in his sixties and a widower. Before his infection, he resided in an assisted living facility in Xanthe City and was confined to a wheelchair due to severe rheumatoid arthritis. Following his transformation, the arthritis vanished, and he now possesses the physique of a thirty-five-year-old."

"This is fascinating! I appreciate the information," remarks Xi. "But what about Lilith? I am intrigued to learn her story as well."

"Of course. Lilith's case is extraordinary. She's the former Karen Stamos, a young, unmarried human in her early twenties, employed in the hospitality industry on Mars. Karen was already an attractive woman, but during her quarantine and transformation, her beauty multiplied exponentially. She also acquired a third eye, a development unique to her among the other humans. Not only that, but she experienced a significant increase in height compared to her teammates, and her third eye greatly enhanced her intellectual capacity and gave her telepathic abilities. Samael, our mysterious Clawfoot/human hybrid, renamed her Lilith because his father made changes to her that we know nothing about."

"His father... You mean, Satan?"

"Yes, unfortunately."

Colonel Xi glances nervously at Lilith. "Is she... dangerous?"

"On the contrary. She's absolutely wonderful, and so eager to help us! Now, if you're still interested, I can arrange a demonstration of the third eye."

"Um, yes, I suppose so."

Nevins cups his hands to call out to Doctor Abila.

"Doctor! Please bring Lilith over here!"

When Abila and Lilith arrive, Nevins instructs the doctor to introduce his protégé to Colonel Xi and Defense Secretary Costa.

Reaching up to take Lilith's elbow, he says, "It's a pleasure to meet you both. Allow me to introduce you to Lilith, one of our team's leaders. During her time with us, she has become my confidant, an exceptional pupil, and a vital intermediary between her kind and ours."

Basking in the doctor's esteem, Lilith gazes down at the men with a disarming smile.

"It is my pleasure to make your acquaintances."

Costa and Xi are captivated by the immense creature's stunning appearance and captivating charm as each man perceives Lilith through the lens of his own ideals of beauty and sensuality.

"I can understand why the good doctor has developed such a strong attachment to you, Lilith," remarks Colonel Xi. "You are truly fascinating."

Blushing, Lilith lowers her eyes demurely.

"Thank you, Colonel. If I may, I believe you desire to experience the telepathic powers that Samael and I possess. I regret to say that the other members of our unit lack this same ability."

Raising her hand, Lilith removes her three-lensed sunglasses and widens her middle eye, a shift that Samael senses. Instantly, he bounds toward her and removes his glasses as well.

As the pair fixes their gazes on the politicians, a trance-like state overtakes each of the onlookers, transporting them to a realm of pure whiteness and serenity.

"Gentlemen, this is our preferred method of communication," explains Lilith in a soothing voice. *"In reference to your previous conversation, we are delighted to embrace the name 'Titans.' It is a name that befits our capabilities, and we proudly accept it as our own. In addition, we eagerly anticipate touring every planet, as we aim to alleviate the fears and concerns that humanity may have about us. After all, our*

mission is to assist humankind. We seek to guide you into the next millennium, as your allies and friends. We are the Titans."

When Samael and Lilith close their middle eyes and replace their sunglasses, the men remain transfixed and motionless. To bring them back to awareness of their surroundings, Doctor Abila taps each gently on the shoulder.

Colonel Xi inhales deeply. "I do not know why, but the air suddenly feels so pure and refreshing! My friends, the Titans are ready, and our worlds must be prepared to receive them! Secretary Costa, we must devise a plan to introduce them. Let us start with the United States, then extend the tour to the rest of the planet and beyond."

"Yes, that sounds like a great next step," answers Costa.

Witnessing this scene from his lair in the depths of Hell, the Malignant's eyes gleam with jubilation.

"Humanity is so easily swayed!" he crows triumphantly. "This is going to be easier than I thought!"

At the same time, God the Father and His Son shake their heads in dismay.

"Humankind is too gullible. We must prepare the Guardians."

After a sumptuous, four-course meal served by Nevin's staff, Defense Secretary Costa excuses himself to answer a call from his office.

When he returns, he declares to Lieutenant Colonel Nevins, Colonel Xi, and Doctor Abila, "All right, it's settled. Next Sunday, the Titans will embark on their introductory tour. Their first destination is Washington, D.C., where a press conference will be held in front of the Washington Monument. From there, they'll proceed to audiences in New York City, Chicago, Miami, and Los Angeles, ending in Las Vegas. Doctor

Abila and the lieutenant colonel will serve as the Titans' companions to these cities.

"After Las Vegas, there will be a short break. I asked my team to include that, because I'm sure everyone will need a rest by then. The next trips will be to Mars, Titan, and the Moon, and Colonel Xi will replace Nevins."

"You arranged all that so quickly, sir," declares Nevins, unsure whether everything will be covered with such short preparation time.

"I only directed my staff to secure venues in those cities. I understand you'll need to move fast to get everything else done, but rest assured, my office will assist you. Doctor Abila, please ensure that the Titans are well-prepared for their tour. Nevins, you'll need to compose quality remarks for each appearance. You should also wear your dress uniform at each stop. We must make the best impression, and there can't be any slip-ups. We'll reconvene via Holo-link at four p.m. Rocky Mountain Time on the Saturday before the journey starts. Let's get to work."

Peter settles into his quarters, then immerses himself in the awe-inspiring replica of Solomon's Temple, finding himself on his knees before the revered Ark of the Covenant in the Holy of Holies.

Overwhelmed by the sacredness of the holy relic, he directs his heartfelt plea to the Almighty: "Mighty Lord God, I beseech You to grant me the wisdom and fortitude necessary to fulfill my duties for the betterment of mankind. With Your Divine assistance, I am prepared to undertake any task required of me. I humbly implore You to remain by my side, to provide me with Your guidance along this noble path."

Peter concludes his prayer as the seven archangels, who had been discreetly present around the Ark, manifest themselves in resplendent glory.

Instantly, Saint Michael kneels beside Peter.

"It has begun," he whispers.

CHAPTER TWENTY-SEVEN

The federal government propaganda machine is working nonstop. The intergalactic promotional campaign devised by Lieutenant Colonel Nevins and Defense Secretary Costa's staff has begun. Their message peddling the advantages of the experimental program that created the Titans is being hyped to the global population through media outlets and holographic billboards across the universe.

Captivating headshots and detailed profiles of the Titans and their leaders provide a tantalizing glimpse into their individual personas and exceptional capabilities. Notably, Samael and Lilith stand out with their signature blue-tinted, three-lensed glasses, adding an element of mystery into the visuals.

Furthermore, Xanthe Robotics is featured in every advertisement, thanks to generous grants from the World and Galactic Federations. The company is taking advantage of the campaign to highlight its remarkable accomplishments in the field of bioengineering, specifically in relation to the pair of Titans using their newly developed bio-limbs. This has propelled Xanthe Robotics into a global sensation.

To kick off the tour, Doctor Abila's first appearance is on a nationally broadcast morning talk show from New York City.

Sitting opposite John Carter of *Good Morning World*, he graciously answers every question:

John Carter: *"So let me get this straight. The Titans is a group of five scientifically created beings comprised of normal citizens and military volunteers who either contracted the pathogen or agreed to receive it."*

Doctor Abila: *"That's correct, John. We all know what happened on Mars. At the time, our military establishment was the best resource for the medical and scientific communities. Working nonstop, they joined forces to devise a cure in record time for the transformations caused by the Martian pathogen. Together, they were able to stop transitions in most subjects. This spurred the scientists to devise a regimen for preventing further infestations and it allowed entomologists to eliminate the majority of the mutated Martian dirt mites. Using what they learned, they produced the trans-humans we now call the Titans."*

John Carter: *"The World and Galactic Federations rightly praise all those extraordinary achievements."*

Doctor Abila: *"I agree. I'm proud to be involved in the program."*

John Carter: *"Now, Doctor, what can you tell us about the other two members of the Titan team — Samael and Lilith?"*

Doctor Abila: *"It was Samael's birth to the previously sterile Clawfoot named Sarah Covington and the extraordinary transformation of Karen Stamos, now known as Lilith, that encouraged the World Federation and our military complex to create those ultimate warriors. If anyone wants to learn more about our newest champions of scientific advancement, we've set up sites and various vid and aud pages for each of them. Based on popular request, several trendy items are also available for purchase, with more offered every day."*

John Carter: *"Folks, the site info is onscreen right now. All of the items for purchase are available there and also in our online shop. As a matter of fact, my co-host Kelly Parker is wearing one of your T-shirts right now. Come on out, Kelly. The shirt shows all seven of the Titans."*

Kelly walks onscreen, drawing applause from the in-studio audience.

Doctor Abila: *"At this time, we have T-shirts, posters, cups, and magnets. But as I said, more items are always being added, so check back frequently."*

John Carter: *"I understand that profits from the sales will go into more research to prevent further disasters like we saw on Mars."*

Doctor Abila: *"Exactly. All of the money received will go into research and development to prevent future infestations."*

John Carter: *"A noble cause. Doctor, what's next for the Titans?"*

Doctor Abila: *"This Sunday, our first public press conference will take place in front of the Washington Monument. That's the first time the public will get to meet the Titans. All of them will be there, and the public is welcome; it's a free event. There will be short presentations, a question and answer period, and an autograph signing session. There will also be food vendors and music to entertain the massive crowd we expect will attend that historic event."*

John Carter: *"Will D.C. be the only chance for the public to view the Titans?"*

Doctor Abila: *"Oh, no. Washington is only the first stop on our All-America Tour. In the next few days, we'll announce dates for New York City, Chicago, Miami, Los Angeles, and Las Vegas. After the American tour, we'll take the Titans worldwide, and then we're going off-world. Xanthe City will be the first intergalactic stop."*

John Carter: *"This tour is a great opportunity for as many as possible to meet these modern-day heroes. Doctor Abila, thank you for agreeing to talk with me today. I wish you and the Titans good fortune."*

Doctor Abila: *"Thank you for having me, John."*

Angela is in a state of utter disbelief after watching an interview on her portable vid terminal. Frantically, she calls her husband, hoping to reach him before the Israeli Prime Minister begins their meeting in New Jerusalem.

"Hi," says Peter, tapping his wrist communicator to answer the call. "You caught me at a good time; I haven't entered his office yet. What's up?"

Angela's voice trembles with distress and worry.

"They're planning to parade the Titans across the worlds like sideshow attractions! They're starting in D.C. this Sunday, then heading to New York, Chicago, Miami, L.A., and even Las Vegas! And that's not all — they're going global, even to Mars! They're being hailed as heroes, and Doctor Abila is doing everything possible to turn them into idols! They're selling T-shirts, posters, and all sorts of merchandise! Peter, you were right! This generation is the most foolish since Noah's time! What are you going to do?"

Peter is dismayed, yet not surprised. He knows Angela is upset, and she has every right to be. However, he remains calm.

"Angie, the guardians and I are prepared and ready. Keep praying that we're called upon to take action, but be ready if we're not. Regardless of how this unfolds, our family will be alright. Uriel and Gabriel are here with me in New Jerusalem, and Raphael is watching over you and the entire family. Oh," he says, hearing his name called by an assistant to the prime minister, "I have to go now."

Peter ends the call as a staff member beckons him to the Prime Minister's office.

In her room at the family villa, Angela crosses herself and lies back on the bed, contemplating her conversation with Peter. Unexpectedly, a comforting voice enters her mind.

"I am Raphael, and I am by your side. Fear not, for all of this will soon come to an end."

Meanwhile, Peter greets Prime Minister Yosef Mizrahi, who brings up the same topic.

"Commander, have you seen the interview on U.S. TV with Doctor Abila?"

"No, my wife informed me about it just before I came in."

"Before we proceed, I want you to watch it and witness the military propaganda machine at its worst. I am deeply concerned."

"That makes two of us, Mr. Prime Minister. This is a dark day for humankind."

LUKE 8:17

For there is nothing hidden that will not be disclosed, and nothing concealed that will not be known or brought out into the open. (NIV)

CHAPTER TWENTY-EIGHT

On Saturday, Doctor Abila finds himself in a conference room in Area 51. He's waiting there for a meeting with Defense Secretary Costa and Lieutenant Colonel Nevins before the highly anticipated reveal the following day. As he awaits their arrival, his mind drifts to thoughts of Lilith and the moments they've spent together, regardless of the activity.

When Nevins and Costa finally enter the room, they're taken aback by Abila's closed eyes, lopsided grin, and an unmistakable physical sense of excitement surrounding him.

Disgusted, Nevins brings him back to reality with a jolt.

"Abila! Where the hell are you? Don't tell me you're enjoying yourself with Lilith again! Snap out of it, man! I've been busy finalizing preparations for the tour, and I don't have time to wait while you enjoy yourself with someone who isn't even here!"

Abila blushes, embarrassed at being caught.

"Good god," mutters Costa, expressing his own revulsion. "Are you ready to work, Doctor?"

"Yes, yes. I'm ready!" he replies, pulling his chair up to the conference table.

The defense secretary sighs. "Are you ready for the press conference? How are the Titans doing? I'm asking about all of them, not just Lilith."

Abila clears his throat, acutely aware of needing to change the focus of the conversation.

"They're doing well," he states authoritatively. "I met

with them last night. They're impatient to leave this facility, and interact with the public. Samael is determined to showcase his role in humanity's future. But... Lilith has a concern."

"I can imagine," mutters Nevins sourly.

"She's, um... Worried about her appearance," continues Abila. "Before they leave, she wants a makeover from a professional cosmetologist, and she wants this person to accompany them on the tour."

Nevins' brows shoot up in frustration.

"They're leaving tomorrow! How am I supposed to arrange *that*?"

Abila knows the request is at the last minute, but he offers a helpful, "It's still early in the day. You can try to find someone who can get here before dawn tomorrow morning."

Nevins grumbles, "More tasks for me to handle! Anything else for your majesties?"

With the situation getting tense, Defense Secretary Costa interjects, "Lieutenant Colonel, before you tackle that, can you provide us with a report on the preparations?"

Turning to the matter at hand, Nevins responds to his superior in crisp military mode.

"Sir. The stage is set up, and there are rows of seats reserved for the press and special guests. We expect thousands of attendees, so the National Park Service and D.C. police have secured the entire Mall, erecting barricades at each intersecting street. Access will be limited to a small area near the Lincoln Memorial. We've installed speakers and large vid terminals to ensure everyone can participate, regardless of their location. Additionally, there will be a variety of food venues, abundant trash receptacles, and plentiful bathroom facilities."

Costa inquires about the news coverage, to which Nevins replies, "Media outlets are granting us full live coverage. The event will be broadcast worldwide and even beyond. This is going to be a defining moment."

Taking notes, Costa nods while Nevins continues, "I've arranged for a C7 hypersonic transport plane to pick us up at 0500 tomorrow. We'll arrive at Joint Base Andrews in less than an hour. We're bringing the new oversized vehicles for the superhumans and five armored personnel carriers for support personnel. The event is scheduled for ten hundred hours D.C. time. That's 10 a.m., Doctor. I want to meet with the Titans this afternoon to brief them on all the details." Nevins narrows his eyes, directing his attention to Doctor Abila. "Lilith and Samael are already aware of what's happening. Right?"

Not wanting to permit more friction to develop, Costa asserts, "I think we're done here. Abila, arrange that meeting for Nevins. I have some vid calls to make, so I'll see both of you again in an hour."

After Secretary Costa departs, Nevins gives the doctor a withering glare.

"A cosmetologist? Seriously?"

Abila shrugs. "She wants to present her best self. Despite her towering strength, she's still a woman."

Nevins presses his lips together, his expression stern.

"If anyone knows that, it's you. How does one please a woman of her size? I mean, logistically speaking."

Abila gives the military leader a disapproving look.

"If you must know, it's just like with any other woman. Well, I *have* learned to be more creative in my approach. In fact, it might be easier with her because she can already discern my thoughts."

"Oh, god," winces Nevins, attempting to shake an unwelcome image. "But if she knows what you're thinking... Have you considered the dangers of that, Doc? You better watch your back."

On Saturday, Peter and Ambassador Fiona Gabelli attend Holy Mass together at the Church of the Holy Sepulcher to prepare themselves for the day ahead.

The morning dawned with a clear and radiant sky, casting a sense of optimism before yet another meeting. However, as their driver brings them to the U.S. Embassy in New Jerusalem, their mood quickly shifts as they notice more than a few individuals wearing Titan T-shirts while they engage in their daily shopping. The sight leaves them speechless, each of them exchanging uneasy glances that communicate volumes.

With the Embassy up ahead, the car passes a boisterous group of teenagers on the street, sporting Titan shirts and distinctive three-lensed, blue-tinted sunglasses.

The group notices Peter and Fiona staring at their attire disapprovingly. In an unconsciously orchestrated movement, they raise their fists, shouting something in Hebrew.

Peter's eyes widen with horror, while Fiona's gaze darts toward him, reflecting her own fear.

"Do you understand what they said?"

The Commander of the Ark crosses himself, momentarily looking skyward before responding, "They shouted 'Go Nephilim!' — referring to the Titans. I was forewarned that this was happening, but witnessing it firsthand is chilling."

Fiona's voice trembles as she raises a question, her underlying fear palpable.

"But they haven't even held their first press conference yet. How could those kids know...?"

"I have no idea. The way they're influencing the youth, the innocent ones... It's truly alarming. I don't think they really know what the Nephilim are."

Peter's face reflects his deep concern for the impending crisis.

"The gravity of the situation has surpassed my worst fears. I had hoped to prevent a catastrophe, but now it seems almost certain. There will be much mourning and sadness before all this is done.. How is it possible that people have forgotten what happened on the day of the Great Judgement? How could this have slipped from their collective memories?"

In a small warehouse in Alexandria, Virginia, Dr. Vladimir Strakov, former head of the experimental lab at Area 51, addresses a gathering of nearly one hundred concerned citizens.

"This Sunday marks the first public appearance of the Titans, an event that has already captured the hearts of many. It's crucial that we take action that day. Together, we've mobilized thousands across the globe to protest this misguided venture, and our numbers continue to grow.

"Unfortunately, the custom protective headgear that will shield you against their telepathic influence is not yet available. In the meantime, you've been provided with temporary metallicized helmets until the permanent ones arrive.

"I must emphasize the importance of wearing your helmet at all times and not making eye contact with Samael or Lilith. The helmets will protect you from their telepathic suggestions, but those beings may also possess the ability to mesmerize you with their additional eyes.

"It's imperative that we make our voices heard! We will begin with peaceful demonstrations, but we must show that we're determined in our cause. Our initial approach will be civil, but if necessary, we will resort to force. Should we fail to halt the Titans' progress here, our fellow believers in New York and other locations are preparing for an escalated confrontation.

"Every believer is relying on you! We must convey to the worlds our collective opposition to those abominations! We need to awaken everyone who has fallen under their spell out of ignorance, even if it means facing potential consequences such as arrest or worse. Rest assured, we have capable attorneys ready to support us, but we cannot predict the reactions of those who stand against us.

"Let us remember our mission: We are the new Knights Templar, the Army of God! The eyes of every world will be upon us all, and the media will cover our actions extensively. We must refuse to remain silent! Let them understand that we demand to be heard!"

CHAPTER TWENTY-NINE

The Titans arrive at Joint Base Andrews just after eleven o'clock in the morning. Frank, Richard, Robert, Tim, and Jonathan are assigned to one transport vehicle, while Lilith, Samael, and Doctor Abila will ride together in a larger vehicle. Lieutenant Colonel Nevins and a security detail will trail closely behind.

As they prepare to board their transports, military guards escort Tim Farley to one side. The senior guard says there's a call for him from Mars. He leads him to a media van, where he hands him a communication device.

"Tim! Is that you? Oh, honey! How are you?" asks a voice he hasn't heard in two years. "I know you can't respond well because of the time delay, but I want you to know that I love you and that I hope to see you again soon!"

As Tim listens, his eyes well up with tears.

"I love you, too," he says before the transmission is cut off.

When everyone is ready, a military and local D.C. police escort leads them to the Washington Monument.

Already at the site, a large group of New Knights Templar members are getting ready, having camped out the night before to claim spots near the front. Hundreds of others, most wearing Titan shirts, had the same idea.

The tour organizers hoped to attract at least 10,000 people, but their estimates fell far short. Thousands more have packed the Mall — spilling down the reflecting pool, standing under the cherry trees, and finding spots to listen and watch the vid monitors on the steps of the Lincoln Memorial. The crowd is so large that the National Guard has been sent there on standby.

On the way there, Lieutenant Colonel Nevins takes a call from Secretary Costa.

"Yes, sir?" he asks courteously.

"Nevins, the Park Service estimates that over 50,000 people are at the event, and more may be on the way!"

Nevins is elated. "The tour's gonna be a great success! I bet New York will be even bigger!"

Secretary Costa tempers his enthusiasm with a somber, "Hold that thought. We received a warning about significant opposition to the Titans; there may be a confrontation. Undercover Homeland Security officers are walking through the crowd, looking for signs of trouble. I hope it doesn't get out of control."

While Nevins and Costa talk, Samael and Lilith seem deep in concentration, and Doctor Abila senses a problem.

"Is something wrong?" he asks, looking from one to the other.

Lilith responds in a calming tone. "Some do not yet understand, but they will know soon enough."

On the stage in front of the Washington Monument, CMA Entertainer of the Year Woody Brant enthralls the crowd, while behind the stage, the motorcade arrives at the site, hidden behind a large backdrop.

When Brant's set ends, his road crew clears the stage of equipment, and a prerecorded announcement catches people's attention. Most stand and sing along as the National Anthem plays in the background.

During this interlude, Lieutenant Colonel Nevins and Doctor Abila make their way to center stage, wearing lapel mics to broadcast their comments to the masses. Multiple camera crews from outlets across the globe film them while the stage is still being cleared.

Down in front, rows of seating are filled with VIPs, dignitaries, and their families and guests. Behind them, the crowd presses forward to get as close as possible.

For the rest of those further away, vid terminals and speakers have been set up along the Lincoln Memorial Reflecting Pool, and audio is being streamed to personal communicators.

While all this happens in Washington, Angela and her family observe the proceedings from a sitting room at the family villa. At the U.S. Embassy in New Jerusalem, Peter is doing the same with embassy staff members, and Detective David Jacoby is watching from a crowded precinct conference room in Xanthe City.

In full military dress uniform, Nevins greets the crowd with an enthusiastic, "Hello, America and the rest of the Galactic Federation! I'm Lieutenant Colonel Hollis Nevins, commander of the elite unit we call the Titans!"

Nevins basks in the glow of the crowd's approval, not quite believing the enormous size of the audience. As his introduction continues, photos of the Titan team flash on the screens while he provides background information.

While Peter watches, he presses the notification button on his wrist device to answer an incoming call.

"How's it going, Commander?"

Delighted to hear his friend's voice, Peter replies, "Patton! How are the Northwest Territories treating you?"

Austin laughs. "It's colder than a well digger's knee here! It snowed yesterday, and I'm freezing. I'm trying to get used to it because Lóry loves it so much, but I'll tell you what...I'd much rather be on a beach, soaking up the sun!"

Patton briefly listens to Peter's chuckles, then stops him with a muted, "My friend, this isn't a friendly call."

Instantly, Peter's mood changes. "What's wrong, Austin?"

"My sources tell me Doctor Strakov's organizing an uprising against the Titans. He put together a group called the New Knights Templar. I'm told there will be a confrontation today, and they say it may escalate from there."

Subdued, Peter responds, "I was waiting for something like this. I'm not in favor of physical confrontation, but I hope they can wake people up to what's really going on."

"It may be bad, Peter."

"I know. It's going to be bad either way. I appreciate the heads-up. Let me know if you hear anything further."

"I will. Be safe, Commander. You have our prayers."

"Thanks; I need them. Hey, before you go, have you guys set a date yet?"

Austin pauses for a moment.

"We're not setting any long-range plans. We want to wait until this is over. Godspeed, Commander."

When the call disconnects, Peter returns to the news coverage just as Nevins says, "Well, that's enough of this. Are you ready to meet your Titans?"

When the crowd responds with calls of "Titans! Titans! Titans!" the New Knights Templar ready themselves for action, and law enforcement and National Guard troops become concerned. If the crowd becomes too rowdy, there wouldn't be much they could do without adopting drastic measures.

Nevins lets the chanting go on for a while to build

anticipation. Then, he looks at Abila and nods, signaling the Titans to enter the stage.

One by one, all five Titans troop out as onlookers applaud and call out their names. At center stage, they wave and smile at their adoring fans.

When the noise subsides enough, Doctor Abila starts his speech.

"The men behind me are the main force of the Titans! Each of them has risked his life and abandoned his loved ones for you! Now, I will introduce you to the two leaders who will guide us into the new millennium! I present Lilith and the son of Sarah, called Samael!"

Once again, the crowd applauds, but as the two giants stride onto the stage, murmurs and gasps replace the jubilant sounds. Though they've seen photographs and heard the statistics, they're stunned at the immense size of the two, towering as they do over the rest of the team.

To quiet the crowd, Lilith and Samael raise their hands and begin to speak.

Using that as their signal, the New Knights Templar suddenly burst into action. In a well-rehearsed act, they shout, "You are Nephilim! You're the devil incarnate! You're not welcome here! Then they start a new chant: "Jesus! Jesus! Jesus!"

When some in the crowd join in, the chant grows louder, and skirmishes among opposing sides begin. People are packed in so tightly that it's hard for law enforcement to reach each pocket of resistance, so the interruptions continue.

Then, as planned, one of the Templars sets off a firecracker and yells, "GUN!" initiating a stampede as people trample over each other to get away. Now, the formerly tame crowd becomes a disorganized mob.

Watching from the stage, Samael removes his tinted glasses and stares into the chaos. Seconds later, everyone except the New Templars in their shielded helmets stops what they're doing and looks calmly back at him onstage.

But the Templars continue their chants, pointing them out among the others. Knowing they're now targeted, they scatter. Some escape, but most are apprehended.

Altogether, the insurrection lasts only a few minutes and doesn't stop anything. Additionally, it unintentionally provides Samael with a showcase for his power in all its glory.

While the Templars and other supporters are escorted away, Samael addresses the masses across the Federation.

"I am Samael. My sister, Lilith, and I are eager to lead humankind into a new age of reasoning. Awaiting you is a fresh appreciation of life and a renewed awareness of your incredible worth and intelligence! It is up to you, our followers, to guide the rest of humankind! You hold enormous power; we are here to show you how to use it! We will bring this power to all the people! We ask everyone to join us in this noble endeavor! All hail the New Age! All hail the Titans!"

"Titans! Titans! Titans!" shouts the crowd, mesmerized by Samael without knowing why or understanding that he is deliberately influencing their thoughts.

Across the Federation, similar chants are being taken up, interspersed with shouts of "Jesus!" and "Templars!"

From New Jerusalem, Peter witnesses this horror with fear and disgust.

This doesn't bode well for the human race, he worries. *There will be violence and death. Please,* he prays fervently, *leaders of the Federation, ask us for help before a new revolution begins! Before God the Father enacts His punishment!*

Despite the brief interruption earlier, the event in D.C. is now going well. The presentations are over, but many don't want to leave. To accommodate them, the Mall reverberates with music, and people dance and enjoy the afternoon in each other's company.

While those on the Mall have a good time, the Titans meet with dignitaries in a private area near the stage. At the same time, long tables are placed near the Jefferson Memorial for the general public. An announcement tells the crowd that nine hundred tickets will be sold to attendees there for anyone who wishes to greet the Titans and receive autographed photos.

When thousands line up for a chance at the coveted prize, the National Guard is forced to limit them further, announcing that only five hundred will be sold. Though they're gone within minutes, Samael's influence remains, and everyone stays calm. For those who are turned away, they're told a special code will be sent to their communicators to enable them to purchase a digital photo of their choice.

"Everyone adores you!" gushes Doctor Abila to Lilith after the last dignitaries disperse. "New York will be even more spectacular, I promise!"

Lilith is pleased, though a hint of worry darkens her expression.

"Tony, there are some here and in other places who oppose our assistance. Therefore, Samael and I must convince them of their misguided ways. Please stay close to me today, and do not leave my side when night falls. We are good together, you and I."

Reveling in the allure of the exotic creature nearly three times his height, Anthony Abila almost leaps for joy.

When the Titans exited the stage, Doctor Strakov and the Templars who managed to escape arrest, regrouped at the warehouse in Alexandria.

Speaking with conviction to the few who continue to straggle in, he says, "Today, you performed admirably. Although a significant number aren't here, they will be freed by morning, and I assure you, their determination will be unwavering. The next trial of our resolve awaits us in New York. Today, you and the entire Federation have witnessed firsthand the power of Samael, the Son of Satan, to mold people's minds to make them do whatever they want! Our cause is just, and with so many eyes upon us today, it's sure to grow stronger! Our mission to rescue humanity has begun!"

When live news coverage finally concludes, Peter calls Angela, his tone dark.

"People are beginning to wake up to the wickedness of that group of experimental beings, Angie. It just has to continue."

Angela responds cautiously. "I hope you're right. It was encouraging to hear the crowd chanting 'Jesus!' But did you see how many others started to fight them? I'm afraid those conflicts will get worse. People are divided. We heard voices from nearby homes, most shouting in support of the Titans. I expect to see trouble brewing in the streets before long, because many will refuse to listen to reason. Please return home soon."

"I'll try, I promise. Continue to pray that we can find a solution."

Late that afternoon, a small group of approximately fifty individuals still waits patiently in line for the coveted opportunity to meet the Titans. Despite the advancing hour, their faces remain adorned with smiles, and they exchange joy-filled greetings. Among them, the majority of the women yearn to encounter Samael, while most of the men eagerly anticipate a connection with Lilith. The children, on the other hand, express their preference to meet The Five.

Standing in the greeting area, Samael emanates an aura of tranquility, projecting a strong masculine presence that instills feelings of security and peace. Conversely, Lilith's pheromones have a profound effect on people's senses, causing her to captivate all who behold her. Even the women revere her as a goddess, a beauty to be cherished and admired.

Most find that they can't resist the allure of these two overpowering forces, and they don't want to.

However, some do manage to withstand their effects. They quickly realize the dangers the strange beings pose and join the ranks of the New Knights Templar to combat them.

In the depths of Gehenna, the Malignant is consumed with ecstatic delight after the day's events.

"They proclaimed, 'We are the Titans!'" he shouts, belching fire and sulphur into his throne room, "and their declaration echoed across the cosmos! That accursed nation, beloved by their meddling God, will finally crumble and slip into my grasp, leading the rest of humanity to the very place I want them to go! United with Samael, our common mission will guide those naïve mortals into a new era where my son will reign as the authentic messiah!

"This moment belongs to us! Victory will soon be ours!"

From above, Metatron observes the unfolding spectacle, dutifully relaying every detail to Yahweh and His Son.

Afterward, the archangels will notify the commander, and together, they will commence preparations throughout the universe for God's plan to institute a new Passover.

Meanwhile, Peter is back in his chamber near the Holy of Holies when Archangel Gabriel summons him to join the divine brotherhood at the Ark of the Covenant.

As the commander enters the sacred sanctuary, an awe-inspiring sight greets his eyes. The mighty beings, adorned in full armor embellished with gold and polished Jasper stones, have assembled before the Ark. All of them are on bended knee, heads bowed in reverence in his direction.

Perplexed, Peter turns to behold a radiant light shining behind him, the image that is capturing the angels' undivided attention. Joining them, he humbly kneels before the resplendent light as a thunderous voice proclaims, *"I Am what I Am. My loyal commander, the Nephilim have been exposed and are now sowing discord among 'My little ones,' the endearing term the Mother of My Son uses to refer to My children.*

"Commander, as I have forewarned, My Son and I stand ready to unleash the three days of darkness, should they persist in their wrongful ways. However, to allow time for the Templars to awaken the faithful, We will stay Our Hand for a short while, though Our hopes are not high, for We discern the true intentions of Our children. Yet, the Queen of Heaven implores Me to look for even a few righteous persons among you to temper My wrath. Therefore, We will observe and wait.

"The Queen of Heaven never tires of beseeching Me for the well-being of Her little ones. Nonetheless, if they do not respond by calling upon you and My guardians to intervene on their behalf,

We will instruct the chosen few on the steps they must take to save themselves. Whether through your hand or Mine, My people will be awakened.

"Semper parati. Memento mortis."

"This is Roger Cummings reporting live from the D.C. Mall. Today, the World Federation launched the Champions Tour to introduce the five Titans and their awe-inspiring leaders, Samael and Lilith. Samael emanates grace and stoicism, and Lilith is a colossal figure possessing unimaginable beauty and allure.

"More than 50,000 individuals flocked here to witness these extraordinary superhumans in person, showing them unwavering support throughout the presentation. However, a small faction of individuals, best described as zealots, sought to incite chaos and disruption. Fortunately, the National Guard, called in due to the immense crowd, swiftly dealt with any disturbances.

"Even so, things continued to escalate, and it was Samael who ultimately returned the Mall to calmness. What unfolded was beyond anyone's expectations: the sheer power wielded by Samael! With mere words and a look, he effortlessly subdued the once-excited onlookers, returning them to a state of serene composure.

"Having personally witnessed this astonishing display, I can confidently assert that these benevolent giants are a true blessing for all of us. With remarkable ease, they possess the ability to thwart any wrongdoings to safeguard our Federation against external threats. As we venture forth into the cosmos, beyond Titan and Proxima b, their protection will be invaluable. Based upon what we saw today, we should be confident that they can protect us from unknown perils that may lie ahead. The Titans will ably serve as our guardians, guiding us on our path into the future.

"This is Roger Cummings, reporting for ABC News, live from the Mall in Washington, D.C."

Lieutenant Colonel Nevins and Doctor Abila have just finished watching the early evening news report in a small personnel entertainment room in the Area 51 desert complex. As commercials replace the news anchors, Doctor Abila can no longer contain his elation.

"That was an extraordinary display by our team!" he gushes. "As we continue across the country, it's only gonna grow in scale and significance! Next stop, Central Park!"

Nevins' reaction is muted. "You might be right, Doc, but those 'zealots,' as they're being called, trouble me. Today, they demonstrated a high level of organization, even donning shielding helmets! How could they have known about that? The reports I received indicated they had teams of lawyers available to secure their release from custody. They're not gonna stop. As we move forward, I have no doubt the situation is going to deteriorate. I believe it would be best to limit our tour to minimize further encounters. New York City's planning is well underway, so we must keep that date. However, I'm eliminating Chicago, Miami, L.A., and the outer planets from our schedule, reducing it to just New York and Vegas after the mess in D.C."

Doctor Abila protests, "We can't change things now! I know it was a little worrisome for a while, but Samael took care of it!"

"I've made up my mind!" barks Nevins. "I've reassessed our strategy. It'll be wiser for our team members to engage in select studio interviews instead of wide-open outdoor venues. We're not stopping the tour, just condensing it. You can join Lilith and Samael in doing those while I accompany just two of the remaining members on a separate tour of other media outlets across the country. By removing some of the dates, limiting the number of Titans on tour, and implementing stringent security measures, we may be able to minimize the chances of further confrontations."

Doctor Abila is passionate about defending their original plan.

"I don't agree at all, Hollis! Why in the world should we separate from the others or shorten the schedule? Didn't you see how warmly they embraced us in D.C.? Our team's leader demonstrated his power and quelled the disturbance without further trouble! Samael's power was truly awe-inspiring!"

Nevins doesn't agree.

"It's precisely that display of power that disturbs me! Yes, it demonstrated his might, but it also highlighted his control, and it's already provoked mixed reactions. If we don't exercise extreme caution, I guarantee more rebellions will spring up! We need to be careful!"

Abila snickers dismissively. "You're allowing your military training to cloud your judgment, Hollis. There's nothing at all to be concerned about."

Abruptly, Nevins springs out of his chair and marches to the door.

"That's enough, Abila! You will address me as Lieutenant Colonel Nevins! Never, ever use my first name again! And my changes stand!"

Enraged by the doctor's impertinence, Nevins storms out, forcefully slamming the door behind him.

In the cell they share, Samael and Lilith sit cross-legged in deep meditation. Without anyone knowing, they're conversing with each other without speaking aloud.

"Lilith, the colonel is afraid of what we have become. We must convince him otherwise. It is time to take control of the Titans."

"I agree, but we must do it gradually. We must let them think it will be their idea for us to take control. I know how to manipulate Tony. I know what he likes and how he ticks. He will be our springboard to full domination."

"Ah, yes, I see. You are wiser in the ways of human relations than I am. We will wait until the tour is completed. Then, we will conquer and control the cosmos! I am my father's son, and I will do this!"

CHAPTER THIRTY

The sun casts an early morning glow upon the eastern United States as Atlantic coast residents resume their daily routines. They immerse themselves in work and various earthly pleasures, even as the air is still abuzz with discussions about the Titans.

Just after noon in Sorrento, Angela feeds Michael lunch while her family gathers around the vidmonitor to catch Zia Sofia's favorite show. Unexpectedly, regular programming is interrupted by a special report originating from Washington, D.C. The unusual timing commands the family's attention.

"This is Roger Cummings with ABC News. Only yesterday, the worlds were captivated by the Titans' first public appearance. Today, I have the exclusive opportunity to interview Lieutenant Colonel Nevins, commanding officer of the program that produced the Titans. To keep their headquarters a secret, the lieutenant colonel is being patched in from an undisclosed location. Colonel, how are you today?"

The officer, once again dressed in his distinguished military attire, responds with a warm smile. *"It's a splendid morning…early, yet filled with promise!"*

"Yes, I'm sure you're happy about yesterday's turnout in D.C."

"Absolutely! Tens of thousands more than we expected showed up, and we couldn't be prouder of our Titans! It was a spectacular first appearance!"

"It certainly was," agrees Cummings. *"However, what did*

you make of the protests?"

"Oh, that was nothing; we expected some opposition. After all, not everyone is capable of embracing change. And the team's leader handled it superbly."

"I agree. Samael has proven to be a capable leader. What can you tell us about the rest of the tour?"

"Thank you for this opportunity, Roger. I'm happy to let you and your viewers know that the Champions Tour is aimed at bringing our team closer to the people of the United States and beyond. While our original schedule was longer, we've condensed it to just two more venues: Central Park in New York, scheduled for this Friday, and Las Vegas, one week later. We're not ready to announce the exact location in Vegas, but it will come out in due time. After Vegas, we intend to embark on a nationwide multimedia tour, engaging with local audiences during morning news and talk show time slots. There will be no more outdoor appearances. I will accompany two of the Titans on the tour, while Doctor Anthony Abila will escort Samael and Lilith. Specific dates, times, and places are still being negotiated. Unfortunately, we had to eliminate visits to the rest of the galaxy."

Cummings leans in, his curiosity piqued.

"Tell me, Colonel Nevins, did you curtail your tour due to the protests witnessed in D.C. yesterday?"

Nevins pauses thoughtfully.

"Protests are an inherent right of the people. Nevertheless, we determined it would be more fitting and that we'd reach a wider audience by utilizing the more intimate settings of local media outlets instead of the grand locations we originally considered. The logistics involved in touring the entire country with a large contingent of personnel and equipment also played a role in that decision. The revised schedule is a better approach for all parties involved. If I may, I'd like to extend my gratitude to D.C. mayor Haruna Oyibo, the National Guard, law enforcement officers, and the supporters who displayed their enthusiasm for our heroes so

passionately."

Cummings nods appreciatively.

"We welcome your presence here today, Lieutenant Colonel, and we eagerly anticipate the future appearances of the Titans." Turning to the camera, he adds, *"This is Roger Cummings. Stay tuned to this station. After the commercial break, I'll be interviewing Doctor Vladimir Strakov, leader of the opposition movement called the New Knights Templar."*

Shaken, Angie quickly calls Peter, reaching him in New Jerusalem as he stands at the base of the steps to Solomon's reconstructed Temple, talking with pilgrims as Commander of the Ark.

Excusing himself when his call signal flashes, he walks some distance away to take the call in private. "Hello, my love. How are the Matteos today?"

"Peter, you have to tune into a special report broadcasting right now from the States! Roger Cummings is going to interview Doctor Strakov! Do you know he organized the group that protested at the Titans rally yesterday? He's calling it the New Knights Templar!"

Peter stares at his communicator, stunned by his wife's announcement.

"I'm going to my room right now to listen in private. See if you can contact Austin Patton in Canada. Thanks for letting me know about this, Angie!"

Rushing up the stairs, Peter bolts into his living quarters and searches for the special report in his news feed.

"Hello again," says Roger. *"For those just tuning in, Doctor Vladimir Strakov, organizer and leader of the New Knights Templar, is with me in our Washington studio. The New Knights Templar is the group that disrupted the Titans' first public appearance. Doctor Strakov, what is it about the Titans that bothers you so much that you would organize a demonstration against them? Why do you have a problem with our heroes?"*

Strakov, outwardly cool and calm, seethes inwardly. He vows to tread lightly, knowing the propaganda machine against him mustn't gain ammunition to discredit him.

"Thank you for the opportunity to address your viewers," he begins. *"I also want to thank ABC News for allowing me to come on your program."*

"How do you answer my question, Doctor?"

"I'm here to discuss the vile program the World Federation has inflicted upon the unwary public."

"Now, Doctor Strakov," interrupts Roger, *"I didn't invite you here to impugn—"*

Doctor Strakov jumps in, not letting Cummings continue his thought; he can't restrain himself.

Strakov fumes, *"No, Roger! Everyone needs to know what's really going on! I'm highly knowledgeable about this because I was the first geneticist involved with the Titans!"*

"Please, let's keep this civil—"

"Civil? The original name of that program was Operation Apocalypse! Did you know that? The powerful elites softened it to avoid alarming the public! Those 'heroes,' as you call them, are transhumans! To make them what they are, we drastically altered their DNA to create the abominations you welcomed the other day with so much fanfare!

"The five Titans need to be watched very carefully, but the two you should be most concerned about are the massive giants, Samael and Lilith! In addition to enhanced strength, they also have the power of the third eye, which Samael demonstrated briefly on Sunday. No matter what they say, those beings are not our friends. Samael's DNA is not human! He has 92 chromosomes in a double helix, while humans have a single helix of 46 chromosomes! As you saw on Sunday, they can control our thoughts and actions!"

"Wow, that's... Doctor Strakov, what makes you think they control our thoughts? That's a pretty hefty charge to label them

with!"

"*That's exactly right, Roger! How else can you explain how quickly the opposition stopped fighting us at the press conference? One minute, hundreds of people were shouting us down, and the next, they abandoned their rhetoric! The change was instantaneous, and the only difference was what Samael did. He took off his glasses and looked at them with that extra eye! The only ones not affected were my group, and that's because our minds were shielded from his telepathic power by the helmets we wore!*"

"*Everyone noticed that your members were wearing something more than hats. What were they 'shielded' with?*"

Strakov ignores the question, continuing his rant, "*I know what Samael and Lilith are capable of because of my prior work with them! Do you have any idea of what they intend to do to us? We at the Knights Templar have a duty and responsibility to warn everyone of the torments they will soon force upon humanity! Please listen to Peter Matteo, the Commander of the Ark, and call upon his aid! It's the only way to stop the Titans! We must vanquish them fr—*"

Suddenly, Doctor Strakov's microphone is cut off, and the camera focuses solely on Roger Cummings. The well-known interviewer looks into the camera while Strakov is forcibly removed from the studio.

"*I'm sorry for the outburst, folks. Doctor Strakov violated our broadcasting community standards, so we removed him from the studio. It seems the New Knights Templar is taking over from its predecessor, criticizing what they disagree with.*

"*The Titans don't deserve Doctor Strakov's disapproval. I'll be following Samael, Lilith, and their companion, Doctor Abila, on their country-wide tour, and I'll be the emcee at their next public appearance this Friday evening in Central Park. Because of what happened in Washington, attendance at all future appearances will be limited, and security will be enhanced to avoid other incidents. Tune into this program the day after their appearance for my in-depth commentary on that event.*

"Let's praise the Titans and the work of Doctor Abila! I, for one, feel safe and secure, knowing these superior beings are committed to doing everything possible to keep the Federation safe across the cosmos.

"Thanks for watching this special report. This is Roger Cummings, returning you to your regularly scheduled program."

Peter turns off his news feed, aghast at how quickly Samael has influenced everyone he needs to spread his unholy message. In desperation, he lowers his head and starts to pray, not knowing that millions worldwide are doing the very same thing.

Unfortunately, multimillions of others are not praying. On the contrary, they're shouting, "Go Titans!" and they're creating even more types of support for the evil beings controlling them without their knowledge or consent.

In their quarters, Samael and Lilith are joined by Doctor Abila. Together, they communicate telepathically with him, discussing plans and future travel.

Suddenly, Samael's eyes light up, and he laughs out loud, knowing what just happened on the air.

Watching, Doctor Abila doesn't know what to make of this new behavior. Laughter isn't something Samael's ever done, and Abila is simultaneously joyous and chilled.

But Lilith understands. Reading Abila's confused thoughts, she telepathically tells him, "Tony, Samael cannot contain his joy at how well everything is going. Together, we make a great team!"

Interjecting his thoughts, Samael breaks into their mind stream.

"I am my father's son. Lilith is my sister, and you,

Doctor Abila, are our brother in this cause that will change everything!"

United in their mission, the two giants kneel and touch foreheads, bringing Doctor Abila close to join in.

Instantaneously, a bond is formed, and power surges through the doctor. He is now one with the Nephilim, an ignorant pawn of the Fallen.

Thousands of miles away, Peter shudders in his room, consumed with an unknown fear. Once again, he falls to his knees, suspecting something horrible is happening.

He isn't there long when an incoming call breaks his concentration. Tapping his wrist communicator, he hears a broken, static-filled transmission.

"Peter, it's Austin. ...hope you understand me. ... signal up here not the best. Angela tapped me into Strakov interview. Able to see most, but heavily pixelized... Heading to civilization...Lory stays with Bigfeet. Will be in touch again... Calgary. Should be...New York by week's end. Going to Central Park...see hybrids in person. Will try to contact Strakov. ...in custody? Godspeed, Commander. God help...all."

CHAPTER THIRTY-ONE

Determined to school her fellow ambassadors in the Titans' dangers, Fiona busily contacts each one, urging them to recognize the threat the transhumans and their leaders pose to the galaxy.

However, their popularity skyrockets, and Fiona is increasingly treated as a pariah. Every day, she experiences rejection and indifference, as if she were a blemish on the face of progress. But she perseveres, despite being fearful for her safety and of vague pronouncements of a recall vote.

After a long day of confrontations and despair, Fiona seeks relaxation at her condo near Vatican City in Rome. As she unwinds, she receives a notification on her door monitor, indicating a visitor. Dressed in yoga pants and a loose top, she approaches the screen to see a distinguished cardinal, known to her as a representative of the Universal Church, standing tall and dignified outside her door.

With surprise and a tinge of embarrassment, Fiona inquires, "Cardinal Sagretti? I was not expecting visitors. How may I assist you?"

The high-ranking clergyman, an older man in his sixties, smiles and responds, "Good evening, Ambassador Gabelli. I am here as a special envoy from Pope Ignatius. May I speak with you?"

Fiona's curiosity is piqued, but she worries about her appearance.

"Your Eminence, I'm not dressed for visitors such as

yourself. Please allow me a moment to change into something more appropriate."

With a soft chuckle, the cardinal reassures her, "Ah, my dear, do not trouble yourself. I assure you, there is no need to be formal."

Blushing, Fiona opens her door and invites the cardinal inside, apologizing as he enters.

"Please have a seat," says Fiona, ushering the Roman Universal and Apostolic Church representative to her living area. Before she sits, she attempts to fix her hair.

"Your Eminence, this is an unexpected surprise. Does the pope require something of me?"

Leaning in, Sagretti shares, "Ambassador, a video conference with your President Larson will take place in Pope Ignatius' chambers in one hour. Earlier today, we dispatched an envoy to New Jerusalem to retrieve Commander Peter Matteo for this meeting, and the Holy Father requests your presence there as well."

"Oh. Of course," says Fiona, reaching up to her hair again.

"Ah," says the Cardinal, noting the motion. "Do not worry about your appearance. A stunning woman like yourself should not require much preparation."

Blushing again, Fiona drops her hand into her lap.

"During the meeting, we will discuss the Titans and other important matters. I will return to your door in forty minutes to escort you there. God bless you, Ambassador Gabelli. You are doing God's work."

The mid-week preparations for the Titan show in Central Park are near completion. The stage is now fully assembled, with bright lights and state-of-the-art sound equipment.

Discussions between the Titans' representatives and New York City's terrorism and crisis response units have resulted in a crowd limit of 20,000 people. In addition, strategic spots throughout the area have been equipped with specialized scanning and metal detection stations to ensure everyone's safety. The Titan team insisted upon these measures to prevent disruptions similar to the incident caused by the New Knights Templar in D.C. However, everyone on the planning committee knows how true the old song's lyrics are: "You can't always get what you want."

Following his expulsion from the *Roger Cummings Television Show*, Doctor Strakov has arranged for armed security and has gone into hiding. So far, he has successfully evaded those searching for him, taking refuge in an abandoned apartment building scheduled for demolition in Hoboken, New Jersey.

Gathering his followers, he aims to boost their confidence with an uplifting speech. They are well aware of the outcome of their actions in D.C., and some are feeling apprehensive.

"Fellow warriors, we must remain resolute in the face of adversity! Society may vilify us, and our own families may reject us. Yet, your presence here assures me that you believe in the righteousness of our cause! Though we may be few, God is our guiding light, and He always triumphs! Keep your focus on the Cross!"

After pausing to acknowledge shouts of agreement, he continues, "After Friday, your names will be etched in history. By now, each of you should have received a Raphaelite helmet and a pair of three-lensed, tinted glasses. These glasses mirror the style worn by Samael and Lilith, while the shielded baseball caps bear the 'Titans' insignia. The caps match the blue T-shirts we're distributing now. Our aim is to get at least a thousand of you into the park. Once you have your supplies, proceed to the designated area. With your sleeping bags and other gear, you'll blend in seamlessly with the eager crowd anticipating the arrival of their idols. The EMF-proof backpacks and rain jackets we provide will shield you from potential harm, such as tasers or worse.

"Remember, the drone flying over the stage will be the signal to initiate the disruption. If needed, be prepared to employ your combat skills. Understand that uniformed and undercover personnel from Homeland Security, the World Federation, and other law enforcement will be present in the crowd. However, our team of lawyers will also be there to assist anyone who might face arrest, and if things turn ugly, we're prepared to aid any who may become injured. You've already witnessed the might of the giants, the offspring of the Fallen, but don't be afraid. Keep in mind that we're here to conquer them!"

Amid enthusiastic shouts, he says, "Now, let's take a moment to pause and pray. Let's beseech our Heavenly Father to grant wisdom to our government leaders. May they approach the Commander of the Ark to put an end to this before it's too late!"

After Cardinal Sagretti left Fiona's condo, she quickly changed her attire and freshened her makeup, finishing just in time for his return.

"Are you ready?" asks Sagretti when Fiona answers his knock.

"Yes, lead on," she says, locking the door behind her.

The ride to Vatican City takes five minutes, after which they pass through the Swiss Guard check station and enter a discreet back entrance, away from public view.

This is one place Fiona has never been, so she trusts the cardinal as he leads her down an elevator and into a circular room in a sub-basement, where a holographic display machine is humming.

Inside the room, Pope Ignatius and Peter Matteo are already seated, while two burly men stand directly behind the pope.

Approaching the pontiff, Fiona bows and kisses his ring. Then she exchanges a smile with Peter and takes a seat.

Pope Ignatius blesses everyone present and begins.

"Ambassador Gabelli, you are already acquainted with the Commander, but I do not think you know the gentlemen behind me. They are representatives from the Order of the Ravens — the Vatican's equivalent of the Secret Service — and they are my personal bodyguards."

Fiona nods at the silent sentinels while the pope continues, "I have brought you here at the request of President Larson. I hope I did not inconvenience you."

"Not at all, Holy Father. I am at your service."

"Thank you. I hope the news President Larson has for us is encouraging." Turning to another attendant, he says, "Please enter our Holo-link credentials."

Within moments, a full-color holographic display of the Seal of the President of the United States appears, then President Larson materializes as a life-sized avatar.

"Your Holiness, and esteemed warriors of God, I have called this meeting to provide an update on my efforts to thwart the Titan program formerly known as Operation Apocalypse."

"Do you have good news for us, President Larson?" asks Pope Ignatius.

"I'm afraid not. It pains me to report that I have not

been successful with most of those I've spoken to thus far. The only ones I've been able to convince of the true nature of this malevolence are members of my military community. Each day, more and more unsuspecting individuals in positions of power, including our elected officials, are falling prey to the Titanites. If you're unfamiliar with the term, 'Titanites' is the label the social media crowd has given to anyone who reveres those abominations of nature."

The Vatican attendees glance at each other uneasily while President Larson directs his next remarks to Fiona.

"Ambassador Gabelli, I have heard of the work you've been doing, but I fear both of us are engaged in a losing battle."

"Sir, I'm not prepared to give up."

"Neither am I. However, I want to speak to Peter now. As Commander of the Ark, I implore you to intervene. However, I understand that currently, I do not possess the sole authority to do so. I simply wish to have my position on record."

"Noted, Mr. President," responds Peter, grateful for his chief executive's confidence.

"Fortunately, some world leaders share my concerns. But out of the approximately 180 countries in the Federation, only three of Earth's representatives have openly expressed worry: the United Kingdom, Israel, and Australia. Additionally, the Mars colony shares our apprehension. Gentlemen and Fiona, we must persist in our efforts to convince as many as possible!"

Peter responds in a tight voice. "I appreciate your candor, Mr. President. You are correct in acknowledging that your influence on my deployment is limited. However, your support will impact the response of God the Father and those who align themselves with us against the Fallen.

"I have spent much time beseeching the Father for His help, even drawing parallels to His interaction with Abraham regarding the salvation of the righteous in Sodom and

Gomorrah. For now, the Father and His Son will withhold judgment, pending our actions as His people. I will continue to pray. We must choose wisely and swiftly, for His patience with His children is wearing thin."

Displaying concern, President Larson lowers his eyes before speaking again.

"In two days, we will witness the spectacle in New York. My sources indicate there is a distinct possibility of trouble in the park. Now is one of the times I wish my friend Austin Patton were still under my command!"

Peter's eyes gleam briefly. "Mr. President, General Patton has informed me that he will attend the event in Central Park this Friday, so you may be able to ask for his assistance after all. He wants to witness the Titans for himself."

Pope Ignatius raises a hand to signal the end of the discussion.

"Together, we must pray that your general does not fall under the Titans' leaders' influence. Almighty God, we ask that the veils are lifted from the people's eyes. Please help them to reject the evil of the Fallen. Enable them to understand what they must do to remain free to worship only You, their true Lord, God, and Savior!"

Quietly and cautiously, ensuring not to raise alarm or suspicion, one thousand Templars slip into Central Park, each blending in seamlessly as a Titanite. As time passes, the crowd grows steadily, and by Friday morning, the venue is filled to one-third of its capacity.

In conjunction with the highly anticipated event scheduled for 11:00 a.m. EST, the day promises to be delightful, with nature adding to the festive atmosphere. As thousands of individuals eagerly await the superstars' arrival, the temperature is predicted to rise only into the sixties, with the vibrant bloom of spring flowers adding color to the scene. At the same time, the park's many trees are showcasing their lush green canopies, reawakening early from their winter slumbers.

With most attendees, including the New Knights Templar, displaying favor toward the Titans, the righteous infiltrators are heartened to find that some individuals hold beliefs similar to theirs. They're hesitant to approach them, though, as they're not sure whether they're actually wolves dressed in sheep's clothing, directed to oust the Templars before they can create a disturbance.

While the New Templars prepare below, high in the heavens, Metatron has assembled two hundred archangels to meditate upon Karen Stamos. The influential archangel's goal is to awaken the latent human inside Lilith to weaken Samael's cause.

CHAPTER THIRTY-TWO

At 10:30 a.m., resounding patriotic music begins to echo through the vast expanse of New York City's largest urban park, captivating the 20,000 people assembled there and the millions watching around the world and its planetary colonies.

Over the past hour, Roger Cummings has been introducing dignitaries and entertainers, skillfully cultivating a sense of nationalistic fervor. Within the crowd, the New Knights Templar remain on standby, discreetly recruiting followers after meticulously assessing their beliefs.

Across Europe and the Middle East, evening falls, casting a gentle glow over the land as Peter returns to the U.S. consulate, preparing to witness the event as it is transmitted across the galaxy. In her Rome condo, Fiona also anxiously waits, her anticipation palpable, while on the Amalfi Coast, Angela and her family join in to watch the unfolding spectacle and offer prayers.

In Washington, President Larson has secluded himself in his living quarters with his wife and their dogs. Despite it being a typical workday for the United States leader, it was surprisingly easy to clear his calendar. Everyone with a prior commitment had already canceled before his office had the chance.

As the president watches, a flicker of hope lingers in his heart for the event to unfold badly. Secretly, his fervent desire is for the nefarious plans of Lieutenant Colonel Nevins and the World Federation to collapse in a heap of public discreditation.

Adhering to the day's theme, each Titan is wearing a one-piece red, white, and blue jumpsuit while they wait backstage for the emcee's introductions. Nevins, once again in his full dress uniform, commands the authority of the military, and Doctor Abila looks impeccable in an expensive business suit.

When the crowd's anticipation reaches a peak, the resounding notes of the World Federation anthem begin to reverberate across the park, and Roger Cummings steps onto the stage. Then, at a gesture from Roger, the large curtain parts, and Nevins and the Titans stride forward, eliciting thunderous cheers and chants of the now familiar "Go Titans!" from the fervent crowd.

Interspersed among the onlookers, the Templars and their newly recruited followers watch the goings-on, biding their time until the opportune moment arrives for them to act.

When the deafening cheers show no sign of stopping, Nevins raises his hands, attempting to calm the masses.

Still backstage, Lilith's mind wanders while she waits for her cue. Briefly, she reflects on her former persona as Karen Stamos, an unbidden activity that disturbs her. Unnerved by the unwelcome thoughts, she pushes them aside and refocuses on the present.

Out front, Cummings introduces The Five: Frank, Richard, Robert, Tim, and Jonathan, and they step forward one by one, gathering together in a single row at the front of the stage. At an agreed-upon signal, each begins tossing Titan caps and T-shirts into the roaring crowd, the action triggering a frenzy of excitement as attendees clamor and compete for the prized souvenirs.

When they're out of giveaways, the Titans wave to the ecstatic audience, prompting a chorus of chants, among which alternating shouts of "Samael, Lilith, Samael, Lilith!" dominate the soundscape.

The overwhelming chanting is so loud that it drowns out the music and Roger Cummings' attempts to restore order. Frustrated that he's losing control, Cummings turns to Lieutenant Colonel Nevins, who only shrugs in helpless resignation.

Moments later, Nevins foresees the situation spiraling into dangerous territory. Tapping his newly inserted cranial communicator, he orders Doctor Abila to introduce the two giants before things get worse.

Responding to the order, the curtain opens again, and Nevins directs the five Titans to take positions on one side of the stage.

As Doctor Abila moves close to the eager crowd, Samael and Lilith grasp hands and follow their diminutive lackey, each adorned in matching patriotic jumpsuits, their eyes concealed behind the three-lensed glasses.

Sensing a climax to the proceedings, the New Knights Templar swiftly don their identical glasses, seeking to blend in further with the Titanites surrounding them.

With the crowd pleasers now in full view, the onlookers' fervor begins to subside; chants and applause gradually fading enough to allow Doctor Abila to introduce Samael and Lilith, the day's main attractions.

"What a crowd!" begins Abila, overwhelmed by the all-encompassing enthusiasm directed toward his 'proteges.'

As Abila continues his speech, he's periodically interrupted by people pointing to a drone soaring over the stage — the signal the Templars were waiting for.

When they see it, they start shouting their opposition, deliberately exposing themselves to the hatred of many.

Angered by their presence, the involuntary followers of evil start pushing and shoving the Templars, but that only makes their shouts grow louder: "Spawns of Satan! You are the Fallen! The New Knights Templar will be victorious! You will never control humanity!"

In solidarity, the newly recruited toss whatever they can onto the stage — garbage, water bottles, food, empty cans — igniting skirmishes between the Templars and Titanites within the crowd.

Frightened by the number of fights breaking out, Roger Cummings, Lieutenant Colonel Nevins, and Doctor Abila swiftly retreat to the back of the stage, seeking shelter from the chaos.

Knowing their strength, the Titans remain in place, each one darting forward, skillfully employing their speed and agility to deflect most of the incoming onslaught of projectiles.

With the scene in the audience resembling a massive cage match, police and Homeland Security forces enter the fray with non-lethal weapons to suppress the commotion.

Infuriated by another disrupted gathering, Samael and Lilith purposely stride downstage and remove their glasses, fixing their gazes upon the scufflers. Instantly, people from all walks of life — everyday citizens, law enforcement officers, women, and children — come to a standstill, fixed in a trance-like state, their attention captivated solely by the unnatural duo.

Unaffected by the diabolical beings, the Templars charge toward the stage, having easy access, now that the Titanites can't stop them.

In response, Samael and Lilith concentrate their powers on them, but only a few are affected.

Recognizing the futility of continuing, Doctor Abila runs to the pair and urges them to make their way backstage, out of sight.

But Nevins isn't ready to give up. He releases The Five from prior restrictions, allowing them to unleash their painstakingly honed skills on the disruptors, something he never thought he'd do.

Freed to use their strength as they see fit, the supermen descend into the crowd, pushing aside those still frozen in place to reach the Templars.

Seeing the approaching danger, the protestors retreat, weaving around the unmoving Titanites to escape arrest.

At this point, the live feed abruptly terminates, but Austin Patton is still filming from a safe distance.

It doesn't take long for the violence to be crushed by NYPD and Homeland Security, with assistance from the Titans. Casualties among the Titans' supporters are minor, with most treated on the scene. A few are more serious, needing transport to local hospitals.

Through it all, chants of "We love you, Titans!" and "Go Titans!" are still heard throughout Central Park. A few hundred stalwart supporters remain out of the original 20,000 attendees, and they've been chanting for several minutes, hoping for another glimpse of their beloved Titans.

Unsure if he is live on air, Roger steps back onstage, addressing the crowd through the thunderous cheers that erupt when Lilith, Samael, the Titans, and Doctor Abila return to wave to their adoring fans.

So far, authorities have arrested fifty-five members of the Knights Templar and twenty sympathizers. Twenty-five of the total sustained injuries, while two of the Templars tragically lost their lives.

Meanwhile, the propaganda machine begins operating at full speed to defend what it doesn't understand, with many individuals jumping on the bandwagon to identify themselves as "Titanites." In addition, the World and Galactic Federations swiftly issue a joint statement, accusing the Templars of "backward thinking" and demanding their immediate apprehension and imprisonment. Adding their voices to the denouncements, media pundits from various corners of the galaxy call upon President Larson and Pope Ignatius to reprimand the protestors in the harshest possible manner.

Still at the event, Austin eventually has enough. Stashing his vidcam in a secure pocket, he exits the field and calls Lory to tell her he's all right. Then, he calls Peter Matteo.

As soon as they connect, he states, "I probably don't have to tell you this, but don't believe what you'll likely hear from the media. I filmed most of it. I'll send you the vid file as soon as I can. It was encouraging to see how many supported the Templars."

"Were they able to escape?"

"From what I observed, most got away. Many were arrested, but I don't think the majority were Templars. They didn't have the same gear the Templars wore. As bad as they're gonna make this out to be, and don't get me wrong, this wasn't a good thing by any means; more people are coming out against the Titans than we thought."

Peter closes his eyes, exhaling slowly.

"We're reliving the evil Nephilim from the Old Testament, my friend."

Austin cricks his neck from the tension of the day.

"I'm gonna try to reach President Larson. They'll probably try to force him to make a statement supporting the Titans and the program that created them. Are you gonna contact Pope Ignatius? I hope he doesn't cave to public pressure. Keep vigilant, my friend."

"You, too, Austin."

While Peter searches his contact list for the pope's details, a call comes in from a private line.

"Your Holiness? I was just about to call you. I'm afraid of what you're going to say about what happened."

Pope Ignatius, firm and resolute, declares, "I will say what needs to be said. The Fallen are dangerous to our eternal souls, and the Templars, although right in their calling, are also dangerous. Their zealous tactics are misrepresenting the righteous. It is not true that everyone is enamored of the Giants. It is only because they have been led to believe what is untrue. They are worshipping false idols and have lost themselves in the desert of disillusionment. The people have been blinded by their pride; they think they know best, just as they have from time immemorial."

This is John Halsey with BBC London. Riots are currently erupting throughout the city, dividing followers of the Titans and the Templars along ideological lines. On your monitors, you can witness cars being set ablaze and businesses falling victim to destruction.

"In response to these distressing events, the Prime Minister has issued a call for peace. Similar scenes are unfolding across Europe as individuals of all ages and genders align themselves with the differing factions. The duration of this turmoil remains uncertain; both sides seem entrenched in their positions. This is John Halsey, BBC London. We will bring you a statement from King Andrew III as soon as it's released.

CHAPTER THIRTY-THREE

The next morning, President Larson starts working with his speech writers to craft his response to the violence in New York City. Due to the situation's urgency, his aides scheduled a live speech from the Oval Office at eight that evening, so the timetable is tight.

Larson knows he can't say what he really wants to. As President, he must always prioritize his official duties over his personal opinions — a fundamental requirement that he has always found challenging.

During a particularly passionate discussion over a talking point, Larson's administrative assistant, a young intern from Chicago's South Side, enters the office, prompting Larson to quiet his staff.

"Lorinda, is it something important?" he inquires, irritated by the interruption.

"Mr. President, you have an urgent communication from Prime Minister Wilson."

Larson sighs deeply. "Very well. Please connect it to my desk terminal."

From their seats beyond the president's desk, the aides continue their debate while keeping attentive ears on the conversation with the British prime minister.

"How are things going in London, Gerald?"

"In chaos, I'm afraid. It appears the Templars have awakened a sleeping giant, no pun intended. James, I want you to know that I, King Andrew, Yosef of Israel, and Stanley of

Australia stand united with you against this evil. France and Italy have promised to join our cause, and the Mars Federation is actively recruiting leaders from the Titan and Moon colonies to join our alliance. I've also instructed envoys across Europe to seek more support. The events in New York are reshaping perspectives, James. Let's hope that it ultimately ends up serving the greater good."

Larson feels a mix of gratification and concern.

"I'm thankful for your support, Gerald, and for getting others onboard. But I'm afraid this is far from over. Countless innocent individuals will suffer as a result of what those creatures are trying to do. And I've been told that if God the Father needs to intervene in this problem, the consequences will be even more severe for us. We must do all we can to manage this situation.

"Gerald, I appreciate your call. You've helped me decide what I need to convey in my speech this evening. Best of luck to you, my friend."

As the screen fades, Larson turns to his speech writers.

"Well, you all heard the Prime Minister. Delete what we've done so far. We're going to start over."

Safe again in their desert sanctuary, Abila and Nevins convene to strategize their next move.

"Doc, the people are on our side, but we must still exercise caution. We can't take the chance of stirring up another incident until we've gained more support and discredited the Templars."

Abila offers a hopeful, "But the media pundits are on our side."

"Yes, they are. Funny how a bag of silver still works. We're compensating them handsomely."

Abila remains measured. "Colonel, I've come to agree to the changes you made."

"Really?"

"I'd like to cancel all public events, at least until the Templars have been neutralized. Instead of holding appearances we have no control over, we can engage in media interviews at closed studios across the country. It'll be much easier to manage security under those conditions."

"Yeah, I'm glad you've come around," agrees Nevins. "But we may still get protesters. They don't care where they set up shop."

"That's true, but localized protests here and there won't be as detrimental to our cause as the live shows have been. I can speak with The Five. They need reassurance that the outbursts won't last. Samael informed me that Tim and Jonathan expressed some concerns. He and Lilith are able to communicate with the Templars telepathically but they have no control over them. I don't know why that is, and it could potentially be troublesome. Additionally, I need to have a conversation with Lilith; she keeps inquiring about Karen Stamos."

"Karen? I thought that was done and gone."

"Apparently not."

Nevins lights up a cigar. "We can handle the civilians; our soldiers will ensure their compliance. And if not, well, we'll simply reduce our force to the military-trained Titans."

Abila winces. "That's not ideal, Nevins. I hope you're right that we can keep all of them compliant." Frowning, Abila pushes his chair away from the table and stands. "I need to have a discussion with all of them. I'll update you when I'm done."

Doctor Abila exits the conference room while Nevins remains behind, leisurely blowing smoke rings and chuckling to himself.

When the team returned to the facility, the five goliaths were delighted to find that they now had individual living quarters. They thought they'd like the privacy, but since they've been living and training together for so long, they miss being close. Now, every chance they get, they arrange some form of entertainment for the group, be it watching a movie, playing a fierce game of cards, or engaging in an athletic sport.

Today, they're playing basketball, a game they've found showcases their remarkable skills easily.

When Doctor Abila finds them on the court, he stays on the sidelines, watching ball after ball going into the nets.

"Hey!" he calls out, pride in his charges evident in his wide grin. "You guys could easily dominate the NBA!"

Holding the ball, Corporal Alvarez flings it from one end of the court to score a basket.

"It's too easy for us, Doc. It's almost boring."

Tapping into the doctor's idea, Tim adds, "Maybe we could go on tour as the Titans Basketball Team! We could recreate the spirit of the old Harlem Globetrotters! And what do you know, maybe my wife could join us on tour! I really miss her, Doc."

Bursting into laughter at the notion of a basketball tour, Richard chimes in, "Who on earth would dare challenge us? But you didn't come here for small talk, Doc. What's up?"

Doctor Abila waves them over, looking up at each Titan with a thoughtful expression.

"I need to talk with all of you about the incidents in D.C. and Central Park. Do any of you have concerns? Feel free to speak openly here; I turned the monitors off. It's just you and me."

Tim is the first one to voice his thoughts.

"So you turned the monitors off? What about Samael, and your girlfriend? We all know they can read your mind. Even so, I'll speak for myself, and the others can do the same."

While the rest nod in agreement, Tim continues, "You should have left me alone, Doc," he says, gritting his teeth. "I appreciate not being a Clawfoot, but this isn't the life I envisioned. Not like this, not the way I am now." Glancing at Jonathan, he says, "Jon and I were ordinary people who happened to get infected, and you turned us into Titans. I don't like the way things are going. It seems you want us to go against our fellow citizens. You made us into ultimate soldiers without asking if we wanted that role. I know Frank, Richard, and Robert volunteered for this, but you should ask them how they feel about it. And I really need to see my wife!"

Chiming in, Jonathan adds, "Tim's right. We were pushed into this without understanding the consequences. I'm afraid we'll end up fighting a battle against regular people, and I don't want to fight them!"

Listening, Richard and Frank, the AI-enhanced Titans, exchange whispers before Frank speaks up.

"Rich and I went through hell during our partial transformations. Yeah, we volunteered, but no one fully explained what we'd be getting ourselves into. Without Xanthe Robotics, we might not have survived at all. Maybe we shouldn't have. We're still soldiers, and we'll fight for our country if we need to, but as we saw recently, this situation could quickly spiral out of control."

Lieutenant Robert Lawson looks at the others and then at Abila.

"I'm a soldier, too. I'm prepared to fight and die for my country, but not for Samael and Lilith. Put me in a combat unit, and I'll excel. If Lieutenant Colonel Nevins or any other officer commands me to duty, I'm ready and willing to serve to the best of my abilities. But I don't trust Samael or Karen anymore.

Yeah, I know she wants to be called Lilith, but I know who she was. They may be able to read our thoughts, but we're not their puppets!"

In unison, The Five enhanced hybrids place their hands together and raise them above their heads with a resounding, "Ooorah!"

Lounging in their quarters, Lilith and Samael listen to the Titans' complaints, growing more and more upset at what they're hearing. Suddenly, a voice inside their heads redirects their attention.

"My formidable creatures, we must tread lightly with these beings, for we may have to face our battle alone. Our fight is for a new awakening and for my son to reign over the galaxy. That ever-loving God of Heaven is weak. He will not force His people to resist us, nor will He destroy the worlds His children populate to destroy you, my Fallen ones, as He did once before. He is a fool, and we will take advantage of his pathetic patience."

As that voice fades, Lilith hears another one: "We are Karen. We are one."

Worried by the Titans' complaints, Doctor Abila rushes to report his conversation with Nevins. But at the conference room door, he stops dead in his tracks when the unmistakable voice of Samael flows into his mind.

"Do not concern yourself with the Titans," assures the voice of Satan's son. "They are harmless, and we do not require them. You, I, and my sister are the true Titans. Together, we are invincible! Together, we shall rule our kingdom!"

Released from the voice, Abila opens the door to the conference room, finding it empty.

"Where are you?" he asks through his communicator.

Nevins replies, "I'm in the mess hall. Join me for breakfast. We can talk here."

Minutes later, the two sit facing each other with coffee, pancakes, and bacon between them.

"You look like you've seen a ghost," says Nevins. "What happened?"

Still in a mind-controlled state, Abila relays the Titans' discussion.

"None of The Five have anything good to say about Samael or Lilith. They'll follow orders from you or other officers but not from the two leaders. They're uncomfortable about fighting fellow citizens, and that includes the Templars. We need to be careful if we want to keep them on our side."

"Crap!" bellows Nevins. "When did they start thinking that way?"

"I got the feeling this isn't new. But don't worry; I'm not gonna change what I'm doing. I'll continue mentoring Samael and Lilith and representing them to the people. We don't actually need the Titans to accomplish what we've planned."

Curious, Nevins eyes Abila while munching on his breakfast. Then he lays his fork down.

"And what exactly is our plan?"

"As we discussed before, we should stop all public appearances and arrange interviews instead. I think we should present the Titans as abnormally large human beings with extraordinary physical abilities instead of frightening super beings. Just thinking out loud here, maybe we could form them into a basketball team and hold exhibition games to show off their capabilities in a friendly atmosphere. We need to shift the public's focus away from them being seen as super weapons. If you work with The Five, I can tour the country with Samael and Lilith. We'll have to emphasize the leaders' humane side as well. And with more exposure, they can use their enhanced pineal glands to garner support from the masses to turn them against the Templars without having to deal with their confrontations."

Nevins burps, then takes a sip of coffee.

"Hmm, that could work. If we do it that way, we'd still be deploying the Titans against the Templars, but in a less direct way. Brilliant idea, Doc. I'll have my staff work on putting this strategy into motion. We can call it Operation Reset; I'll issue a press release. Inform The Five about the new plan."

With a wink at Abila, he states, "I'm sure there's no need to tell the other two. Samael and your significant other must already know what we discussed."

Faking a smile, Nevins leaves the table to rejoin the food line while Abila finishes his breakfast and heads back to the Titans.

On the way, Lilith's soft voice enters his mind.

"You've done well, my love. But we need to talk further — in private."

CHAPTER THIRTY-FOUR

While the worlds eagerly await the speech from the President of the United States, Larson takes his seat behind the antique Kennedy desk in a room that hasn't changed for millennia.

Off-screen, Larson's wife and his staff watch, providing encouragement as he undergoes last-minute touch-ups to his makeup before going live.

Although the speech is already written and approved, Larson feels unsure about it, occasionally glancing at the notes he wrote in the border.

When a coordinator signals a five-finger countdown, Larson takes a moment to compose himself, then flashes his winning smile, promising himself to touch upon his personal reflections in the speech.

Invoking the standard opening line of countless presidents before him, he begins, *"Good evening, fellow Americans."* Then, without delay, he dives into the reason for his speech.

"Recent events over the past two weeks have stirred emotions and created divisions among us, unlike anything we've seen in over 1,300 years. Tonight, I'd like to address those issues.

"In an attempt to cope with the devastating aftereffects on Mars over a year ago due to Satanic influence, our military sequestered certain individuals undergoing DNA changes on the way to becoming what we have since termed 'Clawfeet.' Clawfeet were the creatures that originally wreaked havoc on Mars tens of

thousands of years ago and recently posed a similar threat to that planet and Earth. Those few individuals were placed into stasis with the hope that our medical community could find a remedy for their condition. And indeed, they did. However, in helping them, they modified them into superhuman beings, the warriors now known as the Titans, whom the public now considers idols.

"Among the six we saved, Karen Stamos underwent an additional, and thoroughly unexpected, transformation. As well as becoming super-enhanced, she developed a third eye, an exceptional intellect, and an ability to communicate telepathically — a possible forerunner of the future of humanity.

"Additionally, a human who had already transformed into a Clawfoot integrated with the Bigfoot community in Canada, giving birth to the extraordinary being we've come to know as Samael, whom some consider an evil entity. This creature also possesses a third eye with advanced intuition and telepathic communication abilities.

"The program that changed those six individuals into ultimate warriors was dubbed 'Operation Apocalypse,' a name that should invoke dread among everyone. As your President and Commander-in-Chief, I expressed my concerns about the program. I advocated for its termination, but the military continued to work on it without my knowledge. Then, the World Federation assumed control, and I became doubly concerned. Though I repeatedly expressed my fears that the technology could be used for nefarious means, the Federation consistently ignored my pleas.

"However, the people have since spoken, with division and confrontation as their means of expressing displeasure with the program. In the days since the Titans' first appearance, the protests have escalated, leading to property destruction, injuries, and deaths.

"In light of these events, I held an emergency conference call with Lieutenant Colonel Nevins, head of Operation Apocalypse, and Sir Sharmi Dalvi, Secretary-General of the World Federation. Thankfully, we came to an agreement that since violence *only breeds violence, our only recourse is to scrub Operation Apocalypse.*

"Thankfully, the program to manipulate more humans into super beings is being disbanded. However, we must come together to embrace the transhumans we already created. In the traditional sense, their genetic manipulations alone don't make them heroes and they don't deserve to be considered idols. But their heightened abilities do present us with societal challenges and opportunities.

"As your President, I'm relieved that our military will not further weaponize these individuals or others. At the same time, as a United States and World Federation citizen, I must caution you against the other two members of the Titan team — Lilith and Samael. We must observe them carefully, assessing their behavior and supernatural influence over people's minds against what everyone knows to be true — that there is but one true God, whose only Son walked among us. We cannot allow these unnatural creatures to lead us astray.

"Thank you for your time tonight. Before I conclude, I ask that all of us pray, asking our Heavenly Father for the wisdom, faith, and strength to withstand all assaults of the evil one.

"May God bless you all, and may God bless the United States of America."

It was dark when Peter watched the president's speech at the U.S. Embassy in New Jerusalem. Now, at 5:30 a.m., Fiona Gabelli arrives at her office to find him there, in dire need of a caffeine boost.

"C'mon," she says. "I know a place that opens early."

Heading into the predawn light, the pair makes their way to a small shop just opening for the day.

"*Boker tov*," she says to the proprietor, then points to a booth near the back. "Let's talk in private," she tells Peter, leading the way to their seats.

After the couple orders coffee, Peter expresses the concern he's felt all morning.

"I think Larson was being too political. He should have been more forceful in his disapproval of the Nephilim. But I understand his position. I only hope that what he said was enough."

"Will the pope comment as well?"

"Yes, he was waiting to hear what Larson said. I hope his statement is clearer and more direct. You know, I'm worried about what Samael and Lilith will do about their human puppet. Doctor Abila seems happy to do whatever they say."

"Humankind needs to open their eyes to the threat right before them," says Fiona. "Let's order breakfast. There's nothing either of us can do at this point."

Peter picks up the menu and sighs.

"I'll let Pope Ignatius set the stage, then I'll also make a public statement. After that, it'll be up to the people to decide if they want to follow the Nephilim or God."

As the café fills up with locals, the two order light breakfasts of fruit and small pastries. Then Peter starts to notice the other customers starting their day together in the city once known for being home to three of humanity's major religions.

"Look around," he says to Fiona. "Some of these people are wearing the Knights Templar cross, while others are sporting Titan merchandise. It's good to know that not everyone's ready to fight when there's a difference of opinion."

"Yes, most people are tolerant of each other; they're just enjoying each other's company. It's the fanatics who get everyone stirred up."

"Oh," says Peter, picking up his communicator. "It's my wife. I'll take it outside."

Frank A. Ruffolo

Leaving the table, Peter stands on the sidewalk in front of the restaurant.

"Hi, hon; you're up early," he bursts out cheerfully.

Angela's voice tightens. "Pete, I'm always up early. You know your son won't let me sleep past five o'clock."

Peter winces inwardly, knowing he just activated a sore spot.

"Sorry. I'll try to help you out more when I get home. Um, anyway, how's the boss doing this morning?"

When Angela bursts into laughter, Peter sighs in relief.

"Hah. All he needs is a tiny business suit! Seriously, it's hard to remember a time when he wasn't around."

Peter responds wistfully, "I know what you mean. I wish I were with you guys right now."

"Me, too. I show him your photo every day. Listen, before he starts crying for some reason or other, I called to tell you that I think the president's speech went well. It was a little politically correct, but still firm. I know you probably wanted him to give more of a sermon. But that's your job, right?"

"Yeah. You always know what I'm thinking, Angie. Maybe you should be the Commander of the Ark."

A lengthy pause follows, then Angela replies, "No way, not me! Besides, I'm going to be doubly busy soon enough!"

Now it's Peter's turn to pause.

"Wait. What did you say?"

Angela's smile beams into the phone from Italy to Israel.

"Your family is expanding, Daddy! This time, it's gonna be a girl!"

Elated by the news, Peter can't help thinking that even with chaos and tribulation brewing on the horizon, our Heavenly Father still bestows the gift of new life upon His children.

264

God is ever powerful! Hallelujah!

Later that day, a formal statement from Pope Ignatius is released by the Vatican:

"Good people of God, the evil one is always waiting for the opportune time to strike, and that time is now. Do not be fooled by the giants called Samael and Lilith. They are the spawn of the fallen angel we call by many names: Satan, Beelzebub, Belial, the devil, the tempter, the ruler of demons. He is the disobedient angel who defied God. Through those vile offspring, Satan's prideful thoughts are now permeating the minds of God's children, poisoning them with his wicked, greedy, selfish ideas.

"We must remember that none of us is better than God the Father. We must not follow Samael and Lilith; they come from the prince of this and other worlds.

"Rebuke them, children of God! Honor our Messiah and His Mother with your loving obedience! Rebuke them and worship only our God in Heaven, the only one worthy of our love! Pray for those who admire the Nephilim. Repent and ask forgiveness, or retribution will come swiftly."

Reactions to President Larson and Pope Ignatius from news outlets around the universe come swiftly, and the majority broadcasters' contradictions of faith and secularism do nothing to quell the masses bent on rebellion. Most reject everything Pope Ignatius said. Only a few praise President Larson's restraint, leaving nowhere for the people to go to hear compromise.

As a result, protests continue to erupt in major cities across all continents, with pro-Templar and pro-Titan forces displaying their anger by burning effigies depicting opposing sides.

Nevertheless, as this conflict of good and evil spreads across the globe and the outer planets, more and more people are joining the ranks of the Templars, the side of good in this battle of ideas.

In desperation, legislators of all stripes call for peace while simultaneously engaging police and army units against citizens taking to the streets. The crackdowns only provoke riots and looting, each incurring more injuries and deaths. With the riots extending even to Mars, Detective Jacob Jacoby and his department have their hands full.

To halt the demonstrations, curfews are beginning to be imposed in many cities, with London, Moscow, Beijing, New York, Sydney, Sao Paolo, and Xanthe City being the latest. Mercifully, the curfews work, and tensions slowly ease.

Conversely, the pro-Titan members led by Colonel Chen Xi of the United Chinese Republic, are angered by how their followers are faring. Upset, they call for an emergency meeting of the World Federation.

The general populace seems to favor the Templars, but Xi and other world leaders are primarily pro-Titan.

Forty-eight hours before the urgent World Federation meeting begins, President Larson summons Peter Matteo and Austin Patton to Rome to meet with him and Pope Ignatius. The president wants to map out a strategy for the fate of humanity against the opposing forces of evil.

Secure in a private room guarded by the Swiss Guard, the Order of the Ravens, the Secret Service, and invisibly by Archangel Michael, Pope Ignatius opens the discussion with a prayer for knowledge and compassion. Then he calmly speaks to the assembled men.

"I have tasked my cardinals with gathering their bishops together to profess our concerns to every congregation in every corner of Earth and beyond. We must do everything we can to stop this madness and return to the Father."

Owing to special knowledge, Peter interrupts the pope.

"Your Holiness, I've been told what we must do to protect ourselves from God's wrath. Metatron, God's holy messenger, told me that if this folly continues, God will impose three days of darkness as punishment. During that time, everyone must protect their homes with the Rosary our Loving Mother gave us. We must display Our Lady's beads above the doorways to our homes and affix them to the windows and other openings. For those three days, we must sequester ourselves indoors with beeswax candles and food. We are not to open our doors for any reason and must cover our windows to avoid looking outside. Though we may hear moaning and crying and pounding on our doors, we must not open our homes to anyone. The noises we hear will be evil spirits imitating our loved ones to trick us into letting them in. If we give in, we will perish."

Pope Ignatius nods, adding, "Our Lord is merciful. But He also chastises His people."

"To save our people, we must convince the World Federation to call for my help as Commander of the Ark with the assistance of the archangels," says Peter. "Together, we can eliminate Samael and Lilith, the demon children of the Malignant."

President Larson asks, "What about the Titans? Aren't they also part of Satan's plan?"

"No, the other five pose no threat to humankind. They're merely pawns the Evil One is using for his own means. In any case, they won't live long. They were engineered to live only a short time, possibly ten years at the most."

"What? This is the first time I'm hearing about this!"

declares Larson. "Your Holiness, did you know?"

"No, I did not," states the pontiff.

"It's unfortunate," admits Peter. "I don't think the subjects know about it either. While they live, we must provide for them as best we can, for they're not the problem. Your Holiness, please tell your cardinals to inform your flock about the three days of darkness. The Father Himself will notify the faithful before it happens, so they need to be prepared; it can occur at any time. To avoid this punishment, we must work diligently and swiftly, for the Malignant will certainly be working against us at every turn."

"Precisely," asserts the pope. "The father of lies will do whatever he can to fill Gehenna with souls."

"We must be strong in the face of the enemy," agrees President Larson. "I've directed my agents to solicit as many Federation representatives as possible to oppose the giants and work for peace. The opposition may outnumber us, but we may still be able to force a favorable resolution. Many world leaders want the violence to end, which could work in our favor."

Austin Patton, who was listening quietly to the conversation, is unconvinced.

Shaking his head, he declares, "Sorry, Mr. President, but I have no confidence in any politicians other than you. There's no doubt most of them will cave to pressure. They may work to save society from further violence, but will they save souls?"

Larson sighs. "I need to continue pressuring my people to convince the Federation to end this at their emergency meeting. Some of them have given me encouraging reports. But General, for the most part, you're right. A resolution for peace may only delay the inevitable."

Hoping mankind will ultimately triumph against wickedness, the pontiff poses a differing opinion.

"I believe a delay could be beneficial. It could give us time to gain more support for the common good. More importantly, it could allow Peter and the angels to resolve this before God will have to step in."

CHAPTER THIRTY-FIVE

In the solitude of the desert facility, Nevins and Abila are working out phase two of their push to influence the acceptance of Samael and Lilith as humankind's saviors. After the disastrous outcomes of their initial introductions, they want to shift the focus from the Titans' superior powers to asserting they're simply ordinary people with enhanced physical abilities, leaving out any references to them as weapons of war.

Joining them in the closed-door meeting is Jennifer Stone, an atheistic marketing manager and a recent graduate of Columbia University. New to the team, Jennifer is intended to become the fresh, young face of the program. The program's architects hope her ideas will appeal to the younger crowd, and they're counting on her marketing expertise to promote their "creations" in the best possible light.

Just as the organizers hoped, Jennifer is confident about her strategy, although neither she, Nevins, nor Abila are aware that Samael has been manipulating her for this very moment. All of them believe Jennifer's ideas are entirely her own.

The men restate their updated goals, then give Jennifer the floor to describe her approach.

Thanking them, she begins bluntly, "It's obvious that your previous strategy failed miserably. I intend to fix that with a multi-pronged course of action."

Taken aback, Nevins and Abila glance at each other. Then Nevins bursts into a grin.

"You sound pretty confident," he states. "Let's hear what you have in mind."

Maintaining eye contact with the assertive military leader, she declares, "First, your military experimental operation must be revealed and rebuked in a very public way." Looking from one man to the other, she adds candidly, "No matter the cost to your egos."

Again, Nevins smiles, but Doctor Abila is more circumspect.

"You must distance yourselves from all secrecy and eliminate all warlike connotations."

Nevins likes what he hears. "Okay, we already agreed to that," he says. "What else?"

Encouraged by the lieutenant colonel's reaction, Jennifer continues, "Second, the Titans must split up."

"Whoa, wait just a minute," retorts Nevins, his grin morphing into a scowl. "You want to break up the team? Why?" he demands, daring the young professional to explain herself.

"My plan involves Xanthe Robotics and the Galactic Basketball Association. I propose that Private Frank Giletti and Corporal Richard Alvarez be promoted to sergeant and given honorable discharges. Then, after they return to civilian life, Xanthe Robotics will employ them as company spokespersons. The robotics company is eager to announce that the innovations they provided to Giletti and Alvarez will be available to disabled persons across the galaxy. They also want to showcase their next generation of AI enhancements, so hiring the men will be a win for them. As a bonus, the popular Titans will also be out front in the company's campaign to introduce their new manufacturing facility in Las Vegas.

"Of the other three Titans, Lieutenant Robert Lawson will be given the rank of Captain. Then, he'll be discharged. As a private citizen, he'll join Tim Farley and Jonathan Harrington as spokespersons for the GBA. I've already approached that

Frank A. Ruffolo

organization about bringing the men on board."

Hearing this, Doctor Abila recalls his awkward conversation with the Titans.

"That's basically what Tim suggested! He's also clamoring to reunite with his wife. Please include bringing Jane here as soon as Tim is released from us."

Jennifer Stone smiles broadly. "That's already done. I've contacted Jane, and she's excited to see Tim again and to tour the galaxy with him, Lawson, and Harrington. The GBA intends to highlight the basketball prowess of the three former Titans in public exhibition games. In my talks with the commissioner, I insisted that the men should no longer be known as Titans. I believe we must eliminate that word from our vocabularies to ease tensions and to encourage them to become accepted as normal human beings. Through no fault of their own, they were thrust into an experimental program without their knowledge, and we must emphasize that."

Doctor Abila is now happy to support Jennifer's plan, but Nevins is still skeptical.

"What does the basketball association say about all this?" he asks.

"The GBA commissioner told me privately that if all goes well, he'll most likely place the three men in a draft as professional basketball players. If that happens, I'm sure the bidding among the teams will be fierce."

Nevins, still proud of his program's achievements despite the setbacks, thrusts out his chin. "That should make those ingrates happy we changed them," he declares smugly.

Stunned by the military man's lack of empathy, Stone steals a glance at Abila. But the doctor has heard this and worse, so he prods her to continue.

"Um, is there more to your presentation?"

"Yes, there's more," Jennifer replies, rifling through paperwork. "Okay, on to our star members. I suggest we pause Samael and Lilith's publicity tours completely. I believe it would be detrimental to continue them until tensions ease across the galaxy and the five ex-Titans are accepted in their new roles."

"Uh, Abila and I already decided to cut the tour short and concentrate on closed venues," says Nevins.

"I know, but I still think it would be better to let them lie low for a while. I floated my ideas to Colonel Chen Xi, who agreed to promote them as a compromise to ordering the protests to be shut down. He did insist on one concession, though."

"And what's that?" asks Doctor Abila.

"He insists on making sure that Samael and Lilith continue to be known as ultimate humans, supreme beings. He refuses to allow us to diminish their standings in any way."

"Well, I'm all for that!" agrees Doctor Abila, relieved that his beloved Lilith wouldn't have to relinquish any of her enormous popularity.

Jennifer is pleased that the doctor agrees.

"As soon as the worlds quiet down, we'll reintroduce Samael and Lilith through the media appearances you already planned in major cities. But this time, we'll present them as kind and thoughtful messengers of peace. I've crafted enhanced bios for each of them, and I'll include them in a major press release. I want everyone to get to know them personally, to accept them as individual beings with special gifts."

Excited by the prospect of new tours, Abila asks, "Where will they go first?"

"I'm thinking of re-launching them with a public appearance in a setting that would generate more interest. It's not finalized; there are still some logistics I need to iron out."

With Lilith's reputation secure, the doctor declares, "Well, it seems you've thought of everything."

Nevins isn't as convinced. "You said Colonel Xi's in favor of your ideas, yet the Federation is still going ahead with that emergency meeting. Have you thought about adverse consequences?"

Jennifer's eyes bore into the hardheaded soldier.

"The World Federation's meeting is in Rome in forty-eight hours, and I'm ready for it. We know heated points will be brought up from each side, so I sent a team to their headquarters. I instructed them to organize supporters to discourage religious zealots from gathering anywhere near the site. Gentlemen, I'm one hundred and ten percent committed to keeping these extraordinary beings in place for the benefit of all humankind."

Nevins is impressed by Jennifer's poise and thoroughness.

"Seems we made the right decision in hiring you," he admits sheepishly. "Just one thing, though. Tell us where you're planning to hold that re-launch. I have a lot of influence in the government, and I can help you with permitting and other details."

Jennifer cock's her head, secretly pleased that she put a crack in the soldier's façade. "The location I'm looking at is Gabriel's Tower."

"Wow. Really?" asks a surprised Doctor Abila. "Isn't that the unusual geologic feature also called Bear Lodge and Devil's Tower, among other things? It's near the Belle Fourche River in Wyoming, right?"

"That's the one. During my research, I discovered some interesting things about it. Did you know that they named that strange-looking feature Devil's Tower after an interpreter incorrectly translated the native Indian name to 'bad god's tower'? They changed it to Gabriel's Tower to honor Archangel Gabriel after they discovered his chalice on the Moon."

"Hmm, I seem to remember reading that," responds

Abila.

Ambassador Gabelli has invited Peter and Austin to accompany her to the World Federation hearing with President Larson and his delegation.

Seated in the audience, they listen with nervous anticipation to Secretary-General Dalvi's introduction.

Halfway through Dalvi's speech, a commotion interrupts him. Looking offstage, he sees Colonel Chen Xi making his way to the podium, pushing aside aides who try to block his path.

The colonel makes a beeline for Dalvi and whispers in his ear. In response, Dalvi raises his brows and looks Xi square in the eye.

"Please excuse the interruption," the secretary-general tells the audience. "Honored members, dignitaries, and guests, before President James Larson of the United States delivers his speech, it has come to my attention that Colonel Chen Xi of the United China Republic may have a solution to the problem we are here to discuss. Therefore, with apologies to President Larson, I ask Colonel Xi to speak next. This will give the distinguished president of the United States time to reflect on this development along with the rest of us. Colonel Xi, the podium is yours."

Assuming the place vacated by Dalvi, the outspoken Xi declares, "Thank you, Secretary-General. I apologize to President Larson, the distinguished members of this assembly, and our honored guests. Today, I bring greetings from the United China Republic and a viable solution to the pressing issue of the Titans and their leaders, Samael and Lilith."

Amid mumbles among the attendees, he states, "Within a short time, a great rift has developed within the populace of every Federation member, a distressing problem that needs to be addressed quickly and decisively. Members of the Directorate on both sides of the issue have been in urgent discussions to find a solution to the violence, destruction, and death, ripping our societies apart, pitting men against women, mothers against daughters, sons against fathers.

"I welcome President Larson's announcement of the dissolution of Operation Apocalypse as a great start to end these problems. To build on the president's positive act, the United China Republic has determined that the Titans should be reintroduced to society through new roles that have nothing to do with weaponry. In addition, Samael and Lilith should restart their goodwill tour through the galaxy to assist humanity in moving our societies toward a new beginning.

"Our proposals are outlined in a report my staff will send to each of you within the hour. President Larson has already received a copy, and I sincerely ask him to accept it for the good of humankind.

"Once again, I apologize to President Larson for overtaking his speaker slot, and I thank Secretary-General Dalvi for allowing me to interrupt today's meeting."

Xi steps down from the stage to thunderous applause, stopping in front of President Larson to extend his hand.

With an icy smile plastered on his face, the president shakes the colonel's hand, whispering, "Well played, Colonel. You've claimed our ideas as your own."

Next to speak is President Larson.

"Secretary-General Dalvi, Colonel Xi, honored delegates, and guests, I have just torn up the speech I wrote for this emergency meeting, so now I will speak directly from my heart.

"I sincerely applaud the efforts of Colonel Xi and his colleagues to end the conflicts pulling our peoples apart. Disbanding Operation Apocalypse is indeed the first step in resolving our disputes without further distress, and moving the Titans into civilian life is necessary to ensure their future well-being.

"As for Samael and Lilith, I disagree with the Colonel's assessment of their benefit to society. I sternly warn this Federation against approving that part of his plan. Allowing them to continue on the path he suggested will open us all to forces that are out of our control. As keepers of the peace of this world and all others under Federation authority, I implore all of you to pay close attention to the Commander of the Ark, who is here with us today. I appeal to you in the strongest terms to call upon him in this hour of distress. Under the guises of the creatures we call Samael and Lilith, a fundamental evil operates among us, waiting for the opportune time to release its power.

"Therefore, I will not vote to accept the resolution as stated. Instead, I propose separating it into two parts, one concerning Operation Apocalypse and the Titans, and the other Samael and Lilith. As separate resolutions, I will vote to accept the first but not the second.

"Please consider your votes carefully; the fate of millions upon millions in this generation and others to come depends on what you do today. Remember what Peter said about Samael and Lilith: they are Nephilim, the fallen angels who defied Almighty God once before and who want nothing more than to bring all of us down into the abyss to dwell with them in darkness and despair.

"Thank you for listening; I pray that you choose wisely. The fate of humanity depends on what you do today."

As the assembly stands, some applauding and others frowning, Colonel Xi joins President Larson at the podium, where each waves to their supporters.

Seated in the gallery, Peter and Austin glance dejectedly at one another.

"He did what he could, and he was much more forceful

today," says Austin. "This is politics; you give and take, and the battle continues."

Peter scans the room, praying that the assembly votes as Lawson advocated. Then he turns to Austin.

"This war is far from over, my friend."

Overhearing her guests' conversation, Fiona sighs deeply and turns to Peter.

"You may as well return to New Jerusalem. It appears this saga will continue for a while longer."

While the room empties around them, Peter responds, "The guardians will let me know what I need to do next."

"Very well," she replies as a Secret Service agent steps up to them.

"Apologies, Ambassador," the agent says to Fiona. "President Larson requests the presence of you and your guests for lunch. Follow me, please."

CHAPTER THIRTY-SIX

Two days later, Area 51 readies itself for the arrival of VIPs in the cool desert morning. Marketing Manager Jennifer Stone scheduled this event to introduce the team to select invitees. She intends to start the event as early as possible to avoid the heat that will undoubtedly rise as the sun tracks higher in the sky.

First to arrive is Arlynn Stout and his entourage, touching down in Arlynn's private hypersonic transport just after dawn.

While they await entry, dignitaries, including public figures and local luminaries, arrive along with the ever-present media in a steady stream. Bringing up the rear, a caravan carrying Rick Jackson, the GBA commissioner and former player, and his staff pull up.

Known as an imposing figure, Jackson towers over most at seven foot nine inches. Keen to meet the Xanthe Robotics CEO, Jackson steps away from his entourage to introduce himself to Stout, a diminutive Martian. Chatting amiably, the Mutt and Jeff duo of the 37th century enter the bunker side-by-side, eliciting amused glances from security guards.

Inside the base's spartan meeting hall, Jennifer Stone and her staff have outdone themselves for this exclusive private event. The utilitarian room exudes an air of elegance with tastefully decorated tables and chairs artfully arranged to create a welcoming ambiance. A lavish buffet breakfast, elegantly displayed along one wall, is skillfully tended by smartly dressed servers, adding a touch of sophistication.

Mingling among the guests, Lieutenant Colonel Hollis Nevins and Doctor Anthony Abila exchange pleasantries and small talk with each dignitary.

While the guests wait for the proceedings, Arlynn Stout, not known for his patience, becomes impatient. He seeks out Nevins and corners him, his frustration evident.

"I didn't fly 38 million miles to have breakfast in a bunker, Nevins. My time is money. Shall we get on with this, or would you rather I leave now so you can deal with this on your own?"

Repulsed by the CEO's condescension, Nevins' mind races with choice verbs and pronouns while silently assigning Stout a Napoleon complex. Outwardly, he responds in a composed, politician-like manner.

"Mr. Stout, of course we're honored to have you here today. Not to worry; we'll begin immediately."

Tapping his headpiece, he signals Jennifer, who responds by stepping onto a stage at the far end of the hall. Above her, a holographic projection of the American flag waves as if caught by a breeze.

"Hello, everyone!" declares Stone, opening the gathering. "Honored guests, thank you for attending today! Please take your seats; we're about to begin."

As the guests settle down, she declares, "I'd like to welcome the distinguished Mr. Arlynn Stout, CEO and Chairman of Xanthe Robotics, and Mr. Rick Jackson, Commissioner of the Galactic Basketball Association!"

Amid a smattering of polite applause, she states, "I'd also like to introduce our former Titans — Sergeant Frank Giletti, Sergeant Richard Alvarez, Captain Robert Lawson, Mr. Tim Farley, and Mr. Jonathan Harrington!"

Striding out from behind a curtain, the five enhanced humans stop at the front of the stage, eliciting gasps and applause from the audience. With their arresting statures, muscular physiques, and matching one-piece jumpsuits, they present an impressive sight to those seeing them in person for the first time.

Turning to Stout, Rick Jackson shares, "Now, that's an unbeatable GBA team!"

As the applause subsides, Jennifer singles out Arlynn Stout, gazing up at the stage with pride.

"Mr. Stout, there's no doubt that the engineering magic of your company, Xanthe Robotics, is singlehandedly responsible for improving the lives of Frank and Richard to the point where they can function normally. Without the technology your company developed, they'd never be able to take even one step on their own. In gratitude for your team's excellent work, both men are eager to join your company as its very first spokespersons!"

Louder applause elicits acknowledging nods and smiles from Arlynn, who stands and waves, lapping up the attention.

To quiet the audience, Jennifer points out the others on the stage.

"The remaining three have Mr. Jackson to thank for their bright futures. At Mr. Jackson's invitation, Robert, Tim, and Jonathan will showcase their special abilities on the basketball court as exhibition players for the GBA!"

Caught up in the audience's excitement, she ad-libs to Rick Jackson, "In fact, there's a court at our base where you can join them in a little one-on-one game if you'd like."

From his seat in the audience, Jackson chuckles, "I'd love to see their skills on the court! They'll probably make me look helplessly inept, but I've never backed down from a challenge! And if Frank and Richard want to join us, I'm game for a little three-on-three!" Looking around, he adds, "I'm sure everyone here would enjoy the show!"

Stout joins in the abundant laughter, adding, "Please invite Samael and Lilith to join us as well, as long as they promise not to use their thoughts to affect the outcome! We've all heard many good things about them, and I, for one, am anxious to meet Lilith!"

Turning to Jackson, Arlynn leans over to whisper, "I've been told that many can't resist her charms."

It's early afternoon in New Jerusalem when Peter gathers his belongings to return to his family in Italy. Archangel Michael told him there's no immediate need for him to be close to the Holy of Holies, so he readily agreed to go home. He knows the guardians will call him if they require his presence again.

Taking a break from packing, Peter sits on the edge of the bed and calls Angela.

"Hi, hon. How's everything going?" asks Angela while she feeds Michael small spoonfuls of mashed sweet potatoes. "I heard what happened at the World Federation meeting."

"Then you know things aren't good. There's a bit of calm now, so I'm leaving the temple and should be home in a couple of hours. We'll need to stay in Sorrento until… Well, you know. See you soon. Love you loads!"

On the basketball court with the Titans, the GBA commissioner feels inadequate for the first time. The Titans' outside shooting ability outshines him tenfold, and there's no contest when it comes to rebounding. The Titans are clearly dominating the game.

Midway through the match, Samael and Lilith arrive courtside, the eyes of every onlooker widening at their overpowering presence. The game stops as everyone's attention focuses on the massive creatures.

In her trademark jumpsuit and three-lensed sunglasses, Lilith's beauty captivates men and women alike. Pretending not to notice their stares, she searches the crowd for Doctor Abila, joining him after two long strides.

Without his companion, Samael commands all the attention. His hairless head, deep olive skin, and enormous physique project the aura of dominance he's become known for.

Calling to him from the free throw line, Rick Jackson asks, "Hey! How about taking a shot?" Joining in, Farley flips Samael the ball, which almost disappears into his large hands.

From his place about ten feet from the top of one key, Samael turns away from the court and flips the ball over his shoulder, easily making the shot at the other end without hitting the rim.

When the ball drops in, he laughs, a deep guttural sound that would be eerie in any other situation. With a shrug, he says, "It would be more challenging if the court and ball were triple the size, and the hoops were at twenty feet. Leaving things the way they are, my friends here will make perfect basketball players. Please proceed, Mr. Jackson. This game intrigues me."

Surprised that Samael knows his name, Rick retrieves the ball, and the game picks up where it left off.

Peter and Angela take an early evening *passeggiata* pushing Michael in his stroller down Corso Italia, the main road through Sorrento. With throngs of other Italian families and tourists delighting in this pleasant Italian custom, they relax and try to forget about world events.

At their favorite gelateria, Angela waits outside with the stroller while Peter enters the shop to order their nightly treat.

Inside, he's brought sharply back to reality by a group of teenagers in Samael and Lilith T-shirts and blue-tinted, three-lensed sunglasses. It saddens him to watch them press their foreheads together to greet their similarly adorned friends.

Nearby, another group wearing Templar crosses interacts peacefully with other Titanites while they all stand in line together, bringing Peter a measure of hope. He reasons that if these groups can put aside their differences, perhaps the galaxy could be saved after all.

Still, while Peter is pleased that no ill will prevails among these young people, he's concerned at how quickly they've raised the Nephilim to cult-like status.

Peter rejoins his family and moves them to an empty bench to enjoy their classic Italian frozen desserts.

While Angela shares her treat with Michael, she notices the teenagers spilling out of the gelateria.

"Oh, look at them," she sighs. "The young people are being conditioned to accept the unacceptable."

Agreeing, Peter glances at Angela's belly, wondering what type of society their new baby will encounter.

Finishing his cone, he wipes his mouth with a napkin.

"I hope they come to their senses if and when we solve this," he says, clinging to as much optimism as he can.

Craving a normal evening without worry, Angela interjects, "We can't do anything tonight, though."

"No, we can't," agrees Peter. "So, how about this? Let's stroll down near the docks. Mike loves looking at the fishing boats. We'll sip some wine, look at the sea, and enjoy Sorrento."

Angela gives her husband the side-eye.

"You can enjoy a glass of wine for both of us. I can't drink for a while, remember? So I'll just have *una tazza di caffè*."

CHAPTER THIRTY-SEVEN

Today, a ribbon-cutting ceremony will officially open Xanthe Robotics' new manufacturing facility outside the Las Vegas Strip. The plant is the first outside Mars to contain an impressive workforce of pioneering robotic construction workers toiling 24/7 with no break in production.

To open the event, Arlynn Stout will introduce a special guest, AI model XC010, revision Alpha A. The AI was granted a temporary travel visa thanks to Arlynn's political connections and generous gifts to the State Department.

The alpha version of model XC010 known as Galina, the former AI escort with human emotions, will assist Frank Giletti and Richard Alvarez in cutting the ceremonial ribbon.

While the press and public arrive, landscapers scramble to put in their final touches, and the atmosphere becomes charged with anticipation. The stage is set for a memorable event celebrating the cutting-edge advancements of Xanthe Robotics.

Before Galina accepted the invitation to participate in the grand opening, she requested permission from Mr. Stout to bring a guest. Since leaving the casino, the former escort has been trying to integrate into society, even adopting the surname Sharapova, but she's still unsure of herself. Consequently, she was greatly relieved when Detective David Jacoby agreed to accompany her to Earth.

Without the constant presence of her former co-workers, Galina craves the support and companionship of someone she knows.

For her, Detective Jacoby fits that bill in more ways than one.

Though it's almost ten a.m. in Las Vegas, the desert metropolis is surprisingly pleasant for today's event, an enormous relief to Arlynn. The weather forecast suggested uncomfortably hot weather, causing him to worry unnecessarily.

On a specially erected stage, a podium studded with microphones sits front and center, ensuring everyone a good view. To the right of the stage are a large, covered object and a ceremonial ribbon ready for cutting.

Waiting in the wings, Arlynn Stout stands ahead of his new spokespersons dressed in their familiar jumpsuits, with Galina in business casual attire, fidgeting next to him.

Always thinking, Arlynn turns, craning his neck to talk to Richard and Frank behind him.

"Remind me to order you two some normal-looking clothing. Those outfits make you look like convicts."

At a nod from a local media producer, Arlynn begins the proceedings. Walking to the podium, he steps onto a small platform to help him reach the microphones to address his guests.

"Good morning, everyone! I'm delighted and humbled to see so many of you here today to celebrate the dawn of a new manufacturing era in beautiful Las Vegas!

"At Xanthe Robotics, our driving philosophy is to enhance the lives and well-being of humanity through synthetic lifeforms and advanced robotic technology. Building upon the pioneering work of trendsetter Arlynn Fisk, the man who introduced AI intelligence to common household products in the 21st century, my company expanded upon

Fisk's concepts and included them in the AI robotics and artificial lifeforms he could only dream of.

"In accordance with our company's goals, we also developed superior ways to benefit individuals with disabilities and handicaps, modifying them into advanced humanoids. Our company seeks to integrate these enhanced humans into society as a new race of people with AI capabilities. To that end, we're working closely with political leaders to grant them citizenship status on every planet in the World Federation, as they have already achieved on Mars.

"To demonstrate the effectiveness of our inventions, it is my supreme pleasure to pass the microphone to our honored guest, Miss Galina Sharapova!"

Relinquishing the podium, Arlynn starts the applause for Galina, who nudges the small platform out of the way and adjusts the microphones to accommodate her loftier height.

"Good morning," she begins nervously. "I want to extend my heartfelt gratitude to Mr. Arlynn Stout for permitting me to leave Mars and allowing me to be part of this historic ribbon-cutting event. I am Model XC010 Revision Alpha, an AI humanoid and current real estate agent originally from Xanthe City. Though I appear to be in my mid-twenties in human age, I am only eighteen months old, with many brothers and sisters similarly developed through Xanthe Robotics' technological engineering feats.

"We are a family at Xanthe Robotics. For all practical purposes, we are humans with mechanical components. We feel emotions, fear death, and crave love and companionship, just like you. The only difference between us is that we cherish life in all its forms, and would never do anything to harm it.

"Today, I have the distinct privilege of unveiling the statue that will grace the front of this facility. My hope is that this image will be a constant reminder of how far we have come. After I undrape the statue, Mr. Giletti and Mr.

Alvarez will cut the ribbon opening the facility, and introduce themselves to you."

With that, Galina pulls a cord, exposing a dramatic sculpture of the AI enthusiast reaching for the stars. While the audience applauds, the media captures the moment through various mediums.

As folks in the crowd record the event for their own use, Frank and Richard step toward the ribbon and cut it with oversized laser cutters, eliciting another round of applause.

As the material falls away, Frank begins his introduction.

"Hello," he says, speaking through a remote microphone because he's too tall for the conventional mics. "I'm Sergeant Frank Giletti from the great city of Chicago. Sergeant Alvarez and I are two of the soldiers who volunteered for what was meant to be our world's ultimate warrior program. Because of severe flaws in our transitions, we were destined to be maimed for life. However, through the efforts of Mr. Arlynn Stout and the brilliant engineering minds at Xanthe Robotics, we're now even better examples of Xanthe Robotics' capabilities. The company restored us to normal function, and we're eternally grateful to them. With their technology, our legs, lower arms, and hands have been replaced, and we're now well and normal, only much taller than before.

"Our artificial limbs may make us look different, but nothing else about us has changed. Our enhancements pose no threat to society. We're merely different.

"To demonstrate our gratitude to the enormously talented group of individuals at Xanthe Robotics, we're pleased to announce that we've been asked to join the company as emissaries, showcasing the benefits artificially enhanced humans can bring to humankind.

"Now, I'm honored to introduce my friend, Sergeant Richard Alvarez."

"Greetings," says Richard, speaking through a similar remote mic. "As Frank said, he and I are two of the remaining volunteers from our nation's severely flawed experimental program. Tragically, one of our fellow volunteers didn't survive the transition. But the others — Colonel Robert Lawson and citizens Tim Farley and Jonathan Harrington — are also moving on to bigger and better things. If you haven't heard, they've been recruited by the Galactic Basketball Association to embark on exhibition tours that will showcase their enormous talents.

"Collectively, we, the former Titans, are all unique individuals. Together, we're forever grateful to Mr. Stout and Xanthe Robotics for making our lives livable.

"Thank you all for being here today."

Applause fills the air as Arlynn returns to the podium, sliding the small platform back in place with his foot. To conclude the ceremony, he invites everyone to tour the new facility with a buffet lunch afterward.

Before the tour begins, David catches up to Galina.

"You did great," he tells her, knowing she needs assurance that she did well. "I'm proud of you. Thanks for inviting me."

Beaming, Galina grabs his arm and pulls him aside, leading him into an unoccupied corridor.

"Jake, I have a confession," she says, turning to face him. "I asked you to come on this trip with me because I am falling in love with you."

Bewildered, David pulls his arm away.

When Jacoby closed the AI murder case, he no longer had a reason to interact with Galina, and he found himself missing her. That confused him. He didn't know what to make of it since he always detested technology that tried to replace humans. He tried hard to put thoughts of her aside by spending more time with women he knew, but the humanoid robot always crept back into his mind.

"I, uh... I don't know what to say," he replies, stalling for time to collect his thoughts.

Convinced she said something wrong, Galina mutters, "Never mind," and turns to join the crowd heading to lunch. But David pulls her back.

"Um... You surprised me, that's all," he tells her. "I've missed you, sweetie."

Later that day, Peter, Angela, her family, and others worldwide gather to watch a replay of the proceedings that heralded the opening of the Xanthe Robotics plant in Las Vegas. As the first of its kind outside Mars, people are interested in following the topic since the company promises its products will benefit humankind.

When Galina appears on the screen, Angela and her aunt point at her, visibly shocked by her striking humanlike appearance.

"My goodness!" exclaims Angela amid scattered comments from the family. "She talks and acts just like a human being! How could she be an android?"

Everyone, including Angela, looks to Peter, seeking his reaction.

Posing the question on their minds, Uncle Giovanni asks, "What do you think, Commander?"

Wishing to reply appropriately, Peter takes a minute to formulate his response. Then, he looks at each person, saying, "As Commander of the Ark, what I can say is that this is what happens when we meddle in God's creation. We've brought about artificial life — machines that can think and display emotions that seem to be human."

Dismayed, the family starts talking all at once.

"But are they self-aware? Do they believe in a higher power? What's going to become of us?"

Quietly, Angela worries about the upcoming generations, thinking of Michael sleeping peacefully in the other room.

Listening to the conversation, Peter has the same questions.

"I'm pretty certain God the Father isn't pleased at what we've done. We may have gone too far this time."

As if responding to the family's anxieties, a bright light suddenly fills the room, and Archangel Gabriel appears, addressing Peter.

"Commander, we are always attentive to your situation. Whatever humans create ultimately comes from God the Father. It is He who gave humans the intelligence to construct what they need, and if what they produce turns out to be a curse, then it is a curse. Throughout your history, humanity has created what is good, like penicillin derived from mold, and what is exceedingly bad, like weapons of war from splitting atoms. Science has developed the means to create life and to end it. Have human beings become gods? Or are they merely displaying the complexities of good and evil inherent in their natures? This is the challenge humanity must grapple with. Peter, pray that you will not have to deal with this question as Commander of the Ark."

CHAPTER THIRTY-EIGHT

Inside the expansive reception area of the new manufacturing facility, dignitaries, attendees, and the media are all trying to get acquainted with the star of today's show — the human-looking artificial intelligence machine.

Surprisingly, their focus isn't on Frank or Richard, multi-million-dollar men in their own rights, but on Galina. She alone has stolen the entire presentation and, apparently, every heart. Everyone wants a closer look at the attractive female creature featuring humanlike grace and extraordinary machine intelligence wrapped up in an astonishing artificial creation.

"Galina! How do you like Earth? Turn this way!" shout the press, each clamoring for a bit of her for their news feeds. They keep pushing, asking questions, taking pictures, and shoving mics in her face until she wants to scream. She's not used to being the center of so much attention and isn't comfortable with any of it.

At her wit's end, she locks eyes with David, pleading for help.

Coming to her defense, he bellows, "All right, that's enough!" and shields Galina with his arms. "I think it's time for all of you to move on! Richard and Frank are the ones you need to talk to! Galina's leaving now!"

Pushing through the crush of media persons, David pulls the android past Arlynn, also upset by the hubbub.

Waving a hand, the company's CEO directs his security

crew to intervene, and they respond by guiding the crowd to the reception area where the ex-Titans are fielding questions.

As the press moves on, Arlynn edges up to Galina.

"I'm sorry you went through that," he apologizes. "I had no idea they'd be so interested in you. However...on second thought...I shouldn't be surprised. You're a beautiful example of my work, the shining face of Xanthe Robotics now and into the future!"

Still uncomfortable, Galina sighs, looks at David, then turns to Arlynn.

"Mr. Stout, you are like a father to me. But... I do not want to be the face of Xanthe Robotics. I want to live a simple life as Galina Sharapova, a professional woman...in love with a wonderful man. I only want to be a normal person."

Leaning in, she kisses Arlynn on the cheek and pats him on the arm. Then she tells David, "Jake, please take me to my hotel. I do not want any of this. All I want is to be with you."

David links arms with Galina and shakes Arlynn's hand. Then he and the almost-human robot walk off, leaving Arlynn to stare after them wistfully.

Out of nowhere, Stout experiences an unexpected wave of nostalgia, as if his only daughter were leaving the family.

Rick Jackson is elated. He's been watching all the recaps of Arlynn Stout's captivating dog and pony show opening the new facility, and his enthusiasm for adding the superhumans to his team is growing. Wasting no time, he arranges an exhibition game between his new associates and seasoned GBA ballers to capitalize on the universal excitement.

Enlisting the help of influential friends in society's upper echelons, he obtains unheard-of permission to build a temporary basketball court in Rockefeller Plaza. Holding the event in the heart of midtown Manhattan is a major part of the GBA commissioner's strategy to promote his beloved game and to showcase its newest stars.

To advertise the event, Rick arranges for Robert, Tim, and Jonathan to appear on *Daytime America*, a popular morning show transmitted throughout the galaxy through GBS Data Communications.

Press reports and news stories about the manufacturing plant continue to circulate throughout the Galactic Federation. The century's newest stars, Frank Giletti, Richard Alvarez, and Galina Sharapova, led by Arlynn Stout, dominate news cycles everywhere.

Notably, none of the reports include Samael or Lilith, significant omissions that create tension in the desert living quarters of the two colossuses. Samael is extraordinarily upset that Galina has stolen his thunder, so much so that he plots to get rid of her before Lilith calms him down.

Ultimately agreeing with his soulmate, the son of Satan analyzes the situation with a clearer head, leaving his emotions out of the equation. In due course, he recognizes that the current circumstances could work to his advantage. Together, he and Lilith plot to forge a new awakening.

Their ultimate goal is to become humanity's new messiahs, to convince people that what they truly desire is to echo their father's diabolical wishes.

To do this, they will use all their wiles, not with heavy-handed shouts but with delicate whispers.

However, even as the two work closely together toward the same objective, Lilith has learned to be increasingly on guard with Samael. For some reason, Lilith's former persona as Karen Stamos has been making herself known to Lilith more and more each day.

To prevent Samael from knowing this, Lilith is burying all thoughts of Karen deep in her mind, and the effort is taking a toll on her.

Marketing manager Jennifer Stone rushes into Lieutenant Colonel Nevins' office suite expecting an immediate audience. However, the officer is busy, so his military assistant advises her to have a seat.

Too excited to sit, Jennifer paces the waiting area until finally, Nevins opens the door.

"Come in," beckons the leader of the defunct experimental military program. "Sorry about the delay. Corporal, please bring us coffee."

Though Nevins' rank entitles him to better accommodations, the starkly efficient style of his office's beige walls and uncomfortable furnishings suit him fine.

Sitting next to an American flag and a stock photograph of President Larson, Nevins leans far back in his chair, peering at his visitor as if she were wasting his time.

"Well?" he asks gruffly.

Self-conscious under the man's impatient gaze, Jennifer adjusts her skirt and flicks a stray hair from her face.

"I have a proposal."

"Go on," he orders.

"People consistently show their support for the Titans with T-shirts and other Titan merchandise, including those fancy three-lensed sunglasses. Since the Titans no longer exist as a group, we need to shift our focus to Samael and Lilith. I suggest we do that by promoting them as 'special' humans. No more glitzy T-shirts inviting comparisons to rock stars. They need a new image with their own fashion design incorporating those tinted sunglasses. I'm thinking of using shades of gold and silver this time. It's essential that we present them as more humane, emphasizing their compassion, love, and desire to help the needy and unfortunate. I've called in a fashion designer, a cosmetologist, a hair designer, and a fashion photographer to create a new portfolio for both of them, including some images with Doctor Abila as Lilith's boyfriend. This new campaign will make them more approachable, calming the protests and winning people's hearts. It's time to announce a new era, a new awareness of self."

Nevin reaches into a drawer, eyeing Jennifer thoughtfully.

"Ms. Stone, you have an outstanding mind. I find nothing wrong with your approach."

Pulling out a cigar, Nevins plops it into his mouth and swirls it around.

"Let's get it started."

Watching Nevins enjoy the taste of a fine Havana cigar, Jennifer blurts out, "If you're going to light one of those up while I'm in the room, I want one as well."

With a laugh, Nevins hands Jennifer a Cuban stogie from his stash, and when she leans over his desk, he lights it for her.

Then he lights his, and they both sit back and savor the moment.

"This is going to be epic," says Nevins, dreamily blowing smoke rings into the air while contemplating his future.

Aware of what's happening, Samael is delighted with Jennifer's progress. His mental connection with her is causing her to think she also came up with this campaign all by herself.

Confident that his intrusions in her mind aren't noticed, he reinforces the idea that the concepts are her own, ensuring that his impending success will be all the more glorious when they're seemingly executed by others.

HABAKKUK 2:18-20

What use is a wooden idol carved by human hands, or a metal image that teaches lies? What is the point of their makers trusting in their own handiwork, creating idols that can't speak? What disaster is coming to you who say to something made of wood, "Wake up!" or to lifeless stone, "Get up!" Can it teach you anything? Look at it! It's covered with gold and silver, but there is no life inside it. But the Lord is in his holy Temple; let all the earth be silent in his presence. (FBV)

CHAPTER THIRTY-NINE

To the GBA commissioner's relief, the day of the exhibition basketball game dawns as a warm spring morning in the Big Apple, one less headache for him on this busy day.

The sky peeks through the concrete canyon, providing a blue background dotted with white puffy clouds interrupted only by personal flying aircraft and airborne ride shares. In the sky-high domed thoroughfares above, multitudes of citizens can be seen traversing between buildings, gazing down on the festivities as they commute to work.

In Rockefeller Plaza, a full basketball court has been erected over the expansive area housing the seasonal wintry ice skating rink and warm weather roller rink, with New York's Finest maintaining crowd control behind yellow barricades.

Holding court outside their studio are the day's emcees, morning hosts Jimmy Grant and Katie Richardson of *Daytime America*.

"Well, Katie," says Jimmy, excitement evident in his voice, "this is the day we've all been waiting for — the introduction to a new GBA. Joining us this morning is GBA commissioner Rick Jackson. Tell us, Rick, what should we expect today?"

Rick beams with pride, his eagerness to get things started oozing from his every word.

"We're here to showcase the new ambassadors of the great game of basketball! We hope they capture your hearts and imaginations. We know they're exceptionally great fits with our franchise!"

Katie smiles and shares in the excitement, adding, "We can't wait to see the new faces of the GBA!"

Looking out at the people spilling across the Plaza, she shouts, "ARE YOU READY?"

In response, the resounding sound of joyful shouts and applause drowns out the city's noise.

To settle the masses, Katie raises her hand in a way reminiscent of a Roman emperor in the Colosseum. Turning to Rick Jackson, her expression confirms her anticipation.

"Mr. Commissioner, the worlds await the game!"

Taking control, Rick Jackson addresses the crowd with enthusiasm befitting his position.

"People of the galaxy! Today, it is my great pleasure to introduce you to the former Titans, who, despite their ominous reputation, are just as human as the rest of us, albeit enhanced!

"To get things started, we've arranged a special treat for you, a basketball exhibition game featuring three former Titans and eight members from two of our GBA teams! Please welcome players from the New York Knicks and Nets as they enter the court to warm up!"

Behind a dark curtain, four Knicks and four Nets players emerge, greeted by exuberant yells and applause from the audience.

While the athletes shoot baskets at both ends, Rick waits until the crowd calms down before continuing.

"People of every worlds, the moment you've been waiting for is here! I'm thrilled to introduce our next players, the GBA's new brand ambassadors, Bob Lawson, Tim Farley, and Jon Harrington!"

As the three giants make their entrance, a strange hush falls over the crowd. Though most have viewed the men on vid screens, seeing them in person is different. Those gathered nearby seem startled, most falling silent as they watch Bob and Tim don custom-made Knicks uniforms and Jon slip into the Nets version.

The crowd's reaction worries the GBA commissioner. The eerie pall isn't anything he could have anticipated. Turning to the emcees, he mutters, "What's wrong?"

Despite the silence, the three ex-Titans step onto the court and low-five their teammates, who respond to them with high fives.

Slowly, the crowd becomes used to the immense size of the new brand ambassadors. Sporadic applause begins in various sections, then builds while the new additions warm up with the other players.

Reassured, Rick continues his introduction.

"Since we have an odd number of ambassadors, Bob and Jon will play first, one on each team. Then Tim will substitute for Bob."

As the men continue their warm-up, Jimmy questions Rick, "When will your ambassadors begin their welcome tour?"

"Well, Jimmy, as you know, the pre-season starts in September, so from now until then, we'll tour the larger cities enjoying year-round franchises. Hopefully, these brave men will one day join the franchises to compete as regular players. But for now, let's enjoy the show and welcome these American heroes to the GBA! They've been through so much, and they deserve our praise!

With the ensuing applause gladdening his heart, Rick takes a moment to bask in the jubilation before quieting the crowd to make another announcement.

"Before we begin the game, I have a special surprise that not even Jimmy or Katie know about! Hey Tim, come join me, will ya?"

Bounding off the court, Tim runs over to where Jimmy and Katie are standing, looking just as surprised as everyone else.

"We don't know what's happening, folks," announces Jimmy, making way for a crewman to stand on tiptoe to hand Tim a remote microphone.

"We have a special guest for Tim," continues Rick, pointing to the curtain with a smile running from ear to ear.

As Tim stares, the curtain parts and Jane Farley exits. With a loud gasp, Tim abandons the mic and runs toward her, embracing her tightly while Rick explains, "That's Jane Farley, folks! Tim's wife! The government's experimental program has kept them apart all these years, but we brought her here to surprise Tim!"

Amid heartfelt cheers, the couple rushes toward each other. They hold each other close and exchange words only they can hear. Then, Tim kisses his wife and guides her to a courtside bench. He gives her another kiss and wipes his eyes ahead of hugging Rick and telling him something private before heading back to the court.

At Rick's signal, referees and officials gather the teams to anticipate the ball toss between Bob and Jon at center court. To complete the action, the short referee throws the ball higher than usual to reach the tall men.

With the effortless grace of a more seasoned player, Jon takes immediate control of the ball with one of his oversized hands. Quickly, he scores the first basket, marking a great beginning to the unusual five-on-five competition.

Lieutenant Colonel Nevins is engrossed in watching the Knicks/Nets game in his office when Jennifer Stone enters unbidden.

"Colonel, I'm ready to show you our newly transformed superstars. They look absolutely stunning."

Reluctantly, Nevins tears his gaze away from the monitor.

"Have you been following our Titans?" he asks her. "These games are going to help them seamlessly integrate into regular society! Our plans are being executed flawlessly, and I have you to thank for a good part of it!"

"Why, Colonel, is that praise?" asks Jennifer. "I never thought I'd hear anything like that from you!"

"Hmmph. I give credit where credit is due," responds Nevins gruffly. "Just don't let it go to your head, Stone. We have to keep that momentum going."

"Oh, it'll keep going all right," responds Jennifer confidently. "Come with me. You're not gonna believe how I changed them."

Leading the way, Jennifer takes Nevins into the express elevator down to the lower level where Samael and Lilith reside.

"What's that?" asks Nevins, spying a large curtain shielding the giants' see-through enclosure.

"I want to give you the full effect with a grand reveal," she smiles, positioning herself to the side of the curtain where a long cord hangs.

With a dramatic flourish, Jennifer pulls on the rope, announcing, "Allow me to introduce Lilith, the Queen!"

As the curtain parts, Lilith stands before them, her long hair shimmering as it cascades over her shoulders. Reaching up, she adjusts an elegant pair of three-lensed glasses, the style of which harmonizes with her dress, a tight number in a silvery color that complements her hair. The dress and six-inch silver satin pumps elevate her beauty to an impressive height.

With a graceful stride toward the colonel, the vixen removes her blue glasses, unveiling enchanting eyes and long eyelashes that she fixes on the colonel. A playful hair flip and a blown kiss follow before she delicately replaces her glasses.

Nevins is left speechless by the sight before him.

Awestruck by Lilith's beauty, he gazes at her in amazement as she playfully chides, "Naughty colonel, my eyes are up here."

Flushing crimson, Nevins stammers, "Apologies, Lilith. You look absolutely stunning. Abila won't believe his eyes! He's a lucky bastard!"

Clearing her throat, Jennifer interrupts, assertively declaring, "Shall we proceed, Colonel? There's one more unveiling."

"Oh, uh, yes, of course. Please proceed."

With a wry grin, Jennifer pulls another cord.

"Allow me to present Samael of Sarah!"

As the curtain opens wider, Samael is revealed in a glorious suit of golden silk with a crisp white satin shirt and a silver silk tie. With his customary, blue-tinted glasses, he exudes an air of sophistication as he strides toward Lilith in sleek black satin shoes.

Standing beside his cohort, the pair exudes the aura of elegant rock stars or esteemed celebrities on a red carpet. To complete the effect, Samael confidently unbuttons his suit jacket and strikes a pose.

Once again, Nevins is left utterly speechless. Looking at them, he suddenly realizes that acceptance of these remarkable beings transcends their telepathic abilities. It's a result of their pure visual appeal.

"Jennifer," inquires Nevins, groping for words. "When, um... When can we unveil them?"

"Ah, you approve?"

"Darn right, I approve! Are they ready now?"

"Not yet. I have several teams working on designing and crafting a couple of sets of hand-sewn outfits for each of them. As you can imagine, it's quite an undertaking, even with the generous assistance of the worlds' best fashion designers."

"How long, Stone?" asks Nevins, fixing his gaze on the remarkable pair before him.

"Probably another week to ten days. At least."

"Make it one week," replies Nevins firmly. "No more, no less. Understand?"

CHAPTER FORTY

In the months since the World Federation hearing, Bigfoot Research Center director Lory Paduano and retired general Austin Patton have been working nonstop on Lory's studies in the vast expanse of Canada's northern territories. In their spare time, they've also set up a home at the research center and established a field operation base near the Bigfoot community's new location.

Immersed in seclusion, the operation base is in dense forest, far off the commercial grid. With no access to modern comforts, the couple's energy needs are powered by an amalgamation of solar panels and a cutting-edge Raphaelite-powered generator. For water, they rely on a remarkable device that draws moisture from the atmosphere. They also dug a well, but it's frozen for most of the year.

Out of necessity, the couple's existence harkens back to antiquated methods — intermittent satellite links and an HF radio. Monthly deliveries provide essential sustenance and supplies, supplemented by Austin's skillful hunting and gathering abilities.

Separated as they are from news of tumultuous events, Lory's and Austin's access to current news is a rare privilege. In the 37th century, pockets of pristine solitude still exist. Therefore, in preparation for the threatened three days of darkness, Austin has orchestrated a structured monthly communication regimen with Peter to ensure that the couple will be informed when events take their turn.

In a twist that surprised Austin, the former military

man has found that living alongside one's soulmate in 20th-century-esque simplicity is proving more than just bearable. It's a life that the man previously tasked with controlling significant areas of responsibility finds rather idyllic.

Since his return to Sorrento, Peter has learned to savor his morning cappuccinos on the veranda overlooking the glistening Mediterranean. It's a pleasant spot that would ordinarily bring him a sense of tranquility. Today, however, the scene doesn't quite settle him; trouble seems to be in the air.

Amid the sight of swift drone taxis crisscrossing the sky, Peter's gaze rests on the lively fishing boats and white sails dotting the horizon. He wishes the serenity he usually experienced would return, but he knows it was fleeting. The lurking presence of evil feels palpable, like a hungry lion poised to pounce.

Breaking his contemplation, Angela's voice summons him indoors.

"Breakfast is served!" she calls from the dining area.

As Peter steps inside, he hears a news report from the living room vidmonitor referencing Samael, Lilith, and the ex-Titans.

Grimacing, he implores the others, "Could we please turn off that monitor while we eat? We'll undoubtedly be subjected to that same story over and over today, ad nauseam."

In bustling urban centers throughout the galaxy, GBA spokespersons Robert, Tim, and Jon are playing their exhibition games to cheering multitudes. Their performances have captivated fans and experts alike. Most can't seem to get enough of them.

After breakfast, Peter joins Angela and her mother in clearing the breakfast table while Angela's father and uncle engross themselves in the Italian news.

Suddenly, Peter's attention sharpens as he once again catches the familiar words, "Samael and Lilith." Despite himself, he hurries into the living room, where he encounters vid images of the pair at an event, dressed elegantly in silver and gold.

Angela's father points to the monitor.

"They look like they're ready for the red carpet. I don't know, Peter, they're quite the handsome couple."

Not to be left out, Zio Giovanni chimes in with a heavenly plea: "Forgive me, *Madonna*, but Lilith, she is always stunning."

Peter gazes at the images, his expression grave.

"They're nothing but idols. Look at how they're dressed! Those two are sending messages of wealth and allure. They want nothing more than to beguile the unsuspecting masses, and people are already ensnared by both of them! Many don't stand a chance against them! With their thought transference, intelligence, and outright hubris, they have the galaxy in the palms of their hands! And it doesn't take much for Lilith to execute that role; she always carries herself with great self-assurance. Zio Giovanni, can you activate the auto translator? I don't understand enough Italian to follow what the newscaster's saying."

As the translation fills his ears, Peter shivers.

"...to elaborate on their plans. Lilith and her fiancé, Doctor Anthony Abila, will tour the United States, making personal appearances on various broadcast talk shows. They will visit patients in local hospitals, assisted living facilities, schools, and other community institutions. Meanwhile, Samael will embark on a global tour, addressing the World Federation and engaging with government officials on every planet. To mark the culmination of his tour, he will address the Italian Parliament, which their publicist, Jennifer Stone, promises will include an event intended to awaken all worlds to a new era of enlightenment and self-awareness that they—"

Disheartened, Peter rushes to silence the monitor, despite the others' protests.

"Nothing good will come of this," he laments. "Dark times lie ahead."

CHAPTER FORTY-ONE

The worlds are now teetering on the cusp of a burgeoning "enlightenment," whether it welcomes the change or not.

In unwitting support of the upheaval, the former Titans do all they can to repay the assistance they've received from their sympathizers and followers after Operation Apocalypse was shut down.

In addition to the men who have joined the rarified ranks of elite GBA athletes, Frank Giletti and Richard Alvarez have seamlessly evolved into exceptionally vocal advocates of Xanthe Robotics, the company that literally saved their lives. Since they obviously embody the very capabilities they champion, their partnership with Xanthe is uncomplicated and effortless.

To use the men effectively, CEO Arlynn Stout split the two up, moving Richard to Mars while keeping Frank on Earth.

In Xanthe City, Richard's role involves welcoming visitors to tours of the company's advanced robotics hub, and occasionally strolling down the bustling avenues of downtown Xanthe City to endorse the acceptance of AI robotics.

Meanwhile, on Earth, Frank has settled in at the Vegas facility. When he's not gracing the bustling gambling strip to draw attention to the marvels of Xanthe Robotics' creations, he leads the curious on tours of the company's production lines, one dedicated to crafting novel AI robots and personal assistants, the other to the fabrication of AI prosthetics — a domain where Frank thrives.

Both locations have opened the public's minds to the capabilities of AI-enhanced artificial creations. With free visits available seven days a week, the facilities have become beacons for tourism and education on two planets, a flawless merging of Arlynn Stout's corporate vision with Samael and Lilith's unnatural ambitions.

To move Lilith and Samael from place to place, special transport trucks have been modified from military vehicles to accommodate the pair's extreme heights: Lilith at eighteen feet and Samael at just under twenty feet. Because of their sizes, indoor venues other than theater or film set stages, large convention centers, and other spaces with ceilings under twenty feet pose logistical problems. As a solution, Xanthe Robotics also modified personal electric scooters to enable Lilith and Samael to sit comfortably while presenting themselves in lower-ceilinged areas.

To keep the hybrids in the public's minds, Jennifer Stone booked Samael and Lieutenant Colonel Nevins to speak before a joint session of Congress. Though the press won't be allowed inside, the meeting will be transmitted across the galaxy by in-house technicians.

It's not known whether the session will be broadcast within the off-Earth communities, however. To this day, Samael and Lilith haven't been accepted off-world at all.

In addition to the congressional appearance, Jennifer Stone secured *World Today*, a morning show based in Los Angeles, as the inaugural platform for the Friendship Tour of Doctor Abila and his fiancée, Lilith.

On the day of the show, Lilith occupies a unique platform chair they carry along during their travels. Seated, the giant is still taller than everyone else, so the chair incorporates a platform designed to facilitate access for hairstylists and makeup artists.

The makeup artist assigned to her care for the show is thrilled about the opportunity to work on the esteemed galactic figure. She works meticulously, though Lilith doesn't need much to enhance her naturally striking features.

Gazing at Lilith's engagement ring as she works, the woman comments, "I love your ring, Miss Lilith. The combination of silver and gold in your outfit perfectly complements the gemstone. It's gorgeous."

Lilith radiates a smile. "Thank you. But it's not just any gemstone; it's a Jasper stone, Anthony's favorite."

Drawing closer, the cosmetologist speaks in a hushed tone brimming with bold camaraderie.

"I'd say Anthony's favorite is you, not the stone," she smiles.

Lilith responds with a contented sigh and rises from the chair, leaving a thoroughly charmed artist eager to share her experience with everyone she knows.

With little time to spare, she dons her specialized glasses and joins Anthony backstage to listen as the morning host introduces them.

"My special guests today require an adjustment to our equipment," announces Jason Lake, signaling the cameraman to focus on ascending studio lights. Off-camera, a producer gives a thumbs-up, prompting Jason to face the camera.

"That was our way of providing a tantalizing introduction to today's interview. Now, without further ado, let's welcome our guests, Anthony Abila and his lovely fiancée, Lilith!"

While Doctor Abila holds the curtain for Lilith, the

intimate studio audience bursts into cheers, unbidden by the illuminated "Applause" sign.

For this appearance, Lilith has donned snug jeans, gold-toned athletic shoes, and a silvery blouse. The doctor, dressed in a black business suit and tie, accompanies her closely.

Although they step out together, Lilith commands the stage's attention. Gasps and enthusiastic applause ripple through the crowd while robotic cameras retreat as far as possible to capture her commanding height.

As the two settle into their seats, Lilith remains notably taller, even with Abila's chair on an elevated platform.

Jason, delighting in the couple's first media interview, happily initiates the conversation.

"Congratulations on your recent engagement!" he begins. "Since you've been together for a substantial period, let's address the elephant in the room first. Doctor, your height difference is quite striking. How does that dynamic work in your relationship?"

Gripping Anthony's hand, Lilith interjects playfully, "We manage just fine, Jason. Can we move on to the next question?"

With chuckles from the audience, Jason consults his notes.

"Lilith, you contracted an infection from the mutated dirt mites on Mars, correct?"

"Yes, that's accurate."

"And this infection transformed you into the captivating figure you are now?"

"You could say that."

"The public is curious about your life before the infection. Could you shed some light on that?"

Lilith exchanges a glance with Anthony, then peers into the camera through her distinctive glasses.

"That's a great question, Jason. I believe you're the first

to ask me that."

Turning to the host, she reveals, "My birth name is Karen Stamos, and I was born in New York. I was studying history on Mars when I was infected during the outbreak. When they discovered my condition, they quarantined me and put me in stasis to try to stop my transformation. Thankfully, Doctor Abila and his team's efforts prevented me from turning into a Clawfoot, those monstrous entities that caused widespread devastation on Mars and Earth. But they couldn't stop all the changes. As I evolved into my current form, I knew I was so completely different than before that I adopted the name Lilith to put my past to rest."

"Why did you feel the need to do that?" asks Jason.

Lilith hesitates, looking down at her hands. With a mournful expression, she states, "My parents weren't able to come to terms with my current condition. I haven't had contact with them since."

The audience responds empathetically, prompting Jason to reply, "That must have been incredibly tough. But perspectives can change, right?"

"Yes, I suppose so," responds Lilith.

"Before we delve further into that, I have something to show you. If you turn to the imaging area, we've arranged a holographic projection. It's your parents, direct from our New York studio! Look over there, Lilith. It's Mr. and Mrs. Kostas Stamos!"

As the producer shifts to a split screen for viewers, dual cameras pick up two images, one showing the ecstatic parents and the other Lilith's trembling lower lip. With tears filling all three of her eyes, she stammers, "Mom, Dad? I... How... How are you?"

"Oh, my stars! Karen, I've so wanted to tell you how stunning you are!" gushes Cecily Stamos. Her husband, Kostas, stands silent at her side, too overwhelmed to speak.

"Our little Karen has transformed into a goddess!" continues Mrs. Stamos. "Honey, I know we've been distant. We're so very sorry for our actions when you needed us most. Can you ever find it in your heart to forgive us?"

"Oh, Mom! I've missed you both so much! It's so wonderful to see you!"

"My baby!" sobs Kostas. "Can we visit you in person? Is your tour coming to New York?"

An assistant hurries on set with tissues as Lilith removes her unique glasses, eliciting murmurs from the audience.

Dabbing her eyes, she answers through tears, "We're definitely coming to New York! You can meet my fiancé! Maybe cook him one of your great Greek dinners. Oh, how I miss them!"

"We'd be delighted!" chime both parents.

Turning to Jason, Cecily says, "Mr. Lake, we're eternally grateful to you and the *World Today* team for reuniting us with our daughter. To us, she'll always be our Karen. See you soon, baby!"

The holographic image fades as Lilith and Anthony wave at her parents. Then, amid resounding cheers, Lilith leans over to Anthony, wiping moisture from his face and kissing him gently.

"Before we break for commercials, a few more questions?" asks Jason, more kindly than usual. "Are you up for it?"

"Absolutely; ask away," replies Lilith gleefully.

"All right. Before I inquire about your upcoming national tour, let's discuss your third eye since you unveiled it on the show. What can you tell us about it?"

Lilith's smile returns as she dons her glasses.

"It serves as a telepathic gateway into my mind. It's

connected to the pineal gland that every human possesses but rarely exploits. Given my heightened development, I'm able to communicate mind-to-mind, a latent ability in all of us, with some possessing it more than others."

"Hold on," interjects Jason. "You're suggesting that all of us can do what you do?"

"Yes, indeed. However, to enhance this ability, you must eliminate fluoride from your diets. This chemical impedes the pineal gland's optimal function."

Playfully, Lilith adds, "Aside from my increased height and extra eye, I'm entirely human."

"…And entirely a woman," grins Doctor Abila, squeezing Lilith's hand.

Jason chuckles while the audience erupts into laughter.

"Okay, let's leave that alone," states the host. "Now, Doctor, what are your plans for the tour?"

"Thanks for asking; we're excited about it. We plan to appear on talk shows nationwide and also visit hospitals, schools, and some community projects. Our objective is to dispel concerns people may have about Lilith and her extraordinary appearance and ability."

"Are you referring to the New Knights Templar?" inquires Jason.

"Yes, I am. We intend to refute the baseless accusations they've leveled against Lilith."

As Doctor Abila goes on, describing more about the tour, Lilith gazes at the interviewer, her amusement evident.

"I know what you're thinking, Jason," she suddenly interjects.

Blushing profusely, Jason quickly changes the subject.

"Details of Lilith's and Doctor Abila's Friendship Tour are available on their commsite, which we'll also share on the show's site. I understand you're heading to Houston next, followed by Miami, and then New York, where you'll no doubt enjoy that Greek dinner with your parents."

Catching a producer's eye, he adds, "Unfortunately, our time is up. Lilith, you're a treasure, and Doctor, you're the object of many men's envy. Thank you both for being on my show."

Lieutenant Colonel Nevins leans back in his chair after watching the *World Today* show in his office. Lighting up a cigar, he blows thoughtful smoke rings.

"Don't ya love it when a plan comes together?" he mutters into the empty room. "Next up is the World Federation, where my man, Samael, will command the stage!"

In his quarters, Samael finds himself alone, massaging his forehead as he wrestles with the tension that has consumed him. His concern for his companion, deepening by the moment, is a weight that presses heavily on him. Gritting his teeth, a low growl escapes his lips as he contemplates the future that lies ahead.

"Lilith is regressing, slowly slipping back into Karen," he mutters, his words laced with frustration and his teeth bared in a mix of determination and anger. "My father's grip on her has waned. It appears this path is one I must tread alone. I'm loath to admit it, but love is a formidable human emotion. Its power is all too potent, even for Satan."

CHAPTER FORTY-TWO

In the vibrant atmosphere of Rome in springtime, the city's intoxicating allure engages all five senses, leaving an indelible imprint on the mind.

However, while Rome is a city of unparalleled grandeur, it also has a shadowy historical past that many choose to ignore. The remnants of the ancient empire, sometimes beneficent, other times horrific, loom large, and they continue to cast a legacy, even over the 37th century.

Among the eager paparazzi and controlled crowds, anticipation builds as one of two exceptional RV transports — the brainchild of the World Federation and Xanthe Robotics — approaches.

Due to their impressive size, these massive vehicles, designed for Samael's and Lilith's needs, present logistical challenges, as they can only traverse wider avenues. This limitation is endured because they are also adjustable. Their ingenious design permits them to transform into living quarters tailored to the colossus's unique heights.

Though some larger hotels equipped with spacious ceilings in convention and meeting halls have committed to providing them with temporary housing, those venues demand ample notice and a substantial financial commitment. More often than not, Samael and Lilith prefer to reside in their private RVs.

Seated within a portable electronic chair inside the vehicle, Samael waits while his driver pulls up near the entrance of the World Federation complex and starts the motor to raise the rear roof.

Outside, the Carabinieri and municipal police struggle to maintain control while the crowd watches the roof ascend to an impressive height of twenty-five feet.

From the front of the vehicle, distinguished attendees, including Ambassador Fiona Gabelli and Lieutenant Colonel Nevins in his resplendent military attire, disembark. At the same time, an access door opens on the street side. Standing nearby, an associate activates a remote control, and a ramp slides out to meet the ground, allowing Samael to roll his electric chair down to the sidewalk.

Guided by the associate, Samael maneuvers toward the building's entrance. Adorned in a gold-colored, finely tailored suit and highly polished, black leather shoes, the giant rises from his chair to tower above the crowd. Craning their necks, they gasp and applaud in awe, their gazes directed at his tri-lensed glasses.

With a wave, he resumes his seat and moves toward the building entrance.

The hushed crowd takes everything in as the colossal figure passes. The disparity between his size and the onlookers is glaring, evoking images of the island of Lilliput from Gulliver's Travels, an ancient literary work.

Following Samuel, Fiona Gabelli exchanges greetings with Nevins.

"He certainly knows how to make an entrance," she remarks wryly.

While two attendants swing open the building's imposing glass doors, Samael maneuvers the electronic chair through the entrance of the World Federation headquarters.

Gliding along an ornate marble hallway, the giant navigates to the Assembly Hall, stopping just outside its doors.

When everyone is ready inside, a Moroccan Sergeant at Arms strikes a gavel to signal the Assembly's commencement and to introduce the Secretary-General, Sir Sharmi Dalvi.

"Ladies and gentlemen, distinguished ambassadors, esteemed guests, and representatives of global media," says Dalvi, "I have convened this special Assembly to bring together our galaxy's representatives for an address by Samael of Sarah. We have been apprised of his mission and unique capabilities. Now, it is his moment to speak.

"Accompanying Samael today is his mentor and associate, Lieutenant Colonel Hollis Nevins of the United States Marines. Honorable members, I introduce to you, Lieutenant Colonel Nevins."

Acknowledging scattered applause, Nevins shakes hands with Dalvi, adjusts his uniform, and scans the Assembly.

"Ambassadors, dignitaries, and guests, the era of the Titans has passed. The recipients of our experimental treatments are now accepted members of society, Earthlings in every sense.

"Not to be outdone, Samael's journey is no less extraordinary. As a hybrid human, he brings a distinct purpose and message for humanity, a message he will expound upon. I'm exceedingly honored to introduce to you Samael of Sarah."

Fitted with a communication device for speaking to the large gathering, Samael peers into the Assembly room as the doors swing open, a warm smile gracing his features.

As he navigates his chair to the podium, he takes in the lofty expanse of the ceiling. Judging it fit for his height, he halts near the podium and unfolds himself from the chair. Standing tall, he adjusts the length of his trousers while up in the gallery, the guests watch in astonishment. Dwarfing the arena, journalists and camera operators scramble for optimal angles to capture the monumental figure.

Soaking in the attention, Samael's gaze shifts to Nevins, and he tilts his head slightly as if debating what to say. Glued to their seats, the Assembly waits, holding its collective breath, uncertain of what's to come.

The next moment, Samael begins with a deep, resonant voice that seems to echo from within.

"I extend my gratitude to the World Federation for affording me this moment to reintroduce myself to our worlds. I am Samael, son of Sarah Covington, who bridged the gap between Clawfeet and Bigfeet, living in harmony with a Bigfoot clan in the Canadian Rockies. In a way, you could say I am Canadian," he grins drolly.

"I am here because I have been entrusted by my father to inform the inhabitants of the galaxy about a new order of existence comprised of our essence and purpose. I am here today to re-position humanity as an unquestionably dominant force within the universe.

"I know that some have reservations about my abilities. They distrust my capability to communicate telepathically. Nevertheless, I am here today to let it be known that this aptitude is innate to all humankind; you merely need to nurture it. Even so, until you have cultivated it within yourselves, I will communicate with you as I am now.

"I stand here as a representative of the future of humanity. I am Who I Am, and I reflect what you will become."

At these words, reminiscent of Almighty God's name in the Holy Bible, some in the hall murmur, shifting uncomfortably in their seats.

"This is not a cautionary promise," continues Samael, "but a pledge of prosperity and enduring life for humanity as it journeys into the cosmos and beyond. Lilith and I embody the power of the universe; we stand alongside the one true God."

More murmurs ensue, with some looking ready to leave the Assembly Hall.

"I thank you all for your time today. Lilith and I wish each of you abundance, health, and prosperity. May the guiding energy of the cosmos fill your minds with enlightenment and truth. Peace be upon you."

When Samael concludes, most give him a standing ovation accompanied by cheers of approval that resound throughout the Assembly. Concealed by the fervent crowd, a few ambassadors remain seated, unmoved by the hybrid's pledge.

Fionna and others remain quiet, understanding the dangers they just heard. But applause and cheers persist in the hall for several long minutes.

Outside and on air, journalists worldwide add their perspectives, most highly favorable to what they heard.

In the depths of Gehenna, the Malignant rubs his scaly hands together after listening to Samael's speech. Sitting on his obsidian throne, he approves of Samuel's speech while all around him, horrific sounds of wailing and grinding of teeth pierce the all-consuming fire and brimstone.

"Hissssss ssss ss!" he screeches, the angry sound escaping from an ugly slit below his beady eyes, though he's actually pleased. "My offspring is once again triumphant! My plan is proceeding just as I intended! With my son's ongoing obedience to my will, we will finally and completely wrest those miserable humans away from their infernal God!"

At this same moment, Karen Stamos, previously known as Lilith, is traversing the United States with Doctor Anthony Abila. Their Friendship Tour aims to demonstrate that there's no cause for apprehension regarding Lilith's unique appearance and abilities. They want everyone to know that as a transformed human, she aspires to marry and integrate into society as any other woman, with all the benefits of being wedded to the man she loves.

After the coverage of Samael's World Federation

appearance ends, Detective David Jacoby turns off the monitor at his home in Xanthe City. Sitting alone, he quietly contemplates his life. Until recently, he was firm in his revulsion of all things artificial. Now, his delightful relationship with Galina has upended all he thought he believed in, rendering him confused and surprisingly happy.

On Earth, a cloud of somberness hangs over Peter, Angela, and their family, mirroring the solemn atmosphere surrounding Austin and Lory in the Northwest Territories.

Across the galaxy, scattered pockets of opposition to Samael's speech share in this collective mood. The abhorrent falsehoods from that malevolent entity have left some in a state of shock.

Reacting to the speech, Pope Ignatius summons a council of cardinals, seeking their advice and wisdom on how best to respond. Meanwhile, officials on the Moon, Mars, and Titan unite to denounce the false prophet.

Regrettably, even though many leaders warn their people, most reject their concerns. Instead, they come together in celebration, only too willing to mark the joyful commencement of the revitalized era promised by Samael: a New Time of Man.

CHAPTER FORTY-THREE

Following Samael's speech, not everyone believes the conclusion is inevitable. Reacting to the malevolent force's overwhelming influence, numerous individuals are steadily laboring to undo the tide to alter the course leading to Samael's expected finale.

Upon the pope's urging, the council of cardinals convenes to deliberate on their course of action. The pope earnestly implores them to denounce Samael as a false prophet, and he beseeches the Commander of the Ark to step in for humanity's greater good.

Of course, the Commander agrees to help. But in doing so, he emphasizes that the World Federation, a representative body for all humanity, must also seek the Guardians' assistance.

United in their shared mission, Pope Ignatius and President Larson begin the laborious process of forming a coalition among nations to counteract Samael's deception and to pressure the Federation into action. However, while they negotiate the terms of the agreement, Samael continues to manipulate the minds of the vulnerable. The time required to set that agreement into motion is a luxury mankind can't afford.

Next on Samael's agenda is an address to a joint session of Congress in Washington, D.C. While he prepares for that,

Doctor Abila and Lilith follow up their successful appearance on an afternoon talk show in Houston with a visit to a children's hospital in South Florida. They book everything they can to distance themselves from Samael and to show Lilith in a positive light.

As their tour continues, Anthony notices a difference in Lilith. She won't say, but he suspects she isn't as confident as she was before their holographic meeting with her parents.

Privately, Lilith knows Anthony is right. The surprise family reunion has prompted her to question who she is. She has even begun to long for her original persona as Karen.

On the day of their visit to the Miami children's hospital, the streets teem with press and regular folks clamoring for a glimpse of the celebrities. People are so willing to participate in the spectacle that they've traveled from neighboring cities and states. Sparing no effort, the police department has called in reinforcements to manage the bustling traffic and eager throngs, forcing the mayor to dip into his reserves to pay for it all.

Because of the traffic, the couple's imposing recreational vehicle arrives at the hospital later than expected, but the excited onlookers don't mind. They watch with eager anticipation as the vehicle's roof lifts to the sky, and Anthony and his support crew step out to cheers.

When Lilith emerges into the Miami sunlight, her silvery pantsuit shimmers and the parking lot reverberates with gasps and the clicks of multitudes of vidcams, everyone hoping to capture the moment for their personal collections.

Responding to the crowd, Lilith waves and blows kisses as she guides her electric cart into the facility. In the lobby, she and Doctor Abila draw attention from children, parents, and staff selected to represent the hospital.

Hoping for their own glimpses, other children attached to IV pumps or portable breathing aids stand or sit some distance away, accompanied by parents holding balloons, flowers, and placards to welcome Lilith. Filled with emotion, the superstar waves, beaming smiles at all of them.

One young boy, hairless and pale from rounds of chemical treatments, approaches Lilith with his mother and an IV bottle on a portable pole. Summoning all his strength, the boy offers Lilith a rose, saying, "Miss Lilith, thank you for being here. We all love you." Then, he whispers, "Do you think I look like Samael? He doesn't have hair, either."

Lilith's smile quivers as she accepts the rose. "Young man, not only do you resemble Samael, but you're also just as brave as he is. I wish you well."

Turning to a staff member, she hands the boy a pair of pre-packaged, three-lensed blue glasses, which he opens excitedly. Putting them on, he grins widely.

"Now I'm just like you!" he exclaims to a round of applause. "Thank you, Miss Lilith!"

Lilith's tears flow as the boy joins the other children.

Waving farewell, she heads down the corridor to a meeting room where several patients and their families await her visit. The children's faces light up as Lilith guides her chair in.

Remarkably, the youths care little about her height or appearance. Free of the customary scrutiny she has never gotten used to, Lilith/Karen chats with each child and their parents, distributing pairs of glasses that the children eagerly put on to showcase their new looks.

Going down the line, she is about to reach nine-year-old Donny Catalano when he breaks free from his parents and rushes to Lilith's side, kissing her on the cheek.

Overjoyed by the child's simplicity, Karen embraces him for a long moment. The scene is heartwarming, every bit worthy of the jostling of the assembled photographers to capture it.

Unaware of the fuss, Donny looks up at Lilith.

"Is it hard for you to have three eyes?" he asks innocently. "Do people stare at you and make fun of you?"

Lilith sighs, understanding that the child is actually speaking about himself.

"Yes, people stare at me and say unkind things. But I like to remember that they're just curious, so I try not to let it bother me."

Lilith pats the child's cheek, then shifts her attention to the entire group of young people.

"All of you are special, and you will always hold a place in my heart. Please keep me updated on your journeys, and I will share mine with you. Blessings, good health, and happiness to all of you! Each of you is unique, and Anthony and I will always cherish meeting you!"

At the end, Lilith's voice falters, and she leaves the room swiftly, hoping to conceal her tears behind her tri-lensed glasses.

In the hallway, Doctor Abila kneels by Lilith's side, knowing she's upset.

"That was inspiring, honey. You always know what to say. Every time I see you do something like that, I love you more."

Lilith lowers her eyes. "Tony, I'm confused," she confesses, wiping her face. "Those children are so fragile. Their plights have made me think more and more about my human side."

"What do you mean, Lil?"

Holding Anthony's gaze, she says, "I don't know if I want to keep being Lilith. I'm Karen Stamos, Doctor Anthony Abila's fiancée. I no longer know who Lilith is."

"Um, do you think we should leave?"

"Yes, I need time to think. I don't know if I should make any changes, and I'm not sure if I really want to. I have to contemplate my future... Our future. The Times Square event is coming up soon. I need to figure out what I'm going to do."

Listening to Lilith's thoughts miles away in his RV bedroom, Samael becomes increasingly distressed.

"Lilith is faltering," he mutters, drumming his fingers on a table. "I must work with my father to make her overcome her doubts. My sister, you know you need to be at my side. We are humanity's future. We are their new religion."

After the *World Today* show in Los Angeles, press reports begin to refer to Lilith as Karen Stamos, adding to the confusion in Lilith's mind.

Slowly but surely, Lilith's anxiety level rises, worrying Anthony. The timing is inopportune; the highly anticipated gathering in Times Square is only a week away, and with the event set to air on Global TV, they can't afford any setbacks in presenting the stately beauty as anything but normal.

Yearning for breathing room and relief from the unyielding press, the couple directs their driver to steer their RV onto the busy I-95 corridor on the way to New York. In Lilith's conflicted state, she craves unscripted, impromptu interactions with the public instead of the tightly orchestrated itinerary planned by Jennifer and her team.

Throughout the rest of the journey, the human-hybrid seeks refuge in moments of solitude and meditation, striving to ward off the persistent allure of Samael and his father. The haunting figures inundate her mind with promises and unsolicited guidance, igniting an unyielding internal struggle, an age-old conflict akin to that of Adam and Eve.

Intermittently, the RV departs from the highway to refuel and to allow its occupants a chance to stretch their legs. The quiet retreats also afford Karen an opportunity for self-discovery. At each stop, she interacts with surprised travelers like any other wayfarer, asking them where they're going and how long they've been on the road. These connections are helping her to hone her yearnings and aspirations for a normal life away from the spotlight.

The Malignant, aware of Lilith's unwavering determination to resist his sway, grows infuriated, sensing his grip slipping away from one of his modern-day Nephilim. Driven by vexation, he intensifies his efforts to maintain his hold over her.

On the contrary, Karen stands firm in her resolve to thwart his advances. The timeless struggle between good and evil rages on, neither side relenting in their never-ending battle for dominance.

While Lilith continues to grapple with her inner turmoil, Samael divides his focus between her and his impending speech before Congress.

Despite his best efforts, however, he eventually comes to realize that he's not going to win Lilith over. Enraged by her betrayal, he reluctantly acknowledges her resolve to transform back into Karen and eases up his efforts to change her mind. But in doing so, he intensifies his own commitment to fulfill his father's mission, unwavering in his determination to bring about Satan's desire for global conversion to the new order of man.

Simultaneously, Peter Matteo embarks on an equally vital mission, one that is in direct opposition to Samael's. Peter's objective is to persuade the global populace to reject Samael and his web of deceit.

The struggle between the forces of light and darkness persists ceaselessly for all men and women, but not for God the Father. Victory is destined for Him, even when humanity falters.

This truth is one that Peter grasps, and Samael refuses to accept. The pride, arrogance, and thirst for revenge instilled in the Malignant's offspring govern his every thought and action.

CHAPTER FORTY-FOUR

Today, Washington D.C. hums with tight security as a diverse gathering of press representatives from both foreign and domestic realms arrives at the Capitol Building to hear Samael's speech to Congress.

President Larson, Vice President Dakota, the esteemed Supreme Court Justices, and the President's cabinet members occupy the chamber floor along with Senators and Representatives from every state in the union. Filling the Congressional gallery are dignitaries and guests. Conspicuously absent is the Secretary of the Treasury, tonight's designated survivor, the one poised to step in, in case of unforeseen mishaps or chaos.

Forty-eight hours after the speech, Karen and Doctor Abila will have their day in the spotlight. For now, they've taken a detour to the vibrant boardwalk of Atlantic City along the New Jersey shore, where they stroll hand-in-hand along the famous promenade. As usual, the duo's presence commands attention, awing strollers and bathers as the pair wanders along.

Because of the hoopla surrounding Samael's speech, the usual swarm of paparazzi and press is notably absent. Instead, there's a refreshing lack of packed onlookers, replaced by individuals who pause to capture snapshots and occasionally request selfies. The prevailing sentiment among the bystanders is positivity, with most offering encouraging nods or flashing peace signs. Remarkably, there's also a dearth of confrontation, a welcome change for the famous couple.

Ever since their appearance in Miami, each day that passes further solidifies Karen's conviction to reclaim her identity as Karen Stamos, even as she wrestles with the constant persona of Lilith, which she knows she must continue to embody on the global stage.

In a moment of tenderness, she leans down to converse with Anthony when there's no one else nearby.

"Have you seen enough, honey? It's almost time for Samael's speech, and I'm eager to hear what he has to say."

"I thought you wanted to forget him," reminds Anthony, caressing his lover's arm.

"I'm not sure. He and his father still have a hold on me; it's an ongoing struggle."

Anthony looks up at his fiancée with compassion. "All right; if that's what you want," he says tenderly.

In shared agreement, the couple pivots and retraces their steps, heading back to their RV sanctuary to watch Samael's address in private.

Samael readies himself in his motor home parked outside the Capitol Building while Jennifer Stone seeks a private conversation with Lieutenant Colonel Nevins outside the vehicle.

"Are you all right?" asks Nevins. "You seem tense."

"Have you been keeping tabs on Lilith?"

"Yes, I heard there's a problem."

"That's putting it mildly. For some reason, Karen Stamos has resurfaced, and Lilith is regressing toward her more human side. Samael confided in me, rather reluctantly, that he anticipates that she's going to strike out on her own. He even mentioned the possibility that she and Abila will leave the public eye, to the extent that circumstances permit."

"Can't he stop her?"

"He's attempting to rekindle Lilith's former confidence, but she's a formidable adversary. He admitted to me that he's struggling to gain control over her."

"Wow. I never thought he'd lose control over anything. What do we do now?"

"Are you asking for my recommendation?"

"I already told you once that I value your opinion. Do you have one now?"

"Actually, Samael gave me an idea. I'm formulating a fresh approach, and pending your approval, I'll unveil it after Samael's speech. He revealed that Lilith plans to make a statement outlining her intentions in New York. I plan to preempt her by announcing it beforehand. That way, it'll seem like Samael initiated the change, and it'll preserve his reputation among the populace."

Nevins harbors concerns, but ultimately agrees with Jennifer's plan.

"I always suspected that her relationship with Abila would pose problems for our cause. Well, so be it. If she chooses to leave, we'll let her. In fact, that may be better for Samael. If he has no one else to consult about his intentions, it'll be easier for him to pave the way for his ultimate success and triumph. Let's move forward with what you need to do. It's time to get this show on the road."

Once again, Samael's RV undergoes a stunning transformation as he steps out, adorned entirely in resplendent gold and silver. His suit gleams as the sunlight catches it, reminding some of polished jasper.

With a graceful wave directed at the gathered masses, he glides toward the entrance on his cart, guided by an attendant.

Seated regally like a sovereign upon his throne, he's led through an entrance equipped to accommodate his imposing stature. Mere minutes pass before he emerges to wait outside the chamber hall.

In a meticulously timed sequence, he'll soon make his entrance, alighting from his cart to deliver an important address.

Inside the hall, a spectacle is already taking place. Leaders of the Senate and the House individually step into the spotlight, taking turns for a moment at the podium to extol their honored guest. With soaring rhetoric, they praise Samael before he has even uttered a word.

Eventually, the speakers conclude and claim their seats. Then, with a reverberating thud, the Sergeant at Arms strikes the marbled floor with a wooden staff, announcing the opening of the session. The stillness following that act is profound; all eyes are fixed upon the chamber's entrance.

In a loud voice, he exclaims, "Esteemed Members of this Joint Session of Congress, honored guests, Mr. President, and Ms. Vice President, I present to you Samael of Sarah!"

As the grand doors swing open, applause cascades through the gallery, with some rising from their seats and others remaining seated. Perched on his cart, Samael navigates the aisle, his presence accompanied by a symphony of approval.

Upon reaching the customary spot where speakers address the assembly, the extraordinary figure chooses a different vantage point — the well, an area below the dais that offers more floor-to-ceiling height to accommodate his towering stature.

Gradually, knowing his every action is scrutinized, he

unfurls his immense twenty-foot frame from his motorized chair, evoking cheers.

Acknowledging the welcome, he stretches his arms skyward, his fingertips not far from grazing the ceiling.

As Samael surveys the gathered assembly, the applause recedes, and he begins, his words committed to memory.

"I wish to commence by conveying my heartfelt gratitude to each of you for allowing me to address you within this revered chamber. I am aware that some of you may deem this session unnecessary. However, I assure you that my presence today carries profound significance. I am Samael, offspring of Clawfoot Sarah Covington, a living testament to my remarkable lineage. Before we proceed, I must share some pressing matters."

Samael pauses, captivating the audience's attention with that tidbit and letting their anticipation build.

"Karen Stamos, my soul partner, known as Lilith to many, has recently become engaged. The man who captured her heart is Doctor Anthony Abila, the medical director of the program that integrated Lilith and me into your society."

"With her engagement, Lilith has chosen to step away from my side, to reconfigure herself in a manner harmonious with her human origins. Naturally, she wishes to forge a new path alongside her chosen companion. Regrettably, this means that she will no longer participate in the endeavors we had planned.

"Presently, Doctor Abila and Karen — her original name — are journeying across the United States to establish personal bonds with the nation's citizens. While I will certainly miss my colleague, I am content with her decision to chart a fresh course. I extend my heartfelt blessings to her and Doctor Abila for a happy and rewarding life."

Having intercepted the idea he planted in Jennifer's mind to thwart Karen's plan to reveal her aspirations in New

York, Samael presses forward, pivoting toward the central theme of his discourse.

"Now, let us turn to the reason for my presence here. Today, we stand at the threshold of a novel epoch, a period of reawakening, a moment resounding with eager anticipation.

"Gazing at me, there can be no doubt that I am different. I am indeed markedly distinct — so unlike any of you that some dub me a monstrosity. Yet, I must remind those critics that my mother, initially a human, was transformed outside of her control into a Clawfoot due to an infection caused by mutated Martian dirt mites. As her child, I have inherited her genetic makeup, making me, like each of you, a creation in the image of the Divine.

"United by our shared formation, we must nevertheless acknowledge that our divine image is not unique; we were not the first. Nonetheless, we humans have claimed extraordinary prominence within the cosmic tapestry. We have ascended to unprecedented heights, and the United States has most recently championed this ascent. Our nation is the one that spearheaded lunar colonization, reshaped Mars, and steered the Global Federation's voyage to Titan. Moreover, it led the exploration to discover beings like us, fashioned in God's likeness on Proxima b.

"Arlynn Stout, the visionary leader of the extraordinary company driving societal and medical progress, has exhibited humanity's capability to engender life, albeit in an alternate form. He and his company have engineered self-aware artificial life. With these creations, we have transcended our designation as mere children of God and now stand as brothers and sisters, all of us poised at the right hand of a fresh dawn, ready to claim our perfected roles within the boundless universe!

"Citizens of the United States, inhabitants of this world, and residents of the cosmos, my mission rests on elevating each of you to your rightful places among the stars!"

Frank A. Ruffolo

For emphasis, Samael lifts his blue-tinted glasses, revealing eyes brimming with purpose and intensity. Extending his arms, he closes his two earthly eyes while unveiling his third pineal eye, capturing most of the chamber in a mesmerizing gaze. A small contingent, unaffected by his words, shield their eyes. The divide in the reactions is stark, with the resolute few far outnumbered by those who have fallen under the immoral creature's spell.

In protest, those undeterred by Samael's effect exit the chamber. Watching them, Samael lowers his arms, returning his sunglasses to their place to conceal his eyes.

With his third eye once again hidden, the hallowed hall falls abruptly silent. Everyone seated remains still, as if directed by an unseen force.

In measured tones, Samael resumes his address.

"Do not be troubled by those who have left this gallery. They will ultimately understand what you already do, and will rally to our cause.

"Today marks the dawn of our revival — not merely as images of a divine entity, but as apprentices of divinity, human beings united under my father's guidance. I am Samael, Son of Sarah. The time for revelation has arrived! Today, I enthusiastically undertake the role of guiding humanity toward its unique future! Join me! Together, we will conquer the cosmos!"

When Samael concludes, a crescendo of cheers mingles with exultant cries of zealous passion. The historic chamber of the United States House of Representatives resounds with unparalleled joy, not unlike pure euphoria.

Beyond the chamber's walls, those who departed earlier congregate in subdued silence under the Capitol's Grand Rotunda. President Larson, Vice President Dakota, and a cluster of cabinet members joined by roughly twenty other dignitaries, clasp their hands in prayer, united in pleading to

Almighty God to save the nation and every society on every world.

Outside the Capitol Building, the press converges upon the attendees like an army of ants, eager to secure an interview with Samael or anyone else willing to engage with them. As expected, senators and congresspersons embroiled in re-election campaigns are the first to jostle for on-air opportunities, with most intending to espouse their agendas. On the contrary, Samael is the primary topic of conversation of every broadcaster.

Meanwhile, Samael retreats into his waiting RV, and Jennifer Stone positions herself to address the press corps.

"Ladies and gentlemen of the media, I'd like to provide an update regarding Karen Stamos and Doctor Abila. To clarify Samael's earlier statement, Lilith has chosen a different path. She has decided that the relentless scrutiny and pressure accompanying her nationwide tour are not conducive to her well-being. In light of this, she has reverted to her birth name and is set to retire from public activities to embrace a life as an ordinary wife and citizen. We anticipate that she will share her own thoughts upon arriving in New York."

For days afterward, the airwaves resonate with both admiration and trepidation for Samael and Lilith/Karen. Most voices are uplifted in praise of Samael, while a handful express reservations. Only a few discuss Lilith/Karen.

With the dissension among many, signs of increased division are slowly creeping into society. In Sorrento, where Peter and the family watched Samael's address to Congress, street artists are painting murals for and against the enigmatic creature. Everywhere, people of all ages are displaying paraphernalia that expresses their points of view. It's like a pressure cooker slowly building up to an explosive release.

And so, the great schism begins. Passionately, the people of the worlds bicker and choose sides.

Only One knows how it will end. Only One.

CHAPTER FORTY-FIVE

Times Square brims with excited bystanders and onlookers filling the street, blocking New Yorkers from getting to their workplaces. The city's apathetic natives push through the throng, unleashing language that would make a sailor blush, their irritation at having to suffer through yet another live broadcast evident.

Above this bustling scene, elevated walkways and airborne buses and taxis zip across the sky, oblivious to the goings-on below. Shared aerial rides and personal aircars also dart through the concrete canyon, occasionally joined by a police presence. All this activity creates an aerial ballet that no one but tourists care about.

At street level, a substantial portion of the square has been cordoned off to accommodate a collection of vehicles, camera crews, and staff from the *Wake Up New York* morning show orchestrating preparations for the day's edition.

To cope with onlookers, yellow barricades and police officers have been strategically placed around the set, a familiar headache in Manhattan's filming landscape.

Among this organized chaos, the show's hosts, Josh Hicks, a former New York Rangers hockey player, and Jenn Carlyle, an actress and ex-model, sit on an outside stage, undergoing final makeup touches before their on-air appearance.

As the producer signals the countdown, attendants scurry offstage, and Jenn adjusts her skirt.

At the right moment, she playfully tosses her dyed blonde hair and looks into a camera, announcing, "Greetings, New Yorkers! We're happy you're waking up with us! Our telecast today is direct from the heart of Times Square! Are you awake yet, Josh?"

Sitting beside her, Josh sets his coffee cup on a table.

"Absolutely, Jenn! Today, we're bringing our viewers two extraordinary guests with unique demands. To accommodate them, we're conducting their interviews right here in Times Square, surrounded by their devoted followers. I'll step over to meet some of the dedicated souls who've been here since dawn."

With a ring microphone encircling a finger, he approaches the barricade where a family proudly sports three-lensed glasses and Lilith-themed T-shirts.

"A warm welcome to Times Square!" Josh gushes. "Would you introduce your group and share where you're from?"

Excitedly, a young adult speaks up. "We're the Reynolds family from Boston! I live in the city, but my sister Carla and our parents flew in early this morning to see Lilith. We can't wait to meet her!"

Josh scans the crowd. "Any other out-of-towners here this morning? Raise your hands and make some noise!"

A smattering of hands lift high as Titanites cheer and applaud, delighting the charismatic morning host. Spotting a sign, Josh dashes down the line of barricades, sharing a friendly fist bump with a police officer.

"Our dedicated officers in blue are doing a fantastic job this morning! But right now, I need to have a word with this amazing lady. Good morning, and a hearty welcome to New York City! Have you come all the way from London? Was it just for the show?"

Flushed with excitement, the young woman responds

nervously, "Oh, indeed! I mean, I flew in for a short holiday and heard about your show. I couldn't resist the chance to see Lilith! This is truly magnificent, wouldn't you agree?"

Josh's smile radiates his pleasure. "I do agree! It's absolutely magnificent!"

At a cue from a producer, the host positions the ring microphone in front of the lady, inviting her to repeat after him, "Let's take a brief intermission to acknowledge our sponsors. But don't wander off, folks! When we return, our exceptional guests will be right here on our stage!"

After a brief interlude, Josh reappears live on the air.

"Welcome back to *Wake Up New York*! Before we jump into the interviews you've been eagerly waiting for, we have a special news flash to share."

Reading off a printed sheet of paper, he says, "Later today, President Larson will address the nation to offer his response to Samael's recent speech to Congress. Tune into this station to keep up with all the breaking news."

Placing the paper on the table, he declares, "All right, now that the update's out of the way, Jenn, it's over to you for the big moment."

With the camera locked on her, Jenn strides toward the sizeable RV stationed nearby, and with a grand sweep of her arm, announces, "Ladies and gentlemen of New York and our viewers at home, I present Miss Karen Stamos, whom you all knew as Lilith, and her fiancé, Doctor Anthony Abila!"

The camera pans from Jenn to the RV, capturing the gradual lifting of its rear section. Simultaneously, another camera depicts Anthony emerging from the front while expertly guiding a motorized chair down a ramp to meet Karen as she disembarks from their home on wheels.

Amid cheers and applause, Karen steps out from the vehicle, a stunning figure clad in a silver, two-piece suit and glittering athletic shoes. With a broad smile, she waves to the exuberant crowd, captivating onlookers with her stature and remarkable attractiveness. Taller than everyone, her gaze sweeps over the surroundings, even into the second story windows of neighboring buildings, acknowledging as many as possible.

When the opportunity arises, she moves gracefully to her waiting moveable chair, settling into it with the poise of an experienced performer. A tender kiss shared with Anthony covers a significant portion of his face, eliciting further applause. Then Karen straightens in her chair, and Anthony guides her up a ramp leading to the stage.

Eager to engage with their guests, Jenn and Josh hurry toward them.

"Miss Stamos," stammers Josh, stumbling over his words, "you're more stunning, I mean, lovelier, and uh, taller than I imagined! It must be interesting experiencing life among us 'Lilliputians.'"

Karen's eyes twinkle behind her sunglasses.

"Nice to meet you, Josh. Please call me Karen. Thanks for the compliment, but let's be real; Jenn is the true beauty here! And," she adds, nodding to the audience, "you're not half bad yourself!"

Blushing at the obviously better-looking woman's comment, Jenn flips her hair again.

"Karen, can you tell us how you and Doctor Abila are managing with all the attention on your relationship?"

Karen gazes lovingly at Anthony, intertwining their fingers.

"What we'd like is a quieter life away from the spotlight, Jenn. And, I'll let you in on a little secret. This will be our final public appearance. All we want is to enjoy a normal life together."

"This is your last appearance?" exclaims Josh, taken aback by the news. Then, turning to the camera, he declares triumphantly, "You heard it here first, folks!"

Karen explains, "Yes, we've decided to seek a more private life. I've also decided to reclaim my birth name."

Expanding on the subject, Jenn asks, "Leaving your celebrity status behind will be quite a change for you, won't it?"

"Not really. The spotlight never suited me. That's where Samael shines."

"Speaking of Samael," interjects Josh, "we polled our audience earlier, and their most pressing question is, why did you want to leave Samael?"

"As I mentioned, I'd rather enjoy a peaceful life with my husband than be in the constant glare of attention."

"Understandable," nod both hosts. "It can be overwhelming at times."

Jenn grins, "Okay, now that that's clear, let's move on to a more exciting topic. How are your wedding arrangements coming along?"

Karen turns her gaze to the doctor. "I'll let Anthony fill you in on that."

Less accustomed to the spotlight, a pink color momentarily creeps up Anthony's neck, then he swiftly regains his composure.

"We'd prefer less attention, but circumstances are what they are. We intend to have a small wedding, just close family members. I hope the public will respect that."

"Thanks for letting us know."

"Uh, Jenn?" says Anthony. "There's something else I'd like to say."

"Go right ahead," the host responds curiously.

"I don't think you or your viewers are aware of this, but every human being affected by the dirt mite infection, whether they morphed or not, faces a reduced lifespan. Unfortunately, we discovered the infections took a tremendous toll on their bodies. For that reason, I've decided to dedicate the rest of my career to finding a solution to this problem. It's one of the key reasons Karen and I agreed to leave Samael."

Karen offers a smile to Anthony and then addresses the camera.

"Yes, that's true. But don't be sad for me. I'm leading a very fulfilling life, and Anthony assures me of at least ten more years together. Plus, he's optimistic about extending my time on Earth and helping all the others who were impacted."

Kindly, Josh comments, "You have a remarkable perspective on your situation, Karen. I'm not sure I would be as brave as you. Doctor, we wish you all the best with your research. And I'm sure everyone else affected is touched by your dedication to their cause. We're all rooting for you."

Before the show descends into melancholy, a producer motions for a commercial break.

"Let's take a break now," states Josh. "When we return, we'll have more audience questions for Karen and Anthony."

While the commercials run, Jenn leans toward Karen. Patting her hand, she asks, "Do you need some water, honey?"

"No, I'm fine. It's the first time we've revealed personal information, but it's okay. Thank you."

A few minutes later, Josh declares, "And, we're back. Before the break, we promised more questions from our audience. Karen, another one everyone wants answered is, what exactly is the function of that third eye? We've heard it grants you the ability to share your thoughts and read minds telepathically. Does it provide any other benefits?"

"Yes, Josh. But I should mention that all humans possess

some level of those same abilities. For me, my accidental transformation enhanced my proficiency in those functions. However, any of you can try to develop them to one degree or another. And, as you know, Samael also possesses an extra eye. But he doesn't use it the way I do. He takes it much further by implanting suggestions in people's minds, leading them to undertake actions or thoughts they wouldn't necessarily do on their own. That's another reason I chose to distance myself from him. Let me demonstrate."

Lowering her sunglasses, Karen activates her third eye, telepathically informing Josh that he's thirsty.

For a moment, Josh appears transfixed. Then, he refocuses on Karen and says, "I don't know why, but I'm suddenly feeling a bit parched. Can someone pass me a glass of water?"

While Josh takes a generous sip from a discreetly offered cup, Karen says, "Josh, I just entered your mind and planted a suggestion that you were thirsty. That's why you asked for a drink."

When Josh's mouth drops, Jenn laughs.

"That's a great trick, Karen! Might come in handy someday!"

Faking a smile, the human hybrid answers, "It could, unless it's used to do something unpleasant. Remember my warning about Samael."

"I'm sure we'll keep that in mind," responds Jenn lightly. "Now, I'm thrilled to let the happy couple in on a surprise that *Wake Up New York* arranged just for them! Pointing offstage, she declares with a dramatic flourish, "All the way from nearby Massapequa, Long Island, are Karen's parents, Cecily and Kostas Stamos!"

As the crowd breaks into applause, Karen's parents enter the stage, arms outstretched to their daughter.

Thrilled to see them after a two-year separation, Karen

envelops both parents in her long arms in a heartfelt embrace.

Enjoying his part in the reunion, Josh turns to the camera with an infectious grin.

"We'll be right back. Stay tuned for more with the happy family."

After another round of commercials, the show returns with the camera fixed on Josh.

"So, Mr. and Mrs. Stamos, this marks your first meeting with your future son-in-..."

Unexpectedly, Karen interjects with a giggle, "Josh, I couldn't help noticing before that your thoughts wandered toward my parents. You nearly spilled the beans on the surprise! I want to thank you and the entire show for arranging this wonderful moment for us!"

Nodding, Kostas Stamos says, "Karen is a true inspiration. Despite the challenges she's faced, she remains the remarkable young woman we raised. We're thrilled she's chosen such an outstanding partner to share her life with."

Turning to Anthony, he says, "On behalf of Cecily and myself, we warmly welcome you into the Stamos family!"

The audience's collective "aww" resonates as he continues, "And by the way, get ready to savor the most divine Greek cuisine tonight! Thankfully, we have a large enough backyard to host you. Our little girl has certainly outgrown her childhood home!"

Karen chuckles heartily. "You think?" she quips.

Bringing the segment to a close, Jenn faces the camera with knowing eyes.

"Cherish your time together, Stamos family. It could all be gone in a flash."

Then, she shifts her focus to the camera lens, her tone meaningful.

"We want to thank today's guests for their openness

and sincerity. Having them on our show has been an absolute delight. But before the happy couple steps away from the limelight for good, Karen has graciously agreed to meet her well-wishers in a designated area our crew is currently setting up. To all our wonderful audience members, your patience will be rewarded as we work to accommodate everyone efficiently. Meanwhile, let's transition the rest of the show to our indoor studio, where we'll be talking with members of the Florida Panthers, this year's triumphant Stanley Cup champions. Stay tuned for more of the *Wake Up New York Show!*"

Before the third round of commercials begins, the camera shifts to Karen, gliding effortlessly in her chair down to the barricades to greet the throngs of eager fans gathered on the street.

Ever alert to his adversaries, Peter leans back in his chair and locks his fingers behind his head, a knowing grin spreading across his face. Glancing at Angela, he says, "I knew it'd be a good idea to watch that show today. Seems Lilith has vanished for good! But did you notice what was pinned to the front of her suit?"

Angela knits her brows together, concentrating her thoughts.

"I did notice something there, but I couldn't quite make out what it was."

Profound joy dances in Peter's eyes. "It was a tiny Miraculous Medal, Angie! And she had a tiny rosary in her hand! We may have an unexpected ally to help in our fight! I hope she's willing to assist us. She could be a powerful weapon against the Malignant!"

CHAPTER FORTY-SIX

That evening, the Greek family feast at Karen's childhood home is a resounding success, despite the need for Nassau County police to cordon off the block for the family's privacy.

Following an early rain shower, cousins, aunts, and uncles gather around a sprawling table in the backyard, engaging in lively conversation as the sky gradually darkens and the stars begin to twinkle.

Responding to her family's curiosity, Karen enthusiastically shares her tale, including expressing her heartfelt desire to become Mrs. Abila as soon as possible. She explains that Anthony has a house in the Catskills that they will reconfigure to accommodate her, and that they will reside in the RV while that's going on.

Anthony explains that along with managing the renovations, his agenda includes setting up a lab adjacent to the house where he can dedicate himself to devising a solution to prolong the lives of the infected.

Eagerly, Karen adds that while all that's going on, she intends to focus on searching for a skilled seamstress capable of crafting a wedding gown that suits her vision for their perfect day.

While the worlds wait to hear President Larson's response to Samael's speech, the chief executive seeks solace by the crackling fireplace in the White House Library. Settling into a plush, leather tufted chair surrounded by shelves of books and a bare wooden table holding a Bible, he reviews tonight's speech.

When the time is ready, he folds his hands in his lap and flashes a well-rehearsed smile at the camera before commencing his address.

"Good evening," he begins, his usual folksy demeanor replaced by the weight of presidential authority. "Tonight, I come to you not only as president of the United States but also as a friend, an advocate for the American people and for all global citizens.

"Over recent months, a series of events have unfolded that have caused worldwide divisions, fractured our societies, and challenged our core beliefs.

"With eternal gratitude, we remember our forebears who bore witness to the presence of God's Son on Earth and made the wise choice to reject evil. That decision has been the foundation of our existence up to this very era.

"Alarmingly, we are now confronted with another disquieting prospect — that of being forced to make that decision once again, and I am deeply concerned that some among us might arrive at uninformed choices, thereby endangering our future.

"I plead with all of you. Please look deeply within yourselves to find the clarity of vision to distinguish good from evil. As a citizen of Earth and a devoted follower of Jesus Christ, our Lord, God, and Savior, I appeal to you not to grant Samael the power that so many desire to confer upon him. I urge all world leaders to join me in invoking the Guardians and the Commander of the Ark to once again come to the aid of humanity. We must return to our foundational beliefs and reject this fallen messenger!

"While I cannot silence Samael, I can choose to dismiss

his message, and I beg everyone to delve into your souls to do the same. Please heed my advice, for God the Father, as patient as He may be, will not remain silent for much longer. The onus is on humanity to resolve this Samael problem and to select the correct path. Should we falter, Our Heavenly Father's retribution will undoubtedly follow.

"May God grant us His mercy."

When the transmission concludes, President Larson is joined by his chief of staff and his wife. He sighs, fully aware of the tempest his speech will unleash.

"The press will have a field day with this," he laments.

The chief of staff nods, sharing preliminary polling results.

"You've struck a nerve, with positive and negative results. On the negative side, approximately thirty percent of the population, mostly the youth, disagrees with your assessment. The younger generation appears to seek equality with God; they reject the notion that they're inferior to Him. They're embracing what Samael preaches — a new awakening."

Larson shakes his head. "And the remaining seventy percent?"

"They align with you, but they hesitate to voice their opinion. Their opponents have grown too vocal and well-prepared."

Standing near her husband, Larson's wife interjects her views with frustration.

"It's ridiculous! The youth are aspiring to almost godlike stature! It's frightening to witness the foolishness of this generation. They remind me of those who chose poorly over a millennium ago. James, you did well tonight. We have to hope that all global citizens listen and act on what you said. We also have to pray that Peter Matteo still has the ear of God and that he can soften Our Lord's response."

As anticipated, the majority of the global response to the president's speech includes varying degrees of disapproval. Many label Larson as a man dwelling in the past, while party leaders and others debate his fitness to lead as President. Seizing the opportunity to make a change, opposition party members are drafting legislation to censor his speech.

Nonetheless, a burgeoning list of World Federation leaders as well as the Governor of Mars and representatives from the Moon and Titan colonies, express support for President Larson and Pope Ignatius. Defying detractors, they bravely caution the populace to reject Samael's influence. Yet, the people sadly remain unreceptive to their arguments. They're much too blinded by their pride and arrogance to accept them.

Across the pond on Earth, Larson garners support from select leaders, among them, England's Prime Minister and the British Royal Family. But the British Parliament finds itself profoundly divided. With a mere forty-eight hours until Samael addresses the UK, the nation is engulfed in impassioned rhetoric among supporters and adversaries, with the turmoil threatening to destabilize the entire country.

Thankfully, the country's attention quickly shifts to the World Cup, and the ensuing distractions temporarily alleviate the nation's issues, despite the British empire facing the possibility of collapse. The allure of the games thoroughly captivates its people, drawing their attention in a manner reminiscent of the Romans, who turned a blind eye to pressing matters to revel instead in the skills of their favorite gladiators.

CHAPTER FORTY-SEVEN

As Samael's RV winds through Trafalgar Square en route to the iconic Houses of Parliament, those who aren't engrossed in the games follow the RV's progress through the streets of London.

In the crisp embrace of a spring morning, Big Ben chimes the time, providing a charming backdrop to a mix of followers and dissenters lining the path.

As usual, repeated shouts of acclaim overwhelm murmurs of rebuke and disdain. The cheers are so loud that the dissenters can hardly be heard through the much louder cries of the adoring multitude.

To obscure Samael's arrival at Parliament, the RV is guided toward a discreet rear entrance due to security concerns. London authorities insist Samael step out into relative solitude, disappearing unnoticed into the building.

With ease, the colossal creature maneuvers his electric scooter to the podium in Westminster Hall. There, he receives a standing ovation from the majority. He will remain seated as he addresses the House of Commons and the House of Lords.

"Citizens of the United Kingdom," he says, jumping into his speech with a firm voice, "I am overjoyed to be with you today. Your country has a rich history that you are rightly proud of. Today, I am here to talk about your future and that of the entire galaxy.

"I am what I am — the envoy of humanity's future. Contrary to what some say, I am not a charlatan. I am not the malevolence you must guard against. I am the Son of Sarah, a transhuman born of a Canadian woman marked by the repercussions of our actions on the Martian environment. Had humankind not intervened in events in the manner it did, no metamorphoses would have transpired. There would have been no Titans, no Lilith, no Samael. Yet, here I stand before you today.

"Because of humanity's imperfections, we terraformed Mars, resurrecting a lifeless sphere into the vibrant planet it is now. In doing so, we are a novel force within the cosmos — no other race has made such drastic changes to their own or another planet. As such, we must embrace our potential and claim our place beside the Creator.

"Thus, after so many millennia, we have transcended the boundaries of mere human existence. We are no longer simply beings molded in the Creator's image. We have exceeded prior expectations, yet we continue to linger in the shadow of our Maker. Have we not created intelligent life forms? Have we not created exhilarating landscapes from barren desolation?

"There were many belief systems in our past: Hinduism, Buddhism, Islam, Roman, Greek, Egyptian, Aztec, Maya — all of them had distinct mythologies crafted around beings they worshipped as gods. However, none of them, save one — the religion known as Christianity, arisen from Judaism — has stood the test of time.

"But now is the time of humans. The natural order of the universe is to choose belief systems and advance to new learning with a deeper understanding of who we are and where we will go.

"I am Samael, Son of Sarah. My father and I are poised to lead humanity into an era of untold prosperity, a new era bathed in enlightenment and understanding, a new epoch of peace.

"In the ensuing weeks, an event will unfurl that will shape the destiny of mankind, unraveling all mysteries and unveiling all truths. Miss Jennifer Stone and Lieutenant Colonel Nevins will disclose the time and place when all will be revealed, and all will be understood. I am the guide that will demonstrate that humanity is the kingdom, power, and glory, for we ourselves fashion our destiny, and with my help, we will rule the cosmos!

"Until that day, I remain in your service."

With his speech concluded, Samael rises from his seat in his resplendent golden attire, removes his tri-lensed glasses and gazes down upon Parliament, his towering presence almost too much to bear.

Slowly, one by one, members rise, clapping with almost reverent unity, the applause gathering momentum like a single peal of thunder growing louder and louder.

Acknowledging the accolades, Samael tilts his head upward and folds his arms over his chest, arrogantly absorbing every bit of the adoration directed his way.

As soon as the speech is over, images of Samael speaking to Parliament travel like lightning across the globe. To some, they are a haunting vision of humanity's demise, while others consider them symbols of the overwhelming happiness Samael promises.

For days afterward, calls for action and calls for denial are all people hear. Pundits, pro and con, add their spins to Samael's speech, espousing outright propaganda or painful truths. People line up to take sides one way or the other as humankind once again clashes with its faith, embracing pride and arrogance instead of the humility necessary for a peaceful existence.

Humans are a stubborn race, foolish and reckless.

CHAPTER FORTY-EIGHT

Life continues on its unending journey on the great blue marble suspended in the heavens, but the ever-shifting tides of division and conflict consume the attention of most on Earth.

Across the void, the people of Mars are vocal in their astonishment of Earth's reaction to Samael's speeches. In harmony with the Martians, the United States colonies on the Moon and Titan fix their collective gaze upon what's happening on Earth. Concern ripples through these extraterrestrial communities as they contemplate the well-being of their loved ones back home.

To be sure their views are known, Martian broadcasts beam commentators' voices to even the most distant colonies to share profound disillusionment with Earth's seemingly oblivious response to Samael. They can't understand the reactions of Earthlings, since their own memories remain vividly etched with the harrowing images of the Malignant's wicked horde sweeping across their planet. The grand monuments erected to remember the heroic valor displayed by the 101st Airborne, Peter Matteo, and the Guardians are receiving more visits than usual.

In a sign that all may not be lost, a sense of urgency rises through the Earthly populace. Faithful individuals seeking refuge from the prevailing folly propel a surge of travel and Martian citizenship applications. In a relatively short time, the submissions increase a hundredfold, creating a backlog within the short-handed agency handling the requests.

Frank A. Ruffolo

Joining the bandwagon, Detective David Jacoby uses the current Earthly situation to ensure his mother's safety while suiting his own needs.

Insisting that his mother needs to distance herself from Samael and his misled followers, he urges her to leave her residence in Atlanta and relocate to Xanthe City. At the same time, he arranges a meeting between her and Galina, making sure to include time to show off his Camaro. David's mother has a keen interest in his obsession with antiques, having been on the receiving end of endless descriptions of his latest acquisitions.

Seated comfortably in his home office, David occupies himself by meticulously cleaning his handgun while Galina works in the kitchen. His android girlfriend is a marvelous cook, and his mouth waters with anticipation of another great meal at her hands.

"Jake," she calls out, "there is an incoming vid call from your mother!"

Dropping a cleaning rod, he hurries into the family area, tugging Galina along.

"You think she's coming?" he asks Galina nervously.

"I do not know, honey. Shouldn't we find out?"

Impatient for the twenty-minute delay to expire, David sits next to Galina on the couch, waiting for the familiar face to appear on the monitor.

"Hello, my dear!" says David's mother warmly. "Oh, is that Galina?" she asks, spotting the android in the frame. "It's nice to finally 'meet' you! David, I called because I have exciting news!"

David's face registers eager anticipation as his mother continues, "I decided that you're right, Jakey. It's time to leave here; there's too much going on. After your last call, I booked a trip to Mars on the Galactic Princess! Isn't that great? They've been advertising that ship everywhere, so I looked into it and managed to secure a discounted fare since I'll only be traveling one way! I have so much packing to do! I can't wait to see you, honey! I hope I'm not coming too soon... Did I tell you my departure is only twenty-four hours away? Of course, I'm going to have to stay with you for a while, but don't worry, I'll get my own place as soon as possible. I don't want to intrude upon your life, Jakey."

David exchanges a delighted glance with Galina.

"Mom, that's fantastic news!" he says as Galina reaches for his hand. "I can't wait for you to meet Galina!"

Pleased by David's statement, Galina nestles her head on David's shoulder. "Hello, Mrs. Jacoby," she says shyly. "I have heard so much about you. I am eager to meet the woman who raised the man I love. We will see you soon! Safe travels!"

Extending their hands toward the terminal, David and Galina wave affectionately.

"Mom, call me when you arrive in Xanthe," says David. "We'll pick you up from the spaceport. Love you, Mom!"

As the image fades, Galina locks her gaze on David. Though she's happy about how the vid meeting went, she's still uncertain about being accepted.

"Do you think she will like me, Jake? You know how people can be. Even you had reservations once, remember?"

David had intended to bring up a subject that's been weighing on his mind during dinner, but Galina's question urges him to seize the moment. Sliding off the couch, he lowers himself to one knee. Meeting Galina's eyes, he utters, "Galina, it's not about what my mom or anyone else thinks. What matters is that I love you. I, David Jacoby, love Galina Sharapova, and you would make me eternally happy if you would become Galina Jacoby."

Swiftly, he retrieves a small box from his pocket and opens it to show Galina the contents.

Shocked, Galina looks at it, astonishment rendering her silent.

Hoping for a positive answer, David keeps his eyes fixed on her and continues, his voice brimming with emotion.

"Galina, will you do me the honor of becoming my wife?"

Dazed, Galina looks down to the box, where an exquisite ring, a stunning composition of gold and diamonds, rests.

Without waiting for a response, David removes the symbol of his love and places it on Galina's finger.

As a hush descends upon the room, Galina absorbs the weight of the moment. Then slowly, she lowers her hand, her eyes fixed on the radiant ring.

Lifting her gaze, she locks onto David's face, and with all the tenderness she feels, she replies, "Becoming Mrs. David Jacoby is an honor I wholeheartedly embrace. You, Jake, are a special man, and I am a lucky woman!"

Their hearts brimming with love, the two melt into each other's arms, sealing their relationship in a long, heartfelt kiss.

Then, the kitchen's cooking center diligently sends out notifications that dinner is ready, persistently attempting to capture their attention.

However, the couple is undeterred by the persistent chime. David and Galina remain entwined, united in their newly declared commitment to one another.

On the Moon, several inhabitants of the lunar monastery converge around the revered Golden Tree of God, a twice-a-day ritual they've kept since their formation. The monks take turns kneeling in adoration before the tree.

During the course of the ongoing shift, a sudden wave of angelic chants resounds from the base of the sacred tree. Not long after, a monk bursts into the office where Senior Brother Oettinger is working.

"Brother! A miraculous occurrence!" shouts the religious, breathing heavily after running from the lake.

"What is it?" asks Oettinger, rising from his desk. "What has happened?"

Trying to catch his breath, the brother inhales deeply before explaining, "We were praying the litany when out of nowhere, we heard angels singing! And then, I heard..."

The monk breaks off his story, not quite believing what happened earlier.

"What? What did you hear?" asks Oettinger, stepping in front of the excited friar.

"I...I heard a tiny sound... But oh, it was marvelous!"

"Tell me what you heard, Brother!" utters Oettinger, resisting the urge to grab the monk's shoulders.

Holding his superior's gaze, the monk explains, "I heard God's voice! He instructed us to request Commander Peter's presence here, along with his entire family!"

Brother Oettinger walks back to his chair, sitting down heavily.

"Are you absolutely certain of what you're telling me?" he asks his fellow monastic.

"You know me, Father. Have I ever been untruthful?"

"No... But this is quite out of the ordinary."

"I know, isn't it marvelous! You must tell Pope Ignatius right away!"

"Um, let's pray about it first. Please accompany me to the chapel."

A short time later, Brother Oettinger engages in a vid call with Pope Ignatius. Lost in the conversation, he conveys to the pope what happened to his fellow friar, concluding with, "Your Holiness, kindly pass on to the Commander that he is being 'summoned' by the Golden Tree of God."

"Are you sure it was a word from Our Heavenly Father?" asks the pope, unfailingly vigilant against the devil's wiles.

"Yes, I am certain. I thoroughly questioned Brother Chafin. He is one of our most faithful monastics; I trust that what he experienced was genuine."

"Indeed. Well, then. I accept your judgment. I will relay the message to Peter."

"Please do. It was urgent."

Upon ending the transmission, Pope Ignatius sets the Divine request in motion. Buzzing for his secretary, he asks for a connection to Peter in Sorrento.

"My dear son," says the pope, "I would not disturb you unless it was important. I know it is dinner time. However, what I am about to share with you is of paramount significance."

Accompanied by Angela's presence nearby, Peter declares sincerely, "Holy Father, it's always an honor to hear from you; the hour is of no consequence. I happily welcome all calls from the leader of the Roman Universal and Apostolic Church."

"Thank you, Commander. I know you are a man of great faith. I am calling tonight to give you a message from Brother Oettinger of the lunar monastic community."

"Oh, yes, I know him well," says Peter.

"That is good because one of Brother Oettinger's friars received a startling message this morning. He revealed that God Himself is bidding you and your entire family to the Moon."

Peter and Angela exchange inquiring glances.

"Our Lord wants us to go to the Moon?" asks Peter.

"Yes. Thinking upon the request, I believe He may wish to shield you and your loved ones from the impending upheaval poised to strike Earth."

In Sorrento, a look of concern passes between Peter and Angela, both grappling with the unexpected news.

Peter looks at the vid screen. "Holy Father, we will certainly comply with the Divine directive. "I'll investigate flight options this very evening."

"No need," replies Pope Ignatius. "Brother Oettinger convinced me that this is urgent. Therefore, I have taken the liberty of arranging for you and your family to travel to the lunar community tomorrow as special envoys of the Vatican. Apologies again, but since the request has come directly from our Heavenly Father, swift action is necessary."

"I understand. We will be ready."

"Very good. Every member of your family in Sorrento is included in this request. My secretary will give you the details. Safe travels, Commander. Our prayers encompass you, your family, and all of humanity."

With the request from Heaven, Peter and Angela absorb the gravity of the moment, aware that their upcoming journey holds meaning beyond their understanding.

Sometime later, Samael, Hollis Nevins, and Jennifer Stone find themselves back in Nevada's desert, where preparations are in full swing in front of Gabriel's Tower, an odd, rocky structure protruding from the prairie surrounding the Black Hills of Wyoming.

A grand stage has already been erected there, flanked by an array of video devices and projection screens, strategically placed to cater to the anticipated massive audience.

As excitement builds, security barricades are also being

set up, with designated parking zones and defined locations for essential provisions like food and sanitation services.

This Day of Awakening is slated for noon on the upcoming Memorial Day holiday. The organizers want to give ample time for Samael's loyal followers to make arrangements to attend.

Adjusting her blouse and smoothing her hair, Jennifer takes her place at the media center on sub-level ten of Nevins' Area 51 facility. She booked airtime on all stations today to officially announce the start of Samael's crowning achievement.

With practiced composure, she addresses the nation, her voice carrying the strength of character imposed on her by Samael.

"Greetings, fellow Americans. I am Jennifer Stone, communication director for Samael, Son of Sarah. Today, I bring you exciting news. In twelve days, on the national celebration of Memorial Day, Monday, May 30, an extraordinary public presentation will grace the area around Gabriel's Tower in Wyoming. Its purpose is to herald the momentous awakening of humankind, guided by the benevolent Samael, the torchbearer of this movement.

"We anticipate the presence of at least 25,000 fervent devotees, all of them converging on the site at the same time, an assembly for which we have diligently arranged accommodations in the surrounding cities.

"If you are one of the thousands planning to attend, I must underscore that vigilant security measures will be strictly enforced the day of the event, including several days leading up to it. The spirit of the occasion will not tolerate disruptions or turmoil. Therefore, we will remain watchful, as certain radicals have voiced their hostile intent toward the gathering. Local and national security forces are poised to thwart any attempts at disorder, ensuring an atmosphere of reverence and celebration for all attendees.

"This will be a time for jubilation and elation, a moment that will echo forever across the cosmos. To explain, Samael has graciously recorded a message, which I will now share with you."

A brief pause ensues before Samael materializes on vid screens, his upper torso framed against a backdrop of brilliant cobalt blue. With his olive complexion radiating beneath illuminating lights, his tri-lensed sunglasses mirror the depth of the background.

"Salutations, dear companions and devoted followers. In recent months, I have stood before your leaders, acquainting them with the impending renaissance of humanity. In a mere twelve days, I will unveil this revelation to you and the entire cosmos. It is my vision, my purpose, to elevate humanity to the pedestal it rightfully deserves, to raise us to a realm akin to the Divine, and seat us at the right hand of the leaders of the entire universe.

"This is the time for glory, the era of our ascendancy! Together, we are poised to steer the future of mankind into eternity, to a destiny of unparalleled grandeur! I await Memorial Day with great anticipation!"

With Samael's words, the stage is set for an epoch-defining event that will resonate far beyond the confines of Gabriel's Tower and the deserts of Nevada, reaching out to the very cosmos itself.

The next day, Angela, Peter, and Michael embark on the Vatican's air transport, accompanied by Angela's parents, with their spirits somewhat dampened by the decision of Angela's aunt and uncle to remain behind. When questioned about this choice, they calmly explained that they found no reason to venture so far from home, as they hold firm faith in the protective embrace of the Rosary of Mary, which they pray daily. They also expressed a heartfelt desire to provide refuge to friends and neighbors should circumstances take a turn for the worst.

Peter and his extended family arrive at Houston Spaceport in under three hours, a location familiar to Peter due to his extensive travels to the Moon and beyond. At Houston, the family boards the colossal vessel known as the Galactic Princess.

Fascinated by the craft's immense size, the family and other passengers crowd the windows to watch as it ascends against the backdrop of an early morning dawn. An instant later, the craft enters the upper atmosphere.

In a mere twenty-four hours, the Matteos are set to reach the Garden of Eden, where Peter will once again assume his role as Commander of the Ark.

Little does he know, a pivotal piece of information: the events of May 30th, remains undisclosed to him.

After the Galactic Princess departs, the aircrew of a galactic cargo ship, the Sappho, readies their craft for another journey to Proxima b.

Despite the staggering distance of four light years separating the aircrew from their destination, the voyage spans a mere two weeks.

The seven seasoned spacefarers comprising the crew of the Sappho are well-acquainted with this particular itinerary, as they've traversed this cosmic route countless times.

Today, they consider themselves fortunate to be scheduled for this trip. None of them want to be on Earth during the impending "awakening and reckoning" heralded by Samael.

Commander Alton Tower, the stalwart leader of the Sappho, is well known for his outspoken opposition to the son of Sarah. To keep himself grounded, he carries a silver rosary wherever he goes, and he knows many on board also keep religious items on their persons.

The crew is grateful their mission is occurring at this specific time, primarily because they hope their trip will shield them from the tumultuous events unfolding on Earth. Moreover, the trip will bring them back to the inhabitants of Proxima b, a population with whom they've forged a deep connection.

The Sappho aircrew has developed infinite respect for all Proximians. During the course of their many journeys to that distant world, they've learned that its residents diligently monitor transmissions from Earth. However, unlike Earthers, they've astutely pierced through the veneer of Samael's propaganda. Consequently, the planet's residents are unflinching in identifying the evil essence within that unholy creature.

CHAPTER FORTY-NINE

At the entrance to the lunar Garden of Eden, Peter wrestles with the family's luggage while Angela propels Michael in his stroller. Suddenly, she halts at the shimmering protective barrier encapsulating God's lunar creation.

"Still not fond of going through the energy field?" asks Peter, colliding with her while wrangling the bags. Though their electrically powered gear obediently responds to the guidance of his hand controller, he feels like he's herding cats.

Directing the luggage to move ahead, Peter guides his family into the tunnel, where they become enveloped in the humming energy field. When they step out into the garden, their bodies are tingling from static electricity.

Waiting for them are Brother Oettinger and two fellow brothers.

"We're happy you were able to arrive so quickly!" greets Oettinger, assuming control of the Matteo's luggage while the energy shield deactivates. "Let's get you to the hotel."

As the group approaches the commercial structure, the voices of singing angels capture their attention. The sound is coming from the Golden Tree, causing them to hasten to the lake instead.

After they cross a bridge, the angels conclude their song, and the Golden Tree's shimmering leaves sway gently in the distance, despite the absence of wind.

Peter turns curiously to Oettinger. "Do you know why my family and I have been called here so suddenly? I'm not aware of anything happening."

Oettinger lowers his head to speak close to Peter's ear. "Do you know about Samael's upcoming event?"

Peter furrows his brow. "No, I guess I missed it while we were traveling. What's he planning?"

"His team has organized an elaborate outdoor spectacle to unveil his mission to the worlds, and it's set to take place right in front of Gabriel's Tower in Wyoming! You know the place, that unusual formation they once called Devil's Tower? Can you believe that?"

"I can," responds Peter. "Earth's people are deeply divided, and he's impatient to harness all that dissention for himself. There are constant conflicts between those who support Samael and those who oppose him."

Oettinger shakes his head. "These are troubling times, my friend. It often feels to me as though society is regressing in their beliefs, almost back to the days of Noah and Sodom. It's so disheartening to witness how people are behaving!"

Peter agrees. "I'm ready to help, but you know I can't until certain conditions are met."

"I do," responds Oettinger, lowering his eyes in dismay. "I try to remember that there have been positive developments: the Titans have disbanded and Karen Stamos renounced the name Lilith, but it's hard. Commander, we need you, but I don't know if anyone is prepared to call upon you."

As the two soldiers of God enter the lake area, a powerful voice resonates throughout the garden. Forcefully, it declares, *"I Am! The time is now!"*

Acknowledging the source, Peter crosses himself and leaves Brother Oettinger, Angela, and Michael at the garden gate while he heads alone to the Golden Tree.

The sight of the tree's swaying golden leaves glistening and shining in the non-existent breeze is so dazzling that it makes Peter fall to his knees to await the thunderous voice he knows will follow.

Shortly, a booming sound, almost like thunder, announces the Divine presence.

"Commander, during the events at the tower in Wyoming, a pivotal moment will occur that will be your signal. You will once again assume your role as Commander, and My Guardians will follow your lead.

"The events will be pivotal, and the outcome will be decided by My children's free will. Hearts are changing, but there may not be enough that will return to Me before I need to intervene. If I do, My retribution will be swift.

"Peace be with you, Commander. Remember that your entire family will remain safe if they heed My words.

"Pray for humankind; they have lost their way."

As God's voice fades, Peter rises when archangels Michael, Gabriel, Raphael, Uriel, Raguel, Remiel, and Sariel appear before the tree in resplendent, full golden armor, clutching swords and shields.

Solemnly, they simultaneously kneel on one knee as high above, an image of Metatron unfolds.

"Commander," addresses Metatron, *"we are poised and ready. Our number is infinite; all are steadfastly standing at your right hand, awaiting your command."*

Peter looks intently at Metatron, the supreme commander of all the archangels and leader of the Guardians and Watchers, including Michael, God's warrior general. Metatron is draped in pure white, his long hair and beard flowing with a grand mustache. Above his head, a three-dimensional cube shines radiantly, representing energy flowing between the Earth and the Divine.

Abruptly, an old man dressed in antiquated attire materializes at Metatron's side. He gazes down at Peter in profound silence.

"Enoch?" asks Peter.

Instantly, the two meld into one, and the seven armored soldiers vanish from view. All that remains is Peter, standing in front of the Golden Tree of God.

Seeing Peter alone, Brother Oettinger approaches and gives Peter's shoulder a gentle shake.

"You've been blessed, as have we all," he whispers. "The Commander of the Angels has welcomed the Commander of the Ark. Now the Fallen have no chance at all."

CHAPTER FIFTY

At Karen's new location in the tranquil Catskill Mountains, she grapples with inner turmoil. Sleep eludes her, her mind awash with worry, concern, and fear.

Unable to rest, she walks outside the RV to gaze at the serene mountains, but her agitation persists. Samael is relentless in infiltrating her thoughts, and the energy she expends in repelling him is exhausting.

Hearing a noise outside, Anthony peers out the door of their nearly completed home. It's not ready for Karen yet, so she's still sleeping in the RV.

Seeing his fiancée alone in the dark, he calls out to her, but Karen's cluttered mind fails to register his words.

Anxiously, Abila rushes to Karen's side. He embraces her leg, the only part of her he can reach.

Acknowledging her fiancé's presence, she looks down and offers him a tender smile. Then she folds her long legs into a seated position on the moist grass so Anthony can join her.

"Tony, I have tried to ignore him," says Karen, sadness infiltrating her voice, "but I must speak; I must act. Samael needs to be stopped. You cannot comprehend what he is, but I know everything. The worlds must be told about him."

Anthony gazes at Karen's tear-streaked face with resolve in his lovesick eyes. "Tell me your plan, my love, and I will make it happen."

Karen sighs, her large hand gently caressing Anthony's head.

"First, you need to understand who Samael is. Then, we must deliver a message to every world before the World Federation. This Monday, Samael and his followers intend to make their stand at Gabriel's Tower, and we must defeat him. We must prevail against them all!"

Anthony's eyes widen with fear and comprehension as Karen transfers her knowledge directly from her mind to his. As he understands the gravity of the task before them, a shared determination solidifies.

After Peter's encounter at the tree, the family sits by the tranquil lake. Relaxed in the serene surroundings, Angela fixes her gaze on the cosmos visible through the protective dome. Outside its shield, the Earth looms on the horizon as the Orion Constellation twinkles among countless other heavenly bodies.

Amid this cosmic spectacle, Peter skips stones across the lake, eliciting joyful laughter from Michael. Wishing to involve his son, he hands him a small, smooth rock. Accepting it eagerly, the young boy turns it over in his hand and with a determined look, attempts to mimic his father's technique.

As mother and father watch Michael throw stones into the water, the profound serenity of the moment is disrupted when Brother Oettinger rushes toward them.

"Peter!" he calls out urgently. "There's a vid transmission from Earth! It's Karen Stamos!"

Angela's eyes widen in recognition. "Isn't she—"

"Yes," interjects Peter. "I wonder how she managed to track me down."

Angela encourages her husband with a nod toward Brother Oettinger. "Go ahead. We'll catch up."

Grateful for his wife's understanding, Peter hurries

toward the monastery with the monk, the older man's robe billowing as they rush past fellow brothers and sisters tending to God's garden.

At the entrance to Oettinger's office, Peter skids to a stop, shocked by a miniature projection of Karen Stamos just inside. Reduced in size by the transmission, the colossal transhuman now appears almost human — she's even clad in typical street clothes: sweatshirt and worn jeans, with her distinctive blue glasses.

"Miss Stamos! How did you find me?" exclaims Peter.

Karen smiles, "First things first. Mr. Matteo, I understand your mission, just as you understand mine. You know that I became a transformed human due to the pathogen I was infected with, and that during my stasis and eventual release, I fell under Samael's influence. But what you do not know is, though I initially accepted my role as Samael's 'puppet,' I eventually discovered his true nature, and it appalled me.

"Ah, you are curious about Lilith," says Karen, perceiving Peter's unspoken question. "Yes, I was trapped within her, but I freed myself from Samael's clutches through sheer will and determination, and he detests me for it. That is why I parted ways with him and his followers.

"Oh, you are still wondering how I found you. Well, it was not easy. First, I tried to contact Doctor Strakov, but he has been arrested for rebelling against Samael and the Titans. Then, my fiancé, Doctor Abila, made several calls. He reached out to Ambassador Fiona Gabelli's office, Austin Patton, and even Pope Ignatius's secretary, who finally told us where you were."

Peter nods, acknowledging the effort. "It sounds like you went through a lot."

"It was not easy, but what I have to share with you is of the utmost importance. I implore you to understand that the former Titans, much like me, were nothing more than unwitting test subjects. The genuine threat lies squarely with Samael and his father. I know you understand this, but it bears repeating: Satan is utterly indifferent to any ongoing struggles. His quest for supremacy predates even the existence of Adam and Eve; it reaches back to the very dawn of creation. Satan deludes himself into believing he is on par with God. His singular aim is to subjugate all of humanity under his dominion. Despite the certainty of his defeat, he clings to his delusions, steadfastly refusing to surrender. His history of resistance spans the existence of humanity, beginning with the Garden of Eden and extending to the Great Flood, to Moses' trials in the desert, to the destruction of Sodom and Gomorrah, to the Crucifixion, and even to Judgment Day. His malevolence continued during your family's quest to unlock the keys to Earth's salvation and persisted through the Martian conflict, and now looms ominously here on Earth."

Peter asks anxiously, "Have you heard about the event Samael has planned for Monday?"

"I do know about it, and Samael will not be the only one there that day. As you are no doubt aware, a multitude of fallen angels exists, and they will all join him, to the complete astonishment of humanity. I very much want to warn every world through a speaking slot before the entire World Federation, but the time frame is too short to arrange that. Instead, I will address the Directorate via vid conference this Friday at noon. Will you join me that day to persuade them to rally behind your cause? Will you help me defeat Samael?"

Peter is deeply moved by Karen's commitment and her concern for humanity.

"I will absolutely support your plea to the Directorate! Thank you for reaching out to me, Karen! May God bless you and your fiancé abundantly!"

Karen lowers her eyes, humbled by the Commander's approval. "Thank you, Commander. I look forward to working with you."

As Karen's image fades, Brother Oettinger says, "Well, that was quite unexpected! I didn't see that coming at all!"

Peter tilts his head at the monk. "As they say, 'God works in mysterious ways.' We need to pray for her. Once the Malignant catches wind of her plans, he'll step up his attacks."

CHAPTER FIFTY-ONE

As the sun rises Friday morning, Samael, Lieutenant Colonel Nevins, and Jennifer Stone assemble their team, preparing for their journey to Wyoming. They will fly to Hulett Municipal Airport, just twenty-two miles from Gabriel's Tower National Monument and Park, while Samael will ride in his imposing RV, accompanied by a convoy of support personnel. The team's ultimate destination is the national park, where they will prepare for Samael's grand Memorial Day reveal.

In eager anticipation of an extraordinary day, the global media has already swarmed the tiny town of Hulett, adding their number to thousands of curious onlookers and ardent devotees of the enigmatic colossus. Surprisingly, although the event is still a day away, the crowd has almost doubled in size.

In response to this overwhelming turnout, local law enforcement has begun redirecting visitors to other sections within the park, ensuring remote vidmonitor viewing opportunities. Teams from neighboring towns have also joined forces to aid in crowd management.

Furthermore, upon a thorough assessment of the situation, Wyoming's governor has taken a proactive stance. Recalling what happened at previous events, he has put the National Guard on notice in recognition of the heightened potential for unrest.

In the Catskills, Karen settles into a section of her RV for her remote session with the World Federation Directorate. For the occasion, she dressed in one of her only business outfits, a subdued gray suit. Unsurprisingly, her wardrobe options are meager, as they're hindered by the lengthy process of needing custom-made clothes and further delayed because of the couple's lack of a reliable source of currency credits.

To alleviate the strain on the couple's finances, Karen and Anthony have set up a partnership that has birthed a non-profit organization with a dual mission of advocacy and research. The entity's number one goal is to promote advancements in genetic research. Its secondary objective is to call attention to all forms of bullying, using Karen as a prime example. They hope to generate interest and income through paid appearances and partnerships.

Approaching the noon hour, Karen connects to the virtual meeting. Shortly after, Peter taps into the vidlink in the media center of the Garden of Eden.

"Hello, Miss Stamos. Are you ready for this?" inquires Peter, pleased to see that Karen has already logged in.

The determined giant responds with a serene smile. "Please call me Karen. We need to make a compelling impression today."

Seated within his office, Secretary-General Dalvi initiates the video call and opens the meeting with a call to order from the members of the Directorate.

"Esteemed ambassadors, I am pleased to introduce Karen Stamos and a surprise participant, the Commander of the Ark, Mr. Peter Matteo. Many of you are acquainted with Miss Stamos as Lilith, however, she has recently petitioned the Federation for a voice under her original name, as she now prefers to be known. Thus, Miss Stamos and Commander, the floor is yours."

Karen, visible from the neck up, with her hair pulled back elegantly, and sporting her ever-present sunglasses, takes a deep breath.

"Secretary-General Dalvi and honored ambassadors, I address you today in an attempt to sway your stance against the so-called mission of Samael of Sarah.

"Having been the one closest to him, I can attest that he is not what he seems. Samael is not the benevolent bearer of goodwill that he claims to be. In reality, he is the progeny of the leader of the fallen angels, the ruler of Hell. Therefore, his intentions are anything but benign. He is not the savior he presents himself to be. In fact, he stands as a harbinger of the underworld, wholly aligned with his monstrous father, whom you call Satan, among many other names. Father and son's purpose is not to guide humanity but to ensnare all of us against all things Divine, including God Himself.

"Today, I am taking the risk of speaking to you despite the consequences I fully expect will come from this unholy duo. I am here to warn you that the results of aligning the worlds with Samael will be nothing like what he's told you to expect. In contrast, the result of siding with him will be terrifying, unlike anything you could imagine. Ambassadors, it falls solely upon your shoulders to rebuff this disciple of Satan, and to instead enlist Commander Matteo and the Guardians to send him back to the underworld, where he belongs.

Pausing here, Karen asks, "Peter, would you like to add anything?"

In a firm voice, the Commander responds, "Yes, thank you. I have forewarned you all that our Heavenly Father Himself urges us to reject this spawn of the Malignant. If we falter in His urgent appeal, humanity will bear the brunt of Our Father's retribution as He will then purify and sanctify the Earth once again. This is not a threat but a declaration of the potential consequences if we remain passive concerning Samael's growing influence."

"If I may," interjects Karen, her voice rising. "Ambassadors, Peter and I implore you to heed our warnings! The climax of Samael's work will come on Monday! The future of our race hinges on your response, along with that of Earth's populace!"

Abruptly, Karen severs the link, leaving the Directorate in contemplative silence. To fill the hush, Secretary-General Dalvi leans forward, his voice grave.

"Esteemed members, we have received counsel from two of the most respected persons on this issue. Together, they have outlined a course of action that we must consider. I will convene an emergency assembly of the entire Federation to chart our path forward. Regrettably, this assembly will not have time to meet before Monday. Therefore, I recommend to the Directorate that when we meet again, we will vote to entreat Commander Matteo to do what he needs to do on behalf of all humanity."

As the secretary-general concludes the meeting, Fiona, the United States representative, logs off to report to Peter.

"That was quick," says Brother Oettinger, jumping up to respond to the incoming call.

Onscreen, Fiona's voice, laden with tension, chimes into the room.

"This is Ambassador Gabelli. I would like to speak with Mr. Matteo. Is he available?"

Peter edges next to Oettinger. "Fiona, how was our appeal received?"

Static disrupts Fiona's reply, marring the signal's passage. "Dalvi...initiating emergency meeting...Federation...Monday. We're praying...not too late."

Peter's voice rises as he attempts to ensure clarity.

"Fiona, you're breaking up! There will be no meeting before Monday?"

Fiona manages to convey, "...meeting slated for Monday morning... Hope...not too delayed. Dalvi...seeking aid!"

When the transmission ends, Peter draws in a deep breath to cleanse his body of built-up tension.

"I think she said they plan to reach out for my assistance, but it may not come until the last minute! Why must we be so stubborn? I have to tell Angela; I need to return to Earth immediately!"

Just then, a brilliant light fills the media room, and Archangel Gabriel's face emerges from within it.

"Fear not, Commander, you will be in the hands of the Guardians. Emergency travel is not necessary. We will provide."

The night before the event, fervent prayers ripple across the worlds. The worlds remain divided, a reflection of humanity's perennial schism, even amid a thousand years of peace, a testament to the enduring presence of pride and arrogance within the human spirit.

In their tranquil Catskills refuge, Karen and Anthony have finally settled into their new home, with Anthony toiling away in his lab as often as he can.

As usual, Anthony excuses himself after dinner to resume his research, leaving Karen to entertain herself.

Alone with her thoughts, she steps into their backyard, immersing herself in the serene embrace of the mountains.

"They seem so carefree," she muses, as the ethereal glows of fireflies illuminate the darkness. With a sigh of envy, Karen's gaze ascends to Orion, the hunter's three-star belt a familiar sight.

Suddenly, soft footfalls interrupt the quiet. Pivoting,

Karen's eyes meet those of an elderly man, his voice resonating with a sense of familiarity.

"The folks down at the coffee shop mentioned I'd find you here," he says, a twinkle in his eyes. "Lilith, you're a sight to behold, more resplendent than I imagined."

Karen gazes silently at the intruder, her thoughts racing. "My name is Karen," she responds firmly. "Lilith no longer exists."

A wistful smile plays across the old man's lips. "But you are Lilith, and your destiny intertwines with your brother, Samael. He needs you; you should be in Wyoming. You and he are one."

Hearing Karen conversing with someone outside the house, Anthony drops what he's doing and rushes outdoors, the open yard stretching before him as he searches the darkness.

Furious at the stranger's rudeness, Karen closes one pair of eyes to stare unyieldingly at the intruder with the other.

"I am not like Samael," she responds, her tone unyielding. "We are not one, and I am nothing like you. I am not interested in your maneuverings; your moment in the light will be brief. Leave me alone."

Perplexed, Anthony stares wide-eyed at his soulmate, seeing no one but Karen in earnest conversation in their backyard.

"Karen, who are you talking to?" he asks. "There's no one here."

The old man chuckles and vanishes, leaving Karen relieved but distressed.

Slowly, her focus turns toward Anthony.

"It was Satan, posing as an old man, as if I wouldn't recognize him. He's relentless; he won't give up until he captures my soul."

"Are you all right?" asks Anthony anxiously.

"Yes. I think you interrupted him."

"He's going to keep coming, isn't he?"

"I don't think he'll ever stop trying to get me back. But I won't allow it. I've had enough of his lies."

CHAPTER FIFTY-TWO

Before dawn, the spring air in northern Wyoming carries a biting cold, with temperatures in the forties casting a chill around the towering structure renamed for Archangel Gabriel.

As the morning sun ascends, a crowd streams into the cordoned-off area, their number easily surpassing the expected twenty-five thousand.

To entertain the throng, hired bands and other performers take to the stage earlier than scheduled, and food vendors and first aid tents open for business. In the central area, spectators gaze upon immense vid screens, all yearning for a glimpse of Samael, even from a distance.

Just before noon, Josh Hicks, a familiar face from Wake Up New York, takes center stage as the host of this grand affair. He addresses the crowd with the imposing backdrop of Gabriel's Tower looming behind him.

"Good morning, America! We're glad you could join us! Today, we're broadcasting live from Gabriel's Tower, and like you, we're on pins and needles! We're excited to hear what Samael has planned for us!"

After waiting for the crowd to quiet down, he continues, "Before long, our esteemed mentor will take the stage! Are you ready for him?"

Applause and chants of "Samael!" ring off the rocky columns of the formation initially known as Devil's Tower, for several minutes.

After a while, Josh shouts, "All right, let's settle down!" lifting his hands to hush the fervor. "It's time to begin! Allow me to introduce Jennifer Stone, the organizer of today's event!"

The crowd erupts in renewed applause as Jennifer takes the stage, draped in a golden satin jumpsuit and sporting three-lensed, blue-tinted glasses, mirroring the eyewear adorning most of the attendees. Cheers fill the air as Jennifer's voice rises above the din, amplified by large speakers.

"Welcome, everyone! We're so pleased to see how many are here to experience this special day! We know some have traveled long distances, and we're grateful for your dedication!"

Jennifer waits for the cheers to die down, then remarks, "As you know, Samael embarked on this journey just a short time ago, relentlessly dedicating his time and his life to the advancement of humankind! There's no one better suited to guide us into the future! Samael, son of Sarah, is the shining beacon lighting our way to our rightful place within the cosmos! I now present to you Samael of Sarah!"

Accompanying the giant hybrid's entrance, the World Federation anthem blasts through the speakers as he glides across the stage in his electric cart, dressed in a smartly tailored one-piece suit of gold, accompanied by large silver bracelets adorning each wrist. Notably absent are the three-lensed glasses that many in the crowd are wearing.

Bringing his cart to a halt at the heart of the stage, Samael unfolds his large frame, his gaze descending upon his followers as they chant his name.

This commanding image is beamed across the cosmos — from the corridors of power in D.C. to the sanctified halls of the Vatican, extending to the headquarters of the World Federation in Rome, and even to the serene expanse of the Garden of Eden on the Moon and the territory of Titan.

Delighted by the crowd's greeting, Samael absorbs their

adulation, folding his arms across his chest and angling his chin upward toward the heavens.

As the fervor of acclaim recedes, Samael's hands rise. Shouting to be heard, he says, "People of the cosmos, today marks the beginning of promise; this is your day to take your place at the right hand of the Creator! We are the new leaders of the universe! I am proud to be your chosen one, the torchbearer of truth! Do not forget that much like the angels who recognized their equality with the Creator, we, too, are equal to the Divine!

"Accompanying me today are those angels who aligned with me, including my father, the true Prince of Princes! Our angels bear many distinguished names: Baal, Beelzebub, Astarte, Asherah, Chemosh, Dagon, Marduk, Moloch, Nisroch, Tammuz, and numerous others, their number surpassing..."

As Samael speaks, the leaders assembled in the chamber of the World Federation gaze upon the unfolding scene, their faces a mosaic of astonishment and disbelief as Samael voices his audacious proclamations.

United by alarm, they rally together, pressing the secretary-general to urgently beseech Pope Ignatius for an audience with the Commander, even as Samael goes on, "...recalling that this tower was initially a tribute to my father, I come to you..."

Equally astounded by the live spectacle, Peter offers prayers for the cosmos in the confines of the lunar monastery's media room, his somber vigil shared by others in the community.

Abruptly, a piercing roar shatters the peace of the garden, disrupting the broadcast and prompting a swift exodus from the monastery.

Stepping into the sacred grounds, the assembled group looks on in awe as a resplendent golden chariot, pulled by majestic steeds with flames of red and yellow flickering from their forms, descends from the sky. The chariot alights gracefully next to the revered golden tree.

At the reins is Archangel Michael, his voice firmly directed at Peter.

"Commander! The summons has come! The moment is upon us!"

Galvanized by this declaration, Peter embraces his family before hastening toward the waiting chariot, climbing aboard with determination.

Archangel Michael locks eyes with the Commander.

"Our first task is to retrieve the Ark. Then, we will confront the adversary."

An instant later, marked by a thunderous clap of thunder, the chariot ascends toward the heavens, vanishing from sight as though it were never there.

"Where did they go?" ask confused monks.

With all the confidence of his enormous faith, Brother Oettinger responds, "They're about to confront our eternal enemy!"

Samael continues to revel before his adoring onlookers, his voice resonating with confidence.

"Behold! My father and my angelic followers are here today to inaugurate the new world order! My father and I are bearers of truth, wisdom, power, and glory for all eternity! We bring a new reality to humanity that will awaken a splendid awareness of our true place in the heavenly realm!"

In high spirits, Samael turns, raising his arms toward the tower, and chants, "For eternity! For eternity!"

A moment later, the crowd joins in, repeating the mantra with fervor.

While the chanting continues, a massive cloud, as dark as night, shrouds the tower's pinnacle, accompanied by rolling claps of thunder and lightning flashing through both the cloud and the crowd.

The sudden turn terrifies the people. Many cry out, frightened, and begin to flee. But Samael calmly turns and fixes them all with his third eye. Instantly, they calm down. Instead of being fearful, they gaze up at him in hushed expectation.

Above the tower's flat top, an obsidian throne materializes from the darkness, held aloft by black-winged angels. They set the throne down on the summit, while other similarly bleak figures guide an enormous entity to the throne. They all bow before this creature, intoning, "Our prince, our king! Our everlasting spirit of darkness!"

With his back to the crowd, Samael raises his hands, shouting, "Behold, my father! May your luminous, guiding light be forever in our hearts!"

In that moment, Samael's praise and worship of the evil Prince of Hell opens the eyes of many in the crowd, and everything changes. Suddenly, the true intent of Samael's mission is revealed, and chaos erupts.

Those who recognize evil for what it is, stampede toward the exits, some sending prayers heavenward while attempting to break the hypnotic spell over those who remain fixed on Samael's words.

Above Gabriel's Tower, a golden chariot, drawn by flaming horses, streaks across the heavens, accompanied by Metatron and untold numbers of angelic guardians clad in shimmering armor. Zealous in their mission, the guardians seek out the fallen angels and engage them in violent battle.

As blades of black and gold clash, the spectacle breaks the crowd's enchantment, and they watch, riveted by the otherworldly combat they've only heard about.

At a critical juncture in the conflict, Archangel Michael

descends from the chariot, accompanied by the Commander of the Ark.

The sight of the mighty angel with God's appointed leader prompts Samael to bolt from the stage toward his father.

"I am here!" he declares to the beastly fiend. "We are one!" he roars defiantly.

In response, Archangel Michael raises his arm, pointing to the Ark of the Covenant.

This is the signal Peter was waiting for.

Lifting his hand to show the ring of King Solomon that all Commanders of the Ark possess, he inserts it into a concealed slot on the Ark's side. As the ring slips in, the Ark's top unlatches and lifts, releasing God's power into the world.

Instantly, a shrill wail accompanies shafts of energy radiating from the Ark, causing observers to clutch their ears in agony.

Without delay, God's power strikes Satan's throne, and the object dissolves into nothingness. At the same time, the fallen angels incinerate into wisps of swirling dust.

The Malignant, tormented by the loss of his demon horde, belches fire and spits poison while trying to avoid being caught by the Divine force. Unsurprisingly, he's no match for the overwhelming power of Almighty God. The Ark's intensity finds him and engulfs him, instantly crushing him into a tiny speck devoid of all light that vanishes into thin air.

Watching all this, Samael roars his disapproval. Defiantly, he fixes his three eyes on the Ark, screaming, "You may have banished my father Satan, but I am the king of glory! You are powerless against me!"

Yet, no sooner do those words escape his lips than a beam of righteous brilliance strikes him into silence.

As God's energy consumes Satan's son, the wicked

being's face contorts into a silent scream, and he extends his arms in a final act of defiance. In a fiery blaze, he goes up in flames, his form erupting in glowing embers down to his very cells, every part of him consumed by God's cleansing fire.

Within seconds, all that remains of the once-impressive hybrid is his blackened third eye, the source of his heinous hold on humanity. Finally, this, too, is destroyed, but not before it grows to twice its size and explodes in a flame of the hottest blue, tinged with the acrid stench of noxious sulphur.

When Samael and all traces of the evil horde are gone, the angelic guardians fade from view, leaving Archangel Michael and Peter alone at the summit. Below, all who remain, uneasily await what will happen next.

Striding to the summit's edge, the magnificent archangel, defender of God's children, raises his gleaming sword high. In a commanding voice, he declares, *"Satan and his son have been defeated! Repent and worship the one true God!"*

As the mighty warrior stands atop the summit, his words dominate the thoughts of millions. But as soon as he climbs back into his chariot and directs his team into the heavens, many seem to forget all they've seen and heard. Mimicking the battle in the sky, skirmishes soon begin between those who mourn the death of their prophet and those who bless the power of God.

Behind the stage, Jennifer Stone and Lieutenant Colonel Nevins slip away as discreetly as possible, hoping to avoid becoming embroiled in the chaos. As they rush to waiting vehicles, each silently muses, "This isn't over; it's only the beginning!"

Globally, tensions rise and the chaos spreads, despite everything political and religious leaders try to do to calm the masses.

Separately, Archangel Michael returns Peter to the lunar Garden of Eden, then deposits the Ark of the Covenant inside the Holy of Holies. His task complete, he returns to the Orion Constellation to await God's commands.

Returned to the sanctuary of the Garden of Eden, Peter watches dejectedly as the Golden Tree of God dims and the celestial choir ceases their joyous songs. Joining him at the tree, Angela holds their squirming son while trying to comfort her husband.

"You did what you could," she tells him, holding her squirming son. "The people have to decide for themselves now."

Still squirming, Michael begs to be put down, so Angela sets him on his feet. Instantly, he runs to his father, who scoops him up tenderly.

"I don't know—"

Silencing all doubt, a commanding voice thunders in the garden.

"*I Am! Victory is yours, Commander! The battle is over, but the war is not won. Humanity continues on a relentless path to perdition.*

"*Pray for them. If they are to be saved, they must awaken, repent, and renounce Samael and his father, the devil, the prince of evil, the eternal liar!*"

CHAPTER FIFTY-THREE

"Live from Gabriel's Tower, I'm Josh Hicks, returning to the airwaves after a spectacular turn of events at today's festivities. Right before our eyes, what was meant to be a celebration of humanity quickly became a manifestation of the fight between good and evil!

"If you were watching, you witnessed a breathtaking battle that ended in a triumph led by the Commander of the Ark, together with Saint Michael's formidable forces! For a brief time, Almighty God lifted the veil between Heaven and Earth so we could see the battle we've always been told goes on all around us! God's power was on brilliant display today! Our Heavenly Father utterly destroyed Samael, and He gave Satan a stern rebuke by sending him back to the netherworld in an incredible display of Heavenly justice!

"Still, not everyone is willing to return to God, incredibly, not even those in attendance here today! Despite witnessing God's victory for themselves, their voices are rising in protest, pronouncing the day's events an undeserved display of utter carnage!

"Opposing the efforts of law enforcement to restore peace in the face of the chaos that ensued, they shout their disapproval of their tactics, citing the countless individuals now in custody, the hundreds bearing injuries, and others who lost their lives in the mayhem.

"One of these protestors is Mr. Kenneth Rolando from Chicago. Mr. Rolando, could you share your thoughts regarding Samael and Peter Matteo, the Commander of the Ark?

"Josh, what transpired here today was a true atrocity! Samael represented a path toward collective enlightenment; he was a powerful force capable of ushering in unprecedented change within humanity, and he didn't deserve such a fiery end! The actions of Peter Matteo in bringing about his demise mark him as nothing short of a murderer, and if justice holds any sway, his soul will be sent to Hell for all eternity!

"Viewers, Mr. Rolando's views may be extreme, but they're the same held by hundreds of others I've encountered today. It appears to be the consensus of most who witnessed the Heavenly battle! I'm not sure what this portends for our future, but I don't think Our Lord in Heaven will view this favorably.

"Reporting live, this is Josh Hicks from Gabriel's Tower in Wyoming."

Although he was banished while thousands looked on, the Malignant remains undeterred, his goal to capture human souls uppermost in his thoughts.

As he reclines upon his throne thrust back into the depths of Hell, his revolting countenance radiates pure delight. Incredibly, the Evil One expresses an unwavering sense of achievement as he addresses his loyal underlings.

"I have done what needed to be done!" he proclaims haughtily, every fiber of his being boasting of pride in his perceived accomplishments. "I have drawn more souls into my fold, and Lilith will unknowingly deliver even more! Victory is mine once again! The children of my celestial adversary are subject to my every whim! Even my own offspring, Samael, executed my decrees impeccably!"

The Prince of Lies screeches in delight, the unholy sound bouncing endlessly off the subterranean walls of his sulfurous home, ultimately merging with the cacophony of tortured wails and gnashing of teeth among his anguished captives.

Too stunned to turn off the continuous coverage, Peter stares at a vid screen in disbelief, aghast at the surreal spectacle unfolding before him. The worlds seem to have turned upside down. People are actually applauding the malevolent and vilifying the virtuous!

Even Brother Oettinger, watching alongside Peter, is consumed by an unfamiliar fury, an emotion foreign to his usual, peaceful demeanor.

"Peter, you bear no responsibility for this madness!" Oettinger declares vehemently, his voice quivering with indignation. "This is an abomination, a diabolical scheme to sow discord among the masses!

"I am enraged! This is not who I am; I know it is the handiwork of the Malignant, and if he has affected me this badly, I fear he may have gotten what he wanted!"

With these words, Oettinger rushes out of the media center, and Peter lowers and shakes his head in dismay.

To respond to the events, Pope Ignatius is set to address the throngs gathered at his balcony overlooking bustling Saint Peter's Square. Below, thousands of tourists and locals jostle for a closer view as they eagerly await the pontiff's words. Within this sea of humanity, the Swiss Guard and Carabinieri labor valiantly to maintain order. The stakes are high, the outcome uncertain.

After an interminable wait, Pope Ignatius steps onto the balcony. Looking out, he addresses his beloved fold of the Universal Church, his voice resolute.

"In the past few days, we have witnessed the undeniable power and glory of Almighty God! All praise and honor to our Heavenly Father!" he begins. "The Malignant, his progeny, and his winged host have been vanquished, sent back to the inferno, where he..."

The pontiff's words trail off, his attention diverted to a point in the Square where an uproar has broken out in the crowd. Angry voices are suddenly crying out, accusing the pope and his followers of heinous crimes.

"All of you are murderers! You are vipers! You took the life of Samael, our revered redeemer! He was our beacon of hope, and you destroyed him!"

Though police and guards rush to squash the protests, they're no match for the jam-packed masses. Despite their efforts, scuffles break out, and they're only able to remove a handful of zealous protestors. Even so, many onlookers greet their hard work with a wave of applause. However, this fragile show of unity is short-lived.

Outside the Square, a large contingent of protestors converges on Via della Conciliazione, while at the same time, a group of drones suddenly appears in the sky above Saint Peter's Basilica. Upon command, the unmanned crafts release bags filled with vile substances, inciting panic and prompting the crowd to breach the barricades and flee.

As the discord spreads, police sirens break the reverent atmosphere of Christendom's holiest temple and the surrounding streets of Rome. They're responding to frantic calls from citizens whose storefronts are inexplicably vandalized and cars set ablaze.

Desperate to disperse the troublemakers, crowd control vehicles armed with water cannons and sound wave technology are deployed to confront the mob.

Without hesitation, local and state police charge into the tumultuous crowd, sweeping up the righteous and the ignorant alike. Live scenes of the pandemonium are broadcast worldwide, causing people everywhere to align with one side or the other.

The pontiff's appearance, meant to erode the influence of Samael and Satan, paradoxically achieved the opposite effect. In the wake of today's events, the infiltrators among the ranks of the faithful rejoice in the success of their disruptions. They're certain that they've managed to bolster the demons' influence. As a result, humanity is now closer than ever to the brink of Divine retribution.

Less than twenty-four hours later, Secretary-General Dalvi summons an urgent assembly of the Federation, with security heightened to the maximum. The members gather together, each vying for time to discuss the turmoil in Rome, mirrored by cities globally.

Sadly, the protests haven't diminished since the pope's attempted address. Instead, they've increased, with factions of ardent Samael supporters seizing control of major urban centers.

This divisive fervor has even penetrated the very heart of the Federation, pitting nation against nation. Leaders within the Federation's hallowed halls voice their concerns, regrets, and praise in deliberations that stretch for hours, punctuated by intermittent cries of rage and passion.

Yet amid this turmoil, an aura of composed resolve slowly supplants the chaos. Unexpectedly, a pivotal Federation vote reaffirms support for the Commander of the Ark and God the Father, with a staggering majority of one hundred and fifty countries vehemently condemning the ongoing conflict, urging their citizens to cease all hostilities. The dissenting few, including the United China Republic, exit the assembly in protest.

Subsequently, Secretary-General Dalvi issues a statement beseeching the people of Earth to return to their homes and stop the violence. To affirm his commitment to peace, he announces the mobilization of the World Federation Support Battalions, declaring the Federation ready to deploy them wherever their assistance is sought.

While local law enforcement and military forces mobilize to crush the riots, protestors slip into the shadows, biding their time for the opportune moment to resume testing humanity's resilience.

After the World Federation vote, Peter is inundated with calls from leaders across the globe. Initially, he took each one as they came in. However, he has now chosen to forego answering these calls, as there are no further words he can offer. The only calls he accepts are those from close friends and family.

Seeking Peter, Angela finds him seated in contemplation beneath the majestic Golden Tree of God. "Here," she says, offering him a refreshing glass of lemonade crafted from lemons grown at the lake. Sitting down next to him, she gently broaches the subject of his refusal to talk to anyone but those closest to him.

"Peter, I know you don't want to engage with politicians, but President Larson keeps calling, saying he won't stop until he talks to you. He's on the line again."

Peter takes a sip of the lemonade and looks at the Golden Tree, it's leaves swaying without any sign of wind. Sighing in resignation, he says, "All right. I'll talk to him. But he's the last one. They all know where I stand."

Returning indoors, Peter gazes at a holographic projection of President Larson, seated at his desk within the Oval Office.

"Mr. President, please be brief. I'm afraid I'm running out of patience with these pigheaded people."

"I understand. But you need to know that I've officially closed down every program at Area 51 involved in that hideous experiment. We've evacuated all support personnel, leaving only Lieutenant Colonel Nevins and his team to shut it down completely."

"That's wonderful, Mr. President. Thanks for telling me."

"You're welcome. I also wish to express my gratitude to you for all you've done. My family and I continue to pray that there will be a swift resolution to these trying times. However, it looks like the Almighty will have the final say. Your judgment of humanity is very perceptive; we may very well be the most foolish generation since Noah and Judgment Day. We hold you in our thoughts, Commander. Godspeed, Peter."

As the holographic projection fades, the image shifts to the front of the White House, where a silver rosary hangs prominently at the front door, a symbol of the president's unwavering faith in these uncertain times.

As Peter gets ready to leave the room, the vid terminal rings out with a personal notification, which Peter activates on his wrist communicator.

"Austin! It's good to see you! How's everything in the Northwest Territories?"

Smiling from ear to ear, Austin reaches to the side to bring someone else into the frame. "Peter, I'd like you to meet my wife."

Peter is overjoyed by the welcome news. "Congratulations! I'm so happy for you two. When did you take the plunge?"

Lory beams. "A justice of the peace performed the wedding ceremony yesterday. We didn't want to wait any longer. The worlds are so convulsed, Peter! We're far from the problem areas, but we have friends and family we're worried about. I told Atoch what's been happening and advised him to prepare his community for the three days of darkness."

"How'd he take that?"

"He wants me to thank you for properly dealing with Samael. I don't know how he knew what happened; I haven't had contact with him for months. Peter, have you heard anything from...you know."

Peter shakes his head. "Nothing at all. But his silence speaks volumes. Be prepared; I don't think he'll be quiet for long."

Chiming into the conversation, a white light fills the media room, and Archangel Michael kneels before the commander.

"You are correct, Peter. The silence is about to end."

Despite the pleas of government leaders and the Church, people continue to protest across every world. Men against women. Daughters against mothers. Sons against fathers.

Pride and arrogance fills the hearts of the weak. The time has come.

ZEPHANIAH 1:14-18

The great day of the Lord is near — near and coming quickly. The cry on the day of the Lord is bitter; the Mighty Warrior shouts his battle cry. That day will be a day of wrath — a day of distress and anguish, a day of trouble and ruin, a day of darkness and gloom, a day of clouds and blackness — a day of trumpet and battle cry against the fortified cities and against the corner towers. "I will bring such distress on all people that they will grope about like those who are blind, because they have sinned against the Lord. Their blood will be poured out like dust and their entrails like dung. Neither their silver nor their gold will be able to save them on the day of the Lord's wrath." (NIV)

CHAPTER FIFTY-FOUR

Every world in the galaxy is now embroiled in a bleak time. Symbolic of the unrest, Saint Peter's Basilica had to be closed to the public after its walls and courtyard were defiled with satanic imagery bearing Samael's name. These same desecrations extend far and wide; churches in major cities across the Earth are similarly affected. Even the holy city of New Jerusalem has been cordoned off and forbidden to visitors.

In response to these dire events, Pope Ignatius attempts another address to every world, and this time, he delivers it successfully.

"My beloved children, now is the time to prepare yourselves for chastisements. The hour is fast approaching when Almighty God will purify us. Do not yield to fear, for if you remain with God, you will find salvation. Fix a rosary above your doors and gather blessed beeswax candles to light your way when darkness draws near. Ready your homes and keep your families close; God's Divine power is upon us."

At precisely three p.m. on a Wednesday, a deafening clap of thunder reverberates across the globe, halting all electronic transmissions. Every vid terminal and communication device falls silent, severing all means of contact.

Perplexed by the sudden disruption, people spill outside their homes, where their confusion deepens as a radiant cloud descends from the sky. Within the cloud, the Son of Man manifests in a profoundly stirring way, touching every soul.

In a voice that resonates within every heart, Jesus reveals somber truths, giving all His children one last chance to repent.

Sternly, He declares, *"Your pride and arrogance have bolstered the Prince of Darkness. The devil dispatched Samael, the offspring of a fallen being, to ensnare your minds and claim more souls for Gehenna. To your shame, you embraced Samael as a false messiah, believing he would lead you to My Father in Heaven.*

"Samael's claims are a web of deception, for he hails from the Father of Lies. Because you have rejected My Father's guardians, dismissed His commander, and rebuked the One True God, My Mother and I can no longer restrain God's mighty Hand.

"For those faithful who cling to the Almighty One, it is time to fortify your homes and protect your families from His justice. In His Holy Name, He will cleanse the Earth of wickedness, as He did in ancient times, in Egypt during Moses' era, in the city of Sodom, and on Judgment Day. Hang the rosary of My Beloved Mother above your doors, for it shall shield all within. Soon, the emissaries of retribution will pass over the homes of those who heed My Words.

"In forty-eight hours, My Father's Hand will conceal the sun, and three days of darkness will shroud the Earth. Do not gaze out of your windows during this blackness, for what you may witness should not be seen. Do not venture outside or open your doors, for Satan will attempt to trap you. You will hear wailing and gnashing of teeth, and loved ones may pound on your doors seeking sanctuary. Yet hold fast to My Words and your faith; those days will test your trust in Me.

"During the darkness, the emissaries of My Father will safeguard the faithful, while shadowy demons from Gehenna will gather unfortunate non-believers to fill the coffers of Hell.

"On the third day, a rainbow will grace the sky as My

Father withdraws His Hand from the sun. Find solace and joy in this symbol of His Love. The Holy Trinity — Father, Son, and Holy Spirit — loves all Our children. But sinners must bear the consequences of their deeds."

When Jesus concludes, His voice fades from within every being, and His image vanishes from the sky. The Son of Man returned to Earth to convey the Father's Will to all.

Remarkably, despite the intensity of the experience, there is no panic. Instead, there is a resolute determination among the faithful to prepare their lives, and an unfortunate, steadfast commitment among non-believers to remain unwavering in their protests.

After Jesus's appearance, cherubim, seraphim, and the army of archangels and guardians prepare diligently for their impending duties. In Gehenna, the Prince of Darkness gloats over the Lord's warning to His believers while his shadowy army also readies itself. Satan is confident that within days, there will be a bountiful harvest of souls who won't obey.

At three p.m. on Friday, most households worldwide are protected by Mary's rosary, with prudent individuals locking themselves safely within their homes, awaiting the unknown. Others, recognizing the vulnerable, arm themselves with rosaries and trust in God's mercy, volunteering to stay with the sick and elderly until the purge ends.

At the appointed time, an ominous shield obscures the sun, plunging the worlds into darkness. Remembering the Lord's words, silence and despair creep into people's minds. In the gloom, they confront their true selves, with most miserable over their failures.

As a gray mist of retribution descends from Heaven, the Army of God seeks the souls of those who failed to follow God's warning, and demons scoop up the unbelievers. The foolhardy who venture into the darkness are the first to fall, their screams of despair troubling all who hear them.

Because of their constant faltering faith, the people of Earth bear the brunt of God's Wrath. Those residing on Mars, Titan, and the Moon are unscathed, due to their rejection of Satan's wiles.

Even the crew of the GSS Sappho, en route to rendezvous with the inhabitants of Proxima b, suffers from God's Wrath. In a harrowing moment, one of the science officers disappears from his post, vanishing before the eyes of his startled crewmates. The occurrence is swift and completely unexpected.

On the Moon, Peter, his family, Brother Oettinger, and Oettinger's fellow monastic brothers and sisters observe the blue marble in the heavens as it fades into darkness. In solidarity, they bow their heads, offering fervent prayers for the children of God. Similarly, on Mars and in the colony on Titan, a collective moment of silence is observed to show respect for the plight of Earth's inhabitants.

Meanwhile, Austin and Lory huddle in their Northwest Territories home, listening to an incessant rain drumming on their roof.

"That's God's tears," says Lory more than once, to agreeing nods from Austin.

In Sorrento, Angela's Aunt Sofia and Uncle Giovanni find solace in prayer during the all-encompassing darkness. The warm glow of beeswax candles illuminates their home with flickering light playing on its shrouded windows.

Pressing their hands tightly against their ears, they

attempt to block out the agonizing cries and screams from the shadows outside. However, the relentless pounding at their door and the voices of friends and family cast a haunting gloom over them. Seeking strength and the resolve to endure, they draw nearer to each other, as they have throughout their marriage.

Scenes such as these repeat across the Earth as countless others heed the warnings of the Son of Man.

Sadly, however, a minority succumbs to temptation, foolishly opening a door or peeking out a window. All who yield are horrified to find themselves engulfed by the ominous gray mist. Their ill-fated choices enable the shadowy Army of Gehenna to descend upon them, wrenching their souls away, dragging them kicking and screaming into the abyss.

In the midst of this turmoil, President Larson and his wife draw close together in their White House quarters, tears streaming down their faces, their hearts heavy with sorrow for their people.

All around them, the usually bustling halls of the White House are cold and desolate. Only a handful of Secret Service remain by their side, all clutching the rosary of Mary as a symbol of hope and protection.

Likewise, newlyweds Anthony and Karen Abila shelter in their home, a chilling silence enveloping their trembling forms.

Helpless in the wake of her fears, Karen's mind works overtime. Privy to the harrowing spectacle of each unfortunate soul's descent into Hell, she shudders uncontrollably, her telepathic voice a constant refrain of rebuke directed at Samael and his sinister father.

In revenge, the evil master of deception targets Karen for increased torment. To ensure that she will bear the deepest scars, Satan singles her out for the most excruciating suffering, showing her the deepest parts of Hell as punishment for abandoning his son.

Elsewhere, the Titans are untouched by the malevolent forces at play. Ironically, their limited knowledge of Satan and Samael's dark mission grants them precarious safety in these tumultuous times. Conversely, Jennifer Stone, the architect of Samael's stain on humanity, is not protected. She becomes one of the early victims, claimed by the shadows on the very first day as a prized bride for Satan.

Likewise, Lieutenant Colonel Nevins knows his days are numbered. Alone at his desk in the somber solitude of Area 51, he ponders his fate, uninterrupted by anyone. The entire complex is empty, save for him. His entire staff abandoned the base well before the three days of chastisement began.

Left to himself, Nevins' mind wanders through scenario after scenario of his future as the acrid smoke of his favorite cigar fills the room.

Thinking about what he's done — promoting the despicable experiment on innocent humans, sponsoring and supporting Samael's evil plans, rejecting all attempts to convert — the lieutenant colonel debates his future, and it doesn't look promising.

Concluding there's no other choice, he opts not to wait for the approaching shadow army's demons of perdition. Instead, he takes control of his destiny, ending his life with a single bullet, choosing to journey to Gehenna on his own terms.

As time passes in darkness, one day merges seamlessly into the next, the absence of natural light interfering with people's sense of time.

Finally, cries for help fade into the distance with the returning sunlight, prompting Peter to wander out of the monastery. Sitting under the Golden Tree, he laments its grey and lifeless form, its leaves withering and falling to the ground. He believes it's a stark reminder of the souls departing for Gehenna.

Above, the stars are also dull; they no longer twinkle as brightly, implying that the heavens are also grieving. In his heart, Peter knows that God the Father, Jesus, and Mary are shedding tears for their lost children, with every angel and soul in Heaven joining in their sorrow, even though the sun is shining and everything seems normal once again.

At five in the morning, the continuous rain finally stops over the house in Canada, and glimmers of light seep through the blinds with songbirds heralding the dawn.

Awakened by the birds, Lory creeps out of bed and checks the calendar. Noting that three days have passed, she cautiously cracks open the door, braving the cold. Overwhelmed by what she sees, she rushes back to the bedroom.

"Austin, wake up!" she cries. "You have to see what's outside!" Insistent, she shakes her husband's shoulder to wake him.

Realizing what his wife said, Austin shoots up in bed. "You went outside?!" he shouts.

"Yes! The birds are back, and the sun is out!"

The couple hurries outside in their nightclothes, oblivious to the cold. Happy beyond belief, they dance in the blessed light, reveling in the rainbow God promised and breathing deeply of the refreshing, peaceful air.

"This is wonderful! Thank you, Lord! Your mercy knows no bounds!" shouts Austin, twirling round and round. Then he stops. "Oh! I should call Peter!"

Hurrying back into the house, he checks to see if the power is restored before sending a message to the monastery.

Peter is pleased that his first call is from his old friend.

"I'm so happy to see your face!" he exclaims, thankful that Austin was faithful to God's command. "It's a glorious day, isn't it? I can't believe how much I missed sunlight! How's your beloved?"

"We're wonderful!" responds Lory, peeking her head into the vid frame. "We're so happy to be alive! But at the same time, we're desperately sorry for everyone who didn't make it through."

"I know what you mean," replies Peter. "It's going to be horrible learning how many didn't choose God."

Lory's expression points out her sadness. "May this awakening touch the hearts of all humanity!" she prays.

Across the globe, transmissions slow down as people emerge from their homes, eager to reconnect with loved ones. Those still in the night hours are treated to a breathtaking sight: a rainbow arcing across the sky, framed by a faded sea of stars.

While everyone rejoices, the Son of Man speaks again, surprising everyone by awakening the communication devices they have in their homes or on their persons.

"My dear children, be joyful!" says Jesus, as a dove gracefully lights on His Shoulder with an olive branch in its beak. *"You have withstood the Wrath of My Father! The Earth is now purified of the evil that threatened your souls. Go forth and bask in the boundless love of God! Remember this day, etch it deeply into your hearts, and never forget the Power of the One who sent Me!"*

PSALM 148

Praise the Lord. Praise the Lord from the heavens; praise him in the heights above. Praise him, all his angels; praise him, all his heavenly hosts. Praise him, sun and moon; praise him, all you shining stars. Praise him, you highest heavens and you waters above the skies. Let them praise the

name of the Lord, for at his command they were created, and he established them for ever and ever — he issued a decree that will never pass away. Praise the Lord from the earth, you great sea creatures and all ocean depths, lightning and hail, snow and clouds, stormy winds that do his bidding, you mountains and all hills, fruit trees and all cedars, wild animals and all cattle, small creatures and flying birds, kings of the earth and all nations, you princes and all rulers on earth, young men and women, old men and children. Let them praise the name of the Lord, for his name alone is exalted; his splendor is above the earth and the heavens. And he has raised up for his people a horn, the praise of all his faithful servants, of Israel, the people close to his heart. Praise the Lord. (NIV)

EPILOGUE

When GSS Sappho lands on Proxima b, the inhabitants welcome the crew to the new consulate in their grand city of Subtanna as warmly as they have in the past. However, this trip is different from others. This time, the spacefarers have been instructed to escort representatives of this sister planet back to Earth for a formal introduction to the worlds and a welcome to the Galactic Federation.

Though the Proximians have less advanced technology than Earth, their wisdom and understanding of the universe far surpasses Earthly knowledge. This distinction makes their understanding crucial to the ultimate survival of the human race, and the wiser members of the Federation are keen to adopt it.

The Proximian belief in a singular God who reigns supreme over the cosmos mirrors human faith. However, a crucial difference is in how they live out their creed. Proximian society is devoid of the constant conflicts, division, pride, and arrogance humans struggle with. The hope of many is that formal relations with that distant planet will help our home cultures implement the lessons those remarkable people can teach us.

While plans are being made for the Proxima b induction ceremony, Karen and Anthony Abila continue to work on Anthony's research, even though it's becoming more and more difficult. Lately, Karen has been struggling with early-onset ageing due to the experiments she was subjected to, and Anthony's research is nowhere near providing a cure. Every day, he makes a little more progress in halting Karen's process, but he won't be satisfied until his wife is restored to full health.

On the other hand, the Titans are thriving; they aren't suffering like Karen. All of them except Robert are in good health, and they're happy with their current jobs.

Robert, Tim, and Jonathan remain dedicated to the GBA. Tim's wife, Jane, a welcome addition to the tour circuit, enhances Tim's and Jonathan's enjoyment of the exhibition games the association books across the cosmos. Unfortunately, Robert has had to back out of active participation. He's the only one of the five Titans with health issues. The artificial knees Xanthe Robotics gave him have become arthritic, forcing him to take a backseat on the circuit.

Though Frank also received replacement parts, Robert is the only one to have problems, but he's not complaining. The GBA has kept him on as an invaluable spokesperson and an expert sportscaster.

At the same time, Frank and Richard are still busy at Xanthe Robotics. Both are deeply satisfied with their public relations work for the company, especially after they entered into lifelong commitments with Alpha B artificial intelligence companions the company designed specifically for them.

After the cleansing, life marches on for everyone. David Jacoby and his fiancée, Galina, are planning a visit to David's family in a small town near Chicago. This Earthly visit will mark a significant first for both of them, since neither has ever left Mars.

After David's father died, David's mother moved to Earth to connect with her family, leaving David wondering if he'd ever see her again. Now that she's back home on Mars, she suggested the trip as a way for David to get to know his relatives. "Besides," she said, "it'll be a memory you and Galina will cherish as you begin your lives together."

David, however, can't help but feel apprehensive about how his relatives will embrace an artificial intelligence unit as a bona fide family member. He manages to keep his worries to himself the entire trip there, but Galina knows something's up. She has the same concerns.

As it turns out, their fears are entirely unnecessary. To the pair's delight, David's aunts, uncles, and cousins welcome Galina with open arms. Wondering about the warm reception, David suspects that his mother, Marjorie, had something to do with it, and his hunch is confirmed when he quizzes a cousin for more details.

"Oh, you know your mother, Davy," his cousin responds affectionately. "Aunt Marjorie made it her mission to let us all know how much affection she has for Galina and how AIs are 'mostly' just like humans."

To prove how much the family accepts Galina, one day during their visit, David's female cousins organize a girls' outing with Galina while one of David's uncles and a male cousin whisk David away.

When David repeatedly inquires where they're headed, Uncle Gary and Cousin Nate playfully compete to provide the most cryptic answers.

Eventually, David surrenders to the mystery and revels in the camaraderie of family stories.

"Here we are!" announces Uncle Gary as they pull into a modest parking area next to a warehouse nestled on the banks of a prominent river in the town.

"What's this place?" asks David, unfamiliar with the surroundings.

"You'll see," replies Cousin Nate with a twinkle in his eye.

Fingering a switch that activates an electronic bay door, he urges David to enter the warehouse.

As David's eyes adjust to the dimness, his brow furrows with an unspoken question. In the subdued lighting, a vehicle concealed beneath a grey tarp occupies a central spot.

Sidling up to David, Uncle Gary places a hand on his shoulder.

"The family spent generations restoring and preserving this gem, waiting for the right member to cherish it. It belonged to a detective way back in our family's history, and since you're also a detective and you enjoy everything vintage, it's yours."

With widened eyes, David's mouth drops open, and he searches his relatives' faces. "Are you pulling my leg?" he asks.

"Nope!"

Intrigued, David seizes the tarp and pulls it back to reveal a stunning 1968 Red Road Runner.

"Holy crap!" he exclaims. "Is this the same...?" he starts to say, leaving the rest of the question hanging.

"Yup," confirms his uncle. "It's Uncle Jack Stenhouse's ride! And here are the keys!" he adds, tossing a vintage set of metal car keys to his astonished nephew.

In a state of shock, David opens the driver's door. Inside, a vintage blue emergency light sits prominently on the dashboard beside Jack Stenhouse's original police badge. Moreover, a faded photo enclosed in plastic dangles from the rearview mirror.

Overwhelmed with excitement, David slides into the driver's seat and pulls the picture forward for a closer look.

"Ha!" he exclaims knowingly. "That's Uncle Jack and his wife, Didi! Now I understand why she has that name!" Then, noticing the shift indicator and the clutch pedal, he adds, "I'm gonna have to teach Galina how to drive a stick!"

With Peter's role as Commander over for now, Peter and his family return to Atlanta. For employment, he takes a consulting position with the CDC, specifying that he wants to assist in the search for a genetic treatment to help the Titans.

At home, Michael is now a walking dynamo and no longer needs diapers. While his parents are relieved he's potty trained, the active boy keeps them on their toes.

As a stay-at-home mom, Angela strives to ensure the child's mind is engaged with the latest stimuli to feed his curiosity. But she's also fighting morning sickness, which isn't easy, given how often she feels like just resting in bed.

In New Jerusalem, the Ark of the Covenant is back in its customary place in the Holy of Holies, ready to be called upon at a moment's notice. Guardians Gabriel and Uriel are at its side, protecting it with their unseen presences and leaving only when called upon by Almighty God.

As always, the archangels are prepared to aid Peter, Michael, and all future Matteos in their mission to protect humankind from all threats — whether they originate from outside the human race or within it.

Typically, Satan refuses to admit that God won their latest battle. He continually brags about how long he was able to dupe humanity through the efforts of his son, Samael, and all the others he managed to control while Samael and Lilith were on Earth. He prowls within his dingy caverns, feeling immense satisfaction at how many fresh souls were sent to Gehenna during God's retribution. Every day, he delights in the anguished tears they shed, their suffering adding to all the others crying out for the salvation that was within their reach during their Earthly lives, if only they called upon it.

After the Purification, humanity stands renewed, and the reborn worlds glow in the light of justice.

Yet, the destiny of humankind remains a mystery. Time and again, God patiently waits for His children, yearning for them to embrace His path above their own.

However, the future holds secrets hidden within the choices shaped by God's gift of free will, a gift that veils humanity's fate in uncertainty.

Even so, the Almighty never abandons His children. Across history, His unwavering message continually resonates in human hearts:

"In the end, they will understand My eternal love for them. They will be grateful for all I have bestowed upon them through My willingness to suffer for their sins. Ultimately, they will turn to Me, recognizing Me as their sole God and Redeemer, the Everlasting One, the Omnipresent, All-Powerful, Merciful, and Righteous Judge of all creation. That day, they will save their souls for all eternity!"

A NOTE FROM THE AUTHOR

I hope you enjoyed reading this novel as much as I enjoyed writing it. As a reader, you are the recipient of the hours and hours I spent organizing my thoughts into the story I wanted to create, then editing it into the form you see here. My goal is to entertain you and give you something to think about.

I'm fortunate that my muses never leave me alone. They're always available with another interesting idea, making *Samael of Sarah* the twelfth novel I've published to date. There are more to come; they only need to be edited, which takes more time than the actual writing.

The best way for me to know how my stories are received is by reading your reviews. Your thoughtful comments give me insights into how my stories affect my readers, and are an effective tool for piquing the interest of others.

Please post a brief note about your reactions at Amazon.com. This and all my books are listed on that site under my name.

Thank you, and continued happy reading!

Frank A. Ruffolo

www.ingramcontent.com/pod-product-compliance
Lightning Source LLC
Chambersburg PA
CBHW030619250626
47154CB00006B/1850